UNYIELDING FIRE

Vanessa Stirling whirled by in the arms of a black-clad man who was faceless to Amas Holder; he could see only her. When her partner circled them in the dance, Amas got one dazzled look at her face – blank, indifferent, beautiful beyond the beauty he remembered. Like her dress that afternoon, her evening clothes were dark blue, but now her flawless shoulders and a titillating portion of her generous breasts were naked.

The blue-grey eyes met his; in that breathless second her face absorbed the brilliant light at the end of the dimmer corridor, her skin like white silk. She pulsated with life in contrast to the dead, pale marble of the statues. Those shoulders would have a swansdown softness to the fingers. Amas imagined that proud mouth opening under his. Then Vanessa Stirling smiled at him.

He drew in his breath; his head rang. It was like recovering from a blow . . .

Also by Vivian Lord
ONCE MORE THE SUN
SUMMER KINGDOM

Unyielding Fire

VIVIAN LORD

SEVERN
SH
HOUSE

New edition published in 1987

First published in Great Britain in 1985 by
SEVERN HOUSE PUBLISHERS LTD of
4 Brook Street, London W1Y 1AA
by arrangement with Sphere Books Ltd

British Library Cataloguing in Publication Data

Lord, Vivian
    Unyielding fire.
    I. Title
    813′.54[F]   PS3562.0/

    ISBN 0–7278–1181–9

Printed and bound in Great Britain by
Butler & Tanner Ltd, Frome and London

For Maria T. Suarez and
Eugenie Reidmiller

Part I
The Find

CHAPTER ONE

'You want a lot of money, Mr Holder.' Martin Stirling, financier, studied the man from Kimberley Mine.

He suggested a young lion about to spring. Men asking for money seldom looked like that.

Amas Holder shrugged. 'I can make it back in a week, with the next diamond find.'

The 'can', not 'could', commanded Stirling's respect. So did Holder's calm, his utter lack of servility. Stirling was about to respond when there was a commotion from the outer office. A woman's nasal voice cut off the demur of Stirling's male assistant.

'Never mind, Mr Madden, we can wait. Calm down, Bea.' This was spoken in a low, melodious intonation.

'I can't wait.'

The door shot open. With the air of an angry queen a dark young woman swept in, followed by a tall, fair one in austere clothes. 'You're an hour late,' the dark one accused Stirling. 'You said you'd be home by now, and look what time it is. You must come. Mother can't cope with the musicians.' She held out a topaz-circled watch on a thick gold chain between her high, sharp breasts and glowered.

Amas Holder scrambled to his feet.

He had only glanced at the angry speaker; he could not stop staring at the other woman. Her skin was so white it almost hurt his eyes after the years in South Africa, years of looking at native women, the sun-weathered wives of workmen and miners. That whiteness above the high-necked severity of her navy blue clothes absolutely startled him. His stare took in her generous breasts and curving hips, a waist that looked no wider than his own muscular neck – the hourglass figure that was the ideal in this year of 1885.

But it was her face that attracted him most: her blue-grey eyes, wide-set in a heart-shaped face with prominent cheekbones, had a brilliance he had never associated with that colour of eye. He had always thought of grey eyes as serene, the way his mother's were. But there was nothing serene about this woman. She was as turbulent

3

with life as the rapids of the Orinoco, which he'd ridden on a wager when he was working in Brazil. Her nose was briefly aquiline, her prim pink mouth hinted at strong feeling barely leashed.

Framing the white face with its stunning eyes was a drift of curly golden hair, cut shorter than any woman's hair he'd ever seen. It frothed only inches below her delicate ears, fine as shredded filaments of glowing silk. She wore a turban-like hat with a glorious blue-white diamond in its centre over her brow. Amas had encountered such head-dresses only in India.

'Sorry, Father,' the golden creature said. She was the possessor, then, of that musical, almost husky voice. The timbre of it stroked Amas Holder like warm fingertips. 'I wanted to wait, but Bea . . .'

'Bea can speak for herself,' the other broke in. 'This was my idea. Mother insisted that Vanessa come along.'

Amas glanced at Martin Stirling. The financier had not risen; his face was full of chagrin. 'She is hardly a proper chaperone,' Stirling retorted. 'I am surprised at your mother.' Amas gathered that here, as abroad, young ladies did not come unescorted to a business office. It never happened in the Dutch and English offices back home. He noticed that Stirling's face had reddened with vexation under the smooth wings of his black, grey-threaded hair.

Stirling gestured with a well-tended hand. 'This unmannerly young woman is my daughter Beatrice. The more rational is my younger daughter, Vanessa. Mr Holder.'

Beatrice looked annoyed. She was standing nearer, but instinctively Amas Holder reached for Vanessa Stirling's hand. He noticed that it was hardly wider than a child's, although the fingers were quite long. He murmured a greeting. When their palms met he felt through the thin white leather of her glove a palpable electric shock.

She withdrew her hand from his at once, as if he'd hurt it. There was nothing sensible to say. Politeness obliged him to recognise Beatrice. She was totally unlike the regal Vanessa, bearing a close resemblance to her father. But where Stirling's darkness was positive, hers was merely sharp. His looks had not translated well into her gender.

There was something unpleasant about her shiny black eyes, overlarge in a pointed face with its angular nose, red pouting mouth. Her hair was jet black, coiled into massive loops. A bodice striped in black and mustard-gold seemed to thrust out breasts too heavy for such a thin woman.

She gave Amas a lingering look, a pursed half-smile, as if saying

4

'You'. He was glad to withdraw his hand. Hers had been hot, insinuating in his grasp.

Out of the corner of his vision Amas caught Vanessa studying them with a beautiful, blank face; there was a contemptuous curve on her inviting mouth. He marvelled that she could be so distant and seductive at once, while the blatant sister had no effect upon him at all. Vanessa disturbed him so profoundly he felt the sweat break out along his back.

'Sorry, Holder,' Stirling said, rising. 'Why don't you come over to the house tonight, about ten?'

Amas sensed a surprise in the women as great as his own. Surely it was uncommon for a millionaire to invite a prospective debtor to his house.

'I'll break away from all the social nonsense for a while,' Stirling went on easily, 'and we can finish our discussion.' He gave Amas a Fifth Avenue address.

'Thank you, sir. I appreciate it.'

Amas picked up his soft hat and, with a slight bow to the women, strode out of the office. He was so bowled over by the whole encounter he needed to be alone, to take a walk.

He nodded to the curious Madden with his prissy spectacles and sleek, centre-parted hair. Glancing at the fellow's typewriting machine, Amas thought: what a way to make a living. It was the same for the intent and sober group in the vast outer office, seated at their rolltop desks. They reminded Amas of rabbits in a warren.

He felt smothered, as if his collar were too tight, relieved to get out in the street again. With almost five hours to kill he could take a good long stroll.

Heading west towards Broadway, one of the New York thoroughfares he knew, Amas took grateful breaths of the chill October air. He paused at Broadway for an instant, indecisive. To the north he could see the changing leaves of the park trees bordering the white cupola of the City Hall. Suddenly he ached for the primitive, monotonous landscape of South Africa.

New York was an exciting city, but it was worlds away from the familiar, low-slung buildings, the rumbling ox-drawn carts of Kimberley's market square. And New York made Amas feel hemmed in after all those sweeping spaces. He decided to walk downtown to the harbour; he could breathe there.

A loud bell vibrated in his ears: he waited for a horse-drawn ambulance to clatter by him heading north, then for a group of white-helmeted mounted police trotting southwards before he made his way across the street, populous with carriages and drays.

His long legs propelled him downtown for six or seven blocks before he realised he was hungry. He turned into a lunchroom. It was surprisingly crowded at that late hour by well-dressed men seated on stools at oval counters. They wore bowlers and high silk hats indoors, because there was not a woman in the place, and were drinking beer, eating from heaped plates.

Amas climbed onto an empty stool and read from a chalked blackboard: 'This day, Turtle Soup. Try our famous Beef and Beans'. He ordered the latter. An unsmiling fellow in a white jacket sliced off generous portions from a side of beef, ladled beans onto Amas' plate. 'What'll you drink?' the man asked without expression.

'Beer.' New York fellows didn't stop to pass the time of day the way they did at home. He guessed they were too busy here with their bottles and ladles. The cigar smoke was thick as fog, the marble floors clacked with the hard heels of passers-by.

Amas noticed that a few men gave him curious glances. He knew he looked different in his well-worn clothes, his soft hat cocked carelessly on his brow. His hair was short and, where most of these fellows had whiskers or moustaches, he was clean-shaven. He disliked the burdensome feel of face hair.

The white-coated server had observed him with absent-minded contempt. It always amused Amas Holder to be taken for a tramp, when he could buy most men ten times over and wore a ninety-carat brown rough diamond on his watch-chain. The way a man dressed didn't amount to much in Kimberley the way it did here.

But then his whole life had been different.

His father, Daniel Holder, a frustrated chaser of dreams, had left Pennsylvania for California with the Forty-Niners to prospect for diamonds and gold. Ellen Todd, an aristocratic, well-read Philadelphian as dreamy as Daniel himself, had gone to join him and they were married. They existed in a world of Someday, because Daniel Holder never found his gold. When Amas was born, his mother had pinned all her hopes on him and, as soon as he was old enough to understand, she told him he was marked for greatness. He would be invincible, she said, finding the gold and diamonds his father never had, vindicating the Holder name at last.

When Daniel Holder was killed in an accident they were left with almost nothing. Amas was still a young child. Ellen soon managed to get them to San Francisco, where she was reduced to working as a maidservant in a rich man's house. There, from the children of the house, Amas learned bitter pride and seething rebellion. He left California when he was sixteen. He was big for his age, and lied about it, working his way down the Yucatán Peninsula to Brazil, where he'd heard there were diamonds. He'd heard wrong. The diamond fields were finished there, so he worked his way to South Africa. He did anything to survive – boxed in travelling variety shows, barked in circuses and fleeced their patrons, did odd jobs for merchants and miners. Lifting and hammering, fighting and hauling made him even bigger. His resolve was as hard as the diamonds he sought.

His early efforts as a diamond buyer were defeated for lack of funds. Then four years ago, in 1881, he'd struck 'blue ground', the mother rock of diamonds. A few claims he'd bought for six thousand dollars yielded diamonds worth that amount in just one week. He made an amazing amount of money. He sent a large cheque to a San Francisco bank to open an account in his mother's name. She was able to buy a house as good as the one she'd worked in, have servants of her own. Joyfully she wrote to him, 'I was right. You were marked for success.'

Yes, he'd made a lot of money. But now he needed even more to gain effective control of the Kimberley Central Mine. And he hoped to get it from Martin Stirling of New York . . . the father of Vanessa Stirling. A sudden hotness crawled over Amas' skin. He'd never seen a woman like her, not in all his life.

He shifted his body to free the sticky shirt on his back. There was only one way to get a woman like that. Marry her. Amas wondered what Stirling would think of *that*.

He ordered another beer, reflecting: at least I've got money, probably as much as any of these society johnnies. And he'd have more. When Amas raised his glass he sighted the sleeve of his ancient tweed jacket. He'd have to do something about his clothes. Become like some of these dandies . . .

Amas inventoried the men around him. One impressed him in particular. He was decked out in a grey bowler hat, a darker grey suit of some stuff that was soft as butter and fit him to a tee.

'Excuse me, sir.' Amas leaned over the vacant stool separating him from the elegant stranger.

'Yes?' the man responded coldly.

Amas nearly laughed. The fellow looked as if he was about to be robbed.

'Where do you get a suit of clothes like that?'

The man in the bowler gave Amas an up-and-down scrutiny

compounded of suspicion and disdain. 'Brooks Brothers.'

'And where might they be?'

'On Broadway, corner of Twenty-second Street.' The man got down from his stool and walked away.

Amas turned back to the counter, elated. That was only a step from his hotel. He'd go there in the morning and take a later train to Philadelphia; get fitted out for an evening suit, the whole thing. It would take them time to make the clothes, but he'd pay them well to hurry up. Tailors had done that for him before. Then . . . when he saw Vanessa Stirling . . . *if* he saw her.

He was sweating anew under his clothes in spite of the brisk autumn air that blew in through the constantly swinging door. Better get moving again. There was relief in motion. He paid and left the lunchroom, pushing through the slatted door, joining the crowd on Broadway as he headed downtown.

He walked so fast he soon found himself at the Battery. The wind from the harbour was cold, but it felt good on his heated face. He took off his hat so he could feel it on his bare head. To his left, above the tugs and sailing boats and ferries, Amas could see the gigantic robed figure of that Frenchman's statue still being assembled. Its head was only a goblin framework of metal, its upraised arm not yet completed to the wrist. The hand was merely scaffolding. He'd probably never see it completed.

But she would. Vanessa Stirling. He couldn't get her out of his head.

A ferry slid by. Under its paddle wheel was the name 'Magnolia'.

That's what her skin was like. A magnolia flower. Amas Holder felt an uncomfortable drumming in his loins. A magnolia, white and poreless, so white it could be sullied by the lightest touch. He remembered how his handshake had seemed to hurt her. Yes, he knew what that skin looked like; its feel, its taste and smell he could only imagine.

Soft as a petal. Sweet.

Amas swore and jammed on his hat. The itch, the gnawing had him in its teeth again. He took his watch out of his pocket. Only six. He'd walk back to his hotel at Fifth Avenue and Twenty-third Street. The exercise would scratch that itch a little.

It did. By the time he reached the hotel he felt a little calmer, ready for a bath. He was doing himself proud, staying at this hotel. But he could easily afford it. He smiled, thinking how snooty the desk clerk looked until he took out his money.

8

He'd treat himself to dinner at that Delmonico's he'd heard so much about. They said you got a decent meal there. Later it would be an easy stroll to the Stirling house on Fifth Avenue and Thirty-seventh Street.

He was dressed in a dark suit somewhat more presentable than the tweed when he walked up to the entrance of the marble mansion. He pulled the bell to the right of a stained-glass door framed in garlands and in curlicues.

To his amazement Martin Stirling opened the door. Amas had expected a fish-faced butler. 'Mr Holder, come in. Come in.' Stirling was genial. He led Amas down an echoing corridor between fluted columns and white marble statues to an open door near curving stairs.

Amas heard waltz music, got a lightning glimpse of an enormous room with paintings on the walls where dancing couples circled a floor bright as water. It was the impression of an instant, like a scene viewed from the window of a train, but he couldn't help looking for Vanessa. He didn't see her. His heart pounded.

Stirling apparently misread his stare, for he said, 'I'm keeping you from the festivities, I fear. The ladies are giving a ball, as you see. These things bore me to distraction. But you're much younger.'

Amas said hastily, 'Oh, no, sir. I wouldn't think of . . .' He stopped awkwardly and made a diffident gesture.

'In here,' Stirling directed, smiling. He stood aside to let Amas enter a book-lined room with a high, padded-leather ceiling. Stirling took his hat and put it on a sideboard next to a statue of bronze warriors. Then he shut the door. The waltz music softened.

'Take that chair, why don't you? It's quite comfortable.' Stirling indicated an armless velvet seat with gilded fringe placed near a handsome but businesslike desk.

'Thanks.' Amas did so, looking around. The wall was richly papered over dark wood panelling. There were naked bulbs in wall and ceiling light fixtures powered by electricity. A lamp with untidy cords was set on a corner of the desk's teak surface.

'I haven't seen this light in a private house before,' Amas commented.

'Not many people have it,' Stirling responded. 'Morgan was the first, then we got ours.'

Amas supposed Stirling was referring to the famous J. Pierpont Morgan.

9

'Sorry about the interruption this afternoon,' Stirling said courteously. 'Drink?'

Amas wasn't much of a drinker, but he'd had only a glass of burgundy with his dinner, so he said, 'Yes. Thank you, sir.'

Stirling poured two brandies from a decanter on the sideboard. Amas rose to take his glass. 'I appreciate this interview.'

'Not at all.' Stirling sat down behind the desk and took a sip of brandy. 'Now, Mr Holder, where were we?'

'Call me Amas, sir.'

'Amos?'

Amas pronounced it again, sounding the first A as in 'hammer'. 'My mother named me Adamas, but that's a mouthful. I keep the "Amas", out of respect.'

'I like that kind of respect,' Stirling said. ' "Adamas",' he repeated with a gleam in his eye. 'Greek for "adamant". Like a diamond. The name suits you. You're like a rough diamond yourself.'

Amas laughed. Then he said, 'Not many people know what my name means. But then I guess you're not exactly "many people", considering what you've done.' Stirling was the head of a hundred enterprises turned to enormous profit.

The financier looked gratified. 'I've always been a reader,' he confided. 'And I know a little about diamonds. Frankly, my interest in them is more than financial. There's something about the things,' he admitted, 'that reminds me of those old adventure stories I read as a boy.' He smiled, and added, 'You've had some adventures, I'll wager.'

'A few.' Warmed by the brandy and Stirling's interest, lulled by the fire's warmth, the luxurious surroundings, Amas found himself talking about Brazil and Mexico, the early days in Cape Town.

'So while I was grubbing away in Wall Street, you were pulling a fortune out of Africa's belly.' Amas was struck by his forceful way of putting it, by the man's wistful intonation. He hardly seemed a man to envy another.

'How old are you?' Stirling demanded abruptly.

'I'll be twenty-four, in December.'

'You've got nerve, I'll say that for you. Taking on a man with Rothschild backing. Cecil Rhodes is quite an adversary.' The tall, skinny Englishman had preceded Amas to South Africa by nine years and had had much success with the finds. But now he had political ambitions. A master at creating large capitalist enterprises,

10

he had managed to increase his company's capital to two and a half million pounds in five years.

'But I want money, sir. Rhodes wants a piece of Africa for Britain.' Amas grinned. 'And Britain didn't even get a small piece of this country.'

Stirling looked delighted. 'Exactly.' He slapped the desk top with the palm of his hand. 'I'll tell you something, my people threw the tea in Boston Harbour. We've been leery of the English ever since. I'd hate to see that bastard get ahead of us.' He gave Amas an appraising glance. 'You've got the balls of a brass monkey.'

Amas smiled but made no reply. He liked Stirling's forthright way of putting things, like the men he worked with.

'Now,' the older man said briskly, 'let's have another look at those balance sheets.' Amas took the folded papers from his breast pocket and gave them to Stirling. He'd already checked Amas out on the International Exchange, for sure. Otherwise he'd never have got past the front office of Stirling Enterprise.

'It's all there, sir. What you didn't get from the Exchange.'

Stirling looked up, an appreciative gleam in his dark eyes. 'Not quite all.' He glanced meaningly at Amas' head and his calloused hand holding the brandy glass. 'You've come a long way for the money, son.'

'It's not only that. My mother's in Pennsylvania now. Philadelphia. I haven't seen her for eight years.'

Stirling nodded. 'I like a man who considers his mother.' He went back to his reading. After a few minutes, he handed the papers back to Amas. 'Well, there's a good chance I'll grant you the loan. But of course I'll have to talk it over with some advisers. I pay them dearly for their advice, so I may as well take it.' He gave Amas another of his swift, oddly sad smiles.

Amas set down his glass and got up. 'Thanks again, sir, for your time.'

'Don't go yet. Unless you have an appointment.' Once more Amas was surprised at Stirling's cordiality.

'No, I don't have an appointment.' He settled back in his chair.

'Let me freshen your drink.' At Amas' nod, Stirling did so. He noticed that the brandy had relaxed the older man, loosened his tongue. He'd lost much of the formality he'd had at his office behind the imposing barrier of his desk. 'You see before you,' Stirling remarked lightly, 'a lone man in a household of women.' Somehow the lightness did not quite disguise that peculiar wistfulness Amas

11

had noticed before. It still seemed odd for a man with Martin Stirling's resources to appear so lonely. 'I enjoy your company, son.'

He proceeded to confide in Amas Holder. What he did not say outright Amas was able to infer; he'd learned to read beyond a man's words when he was barely eleven, from dealing with his mother's haughty employers, later from his association with confidence tricksters and the varied men he'd worked for on his travels. Then it had been a weapon for survival. Now it was a tool for understanding. He realised he liked Martin Stirling, very much.

Amas gathered that he had always longed for a son. His older daughter Beatrice, the dark one with the sharp breasts and sharper eyes, had been a foundling, adopted by the family. As sometimes happens, the presumably barren Mrs Stirling had conceived Vanessa a short time after the adoption.

The spoiled Beatrice had been dethroned by Vanessa's birth. And to complicate matters more, the Stirlings had coddled Vanessa to compensate for her junior position. Amas was aware that Stirling favoured Vanessa, although he tried hard not to show it.

'Bea thinks too much about young men,' Stirling said in a burst of frankness. 'Vanessa doesn't think about them enough.'

Amas felt his heartbeat quicken at the constant repetition of her name. He was flattered that Stirling talked to him so freely, seemed to like him.

He ridiculed himself. That was a far cry from letting Amas court his daughter. Some hope. Amas' hand was not quite steady when he reached for his brandy glass again.

Apparently Stirling hadn't noticed.

He went on in a sober tone. 'She concerns me. She's hellbent on becoming a concert pianist. She doesn't have the slightest interest in marrying. A proper young woman should.'

Then Stirling reddened and paused, as if he had said too much. 'I really don't know why I'm going on this way,' he added.

'Believe me, sir, I find it all – extremely interesting,' Amas blurted. He could feel his own cheeks flushing. Stirling gave him a searching look.

He made a dismissive gesture. 'It does me good,' he said, 'to see a youth as devoted to his mother as you are.'

Something in his intonation demanded a change of subject, to Amas' bitter disappointment.

There was no way now to refer to Stirling's daughters again, especially when Stirling added, 'You remind me of myself at your age. I'd really like to hear a bit more about you.'

Obligingly Amas told him his story, ending with the purchase of the San Francisco house, his mother's subsequent move to the city of her birth so she might be among her friends and relatives again.

Stirling listened intently. But Amas saw that he was beginning to tire. Reluctantly he got to his feet, apologising for the lateness of the hour.

When they went into the corridor, Amas got a better look at the mansion's ballroom. He strained for a glimpse of Vanessa, but suddenly his view was blocked by the figure of the dark Beatrice. Amas bowed slightly.

She was wearing a shiny black evening dress with insets of gilt on the bodice. And then Amas realised what she reminded him of – a giant bumble-bee. There was even a nasal whine to her voice, and her big breasts dwarfed her thin shoulders and arms. Tonight the breasts were almost bare.

'Won't you join us, Mr Holder?'

She stepped into the hall, glancing at his suit and hair. It was obvious that she was playing with him, perhaps punishing him, he judged astutely, for noticing her sister first that afternoon. A real queen bee.

'No, thank you, Miss Stirling, I'm afraid I don't dance.' That was literally true. He'd worked all his life and hadn't had any time for things like dancing.

Beatrice was vexed. She stared up into his eyes. 'You're the first man who ever said no to Bea Stirling.' Bringing up her black and gold fan she struck him with it across the cheek.

'Beatrice! Remember yourself.' Stirling was furious.

Amas smiled and bowed to her. 'Then I'm happy to offer you such a novel experience.' Ignoring her as if she were an ill-behaved child, he turned to Stirling to shake his hand. He saw a guarded look of approval on his host's face.

'Thanks for inviting me, sir. I'll call at your office a week from next Monday, as soon as I'm back in the city.'

'Fine.' Stirling walked beside Amas between the marble statues. 'I apologise for my daughter, Holder. She's spoiled rotten. She needs taking down a peg or two. None of these rich boys is man enough to do it. I see that you are.' He grinned at Amas, looking twenty years younger.

That was not a role Amas relished. But he felt a growing affection for the financier. At the door he lingered a bit, unable to resist

13

another backward glance in the hope that he might see Vanessa.

He did.

Vanessa Stirling whirled by in the arms of a black-clad man who was faceless to Amas Holder; he could see only her. When her partner circled them in the dance, Amas got one dazzled look at her face – blank, indifferent, beautiful beyond the beauty he remembered. Like her dress that afternoon, her evening clothes were dark blue, but now her flawless shoulders and a titillating portion of her generous breasts were naked.

The blue-grey eyes met his; in that breathless second her face absorbed the brilliant light at the end of the dimmer corridor, her skin like white silk. She pulsated with life in contrast to the dead, pale marble of the statues. Those arms and shoulders would have a swansdown softness to the fingers. Amas imagined that proud mouth opening under his. Then Vanessa Stirling smiled at him.

He drew in his breath; his head rang. It was like recovering from a blow. It was all he could do to say a sane goodnight to Martin Stirling.

Vanessa Stirling saw the man from Kimberley smile back at her. White teeth flared in his tough, sunburnt face. The hands that held his raffish hat were huge; he seemed immensely tall and big, bigger than any man she was accustomed to. He looked wild, with that disordered mane of sandy hair, those ferocious eyes. Just like a man from one of Haggard's novels. Vanessa's hand, in the respectful grasp of Harvey Boerum, quivered.

Bea hadn't made any impression on Holder that afternoon. He was unique; men always reacted to Beatrice Stirling.

'. . . that enchanting smile?'

'I beg your pardon?' Vanessa looked up blankly into Harvey's watery blue eyes.

Harvey flushed. 'Perhaps I am too bold. I was wondering at the meaning of that enchanting smile of yours.' His grasp on her waist tightened almost imperceptibly.

She drew back a little and her chastened partner relaxed his fingers, resuming the conventional hold, barely touching her curving waist. Vanessa hated conventional contact; touching, she thought, should mean something. She rarely even offered her hand in introductions. Yet she had held out her hand to the Holder man that afternoon. *That* touch, she reflected, was different from anything she'd ever felt. An incredible warmth, a mighty energy had flowed from his hand to hers, and she had thought of it all afternoon.

'I've never known anyone like you, Miss Vanessa.'

She lowered her eyes, to hide her irritation.

'You are unlike any young lady I've ever known.'

Vanessa had heard that often before; she followed Boerum's steps with absent ease, wishing the waltz were over. But then the next man would come to claim her, the man whose name was written on her card; she didn't even remember who now. She wished the whole evening could be over, yearned to sit down at the piano. The only time she ever felt less lonely was when she was playing. Music was her steadfast companion.

Desperately Harvey Boerum tried again. 'Have you read the new Meredith novel, *Diana of the Crossways?*'

Somehow, most of the time, Vanessa felt as if she were alone on the earth, a hollow, desolate feeling. She wondered if the Holder man had ever felt like that. 'I prefer *King Solomon's Mines*,' she said bluntly to Harvey Boerum. With the first amusement of the evening, she waited for his reaction.

Predictably he said, 'My word, Haggard's an unusual author for a lady.'

'Yes, he is.' Vanessa stifled a mighty yawn with a skilful compression of her upper over her lower lip, a trick she'd learned from her father. It made one look ill. Laughter bubbled in Vanessa.

Her poor father. She loved him so much. They had a great deal in common. Both of them hated these affairs of her mother's, and both were devoted to the adventure stories of H. Rider Haggard. She envied her father for his conference with Holder. The man had probably had adventures himself, just like Haggard's men. She'd have liked hearing about them, too, as her father had. Her mother was scandalised at the invitation.

'Even your silence is bewitching,' Harvey murmured. She could feel his stare.

At last he released her to her next partner, and the ball dragged on. Finally, at one o'clock she decided it was late enough to excuse herself without an outcry from her mother. Bea would dance until the last strains of the orchestra died away. Martin Stirling had retired long ago, with the valid excuse of early rising.

After the little Irish maid had undone her ball gown and hung it away, Vanessa dismissed her.

She smiled, looking at her reflection in the cheval-glass. Certainly her hair didn't need brushing. Vanessa ran her fingers through its curly gilt, glorying in the sense of freedom the gesture gave her. She recalled with a delicate shudder the onerous weight of her former hip-length hair. It had always been too curly, unmanageable; even having the gentlest maid brush it was agony. At sixteen, when Vanessa faced the prospect of pinning it up, and the constant attention of hairdressers, she rebelled.

She couldn't bear the idea of those pounds of hair; carrying the weight was like a native woman bearing a heavy basket of fruit on her head. Vanessa's mother often complained of the torture she suffered when a strong wind pulled at the hatpins anchoring a hat to her own coiffure.

Five years ago, when Vanessa was only fourteen, she had asked an outraged hairdresser to cut her hair to its present length. The woman refused. But finally, when presented with an enormous bribe, the hairdresser complied.

Vanessa grinned, remembering the uproar. Her father had chided her, her mother literally fainted. And the precocious Bea, who at fifteen was already quite man-crazy, twitted, 'You'll never get married now.'

Recalling her reply, Vanessa was thoughtful. 'That's fine with me,' she'd retorted. She had never wanted to get married. Since she was twelve years old all she'd ever really wanted was to play the piano. That had been enough. But now she wondered. Why did she have this hollow, lonely feeling if that were so?

She had always considered herself alien from other women. In so many ways she was; this very room was evidence of that. In striking contrast to the fussiness of Bea's room and her mother's, Vanessa's bedroom was almost austere. She had had it done like that despite her mother's strong objections, with the support of her ever loyal father.

In this era when prudishness had reached such a height that the girls' school piano had its naked limbs clothed in pantaloons, Vanessa's dresser was an uncurtained Queen Anne table with a scrolled mirror hanging over it.

The whole room was characterised by subdued detail. Instead of a mantel, which Vanessa had ordered removed, the hearth now had a plainly carved, arched frame. The walls were creamy white, with random pictures. There were lavender-blue satin hangings on the bed and windows, their scrolled valances echoed in the curve of a splat-back chair by the simple marble-topped table. Small rugs were scattered on the polished floor.

16

Usually the room gave Vanessa a sense of security and peace. For some reason tonight it did not have that effect. She was full of strange thoughts, unaccustomed feelings.

She got out of her constricting corset and voluminous under-clothes with relief. Passing the cheval-glass to get her nightgown she glimpsed her naked body.

As if she were appraising a stranger, she looked at the full, shapely breasts, the gradual curve of her narrow waist into the round hips; the patch of golden luxuriance on her lower body, the well-formed legs. The love stories she'd read all hinted that such a body was made for love.

She had never known what love felt like. A memory of that galvanising touch this afternoon assailed her. If a touch of the hand could be so startling, what would . . . the rest be like?

Vanessa slipped her gown over her head and turned out the lamps. Getting into bed she puzzled about the matter of love. She had only seen its results, and they were not reassuring – her father's irritated tolerance of her mother and their lonely separate bedrooms; Bea's avid pursuit of men, so pathetic and embarrassing. Bea was twenty and still not married. Vanessa stirred, feeling uncomfortably warm. She threw off her silken cover.

Perhaps Bea had already experienced what was allowable only in marriage. Vanessa wondered. She marvelled that her mother could remain ignorant of the whispers about Bea . . . or choose to remain so. Vanessa's mother did not like to face unpleasant facts.

And heaven knew she would never offer any information to Vanessa about the act of love. She was far too delicate for that. She'd told Vanessa years ago that the doctor had brought her in his little black bag, and referred to underwear as 'unwhisperables' and 'white sewing'.

Vanessa grinned in the dark. Then she thought, soberly, I wonder what it is like for Bea . . . I wonder what it is like for anyone? What would love be like with the man from Africa?

Abruptly she got up and turned on a light. It was absurd to have such thoughts; she'd only met the man for less than a half hour that very afternoon, glimpsed him at the ball. Then why was she so preoccupied with him now? Before she had been preoccupied like that only with her music. All her emotions had poured into it, leaving nothing for anyone or anything else.

She'd bought a new musical score that afternoon, one she was eager to play, but there hadn't been time. Now it lay on the marble-topped table. She sat down and read the score. Her trained eye transmuted every note to inner audibility, a clear succession of stormy, passionate tones. But now for some reason her customary pleasure in this exercise failed her. That sense of alienation, that awful nibbling loneliness gnawed at her again.

She picked up *King Solomon's Mines* and began reading where she'd left off.

Even that could not divert her. It reminded her of the Holder man from Africa.

He wasn't like anyone she had ever known, with his great strong body, his tanned face and bold eyes.

And for the dozenth time she recalled the touch of his hand, like no other, the touch that had sent that extraordinary sensation through her body, as if for an instant she'd held lightning itself in her palm.

CHAPTER TWO

Amas Holder strode out of the depot and with his bag still in his hand boarded the Battery horsecar No. 323. Another day he would have walked; now time was of the essence and the horsecar would take him within spitting distance of Stirling Enterprise.

He hadn't been on the 323 before, though he'd heard plenty about it around town. It was considered the 'beau ideal' car of the day. He found a place on one of the plush benches and looked around. The clock over the rear central door indicated three-thirty.

Amas hoped he wouldn't be too late. As the car rumbled southward on its eight-mile trip that had begun at Central Park, he observed the passing city scene with absent-minded eye, reviewing the last week in Philadelphia.

The reunion with Ellen Todd Holder had been an emotional one. She seemed to have aged beyond her years, and her hands had not survived the grinding work she'd done when he was a boy, he noticed

18

sadly. The visit had been a pleasant one, though. He liked Philadelphia, a gracious city he had not seen before, even if it lacked the stimulating pace of New York.

And Amas had been gratified by his mother's pleasure in the belated gifts he brought her for her birthday in September – a handsome brooch of Kimberley diamonds which he'd had cut and polished to a blinding brilliance, set in white-gold filigree; a magnificent blue-white diamond ring from the same source.

He had seen too late, from her look of chagrin, that the ring was far too small. She could not slip it over her gnarled, work-roughened knuckles.

'I'll have it made bigger,' he offered hastily. But his mother shook her head and gave him a sombre smile. 'It's much too lovely for these unsightly hands,' she said. 'Save it for the girl that you will marry.'

He protested that that was not going to happen for a long time, and furthermore he would have plenty of diamonds to choose from when that day came. But Ellen insisted that he keep the ring.

With the intention of having it made large enough for his mother's finger, he was carrying it still in his pocket. And he couldn't help thinking of Vanessa Stirling's long, narrow fingers, her childlike hand.

A faint twinge of guilt struck him when he remembered his mother's tears when they parted, his own comparative lack of reluctance to go. But he couldn't wait to get back to New York again.

When the 323 reached City Hall, Amas could no longer contain his impatience. He jumped off, disdaining the metal step, blocks before his destination and rushed off downtown.

This time the clerk in the front office was much more respectful, doubtless owing to Amas' dudish gear. He was wearing a fawn top hat and a perfectly fitting dark brown suit, one of the tailor-mades that were now sweeping America. The disapproving assistant at Brooks Brothers had sold him that suit and a lighter one of greyish-brown, saying emphatically that the 'matter of tailoring' could not be hurried. He would have to wait at least three weeks for his other clothes to be finished. And even that length of time, he seemed to say, was but a hectic instant to a painstaking tailor. Meanwhile, for an 'emergency situation' the tailor-mades might suffice. Amas would be obliged to go back to Brooks tomorrow for his first fitting, and then wait.

Now, however, even the tailor-made apparently impressed the prissy Madden. Amas restrained a grin. After a minimal wait he was shown into Stirling's office.

19

The financier greeted him with great cordiality and asked after his mother. Then he told Amas that Stirling Enterprise had decided to grant him the loan he needed; as a matter of fact the papers were ready for his signature. At the end of the conference Stirling asked him casually to dinner the next night, saying it would be 'informal'.

Amas was so elated by both these pieces of news that he fairly floated out of the building.

The next afternoon he puzzled about some sort of tribute to take the Stirling women; it seemed the thing to do. But he was nervous about choosing. It would not do at all to blunder in with the wrong presents. Then he remembered a shocked remark of his mother to one of his visiting aunts, something about a highly improper gift a young man had made to a young lady. Amas had asked his mother idly what was proper, and she'd answered, 'Flowers, of course, my dear. Or handkerchiefs or candy. At the *most* a thin volume of verse.'

He had nodded solemnly, instructed. At the time it struck him that the whole thing was unreal and absurd, as unreal as the smothering houses of the narrow city, when he thought of the yawning great jaws of the Kimberley mine, the bitter sun and sweating workmen, the stark look of the primitive houses. But now he was grateful to remember the little incident.

After he'd bathed and dressed in his new sand-coloured suit, and visited the hotel barber shop, he bought two small, elaborate boxes of candy for Beatrice and Mrs Stirling. Then, for Vanessa, he bought a box of fragile handkerchiefs in the Lord and Taylor department store. 'Just feel them, sir,' the sales clerk urged him. But they were so frail he was afraid to touch them; his calloused thumb would surely pull the fabric, break the fairylike threads of the fine, thin lace. The handkerchiefs looked almost as soft as the hair of Vanessa Stirling.

'To *dinner*, Martin?' Hester Stirling, in her dismay, let Mrs Leslie's *Lady's Magazine* slip out of her jewelled fingers. It slid off her pink satin lap.

'Why, yes, my dear. You make it sound like an immodest suggestion.' Martin Stirling lit his cigar, pulled at it and exhaled a satisfying cloud of smoke. He retrieved the magazine.

At the piano Vanessa went on softly playing. Her father's mischief, her mother's martyrdom did not bring the usual enjoyment; an odd, quick warmth entered Vanessa's body.

'You might have told me,' Hester Stirling protested. 'We're having dinner in the family room.'

20

'Exactly why I didn't,' Stirling countered. 'Amas Holder is a plain young man.'

' "Ammus?" ' Hester repeated with distaste. 'What sort of name is that, for heaven's sake?'

Stirling told her the story of his name. Vanessa listened closely.

Adamas, she said silently. Amas, savouring the name's lovely strangeness. She began a nocturne of Chopin's.

'Umm, that's nice.' Stirling walked to the instrument and stood there smiling down at her.

'But what on earth do you feed a man like that?' Hester asked sharply, in jarring contrast to the wistful music.

'Cooked food . . . just what we eat. We won't have to throw him raw meat.' Stirling's tone was the one that maddened Hester. Vanessa laughed.

'Are you so sure?' Vanessa saw her father's smile die at the sound of Bea's voice. She rarely joined them in the music room before dinner, making no secret of the fact that Vanessa's playing bored her.

Vanessa stopped playing and turned around on the bench. Surprisingly Bea had joined them tonight, and apparently in time to hear the conversation.

'Are you sure?' Bea repeated, mincing to the sofa to sit by her mother. The tightness of her skirt forced her to lower herself with great caution lest the seams give way. 'If you're talking about that Holder man, he's a perfect barbarian. He was insufferably rude to me the other night.'

'My dear girl,' Martin retorted, 'you were the rude one.'

Vanessa burned with curiosity to know what had happened. But it would do no good to ask her father. Bless him, he never tattled on either Vanessa or Bea.

Now she could tell Bea was sorry she'd brought it up, because Hester demanded, 'What are you talking about?'

'Nothing, Hester, nothing.' Martin made a great show of examining the music sheets on the piano rack.

'Well,' Hester sniffed, 'no one ever tells me anything.' With an intonation of even deeper offence, she added, 'We're not prepared for company, as you see, Martin. Vanessa's not even dressed at *all*.'

She eyed Vanessa's soft grey silk with disdain. In direct contrast to Bea's ruched, gathered and folded mustard satin and her own unbecoming pale pink frilly creation, Vanessa's dress was looser of skirt, modestly bustled and comparatively unadorned.

'Vanessa, go put something on,' Hester directed. 'Good gracious,

21

you look like that little messenger girl in the Renoir painting . . . what is it? *Les Parapluies?* Even if this Holder man isn't . . . anybody in particular, I can't have my daughter looking like a *serf.*'

'Amas Holder,' Stirling said calmly, 'is a very worthy young man indeed. Ten times the man these peacocks are who prance around our daughters.'

'There's no need to be vulgar.' A mottled pink stained Hester's pallid face.

The gilt clock on the mantel chimed its tinkling chime. 'In any case, there's no time for Vanessa to gussy up,' Stirling commented. 'Holder will be here at any moment.'

That quick, alien hotness flooded Vanessa until she felt her veins were dyed with it. She tried to imagine what it would be like . . . seeing him in the company of her mother.

'Father,' Bea began, 'I really don't know what's got into you . . .' They heard the doorbell from the hall.

'You, young woman, had better behave,' her father rejoined.

When the butler announced Amas Holder, Martin Stirling went to the door to greet him.

Vanessa drew in a breath of surprise. Surely this elegant giant, standing on the threshold of the music room, could not be the same dishevelled man she'd met in her father's office, the one who had brought the very wildness of the veld into the corridor on the night of the ball. She was almost sorry to see the flawlessness of his clothes, like anyone else's.

But no, they were not like anyone else's; the meticulous tailoring could not disguise his body's massive strength or diminish his enormous height. Something untameable in him seemed to strain at the very cloth. His dark, ferocious glance swept the room, dismissing it, lighting on her. She was deeply disturbed by the power of those eyes.

Amas Holder smiled, the white teeth flashing in his weathered face. 'Good evening,' he said. She hadn't heard him speak with that same clarity before; his voice was a deep, growling baritone with a gentle intonation. He held three parcels in one big, rough hand.

'Good evening, Amas.' Stirling wrung his hand heartily. 'Please come in.'

Holder obeyed, his long stride disproportionate to the cluttered space.

'You know my daughters . . . Vanessa, Beatrice. May I present my wife.'

Holder bowed courteously over Hester's hand. Then he straight-

22

ened and looked at Vanessa. She put out her hand and he took it with great caution, holding it longer than custom demanded in his big palm. Again there was that faint, galvanic crackle; that astonishing heat flowed from his fingers into her own, as if a minute flame were entering the veins of her wrist, shooting up her arm. Nothing in her experience had readied her for such a thing; she felt her poise slipping, chagrined warmth dyeing her face.

Something bright flickered in his lionlike eyes and he took a gulping, shallow breath. 'Miss Vanessa,' he said softly, his voice sounding strained. He held out a thin, flat package to her.

She took it, barely able to murmur a conventional thanks, almost relieved when he greeted Bea, without touching her, and handed the other parcels to the women.

'How nice,' Hester fluttered, opening the package that revealed a handsome box of candy. Even in her confusion Vanessa enjoyed her mother's apparent change of mind, as if conceding that Amas Holder was not so dreadful after all. Vanessa opened her own package, touched by the sight of the fragile handkerchiefs. When she thanked him the ferocious eyes bored into hers.

At dinner he sat between her father and mother at the round, informal table, roughly opposite Vanessa. He was politely attentive to Hester, warm to Stirling and ignored Bea as much as possible.

Bea seemed to have forgotten her hostility. She leaned across the table insinuatingly, asking numerous questions about the diamond business and South Africa. Holder answered her with perfect, neutral correctness but his glance returned again and again to Vanessa.

She said little, still too overwhelmed by the phenomenon of her reaction to his brief handclasp, even too confused to enter in the talk. But it was impossible not to enjoy her mother's apparent surprise over Amas Holder's good manners.

'This is your first journey to New York, then?' Hester asked him sweetly. There was a calculating light in her pale blue eyes; for an instant Vanessa wondered why. She knew the answer when, after dinner, Hester led them into the music room and asked Vanessa to play. It became obvious that Hester wanted Vanessa safely at the piano, and Bea on the sofa at Holder's side. Her mother was marking Amas Holder down for Bea, Vanessa judged. A rich, unknowing stranger who was unacquainted with Bea's reputation would be a splendid catch, Vanessa supposed. She was amazed at the extent of her resentment.

As much as she shrank from playing to a captive audience, however, she consented, and sat down to play.

23

Something made her choose the wild new music she had bought on the day of the ball.

Amas was not surprised when she began a stormy piece of music, primitive and wild. She was not the type, he thought, for tinkling minuets.

He studied her in half-profile as she played, wishing fervently he could stand beside her, not sit here trapped beside the calculating Beatrice. Her white shoulders almost blinded him above the modest neckline of her soft grey dress, her feathery drift of hair, in the lamplight, like sunlight on summer water. Her only ornament, which his gem-trained eye caught at once, was a simple pair of rose-diamond earrings, flat studs against her exquisitely modelled earlobes, yet regal in comparison to the positive chandeliers of glitter in the ears of Beatrice and their mother.

Listening, Amas was awed by the power of her performance. The music, with its inference of thunder and of native drums, set a barbaric fire ablaze in him. His body burned. He wanted her as he had never wanted another woman, in all his wild and chequered days.

When she finished playing and declined to play more, Vanessa quietly went to a chair near her father's. Amas was hard put to converse the rest of the evening. It was almost with an odd relief that he parted from them; it was too difficult to sit there in the same room with her and not touch her, caress her.

When he bade her goodnight, he realised that her remarkable eyes hinted at a sultry nature repressed below that calm exterior. The eyes haunted him, bedevilled him, as he wandered down Fifth Avenue towards his hotel.

He was far too restless to go to his room, so he walked over to Broadway and went into a bar-room for a drink. He had two or three, more than he usually had, eyeing the oil paintings of voluptuous nudes over the mahogany bar. At last he decided he'd had enough, of both the whiskey and the pictures, and returned dejectedly to his hotel.

He wondered if her passion for her music would be stronger than her feeling for a man. Numbly he took his key from the man at the desk and walked slowly up the stairs, still seeing Vanessa Stirling's face.

When he unlocked the door he was startled to see lights. He hadn't left them on.

Cautiously he stepped in and then quickly closed the door, pre-

24

pared to confront a burglar behind it. With his tightened nerves he'd been ready; it would be a relief to smash something with his fists. But he felt a little foolish. There was no one behind the door.

Then a woman laughed, a high, shrill and excited sound. Amas whirled. Beatrice Stirling was sitting on the sofa, smiling at him.

'What in hell . . .?' he blurted.

'. . . am I doing here?' she supplied, with the same fixed smile. She got up from the sofa and started towards him. 'And how did I get in?' Now she was standing close to him, looking up at him seductively with those huge, peculiar black eyes. 'Well, Amas Holder, I spun quite a tale to the manager. I told him I am your little cousin and that you, you naughty man, were late to meet me. And of course he couldn't let a young lady like me, as he put it, sit in a public lobby.'

Her pouting red mouth was moist and pursed, lifted to him as if she were waiting to be kissed.

Amas recalled now that the fellow downstairs had said something to him, was probably telling him about his visitor, but he'd been so intent on his thoughts he hadn't listened. Beatrice Stirling was very close to him now, her blatant breasts exposed almost to the nipples. He realised dimly that she hadn't been that naked looking at the Stirling house.

She raised her thin arms and put them boldly around his middle; he could smell her heavy, musky scent and for a drunken second his blood pounded, his body, inflamed all evening with the sound and scent and sight of Vanessa, started to respond. Something in him whispered, why not?

Beatrice stroked his sides and emitted a triumphant little chuckle.

She was staring up at him, breathing shallowly; he could see the tip of her small pink tongue between her white teeth, her red parted lips. Her huge black eyes were avid, glittering. 'I knew you wanted this, I knew it,' she said hoarsely.

Almost without volition, he raised his hands and took her by the upper arms. But then as suddenly as it had come, his lust was gone. The close sight of her coarse-grained skin, the heavy, smothering odour of her perfume and another scent – the heat of her arousal – made his gorge rise.

He could see Vanessa's face, with its stormy blue-grey eyes and its flowerlike complexion; the earnest and ironic little mouth. And the nearness of this dark, hot bitch turned him quite cold.

His fingers closed around her bare arms with a determined grasp and pushed her a little backwards.

Now he saw her amorous, drowsy-lidded eyes take on an expression of bewilderment.

'What is it?' she murmured.

'I think you'd better go,' he said bluntly. His voice sounded tight in his own ears.

'What? What did you say?' Her mouth was slack with puzzlement and in the black eyes he saw a fiery point of igniting anger.

'I'll put you in a cab, Miss Stirling.' Amas was having a difficult time keeping his voice calm. He felt a little like a fool. It must have been a month, at least, since he'd had a woman. And here was one, offering herself to him on a plate.

But he couldn't take her, not when his every nerve-end fired with the image of Vanessa. And that idea, in itself, was most disturbing.

Beatrice Stirling was still staring; her rage almost scorched his skin.

He took his hands from her arms and now they hung at his sides.

'You big damned fool, what's wrong with you, anyway?' she demanded. Now her tone was not at all seductive; it grated on him. She was trembling with indignation. 'What's the matter? Aren't you a man, after all? Or maybe you don't know what to do with a woman, after all those sheep and cows you use in the wilderness?'

For a fleeting instant he had a wild desire to hit her. Then he felt only a kind of terrible amusement, a deep weariness. 'It's just that I like to choose my women myself, Miss Stirling.'

The shot went home. Her face crumpled. He was struck with a flash of piercing knowledge, a momentary bolt of illumination, the way a night-scene reveals itself for an eyeblink in a bolt of lightning – this was the human queenbee, to the life. The queen bee whose mate is chosen among the highest flyers; after the frenzy and triumph, the chosen male is destroyed.

Everything about Beatrice Stirling, from her nickname to her pointed face and enormous eyes, her whining tone, and the pathetic choice of clothes in stripes of black and gold, was the queen bee's signature. Even now, Amas realised, the plushy fabric of her very gown had an unpleasant suggestion of the body of that insect with the mortal sting.

He felt a pitying amusement, a deep embarrassment for her.

'Come,' he said more gently, leading her to the sofa where she had tossed her long black cloak. 'I will take you home.'

Amas picked up the cloak and started to put it around her narrow shoulders.

She snatched it from his hands. 'You . . . you rotten eunuch. You're not fit to touch me.' Her anger was so overwhelming that her teeth chattered. Amas was dismayed; she looked as if she might have a fit, right then and there. He began to be very anxious to get her out of his rooms.

Beatrice put on her cloak and fastened it with shaking hands. 'I'll go alone,' she said through tight-clenched teeth. Her face was inordinately pale; he could see that it had been painted, because there were two livid circles on her cheeks standing out against the sallow skin.

'Not at this hour,' he retorted, and took her elbow firmly in his hand. She struggled in his hold, but he was too strong for her.

Picking up his key with his other hand, he led her from the room, down the stairs and through the lobby to the street, conscious of the curious stares of the desk clerk and the doorman.

Forcing a smile, he asked the doorman to whistle for a cab. When it came, Beatrice broke out of his grasp and got in unassisted. Amas heard her give the cabman the Stirling's Fifth Avenue address in a shrill, commanding tone.

He made his way back to his room. He was drained and sore. Damn the bitch, damn her. Now every time he sought out Vanessa she would be there, waiting, and he would have to look at her taunting eyes and evil little face.

The nastiness and absurdity of the whole encounter made him feel unclean. It had certainly, he concluded drily, not relaxed him. He took an ice cold bath, which relieved him a little, and got into bed.

But his whole body began to burn and pound again, when he thought of Vanessa. He had to have her. That he knew. If he didn't soon he would explode into a thousand pieces.

And to hell with that amateur whore. He would just have to cope with her.

In the saner light of day, Amas felt a good deal better. Cool reason told him that there had been another motive for his rejection of Beatrice. He'd be a bigger fool than he realised if he seduced the daughter of a man who was lending him that much money; a man, moreover, he had a real affection for. God knows there were enough light women in New York to take care of any man, even if he had the propensities of a bull. And if worse came to worst, he could surely find them.

His biggest problem at the moment was exercise. Habituated to grinding, backbreaking work for the last twelve years, and early rising, he didn't know what to do with himself in the mornings. He could always walk, but he'd already done plenty of that.

Two mornings after Beatrice's visit, Amas awoke at his customary early hour, feeling as restless as a stallion ready to kick down its stall.

He had filled the hours of the day before, somehow, but he knew there was no point in calling at the Stirlings' before the afternoon. He'd tried that yesterday and was told that Vanessa took music instruction until noon; also, which interested him not at all, that Beatrice and Mrs Stirling were out shopping.

A stallion, Amas repeated silently. Maybe he could hire a horse, and go riding in Central Park. He had found that urban forest early on, and it gave him perpetual delight. Like the waterfront, it was about the only place in the city where he felt he could breathe.

He dressed hurriedly and walked west and north to Thirtieth Street. There was a livery stable there which he'd seen in passing. A fellow had been washing down a horse and was willing to pass the time of day with Amas. No doubt the fellow could tell him where to hire a mount in Central Park.

In another hour Amas was cantering along the bridle path on a patient hack. Not much of a horse, but better than nothing. He felt his flagging vitality renew itself.

After a hearty lunch he walked back to his hotel, bathed and changed his clothes. Buying a bouquet of roses, he walked to the Stirling house.

He was aware that he was moving awfully fast. But time was flying by and time was the only thing he didn't have. He was going to have to go back to Kimberley, and soon. There were just so many weeks that it was safe to leave the mine in a foreman's hands, even a good one like Sam Dillon.

When he rang, the proper butler admitted him into the hall. 'I fear, sir, that Mrs Stirling is not at home,' the man offered in a meaningful way.

In other words, the sisters are unchaperoned, Amas silently translated. 'I've come to see Miss Vanessa,' he retorted. 'Is she in?'

He could hear the loud and steady sound of scales proceeding from the music room.

'I doubt it, sir, but I will ascertain.' The butler gave Amas a reproving look and withdrew. Amas paced the hall.

He stifled an exclamation of disgust. Beatrice was coming down

28

the curving stairs, dressed in her habitual gold and black. 'Well, well,' she drawled. 'Good afternoon. Have you come to make your apologies?'

'I've come to see Vanessa,' Amas responded bluntly.

Beatrice recoiled as if he'd struck her. But she recovered, and snapped, 'She will not see you without a chaperone.' Her twisted smile expressed ridicule, but it could not hide her resentment.

The butler came back with a scandalised air. 'Miss Vanessa will see you in the music room.'

Amas was amused by the omission of the usual respectful 'sir', too elated to give a damn about anything. With pounding heart he hurried off, not even acknowledging Beatrice. When he entered the room he saw Vanessa at the piano. She was no longer practising scales. Soft, liquid sounds greeted him as he went forward.

He sensed in his instinctive way that the new music reflected a changed mood in her. His breath grew short and his collar choked his neck.

Her back was to him. He gloried in the sight of her sunny hair like a golden nimbus around her head; the contours of her curving back, the feminine roundness of her hips undisguised in the narrow skirt of the lilac gown. Even without the deformity of hideous corsets her figure was like an hourglass.

The music ended. She turned around on the piano bench to meet his eyes.

Vanessa stared into the brown eyes of Amas Holder, thinking, this is what I was afraid of. This is why I postponed it. I am undone just by looking into his eyes; I can feel him, all the way across the room.

The very earth seemed to be rocking on its axis. Not a dozen words had passed between them, yet she felt they knew each other deeply, that there was a kinship between them that could not exist between another woman and another man.

Now they were still staring at each other, without uttering a greeting.

Finally he broke the silence with her name. She barely noticed that he spoke it without the preceding title, it sounded so right to her, so true. 'Vanessa,' he said again.

'Hello, Amas.' She saw a bright triumph blaze in his feral eyes at her greeting, and she pounded with excitement. 'I'm glad to see you.' She heard her own words, racked and dazzled with alien feeling. She had never told a man that in all her life.

He seemed too surprised to find an answer. He strode across the carpet and grabbed her by the hands, urging her upward.

His trembling fingers slid up her silk-clad arms and took her by the shoulders, kneading her soft flesh. Then she was moving into him, their bodies melding like mist, losing themselves in each other's nearness. He lowered his wild mouth to her upturned lips and kissed her with a hunger so savage she was dizzy with it, swaying.

Her mouth shook, her whole frame quivered and she felt her will recede, transmuted, dissolved into a foreign, hot submission to his deep, starved, unrelenting kiss.

It lasted less than an instant. Crying out, she pulled herself away and went blindly to the window, staring with unseeing eyes at the grey November light. In one long step he was with her, putting his arms around her body, forcing her to turn to him.

'Marry me, Vanessa,' he said hoarsely. 'Marry me. Come with me.'

Dazed, she looked up into his beseeching and ferocious eyes. 'This is . . . happening too fast,' she gasped. 'I feel such confusion.'

'There's nothing to be confused about,' he insisted, taking her face in his huge hands. The touch sent a swift, mysterious jabbing of liquid fire to her very centre; everything was plausible when he touched her. 'We love each other. We struck each other, like lightning, Vanessa. You saw it, you felt it, from the first time we met. I love you, Vanessa. And you love me. I know it.'

She stared at him, confounded. 'Say it, say it,' he demanded.

She closed out the fire of his hypnotic gaze with her shuttered lids, but the stroke of his calloused fingers on her skin could not be shut out. Her body still throbbed and quickened with that almost painful burning. With her eyes still closed, she whispered, 'All right then, I'll say it. I will say that I am a little mad. With this, with you, Amas Holder. But I do not know if that is love.'

'Of course it is. What else could it be, Vanessa?'

She opened her eyes and smiled at him; she could see moisture in his own eyes, and it touched her unbearably. He was beginning to smile now, too, a tentative, shaky smile that tugged at her emotions as strongly as his embrace.

'Oh, Vanessa.' Still holding her face gently between his hands, he leaned and kissed her again. The force of that caress was even more stunning than the one before; she felt an awful weakness in her legs and arms, leaning against him. His body's strength was massive, protective, all that was certain and secure. Languorously she thought, I would like to stay here, in his arms, forever.

Her softness apparently was his triumph, because he said insistently, 'You see? You belong with me. Marry me, my darling, come back with me to Kimberley. There will never be any confusion for you any more, only happiness, I swear it. Happiness greater than anything you've ever known before.'

He held her tightly; she could feel his hot breath on the top of her head fanning the tendrils of her hair, sense the leashed desire in his hard, trembling frame. 'Oh, God, Vanessa, when I hold you like this . . . I just . . .' He stopped, then went on hoarsely. 'I love you so much, want you so much, it's tearing me apart.'

The sound of the words, the strong vibration of his deep voice against her, aroused a storm of feelings in her mightier than the others; she was afraid she was going to faint, and she had never done that. His steely arms were like a bond around her, holding her with such force she could scarcely breathe.

'Please,' she quavered, 'please, Amas. Let me go a moment. Let me sit down. I can't . . . think when you're doing these things.'

At once he released her and tenderly led her to the sofa. She sat down. He stood above her, fixing her with his bright brown stare. 'You don't need to think,' he said passionately. 'I'll do the thinking for us. Just answer me. Tell me yes, Vanessa.'

When she didn't answer, he went on urgently, 'I've seen it in your eyes – we are the same kind. We don't know how to play. Love is forever for people like us, Vanessa. It is the end of all existence, the end of the world. It will be the end of the world if you don't marry me.'

Involuntarily she nodded; even that made him victorious. He was right. He knew so much about her, sensed so much that no other man ever had, ever could.

He sat down and took her hands. 'We have to be free, Vanessa. We can be free together, in Africa.'

She nodded again.

His face lit up. He had taken her submissive nod for assent. 'You'll love it there, my darling.'

This was like being caught in a whirlwind, she reflected. She was being swept off like a leaf from a tree in a mighty gale, and all at once she knew she had to put a stop to this. He had hypnotised her with his body and his mouth, this man she didn't know at all. She must be given time to get her breath.

The wild emotion that almost brought her pain, it was so

31

strong – how could she be sure that it would last? This very melting tenderness could be a snare that would lead her like a willing, mesmerised animal into a trap. Into the absolute unknown; into a world where her music would be lost forever; into a mysterious wilderness.

Away from her music, the music that had been her sole, solid companion for so long, the thing for which she had worked and suffered and been so alone. He had spoken of freedom. But in that kind of freedom she could lose her very self. She had to be given time, she had to consider.

'What is it?' he asked with desperate anxiety. 'Why do you look like that?'

'You've got to give me time,' she answered weakly. 'I've known you such a little while. Please, Amas. I must be sure.'

'Oh, my dearest, how can you be more sure than this?' He kissed her again with wild roughness and she nearly relented. But when he released her, she shook her head.

'I must have time.'

There was a shining pain in his eyes when he said, 'And I have so little, Vanessa. I have so little time. I've got everything else – strength and health, money and determination. Love enough, desire enough for a hundred men, a thousand. But time – that's what I have the least of. I must go back, and soon. I must. Everything depends on it. Please . . . please don't tell me no. Let me speak to your father. Let me at least hope, Vanessa.'

'Not yet, Amas. Please.'

'Oh, my God.' He got up from the sofa and strode about the room, his hands balled into fists. He turned to her again and pleaded, 'Let me speak to your father.'

His head was rigid on his neck, the posture of his whole body beseeching yet determined. He kept staring into her eyes and she began to feel that helplessness that his look and touch and nearness brought to her confused and weakened will.

But she said, 'Please go, Amas. Go now and let me have a little time.'

He hesitated, fixing her with his piercing stare. Then he took a deep, shaky breath and said in a tight voice, 'All right, Vanessa. I'll go now. But I haven't given up. I'll be back, Vanessa. I'll always keep coming back.'

Amas took her hand and kissed it. She felt her heart fluttering in her throat as he walked out of the room.

CHAPTER THREE

Vanessa ached with unshed tears when she walked to the window to watch Amas' tall, massive figure disappear into the gathering dusk. She saw the golden night-lamps go on, one by one, along Fifth Avenue, feeling torn between agony and elation; remembering the sensation of his mighty arms around her, the pressure of his mouth. But she recalled as well how blithely he had demanded that she change her entire life, asking her to throw everything away in a moment, trading all she knew and held dear for an unknown destiny.

And Amas Holder was a man. The work he loved would go on uninterrupted. She was only a woman, with none of the male prerogatives. Her own work, the music that had been the core of her existence, would be over.

Good God, in South Africa – and the very name was threatening, conjuring up terrifying native drums, ravening cannibals, primitive deprivations – where could she study, how could she perform? Ever since she was thirteen her masters had praised her talent, spoken of her glowing promise.

And yet, on the other side of the balance was that dazzling joy, that alien fire and tempest from his lightest touch upon her. Vanessa put her hand to her face, imagining that his clean male scent still lingered on her skin; inhaling that scent, she was overcome with an inner trembling. Emotion and reason see-sawed for eminence with such an unrelenting regularity that Vanessa was nervously exhausted.

She did not go down to dinner.

In her room, no longer a serene haven, but a lonely cell, she kept repeating to herself the damning fact: the third time he'd been in her company, Amas Holder had asked her to marry him. It was madness. How could he know, so soon?

And she was as mad as he: the third time she had been in his company, her body had responded to his as if they were fated to be together; she talked to him as if they'd known each other all their lives. Perhaps she was meant to marry him.

She hardly slept that night. She did not go down to breakfast, but stayed in her room and breakfasted alone. Her father sought her out with anxious questions about her health, but she told him that she was tired, that she'd been overdoing things.

And then that afternoon, at about the time Amas had called yesterday, she heard the doorbell ring. After an agonising hesitation she sent word that she was not at home, silencing the piano. After the front door closed again she burst into wild weeping. She missed him horribly, yet it was dangerous to see him; his physical presence would burn away her very will, unseat her reason.

Dinner was an uncomfortable affair. Her heart thudded painfully when her mother asked, 'What would you think, Martin, of inviting your African friend to our musicale next week?'

Vanessa saw her mother give Bea a coy look. Bea's lips grew tight.

'Good heavens, my dear girl,' Martin Stirling teased his wife. 'You make it sound as if he'll wear a loincloth and beads and bring a spear. You *are* talking about Amas Holder, I take it?'

'Of course I am. Don't be silly, Martin.' Hester frowned. 'I'm surprised at how civilised he turned out to be. Of course his mother *was* a Philadelphia Todd, and that counts for something, even in these vulgar days. And he seemed to take a very intelligent interest in music.'

'Well, he enjoyed Vanessa's playing,' Stirling remarked, 'as who does not?' Vanessa tried to answer her father's smile. He was studying her keenly.

'I think he's more interested in someone else,' Hester said sweetly, shooting another twinkling glance at Bea.

Vanessa's discomfort struggled with her amusement.

'Well, *this* daughter has no interest in *him*,' Bea snapped. Vanessa's curiosity was aroused. What had got into Bea?

'Nonsense.' Hester dismissed Bea's disclaimer. 'Martin, which is Mr Holder's hotel? I'll write him an invitation.'

'The Fif –,' Beatrice blurted. Then she reddened and fell silent.

Her cut-off reply was lost on Hester, who was listening to Stirling say, 'The Fifth Avenue Hotel.' But Vanessa had caught it.

A suspicion so painful, so grotesque that she could hardly countenance it, overcame her. Amas Holder had taken Bea to his hotel. It couldn't be possible; he had seemed to be impervious to Bea's obvious charms. He had proposed to her, to Vanessa Stirling. How could he? She was stabbed with a pain so numbing that she almost cried aloud. How right she'd been to conclude that she didn't know Amas Holder. He was so obviously a lusty, passionate man; even if he loved her, Vanessa, he was still capable of consoling himself with Bea, deceitfully pretending indifference.

With enormous effort Vanessa kept her expression blank, seemingly indifferent to the conversation. But she could feel the keen stare of her father. And that night, again, her sleep was fitful. The next afternoon she was not at home to Amas Holder when he called. She was certain now that she had made a wise decision. Something had happened between Amas Holder and the avid Beatrice.

Amas put off his departure day by day, gripped in abject misery. For more than a week now Vanessa had refused to receive him. Finally, when he received Mrs Stirling's invitation to a musicale, he had almost given up hope, but his wildest aspirations renewed.

Putting on his new evening suit he arrived at the mansion early, dismayed when Mrs Stirling arranged for him to sit next to the glowering Beatrice, with Vanessa confined to the piano.

He managed to greet Vanessa, but she answered him with such coldness that his heart sank into his shoes. To make matters worse, Beatrice spent a good bit of the evening whispering behind her fan to the man on her other side. Amas was uncomfortably aware of the fellow's nonplussed glances. He could only infer that Beatrice was talking about him, Amas Holder, and not in a complimentary way. He caught a shocked, 'Really? You don't say?' in an undertone from the man.

Silently he cursed the bitch and resolved to ask for Vanessa after the performance. But when he did so he was told she had a headache and had gone upstairs.

The uneasy occasion did serve one purpose – he heard Mrs Stirling tell another lady that the family attended St Thomas Episcopal Church. He was resolved to seek Vanessa out there on Sunday morning. He had only two days left now; he had been forced to make his final arrangements, booking a passage for the following Tuesday afternoon.

On Sunday morning Amas encouraged himself that he looked like any young swell in his light grey top hat, cutaway and striped trousers.

This was his last chance, the last throw of the dice that would decide his happiness. He could think of nothing but Vanessa, the taste and feel, the look and scent of her.

He entered the awesome church unawed except for the sight of Vanessa. She was seated between Martin and Hester Stirling in a pew near the front of the church. Beatrice was on Hester's other side.

Amas doffed his tall hat and strode down the aisle. He sat on the bench just behind the Stirlings where Vanessa could see him if she

35

turned her head. Amas ignored the brass plaque which indicated that his seat was reserved for a member of the VanDyck family. He hoped the VanDycks would stay away this morning.

He was but dimly aware of the splendour around him; he could see only the glory of Vanessa. She was wearing something soft and thick, the colour of lilac, under smoky grey furs. Below a simple hat her drift of golden hair frothed out, frail as the smoke wafted from the bright censer in the processional which he recognised from Catholic services he had attended. He could not tell whether it was the incense or Vanessa's subtle perfume that made his nostrils quiver in sensuous excitement, his pulses throb.

She still had not turned. Apparently none of the Stirlings had seen him. Luckily no VanDycks appeared. The service was Greek to Amas, who did not know the Anglican ritual. When the others stood, he joined them; when they knelt, he sat, keeping his eye trained on Vanessa.

At one point near the end of the endless seeming hour, Amas saw the dark, elegantly-clad Beatrice turn and stare in his direction. He nodded slightly and she gave him an ironic glance.

At last the service seemed to be coming to a close; the priest came marching up the aisle behind a standard-bearer, to the sweet smoke of the swinging censer, the choir in his wake.

Amas put on his hat. He waited until Martin Stirling stepped down and handed the women to the aisle. Amas found himself close to Beatrice, smothered in her cloying scent. Martin saw him, then, and greeted him, smiling.

Vanessa was looking at him now and he was too overwhelmed at first to speak. He stared into her dazzling eyes and touched his hat. Then slowly he joined the procession of worshippers leaving the church.

'Amas, my boy, how are you? I thought we would have lost you by now.' Stirling shook his hand.

'Not yet, sir.' Amas could hardly keep his eyes from Vanessa. He was dumbfounded by the poreless perfection of her skin, the glint of sunlight on her hair. He realised he had never seen her in the light of morning; she was more beautiful now, if anything, than she had been by lamp and candlelight.

He took a step nearer to her; the frail scent of lavender, wafted to him from her person, quickened his nostrils, made his flesh ignite.

'Perhaps you will dine with us soon, Mr Holder,' Hester Stirling said.

36

'I would be honoured, ma'am, but I must leave the country on Tuesday.' Amas shot a quick glance at Vanessa; he imagined consternation on her face, and his hopes rose.

'That's too bad.'

'I wonder, ma'am . . .' Amas began hesitantly, 'if I might have your leave to take Miss Vanessa for a hansom ride in the park?'

'Vanessa?' Mrs Stirling queried. 'Well, really, Mr Holder, I hardly think . . .' She turned to her husband for direction.

'I think it can do no harm,' Stirling said amiably, and gave Amas a compassionate, searching look.

'Thank you.' Amas' elation knew no bounds. 'Would you consider it, Miss Vanessa?'

After a slight hesitation, she nodded. 'Yes.'

From the shocked expression on Mrs Stirling's face Amas gathered that he won an enormous concession. In a daze he summoned a hansom and handed Vanessa in.

They drove across the avenue into the leafy haven of the park. 'Are you . . . too cold?' he asked her anxiously.

'Not at all.' She answered calmly but she still had not looked at him, her breast rose and fell quickly with her breath and he was aware that she was not as placid as she sounded.

He stared down at her, enchanted by the perfection of her chiselled profile, the delicately modelled nose, the long golden lashes resting on her cheek and the small, pink lips. They always reminded him of an unfurled rose. He burned to press their pillowed softness under his own mouth again. The remembrance of their kisses, the sensation of her body close to his, rendered him dumb as he gazed at her.

But he gathered his courage and said quietly, 'It is very kind of you, very good, to come driving with me, Vanessa.'

'I am surprised at your choice,' she said in a clipped tone, and he was bewildered by the remark, by the shuttered blankness of her beautiful eyes. Then a faint pink flooded her cheeks. He must have shown his puzzlement, because she noticed it at once, and the blankness changed to a soft sadness. He was at a loss.

'How could you say that?' he demanded. 'What do you mean?'

Vanessa was stubbornly silent; she wore an expression of reluctance and distaste. At last she spoke in such a low voice that he had to strain to hear. 'I was talking about Bea.'

'Bea!' He reached out for her narrow gloved hand and squeezed her fingers in his grasp, ignoring the small hand's futile attempt to

37

escape. 'Bea,' he repeated, stunned. 'I have never had the slightest interest in Bea, from the first minute, that very first day.'

Vanessa turned her head away from him. Her fingers lay passively in his grasp. This time she said more audibly, 'And yet she knew the name of your hotel.'

Amas strengthened his hold. So that was it. The bitch had said something, then. 'I didn't want to say anything before,' he responded calmly, 'because it was such an . . . awkward situation. Such a thing would wound your parents deeply and,' he added with frankness, 'put me in a bad light with you.' He felt the gloved fingers start against his. 'Yes, Bea came to my hotel, that night after the first dinner at your house. She . . . gave me to understand,' he went on painfully, 'that she found me . . . attractive to her. I sent her home in a cab. That's the sum total of it, Vanessa, I swear to you. I dislike having to tell you such a thing about your own sister. But it's far better than having you think that Bea and I . . . Bea. Good God.'

He could not keep his own distaste, his horrified amusement from his voice. And he saw her face clear, was overjoyed at the new look of tenderness in her eyes. Yet her eyes still did not look happy. What was it, then? He had been so relieved, believing that it was only her suspicions about Bea that were the problem.

No, there was something else. Something deeper, even. Amas felt new apprehension. 'Vanessa. Tell me, please . . . why did you come with me today?'

'I had to, Amas,' she said quietly. 'I had to tell you face to face that I cannot marry you. Any other course would be cowardly.'

He reeled, as if he'd been dealt a hard blow to his solar plexus. 'No,' he said, when he got his breath back again. 'Oh, my God, no, Vanessa. You're killing me. You're killing me.' His voice rose in his agitation.

She looked uneasy and glanced significantly at the coachman so near them on the block of the open hansom.

'I don't care,' he ranted, 'I don't give a damn if the whole city hears me, Vanessa. I love you, I love you with all my heart and soul. I can't make it without you.' Then, aware of her chagrin, seeing her reddened cheeks, he lowered his voice but went on urgently, leaning towards her to stare down into her wonderful eyes. 'I know you care for me. I know it, otherwise you would never have kissed me like that, never have let me hold you like that.'

The colour in her cheeks deepened and she looked away.

'You see? You see?' he declared in triumph. 'You can't look at me and tell me you don't care.'

She turned back then and said slowly, 'Yes. Yes, I do care. But I can't marry a man I don't even know and go running off to the wilderness. You are a stranger to me.'

'We have never been strangers, Vanessa, from the minute we first looked at each other. You know that, your very eyes have said as much to me.'

She was silent and he was heartened; he knew he'd made a telling point. But she murmured, 'It's more than that, Amas. I'm afraid.'

'Afraid? How can that be?'

'I'm afraid I won't belong to myself any more . . . afraid of the very power of my feeling for you. I have lived all my life for my music. I cannot give it up. And with you I would give up everything . . . you would change my life.'

'But that's all wrong,' he blurted. 'Why, Kimberley's got as many pianos as New York.' For the first time that day he was truly able to smile. 'You'd be amazed,' he went on eagerly, 'they love music back home. And I'd buy you a fine piano, the best piano you could want. I know how you feel about your music; I am . . . in awe of your gift. Do you think I'd take a thing like that away? Why, I'd as soon clip the wings off a bird as stop you. How can you think such a thing, Vanessa? How can you?' He grabbed her hand.

She looked away from him again. He squeezed her gloved hand in his. 'Please, give me some hope, Vanessa.'

There was a long silence as the hansom swayed upon the deserted path. Amas thought his heart would burst before she answered.

'That would not be fair, to give you hope. There is none, Amas. I can't marry you.' When she looked up at him, the solemnity of her magnificent eyes devastated him. In vain he searched for a sign of the passion he had seen in them the day he had first kissed her, but there was not a trace. The great grey eyes were merely veiled and sad, empty looking.

'I beg you again, let me hope.'

She shook her head. 'I cannot do that. It is best that you . . . forget me.'

'Forget!' He was almost maddened now.

Forget! How in the name of all that was reasonable could any man with blood ever forget this woman – dismiss the aureola of golden hair, like a sunny mist on a summer morning; the superb eyes full of leashed passion; the flowerlike mouth? Forget how that mouth had tasted, how that body felt in his desperate embrace; not recall his wild imaginings of her naked flesh that would be white and sweet and soft as the unsullied blossom of the magnolia tree? He grabbed her in his arms, kissing her face and the beating hollow below her ear, finding her mouth with his. He could not let her go, although she struggled feebly in his grasp.

'You must not do this,' she gasped. 'You must forget.'

He held her in his steely grip. 'That's insane.'

'Please. Take me home, Amas.'

He stared at her for a long moment. 'No, Vanessa.'

'Take me home.' She was immovable, unreachable.

'Very well. But even if I do, I will never forget, Vanessa, and I will not give up. I never give up on anything. And I will be back. Even if you . . .' his voice shook and nearly broke, 'even if you have married someone else, I'll make you a widow before I give you up.'

She stared at him, gasping, and said no more. The drive to the Stirling mansion proceeded in heavy silence. Without another word, he handed her down to the street and escorted her to her door.

In utter misery he drove away, keeping her in sight as long as he could and promising himself again, in aching repetition, I will make her a widow before I give her up.

When she was 'out' to him the following afternoon, Amas Holder embarked on a wild and drunken evening. He started out at the bar-room with the nudes on Broadway, and found himself in some hotel room later with several boisterous men and three brightly dressed ladies of the evening. All of them, he recalled with chagrin the next morning, had amused themselves taking pot-shots out of the hotel window with a revolver at a passing elevated train.

Amas prayed that he had not hurt anyone; apparently he had not, because he had no memory of a confrontation with the police. He had still less recall of the ladies, sure that he had been too drunk for gallantry, passing out too soon for all that.

Tuesday afternoon he was bleary-eyed, his nerves drawn tight as a bow. He hadn't drunk so much in years, not since he was a reckless adolescent in Brazil. His head pounded with sledgehammer blows, his mouth tasted like the bottom of a mine shaft. He managed to pack up and check out of the hotel. Fortifying himself with food and more than a pot of coffee, Amas took a cab to the waterfront.

He tried not to think of what would happen when he was so far away. The thing was now not to think at all, as far as that was possible.

Amas felt a slight easing when the cab rattled onto the

40

cobblestones of South Street and he got a whiff of the wet, lively wind aromatic with the smells of hemp and canvas, the musty, familiar odour of barnacled pilings. He felt at home in ports, around sailing vessels; he'd worked on a dozen fishing boats out on the west coast. It had been the only way to make a living when he ran away. Inland, in the old days, there was precious little gainful work, so he'd always had to stay somewhere near the water.

The bowsprits, masts and hulls of sailing vessels lined the street on the river side. His ship, the *Walmer Castle*, stood farther down at Pier 10; she was an iron screw steamer of five thousand tons asea for just the last four years. She had sails only fore and aft, with two great red midships funnels rearing sleekly among the nearer ships' masts. The *Walmer* made the voyage from New York to Cape Town in a swift twenty-one days, a record for these times.

Amas paid the cab and jumped down to the pier, burdened now with two big valises instead of one; he'd had to buy another to accommodate the clothes that Brooks had made for him. Feeling the weight of the luggage, he wondered gloomily where he'd ever wear that gear he'd squandered so much money on. As he boarded he felt a deep ache in his body. Now he was really going; he was leaving Vanessa Stirling and New York.

The horn of a departing ship gave out a mournful bellow. It sounded to Amas like a grieving bull being led to the slaughter. A steward showed him to his accommodation, proudly pointing out its luxuries which Amas barely glanced at. He'd been impressed by it on the voyage over but now it meant less than nothing. He was plagued by the ache of awful emptiness.

He tipped the man generously, however, and, leaving his baggage where it was, went out on deck again. Now that he was leaving, he was wild to get it over with. He couldn't stand to linger.

His cabin was on the upper deck that looked like a train running through a cutting. The long, narrow deckhouses that stretched from stern to prow corresponded to the train's coaches, the high bulwarks were like the sides of the cutting. Amas put his fists on the rail and observed the activity on the pier. Funny, standing on the first-class deck like this, he reflected, watching men do the same work he'd done not many years ago – lifting and hauling, driving wagons.

Idly he watched the arrival of other passengers. Most of them looked pretty uninteresting. He was about to walk away to circle the deck for a harbour view when he saw a woman being handed down from a closed cab, two crew members hurrying to gather up her baggage.

41

Amas blinked and shaded his eyes. He stared in utter disbelief, unable to credit his own sight. The woman moved with voluptuous grace, her brief golden hair frothing out from under the sassy brim of a small boater. He would know her anywhere, already knew by heart that proud carriage of head and shoulders, that minuscule waist curving outward into rounded hips; the floating pace so different from the mincing walk of other women.

It couldn't be. And yet is was. It was Vanessa.

Amas was almost paralysed with astonishment; he gripped the rail, staring, staring. As she boarded, she looked up and their eyes met. Her magnificent blue-grey eyes blazed with excitement. She was unsmiling, and her flowerlike face expressed consternation, almost fear.

Dear God, she was coming with him. She was coming. She had brought her baggage. Amas snapped to his senses; he ran down the stairs to the lower deck and by the time she reached him was standing there, waiting, his arms outspread.

The tentative, almost fearful look in her eyes changed to one of burning joy. She came into his arms. In full view of the startled passengers, the grinning deckhands and the fascinated crew, Amas held her bruisingly close; she raised her face to his. He took her small head in his eager hands, and the quick, passionate motion coupled with the brisk wind swept her neat hat off her golden hair. It fell to the deck and blew over the side in spite of the hasty effort of a steward to retrieve it.

Amas and Vanessa began to laugh, hysterically and almost crazily, oblivious to the stares of everyone around them.

It was Amas who got hold of himself at last, saying to Vanessa, 'Come. Come.' He took her gloved hand and led her up the stairs to his cabin. Her furs were slipping off her shoulders, a confused steward following in their wake.

When they reached Amas' rooms he said to the steward, 'Have the lady's baggage put in her cabin.' Fumbling for a note, he pressed it in the man's hand. The pleased steward hurried away.

Amas shut him out. They were alone.

He took both her hands; they stood apart, looking at each other, mesmerised.

Then he said, 'I can't believe this. I can't believe it, Vanessa. You are coming with me, then.' Even when he pronounced the words he could not believe that they were so.

'Oh, yes, Amas. Yes. It has been agony. I was so confused, uncertain. But I'm not uncertain now. I know I've got to be where you are, Amas Holder. Otherwise there is no . . . life for me at all. I love you.'

He released her hands, going to her to take her close in his arms again. His heart was drumming so hard he could barely breathe; he was too stunned with his happiness to say another word. He felt her swansdown softness through the thin wool of her gown; her cloak slipped away, falling to the carpet, and his trembling hands were tracing the form of her magnificent breasts, spanning the tiny waist, stroking the curve of her hips while his mouth opened over hers.

He breathed the fragrance of lavender from her petal-like skin, her drifting hair, and his whole self flamed and hardened, his arms and legs quaking like those of a man with chills and fever.

He feared for an instant that it was all only a dream when she released herself gently from his hold and, with one tender look at him, her eyes huge now and melting, went to draw the curtains over the little round windows of the cabin.

Turning from the porthole Vanessa Stirling looked at Amas Holder. The wonder in his eyes, his astounded realisation, filled her with an almost unbearable tenderness. He could only stare at her, stare as she loosened the belt of her pale grey gown and unbuttoned its jacket. Her body burned with that joyful and alien longing, that new and unknown sensation that had lapped at her senses for the last long days, ever since she had known that this had to be.

Amas said her name, just once, and then strode towards her. His fingers were so shaky that he fumbled at the fastenings of her dress; softly she put aside his hands and undid the fastenings. The dress slid away. She stood before him in her lacy undergarments and she saw his fierce eyes ignite as he gazed hungrily at her arms and shoulders, at the swell of her breasts above the ruffles of her chemise, and wander downward to her slender legs whose shape was revealed through the cambric pantaloons.

She felt the throbbing beat of her pulse, high in her throat, fluttering to her very ears, as she slowly discarded her chemise and peeled the underthings from her lower body.

He made a groaning sound, murmuring, unable for a moment to do anything but look at her, his wild gaze taking in her naked breasts and smooth white skin, the golden luxuriance at the centre of her body. And then with great suddenness he was holding her and she could feel his calloused fingers stroking her, stroking from her satiny neck to her spine, learning the smoothness of her back and haunches, pressing her to his still-clothed body.

His hardness thrilled her to the marrow, the rough, seeking touch set delicious quivers throughout her melting flesh, as he held her vibrant breasts in his huge hands and stroked the skin of her belly.

Now he had released her, and was throwing off his constricting clothes; she sank weakly onto the silken surface of the bed, looking up at him with utter wonder. He had the body of a marble god. But this torso was not of marble; he was tanned almost mahogany to the waist from the long hours spent in the African sun, and his biceps were as powerful as the limbs of a giant oak, the great shoulders and arms narrowing to a sinewy middle without an ounce of superfluous flesh, where corded tendons played and rippled.

He stood on rock-muscled legs, and the lighter loins enclosed his arrowing maleness, that mystery she had expected to fear and shrink from, but which now seemed beautiful.

With a low cry he was kneeling beside her; she closed her eyes and raised her hands to his head, her fingers entering the wild mane of his hair, kneading its thickness; she heard his gasping, almost sobbing breath, felt his mouth on her skin. He was kissing her all over her body then, pulling his head away, kissing her legs and belly, fondling her breasts, lowering his face again to her dazzled loins.

In a daze of joy and disbelief she felt his eager mouth on the very centre of her body; ignoring her half-hearted and puzzled demur, he was rendering a strange, astonishing caress. His firm tongue, caressing, caressing, was leading her to a stunning and barbaric joy; she could feel a narrow flame of pleasure begin to flicker. The flickering went on and on, until it reached, at last, one needle-pointed spark of piercing fire, a peak of pleasuring that so much resembled pain she almost shrank from it, and yet it was not pain at all but finally an ecstasy so profound she thought her whole self would dissolve, that her heart would cease its beating. The tiny point of fire began to widen, the flame turned to wide burning water and the burning wave to a deep, warm sea. She was rocking, rocking, borne on the warm sea's tide, floating with the rhythm of the sea's mighty wave: she heard her own shrill, ecstatic cry.

His mouth was trembling now against her skin and, in the golden dimness, she watched him raise himself to cover her; her body per-ceived a gradual, gentle fullness, all that had been empty fulfilled. To her astounded joy she was stabbed again with that narrow blade of fire, that magically widening circle of pleasure taking her until she drowned, groaning, shaken and appeased.

44

She felt his great frame halt and wince, listened to the outcry tearing from him, caressed him in his trembling as he said her name with a sobbing breath, over and over. Then with slow care, on still quavering arms, he raised his massive body, lowered himself to lie beside her.

Marvelling, overwhelmed, she nestled against him as the floor beneath them trembled; the *Walmer Castle* began to slide from port and head out to the open sea.

I died, I died, he thought, and this . . . is being born again. Looking down at her, beholding her perfection, Amas Holder realised that only her actual warmth pressed close, and the peaceful emptiness of his own vibrating body, could convince him that it had not been just a dream.

If he had hoped for, expected anything, it had not been this: the swift honesty with which she had offered him this overwhelming prize, the astounding passion slumbering beneath her patent innocence. That she had been untouched, in flesh and mind, was clear to him.

He was too staggered to form words; he could only stroke her satiny arm, again and again, and kiss her froth of hair repeatedly.

Men had told him, many times, of their wives' reluctance on the bridal night; Vanessa's sweet compliance, her willingness, had taken Amas' breath away. He had had no experience at all of good women, only of a succession of the other kind. His rolling-stone life had left him no time or desire to settle anywhere.

But now – he gazed down at her once more, dazzled by the sight of her white, bare flesh, the relaxed symmetry of her rose-tipped breasts and voluptuous form, that glint of golden luxuriance, soft as foam . . .

Amazed, Amas felt his body quicken. He turned her gently on her side and moved close to her; the intimate down teased his hardening flesh. With a moan, and a hungry, eager forward motion, he found himself enclosed again, embedded, oh jubilation, in that ineffably sweet softness, that warm and silken pillowed place; found himself almost maddened by her timid, untutored responding, her dear compliance, until there was no more thinking, only feeling, only that quick, ecstatic and irreversible tempo towards the all-absorbing magnitude of letting go.

Drained and sated, he drew her close, kissing her face and mouth until black sleep descended over his fluttering eyes.

Drowsy and weak, Vanessa drew a little away and, leaning on her elbow, studied Amas.

This is the only thing, the only thing, she reflected with wonder, that

45

was ever anything like music. And even that . . . no, not even that had ever quite aroused the tempest of emotion that his body had awakened.

She lay back on the pillows, stroking his big upper arm, seeing him smile in his sleep.

She almost feared that all of this had been a dream from which she was bound to awaken, alone in her chaste and empty suite in the Fifth Avenue house. Strange that already she could not think of it as 'home'. No, oh, no, home was here, with Amas. To reassure herself, she gently grasped his arm. It was solid, comforting.

Feeling more secure, Vanessa closed her eyes, reliving the last swift, amazing and decisive days before her fearful departure.

When Amas had brought her back to the house on Sunday afternoon, walking away from her with dragging steps, she had felt as if her heart had splintered within her body, its sharp, broken pieces stabbing her everywhere with multitudinous and unbearable, narrow pains. She'd almost called him back, but at once her reason intervened: what good would it do? The same difficulties would exist between them. And she had not had the courage to look back at him, even if she felt his stricken gaze on her.

She let herself in with her own key, thankful that she'd been able to forestall the servants. They were usually below stairs at this hour, engaged in luncheon preparation. Furthermore, she blessed the chance of the outside luncheon that afternoon that would keep her family away for some hours still.

The fact that she herself had had no food at all since last night, and only a cup of coffee this morning, did not occur to Vanessa. She was simply glad that the servants' laughter from below masked the smooth unlocking of the big front door, that she could escape undetected to her room. She could not have borne to speak to anyone.

When she reached its haven, she threw off her hat and furs and lay down fully clothed upon her bed, desolate and numb. Today she had thrown away her only chance for happiness; she knew that now, so surely. Yet she also knew that to go away with him, to that wilderness, away from her music and everything that was familiar, would have been sheer madness. They would end by hating each other, she thought darkly.

But then she remembered all the things he'd said, those calm and tender assurances – that he would never stand in the way of her aspirations. Most of all she remembered his saying that they

46

belonged together. That, she concluded, was perfectly true. Never in all her life had she known a man who seemed so attuned to everything that was deepest in her own character. And she wanted him, wanted him so desperately that even now her body was faint and sick with it.

Always, always, however, she returned to the cold, stark fact of their divergent lives and aims. Surely the most profound love could never survive that.

And so her wretched thinking rocked to and fro, for a timeless interval, with the futile rhythm of a dreadful rocking horse with an evilly grinning face that moved in fatuous tempo without making an inch of progress. At last her misery and hunger overcame her; weakly she slipped into a restless sleep.

That night and the next day went by in a blur; she ached for Amas. On Monday afternoon she went for a disconsolate ramble in the park. When she returned she found his card on a tray in the hall. Clutching the card to her breast, she ran upstairs to her room and, alone again, burst into wild weeping. He would be leaving tomorrow. Aware that her father was anxious about her, Vanessa managed to compose herself enough to join the family at dinner, assuming a calm, cheerful manner to hide the turmoil inside her. Her mother and even the sharp-eyed Bea seemed deceived, but Vanessa had a feeling her father was not. She caught him giving her covert glances.

After dinner, playing for Martin Stirling, Vanessa chose the wild, romantic music she had played that night for Amas Holder, hoping that its passionate strains might somehow soothe the deep ache in her. But it brought him so near again, so physically present, that she was hard put not to cry out her longing before her father. And she knew, at last, what it was she had to do. Tomorrow she had to go away with Amas Holder, or she would simply die. How she would manage, how she would dare, she didn't yet know. All she was sure of was that she must go.

She consulted her father's newspaper and discovered the hour of the *Walmer*'s sailing. Then she began desperately to plan. No one must know. Even her father, who liked Amas, might attempt to stop her, to dissuade her. But she would not think of that, not now; the thing was to get away. Vanessa knew her father would be at his office at the hour of the *Walmer*'s sailing; Bea and her mother had mentioned engagements that would, with any luck, ensure their absence.

But how would she manage her grips and trunks? It was impossible. The solution was to take almost nothing; that was it. She would somehow contrive to get everything into one small grip and a larger one. Amas had said it was summer in Africa now; thank God for that. Light garments would weigh so little. Vanessa asked her maid the next morning to bring the bags from the box room, saying casually that she was going away to stay with a friend for the holidays, adding that she would pack on her own. The curious maid left her to the task. While the butler was engaged elsewhere, Vanessa and her maid brought the bags downstairs and set them on the veranda. While the maid summoned a cab Vanessa thought, there is no one, nothing here, that I will ever lack . . . except my father. She was stabbed with tender regret. Only her father had ever loved her, ever understood.

As the cab trundled on its way downtown, she silently repeated to herself the note she'd left him – she knew it now by heart, because it had taken her a long time to think through and compose, although it was very brief:

'Beloved father, I have gone away not for a few, but for many, many days, and I have gone to be with Amas, because he will always have my heart and without him I would no longer even be alive. If the way I have chosen gives you pain, forgive me, but I feared that even you, with your liking and respect for him, might seek to prevent me. You must understand that now he is my life, as you yourself have been for so long, and know that much of my devotion will still belong to you, for always. This will be my great adventure, Father; you and I have always loved adventure. Now I will have the adventures you have so sorely lacked. I love you. Vanessa.'

She smiled to remember those phrases. But now that the adventure was in motion she was struck with new uncertainty: what if she had so pained and angered Amas that he could no longer accept her?

By the time she descended at the pier she was terrified. How humiliating, how terrible it would be if he denounced her. But she would meet whatever came, she resolved, with pride and courage. She squared her shoulders and moved towards the ship. Then she'd seen him on deck, staring at her, still as marble.

When boarding, she met his eyes, and she found there all the answer that she needed; there was nothing in his tawny gaze but love and joy.

Vanessa stroked his arm now, smiling. What a fool she'd been ever to doubt him.

And the lies they had told her – the idiotic lies! Her mother had hinted that marriage was a painful burden, the act of wedded love a 'duty' to one's husband. Dear God, how could she have ever believed such things . . . why had she not known it would be like this instead?

But then her mother had never known a man like Amas Holder. And Bea . . . was this the reason for Bea's embarrassing avidity, her pathetic pursuit of the male?

Surely even Bea had never known such love as this.

Vanessa stared at Amas' face in the gathering dark, and traced with light fingers his thick mane of hair that fell over his broad brow, the hawklike nose, the firm mouth relaxed and softened now in his slumber, as open-looking as a boy's.

His eyes were closed, but his arms reached out for her, and she gladly went into them, delighting in the sensation of his massive, sleep-warm body sheltering her, closing her in their private world. Never, never had she felt so safe and so complete.

Her heavy eyelids fell; she floated like a lazy feather downward into spiralling sleep.

When she woke he was sitting propped against the pillows, studying her with an ineffably tender expression.

'Vanessa, my Vanessa.' He put out his arm, inviting her to lie beside him. She did so, leaning her head on his massive shoulder.

He kissed her on her head, stroking her curved side. 'You are my wife now,' he said solemnly. 'And I am your husband. Tomorrow you will become my wife in name.'

'Yes, oh, yes.' She nodded and buried her face against his chest.

'You have given me the greatest treasure I have ever had, Vanessa.' She could hear his deep voice vibrate against her cheek. She kissed the smooth, warm skin of his hard chest and he pulled her close, his calloused fingers holding her so tight that she gave a small cry.

'Oh, my dear, my dear one,' he said anxiously. 'Have I hurt you? I'm sorry, I'm sorry, Vanessa. I'm just not used to anything as . . . delicate and precious as you are.'

He sounded so chagrined, so self-reproachful that she was flooded with tenderness. 'No, no, you didn't,' she protested. She slid upwards, kissing his neck and the beating hollow under his ear.

'The captain will marry us,' he said eagerly, 'beyond the three-mile limit. I even have the rings,' he continued, sounding boyish, exhilarated, quite proud.

'The rings!' She sat up in the bed. Suddenly, realising that she was naked, she felt her face flush. She pulled up the coverlet over her breasts. He grinned at the gesture.

49

'Yes.' He told her about the ring he'd brought to his mother, and then about a wedding band he'd bought at Tiffany's the very day he'd returned from Philadelphia.

She was silent, thinking, even his mother somehow knew; all of it was fated.

Misinterpreting her stillness, he said hastily, 'Perhaps you should have your own ring, Vanessa. Oh, I'm sorry. What a fool I am.'

Smiling, Vanessa shook her head and told him what she had been thinking. His look of relief touched her so deeply that once more she was washed with a warm wave of utter tenderness, reflecting how strange it was that she should feel this almost maternal protectiveness towards a giant of a man.

'I should have known,' she murmured, 'from the beginning, that this was meant to be. You were wiser than I, Amas – you knew we were kin. And we are. I know that, so surely now.'

He held her close and whispered, 'From this night forward, Vanessa, we will never be apart.'

'From this night forward,' she repeated, looking into the brown eyes whose light was no longer fierce and probing, but gentle as the autumn sun.

The vows they exchanged tomorrow could be no more sacred or binding than these.

CHAPTER FOUR

The intrusion of others, now, was unthinkable, but Amas was prepared to accept her wish to spend the night in her own cabin. She had placed her whole self, her good repute, in his hands and he felt it was a precious trust. So he was moved profoundly when she suggested they have dinner in the cabin, saying, 'I cannot bear to be away from you, not anymore.'

Amas was awed by her courage. Silently he vowed to devote the rest of his life to returning a thousandfold this great gift she had given. He began by outrageously tipping the wise-eyed steward who brought their dinner, to ensure his silence; Amas wanted no comments made about where tomorrow's bride had spent this night. As a matter of fact, if anyone said such a thing in his hearing, Amas didn't like to think what the outcome would be.

Vanessa must have sensed his thoughts, because she smiled and said, 'You want to see the captain, don't you?'

He took her in his arms and kissed her. 'You read me so easily,' he admitted with a grin.

Amas sought out the surprised officer in his quarters, sitting in his shirtsleeves over a book, smoking his pipe, and asked him abruptly to perform the ceremony at the earliest possible hour the next morning. The captain assented at once. He had a twinkle in his farsighted blue eyes, eyes that had the look of staring over immense watery distances. He was a type, with the manner that Amas was long familiar with, and Amas found the whole thing very reassuring. Elated, he hurried back to Vanessa.

Late that night they went up on deck to stand close together at the rail, talking in low voices. Vanessa was wrapped again in her furs.

He caressed her shoulder through the silky pelts. 'It will be warmer before long, when we reach the southern waters.' She snuggled up to him and placed her bare head on his chest.

'Where will we be going?'

'We'll put in at Havana in a few more days, then Trinidad and Rio,' he murmured, drawing her closer.

'The names sound so wonderful, and strange.' Her words were muffled against him. Then she pulled back a little and looked up at him, smiling. Her eyes were wide and excited as a child's; they sparkled at Amas in the vague, gentle light. She was going to be a marvellous companion, he thought, delighted. 'I feel as if this is the greatest adventure I've ever had. That's the very thing I said to my father, in the note I left.'

'He knows then. Good Lord, he must be ready to murder me by now,' Amas added ruefully.

'No, no.' She reached up and caressed his face. 'He is very fond of you, Amas. Didn't you know that? He talked about you all the time, ever since the first night you came to see him.'

'To see *you*, you mean.' Amas chuckled softly. 'I'm glad he likes me. That means a lot to me. We'll cable him in Havana. And I'll cable my mother, too.'

He pulled her close to him again and they stood for an instant in

51

blissful silence. More than ever he felt a burning need to do things for her. He had a sudden inspiration: he'd cable London as well, have them ship a fine piano to Kimberley. With any luck it might arrive before they did. It would be the biggest and best surprise of all. And there certainly wouldn't be any problem about it when they checked him out on the Exchange.

He realised he must be grinning like a monkey, because she laughed up at him, 'You're plotting something.' She stroked his chin.

He moved his head back and forth, enjoying her touch like a petted animal. 'Yes. A surprise.' It also occurred to him then that he could buy her something really nice in Rio. He remembered seeing some decent jewellery in a shop there during the voyage over and fervently hoped it was still there.

But the wind was rising now. 'You'll be cold,' he said protectively. 'Let's go back in.'

He asked her anxiously if she would not need things for the night. 'You are all I need, Amas, for any night.'

He was so overpowered with emotion he was speechless; all he could do was to hold her in his arms and kiss her hair. When they came together again he had the blessed feeling that they had been together all their lives.

Amas woke when it was barely dawn, with a sensation of festive excitement, and rushed off to the galley to consult the chef. He wanted to arrange something very special for a wedding luncheon. And flowers. He recalled that they'd put fresh flowers on the tables, at least during the first part of the voyage over, because a lady had remarked upon it. Amas judged they'd keep the flowers in the galley, under refrigeration.

The chef, a sympathetic and romantic Frenchman, was overjoyed to be consulted. He ordered the galley crew about, having them bring out flowers for Amas' inspection. His face fell: nothing looked like what he wanted. He didn't know a thing about flowers, but he did know that Vanessa looked like a delicate white one. She reminded him of those tiny bell-things; he described them to the chef.

'Ah!' The man said sadly, rolling his dark eyes. 'If this were Paris, now . . . you mean the lilies of the valley. But, as you see, all we have in white is the stiff, uninspired *oeillet*' – he held up a white carnation – 'with which to make a bouquet for the bride.'

'It'll have to do,' Amas said, resigned. 'Some of those, and you know, the other stuff.'

The chef grinned. 'As you say, "the other stuff", absolutely. I will contrive somehow to find ribbons, and . . . Now, the luncheon.' His expression brightened, as if to say, there I will be in my element and no possible ingredient will be lacking.

'I leave that to you,' Amas smiled. 'Just something very nice, for a lady who's accustomed to the best.' Amas offered the man a bill of high denomination. The chef's eyes gleamed.

'I *am* the best,' he retorted. 'Thank you. I assure you that you and the lady will be more than pleased.'

The ceremony was scheduled for eleven; Amas had no idea how he would get through the next several hours. He was reluctant to wake Vanessa at this ungodly hour, so he paced the decks of the entire ship several times, having to restrain himself from shouting out the happy news to every seaman he encountered.

Then he threw himself into a deckchair, feeling a bubbly, drunken elation from lack of sleep, and gave a thought to what kind of gear he should be married in. It might look pretty silly to get all togged out in a cutaway for these simple rites. He suffered a moment of anxiety, wondering if Vanessa would resent not having a big, proper wedding; most women would. But she was not most women, never would be.

He got up and paced the deck some more, then went in to the first service of breakfast, where he drank cup after cup of coffee. He could not swallow a mouthful of food. But at least he was able to kill some time in conversation with a fellow passenger, only half-listening to what the man said.

At last he figured he might return to the cabin without fear of disturbing Vanessa. When he found it empty, and the bed smoothly made, he realised she had returned to her own cabin. Growing more nervously elated by the minute, he bathed and shaved with extreme care – he was jumpy enough to cut his throat – and went to the cubicle where his clothes hung. Each suit had already been pressed, thanks to the line's splendid service. Amas put on a suit of dark grey. He figured that should be about right.

Then he paced the cabin some more, breaking out into a sudden sweat when he remembered he'd forgotten where the wedding ring was. He'd had one made in New York that fitted the dazzling solitaire he'd slipped on her finger last night. At last he found it and put it in his breast pocket.

He looked at his watch for the hundredth time. At last it was late enough to go to her cabin. When she emerged she was wearing a simple morning dress of white velvet, holding the bouquet of white

53

carnations with a streamer of white ribbons. She was so beautiful it almost hurt his eyes to look at her, and in her magnificent eyes there was a brilliant, soft glowing.

'I wanted roses for you, Vanessa. White roses. But it doesn't matter now . . . you are the rose.'

She looked at him with such adoration that he was suddenly fearful in his happiness. She was so great a miracle that he trembled when he touched her, as if she were something infinitely fragile that could be broken in unthinking hands.

The quiet ceremony, witnessed by two of the officers, was the most solemn moment of Amas' life. All he could think of, when he slipped the diamond band onto her slender finger, was how he would care for this supreme treasure, this white, dazzling creature who was the core of all his happiness.

During the succeeding nights and days their strong desire seemed to grow, not abate, with sweet familiarity. Amas was incredulous at her increasing boldness in the marriage bed. He didn't know how he had lived before.

He encouraged Vanessa to practise the piano daily. She derided the tone of the heavily carved piano in the gloomy first-class music room, therefore she often opted for the second-class piano. With its uncarved exterior, its tone was far better. Amas hugged to himself a splendid secret – the perfect, unornamented Steinway he would order from England when they docked at Havana.

They were among the first to disembark. After a breakfast of *caffe con leche* and exotic fruits, they wandered the cobbled streets surrounding the harbour. In a post office Amas cabled the news of their marriage to America and then, suggesting that Vanessa sit at the outdoor café next door, more comfortable than the hot, stuffy office, sent other cables to Cape Town and one to England, ordering the Steinway.

When he rejoined her she seemed overcome with languor; the touch of his calloused fingers on her ungloved hand made her tremble. From somewhere in the drowsy afternoon they heard the titillating beat of hollow drums, the rattle of sticks and gourds, castanets and insinuating brasses.

'Let's go back,' she said in a low voice, staring into Amas' eyes. He felt a new excitement deep in his body, reading her meaning at once. Already her eyes had grown heavy-lidded, her ripe mouth fuller, it seemed to him, from their perpetual satiety. And yet they were never quite satiated. She moved him now more strongly than ever. They boarded the *Walmer* without another word, seeking out their cabin. As the deserted steamer rode at anchor in the sequestered harbour, Vanessa drew the curtains and went to Amas. She slipped his light jacket from his massive shoulders, unbuttoned his shirt with sure and eager hands.

He threw off the rest of his clothes. Still half-dressed, she urged him onto the bed; lying against his startled, hardening body, she pressed her miraculous softness against him. And then, clinging to him, she began to slide downwards, with seductive, excruciating slowness planted a multitude of nibbling kisses on his muscular belly.

He shook all over. 'What are you doing, darling?' His legs quavered, his centre felt like a volcano about to explode.

She only laughed in answer, a low, teasing laugh that made him burn with lust. Her pillowed lips caressed him; he was stabbed with the bladed sharpness of a wild, new need, heating as if with fever.

Looking down at her, he marvelled; she is so beautiful. His eyes feasted on her shapely little head with its golden aureola of hair, the curve of her perfect back and her slender legs through the transparencies of her frail underclothes. Amas shut his eyes, giving himself up to the wonder and the glory of that sweet astonishment. At any second now he would be broken almost asunder.

He tried to lift her upwards, fumbling with the puzzle of her filmy coverings, but she made a catlike sound of dissent. He murmured, 'Oh, my darling, no,' but then he could speak no longer. He felt that irreversible progression, that steady, beating drum of blood that, once struck, demanded the eternal forward beating to the final flourish, the last percussion of the marrow's cymbals; he was going onward, onward, gasping, rising, onward to the last explosion.

It came: his body splintered.

Shuddering all over, he gave a sobbing cry, his maddened fingers writhing in the silk of her curly hair, the hot tears running down his face. And suddenly she was naked, rising to him, pressing her body's full length to his as he felt the jewel-pointed satin of her breasts crush him, the down of her, the warm, writhing silk.

And, lifting her in his quivering arms, he lay her down on the bed, sliding downward to bury his mouth in her, to taste the throbbing bud of her body's core, tasting the clove and honey of her deepest secrecies, caressing until her suave form leaped under his relentless tongue, leaped and shuddered. He heard her own shrill pleasure-cry.

His wondering hands stroked her, tracing every contour from the drowsy, perfect breasts to the narrow, quivering feet.

'I loved you before, Vanessa,' he whispered. 'Now I worship you.'

Preparing to go ashore with Amas in Rio de Janeiro, Vanessa studied her reflection in the glass and thought, I am another woman. Her mouth and eyes had changed: her lips had grown fuller, her eyes were heavy-lidded, seductive, a testament to the constant easement of desire. The farther south they'd sailed, the wilder her longing, and his, had become. There was some magic in the very air of this warmer sea that inspired her to new boldness, achieved for them an overpowering frenzy. Her former ivory whiteness had an overlay of gold.

She was spending more time with Amas on deck, dreamily watching the endless sea. And she noticed that when other men shot covert glances at her, Amas sometimes displayed an almost irrational anger that they dared to look at her with such an expression. His quick, unfounded jealousy pleased her.

Vanessa smiled at her reflection, delighting in the glow of her own eyes, the colour of her skin. She felt alive for the first time in her memory, tingling and sensitised in every nerve, yet with a warm well-being deep inside her. She marvelled that only weeks ago she had been the lonely Vanessa Stirling, restless and remote; now she and Amas were so close they sometimes seemed to live in each other's minds.

And now even her music was different: conscientious daily practice had left her with undiminished technical proficiency, but now the tempest of emotion the music had aroused in her before was awakened only by Amas' presence. The realisation did not disturb her; this was a magic interval, a dream apart. She had no thought today beyond the present.

Amas had told her it would be very warm in Rio, but that there were frequent showers, so she donned a thin pink dress and broad-brimmed hat and carried a dark green umbrella.

'You look exactly like a rose,' Amas said in a low tone as they disembarked. 'Your umbrella's like the leaves.' She'd been surprised at first when he said such things, remarkable for a man like him, but since then she'd learned that he had done an extraordinary amount of reading, that his mother was a sensitive woman who had taught him to revere and notice unlikely matters.

Then, when he led her to an elegant jewellery store in the city's

56

heart, she was delighted with his delight. After an anxious scrutiny of the shop window, his face lit up. 'They still have them,' he said buoyantly. 'Come, let's go in.'

As eagerly as a boy he escorted her into the shop, displaying another lovable quality she'd come to know – the joy of having and spending money, something she had taken for granted all her life, a commodity not mentioned, like the origin of babies or 'white sewing', her mother's euphemism for underwear.

But she could see that to Amas, who had known deprivation, it was a passport to high enjoyment. And more than anything he seemed to love to spend it on her. So she made no protest when he chose certain pieces of jewellery for her approval; his taste was unerring. Among the ornate creations of the day, the pieces were unique, stunningly simple, set with the finest possible gems.

There was a ring in the shape of a primrose whose petals were pink diamonds; a hummingbird brooch formed of brilliant blue-green Australian opals with their flames of orange and gold; another brooch that was a calla lily of baroque pearls and a fragile white-gold chain hung at intervals, like great drops of rain, with perfect blue-white, pear-shaped diamonds. Its matching eardrops were single glittering diamonds of equal flawlessness.

Amas remarked, 'Coals to the lady of Newcastle.' She laughed, infected by his excitement, accepting them all. He slipped the primrose ring on her right hand. 'You didn't have much of a wedding bouquet. This flower won't wither.'

The shopkeeper, stupefied at the sight of Amas' roll of notes, committed the treasures to boxes and Vanessa put them in her reticule before they set out to tour the streets of Rio.

That night at dinner in the first-class saloon, she pleased Amas by wearing the fragile necklace above the low-cut neck of a dark grey gown that set off the glimmering diamonds to perfection. And on succeeding nights and days, with equal enjoyment, she displayed the calla lily brooch on her ivory gown; on dresses of gold and green and then dark blue, the vivid hummingbird that symbolised the swiftness of their magic journey, drawing to its close.

When they stepped from the train into the clamorous station at Kimberley, Vanessa was dazed. In three weeks she had visited so many foreign worlds, it dizzied her – the port of Trinidad, the island of hummingbirds that the Indians called 'Iere', Rio de Janeiro. And last, the bustling port of Cape Town, where they disembarked into a heavy rain. Its muddy streets were lined by ox-drawn carts and tethered mules in grotesque contrast to the great Victorian pile of the British Government House, the walkways a confusion of natives and English soldiers and stolid Dutch farmers called Boers.

Vanessa looked up at Amas. His eyes were blazing with anticipation, his tanned face had the look of confidence and command it had possessed the first time she'd seen him in New York. He reminded her of a captive lion released to its native habitat.

'Sam!' Amas called out. A smiling, stocky man dressed in boots and khaki trousers, a khaki shirt rolled up to his elbows, came striding towards them. Sighting Vanessa, he snatched his light-coloured helmet from his head.

His deeply tanned face was marked by the absence of distinctive features, but his blue eyes twinkled; he looked both shrewd and kind.

'This is my foreman, Vanessa . . . Sam Dillon. Sam, may I present my wife.' Amas seemed about to burst with pride.

Sam Dillon's frank blue glance swept her from head to foot, incredulous. He took her hand gingerly.

'I am honoured, ma'am.' He had an agreeable low voice with an accent something like the Cockney she'd heard in England. Without volition the blue gaze took in her body in the snug travelling dress, then Dillon reddened and looked back quickly to her face. 'Welcome to Kimberley.'

He said to Amas, 'I'll have the boys put the luggage on the ox-cart and drive back with them. I brought the buggy for you.' Sam Dillon put on his helmet and, touching the brim, walked away. Amas handed Vanessa into the buggy.

Observing Kimberley, she was aware that it was only a big mining encampment. Most of the buildings were made of corrugated iron, the streets would be dust on sunny days and mud when it rained. The only regular road was the main thoroughfare, the rest just paths between white tents and tin houses that the diggers moved when they wished to live on a new site. Straggling houses extended along the railway track, almost all made of corrugated iron. Wood, Amas told her, was almost unobtainable because it had to be drawn five hundred miles by oxen.

There was a bar called the 'Digger's Rest' with a questionable-looking set of rooms above; dealers' offices, grocer, pharmacists, a few clothing and general stores, a brewery and a church. The only building of note, besides the train depot, was a long two-storey structure with shaded verandas housing the offices of Amas' competitor, DeVries Consolidated Mines.

They passed through a small valley interspersed with flowering yellow trees. 'Mimosa,' Amas explained, smiling at Vanessa. Between a range of beautiful hills she saw other trees; there was an aromatic odour on the warm air. They crossed a little stream bounded by green willows where some striped animals were grazing.

'Zebras!' Vanessa exclaimed. She'd never seen them outside of a zoo.

'Quachas, actually,' Amas corrected. 'Almost zebras,' he grinned. The quachas looked up at the buggy's approach but did not run away.

Suddenly she saw a sprawling white bungalow at the top of the next rise, surrounded by the ever-present flowering mimosa.

'There it is,' Amas announced with jubilation. 'Home.'

'It looks so big,' she murmured.

'It is. I'm glad I took it, now. It belonged to a man with a family who had to go back to England. But it's pretty . . . bare, after what you've been accustomed to.'

'It's beautiful, Amas.' She squeezed his hand and he gave her a fond, grateful look. As the buggy drew nearer, she saw four Africans, a man and three women, standing in front of the bungalow.

'The servants,' Amas said. 'Assembled to greet the new mistress. They're members of a bush tribe that's scattered now, since the miners came. I came across them one day; they were separated from the rest, almost starving. The man is Salakootoo, my head house man. What you'd call a butler. The women are Sala's mother Sehoiya, his sister, Tattenyana and his wife Waranee.'

'I'll never learn those names!'

'You won't have to,' Amas chuckled. 'I can't call them by those handles every time I need something. They're Sala, Yana and Ranee to me. Sehoiya's another matter, though. She's much too grand for a nickname. She was a princess of the Mashow, daughter of their king.'

'Daughter of a king,' Vanessa murmured. 'I like our country, Amas.'

When she said 'our country', his face lit up. As he halted the buggy a small boy ran up to take the reins. Amas greeted him in a strange, grunting dialect and the little boy grinned widely. Amas and Vanessa walked towards the delegation on the veranda.

'Welcome, sir.' The man Sala greeted Amas in thickly accented English.

'Thank you, Sala,' Amas said solemnly. 'This is the mistress, come home.'

'Welcome, Misses.' Sala bowed his head. He was slender and tall,

59

with a merry expression; his hair was clipped close to his head, although the women's heads, Vanessa saw, were shaved. With great ceremony he presented the women. The two younger were very subdued; Sehoiya, on the other hand, wore her simple cotton like a royal robe. None of the women smiled; they seemed fascinated with Vanessa's hair.

Sala announced, 'The women have gifts for the mistress of the house.' Ceremoniously he gestured to Ranee, his wife. A hint of a smile came to her full lips. She wore sinews in her pierced ears strung with red and green beads and, like the others, several strands of bright beads around her small neck. She offered to Vanessa the mysterious elongated object she had been holding stiffly in her hands – an umbrella of brown ostrich feathers, quite beautiful.

'Thank you!' Vanessa said warmly. 'This is wonderful.'

'To protect Misses from the sun,' Sala said. His sister Yana presented Vanessa with a bonnet woven of reeds. 'Also to shelter Misses,' Sala explained.

Then the queenly Sehoiya stepped forward with her closed hands held out before her; she opened them. On one palm was a small object of bright gold colour, the native African gold. 'This will protect Misses and give her children,' Sala said. 'It belonged to the king of the Mashow.'

'Oh, but I couldn't . . .' Vanessa began. Amas touched her arm, frowning slightly. She realised then that to reject the gift would disgrace Sehoiya.

'Thank you, Sehoiya. I will treasure it.' Sala translated and for the first time the stately woman smiled.

When Amas led Vanessa into the house, she found it as he described, rather bare. But there was a cool serenity to its very bareness. Everything was shining, from the uncarpeted floors to the few pieces of simple furniture. Punkahs were suspended from the ceiling to move the air.

Then Vanessa saw an amazing thing: there in a corner of the stark, clean parlour, gleaming more brightly than the polished floor, was a magnificent baby grand piano, with 'Steinway' in flowing gilt script above the keys.

'Oh, Amas.' Vanessa turned to him and held out her arms. Careless of the presence of the grinning Sala, and the three women behind him, Vanessa held Amas close to her.

Sala said something in his strange dialect and withdrew.

'What did he say?'

60

'He said "your heart is sweet". He meant that you have cheered my heart, Vanessa.'

She was so moved she could feel the quick tears gather under her closed lids. 'My heart is sweet, too, Amas.'

None of Amas' descriptions quite prepared her for her first sight of the 'Big Hole', the Kimberley Central Mine. It seemed to stretch for miles in the blazing sun, like an ancient archaeological dig, the various levels of rocks reminding her of uncovered cities. The cables that transported men and materials to and from the mine formed a giant spider's web over the massive pit. Horse-powered winches brought up the ore from the Big Hole's depth.

She had already seen Amas' map of holdings and knew that the various levels corresponded to claims under different ownership. At greater depths the yellow ground, relatively light rock, gave way to blue 'mother rock', much harder and denser. 'That used to be blue ground,' Amas told her. 'We call it "kimberlite" now, for Kimberley. Now stand exactly where I say and walk where I do,' he added warningly. 'It's a long, long way to fall.'

He was uneasy at first but, noticing her sure-footed gait, her ease in the low-heeled boots and divided skirt she'd made from a pair of his trousers, he relaxed. 'That's the kimberlite, way down there,' he pointed out.

When work began, he explained, it was easy to free the diamonds from the yellow ground. The hard part literally was the depths. From the kimberlite, at first, the rock was carried from the edge of the pipe to the 'floors', or storage areas, left to weather and become more workable. That had taken too much time. Now they had to attack the rock directly, which required heavy equipment, and that was expensive. That was why he'd needed the Stirling loan.

Vanessa saw a trolley running down the cables, taking men down into a pit. She recognised Sam Dillon in the trolley with three Africans. Dillon waved at them, looking surprised to see Vanessa. 'I'd like to ride the trolley,' she said, smiling. Amas frowned. 'Not on your life,' he said firmly. Moreover he insisted on taking her back to the house. The sun would be too much for her.

On the first occasion she meekly assented, but as time went on she started bringing a lunch basket to the site. Before long Amas and Sam took her appearance for granted, greatly enjoying her company for the noontime meal. And every day she stayed a little longer at the site, or arrived a little earlier. She longed to be in on an important

61

find. The care of the house was the least of her interests; she'd seen to the ordering of a few items to relieve its starkness, but generally left it all to the house women, which pleased them exceedingly.

She practised faithfully on the piano each morning, yet gradually she found that her music was not the passionate single concern of her life. Now she was totally preoccupied with Amas and the mine.

One hot afternoon in January, the African summer, Vanessa and Amas were descending into the Big Hole on the trolley, a journey he now allowed her, when she felt an unusual dizziness. She saw black flashes before her eyes and, swaying, leaned against Amas.

'What is it?' His voice was harsh with concern. 'What's the matter?'

'Nothing,' she said weakly. 'It's a little warm, that's all.'

'Damn it, I knew this heat was too much for you.' Despite her adjustment to the climate, the newly golden burnish to her skin, Amas always worried about her reaction to the bitter sun. And now as the trolley sank the heat was increasing, the dust-thickened air unpleasant to inhale. 'We're going up.'

'No,' she protested. 'We're right on the point of a find, and I want to be in on it.'

'There'll be others.' Amas signalled for the trolley to be raised. As it laboured upwards, a strange, quick circle of blackness blotted out Vanessa's sight.

When she came to, she was lying in the shade of one of the great winches with Amas kneeling over her, chafing her hands. Sam Dillon was beside him. Their faces broke into overpowering relief when she opened her eyes. They drove her back to the house in one of the wagons and a doctor was hastily summoned from Kimberley.

The doctor emerged smiling from their room. 'Your wife is fine, Mr Holder. She's going to have a child. Congratulations.'

Amas was exultant. Grinning, Sam pumped Amas' hand.

The nearest Vanessa and Amas ever came to a quarrel was the next morning when she got up at her usual hour, saying she was coming to the mines. Nothing Amas could say would dissuade her. But he was reassured by her air of vitality and well-being. At the end of that week they found diamonds worth twenty thousand American dollars. He repaid the rest of the Stirling loan and sent his mother a large cheque with a letter telling her the joyful news.

Everything seemed to be going their way.

* * *

Vanessa hid her dismay from Amas; she had never had strong maternal feelings and she dreaded the arrival of the baby, who would be an intruder on their paradise. Her life was full and exciting now; too soon it would be crowded. And all too soon she would have to curtail her activities, even stay away from the mine. But for now she was stubbornly resolved to go on exactly as before, her energy unflagging in the brief African winter. The nights with Amas had an even greater splendour than before.

One morning she observed herself in the mirror and realised that her hair had been too long neglected. Moreover, she needed a few more things for the baby and the house. Sala drove Vanessa into Kimberley in the buggy, following her like a fierce, protective shadow from store to store as she made the necessary purchases.

Vanessa bought a new bush hat and some boy's shirts and trousers that would fit her with an alteration in the hips. Questioning revealed that a miner's wife had set up as a dressmaker. Vanessa went to her with the trousers and the scandalised woman fitted them for alteration.

A hairdresser was a nicety unknown to Kimberley, but Vanessa saw a barber shop. She took a deep breath and started in. Sala gave a strangled cry.

'Misses! Please, Misses. Sir told me to take care of you; if you go in this place, he will beat me.'

'Nonsense, Sala,' she said crisply. 'Has my husband ever beaten you?'

'No, Misses. But he will now.'

'I'll take the blame, Sala.' Vanessa smiled at the frightened servant. He was obliged to follow her into the shop. All work ceased when they entered. Hearing the odd silence, two men whose faces were covered with wet towels sat up in their chairs and took away the towels to see.

Quietly Vanessa told the bug-eyed barber that she wanted him to trim her hair. Then she took a chair on which to wait while the uneasy Sala stood guard against the wall. The barber trimmed Vanessa's fine, curly hair while everyone looked on. She was satisfied with the result, tipped the barber well and told him she'd be back in about six weeks. When they returned to the dusty street, Sala's dark skin lost its muddy tinge. 'Oh, Misses,' he gasped, 'nobody ever saw a thing like that in Kimberley.'

When she told Amas about the episode that evening, at first he looked as amazed as the barber had, then annoyed. But at last he burst out laughing. 'I always said you weren't like any other woman. Every day I see how right I was.' However, he suggested that on the next trip Yana or Ranee should go with Vanessa; the presence of a local 'dueña' might ease the situation.

That night before he fell asleep Amas thought of it again, with a kind of perverse delight; his wife was unique in almost everything, great matters as well as small. Holding her close, listening to her peaceful breathing, he reviewed the last swift, full, satisfying months since their arrival at Kimberley.

He marvelled at the fact that, although Vanessa seemed to spend so little time in it, the house had been transformed by her ingenuity and deft administration. Where it had been bare before, it was now simple and serene, full of cosiness and peace. The servants adored her, likely because she had given them new pride in their responsibilities. At first he had feared there might be difficulties with the stately Sehoiya, but Vanessa treated her with great respect, often deferring to her opinions in matters where Vanessa had little knowledge and much less interest. Amas grinned to himself in the dark. Even the meals had improved. How Vanessa had managed that he couldn't imagine, because she was bored with most domestic concerns.

The very dogs and the great tame ostriches, which were never quite tame and would come and go with regularity, loved Vanessa and followed her around the property.

Once she had asked Amas, puzzled, why Sala was so stern with his young wife; they had been married less than a year. Amas had told Vanessa that Sala was in the position of a chief with three wives; if he showed too much favouritism towards one the others would be jealous. 'You and I have a much better arrangement,' Amas had commented.

Vanessa said she'd have a word with Sala. Amas had advised her not to meddle. The natives had their ways and were best left alone. However, Vanessa reported that she had spoken to Sala. 'You are Ranee's husband,' she said, 'as Sir is mine. If the others complain, you must put your foot down, as Sir does. Put your foot down with Yana and Sehoiya.'

'Like this?' Sala stamped on the floor, grinning. Vanessa laughed. 'Not exactly.' But the conference had two results: Sala gladdened Ranee thereafter with greater shows of affection, and the expression 'Put your foot down' became a household joke. Occasional stamping of the floor or ground became a habit with all of them.

64

Vanessa's relations with the people of Kimberley was marked by the same skills. She and Amas had been greeted with open arms at the Kimberley Club, whose doors admitted wives and other respectable women in entertainment-starved Kimberley. Vanessa's company was especially welcome. When the members got over their initial shock at the sight of her brief hair, their observation of her unconventional manner, she was accepted warmly. The wives who might have been jealous of her beauty were reassured by her devotion to Amas, her cool demeanour towards their husbands.

She was often prevailed upon to play and was noticed by the pompous Cecil Rhodes, to Amas' mingled irritation and pride. He detested the fellow for his artificial manner and fanatical look. Not only was he Amas' biggest competitor, but his workers were treated less than liberally. Amas, who had come up the hard way himself, was far more equitable with his crew.

It delighted Amas that Vanessa needed no outside company at all. He and the mines and the 'house family' and animals seemed to be all she required. Sam, of course, was family, too.

Amas smiled now, recalling her consternation that the honeymoon would end with the end of their magical voyage. If anything he loved and wanted her more than ever; she was as ardent as before, making his whole life bloom like the very mimosa that the natives likened to her hair.

And now, he thought, there will be a child. Surely life can offer no more to any man. Yet he thought with a certain wistfulness that she did not seem to share his elation about the child. He himself had felt, especially when he learned that Ranee would also give birth in September, that the whole house burgeoned with life. Vanessa's attitude was less sentimental; in a matter-of-fact way she was preparing for the birth. When she handled small items of clothes he felt overwhelmed with a mighty wonder and tenderness, but she did not appear moved at all.

On the contrary, she had occasionally made half-laughing complaints about the snugness of her trousers, the imminent boredom of confinement.

'Amas.' The soft, sudden sound of his own name broke in on his reflections, startling but welcome. Her silky aureola of hair tickled his chin as she moved in his embrace. 'Are you awake?'

'Yes, darling.' His arm closed around her and he kissed the top of her head.

'I love you, I love you so,' she whispered, turning so that their

65

bodies met. 'I have never been alive before, Amas. I am only alive when I am with you. Tell me that this baby won't make a difference between us.'

He encircled her in his arms, pressing her close, feeling his own body quicken and burn. 'A difference! What do you mean, darling?'

'You won't love the baby more than me?'

She sounded anxious, woebegone. He was flabbergasted.

'More than *you* –' Amas kissed her passionately. 'More than you! Vanessa, that's . . . that's crazy. How could I love anything on earth more than you?'

The relaxation of her body in his grasp told him that she was reassured.

So that was it, he thought. And he recalled all that he had heard of other women, how the coming of children had made them indifferent to their husbands, according the men a second place.

Yes, Vanessa was like no other woman he had ever known. And as they caressed each other, coming wildly together, he had a deeper sense of blessing than he had ever known before.

Vanessa spent the last months of her confinement in arduous piano practice, supervising changes in the house. To compensate her for her imprisonment Amas had an addition built onto the bungalow and ordered some new furnishings from England. Now they would have room for the baby and for guests.

On 23 August 1886 Vanessa was delivered of a daughter. They named her Lesley Stirling Holder.

Ranee's baby was born in September. It was a boy, and they called him Kossee. Ranee glowed with the dignity of her new status; she was now the mother of a family, and she was put in charge of both babies, reigning supreme. Her sister-in-law Yana was married now, gone away.

In October Martin Stirling cabled, asking permission to visit his new grandchild and bring Bea.

'Now why in hell would Bea want to come?' Amas queried.

They were in the nursery. He was holding the baby. Vanessa looked at it with an odd amazement. If only it resembled anyone at all – although Amas swore the child was just like her.

'I can't imagine,' Vanessa said. But perhaps she could. Bea was still unmarried. Maybe that was her mission, to find a husband among men why knew nothing of her reputation.

'She'll be like a peacock in a chicken run.' Vanessa grinned.

Amas put the baby back in her crib, came to Vanessa to put his arms around her and kiss her shoulder. 'Or a hawk.'

'Vanessa, Vanessa.' Martin Stirling held out his arms and she went into his familiar, beloved embrace, realising how sorely she had missed him.

'You look . . . reborn,' he said gently. 'Africa, and Amas, have been good to you, I see.' Martin gave his son-in-law an affectionate glance and, keeping one arm around Vanessa's waist, held out his other hand to Amas.

While the men were seeing to the luggage, Vanessa turned reluctantly to Bea.

'I can't get over how you've changed, Vanessa.' Bea Stirling observed her with the large, dark eyes that were vivid now and less rapacious in the dim light of the Kimberley Club. Her bright yellow dress softened her sharp features, made her sallow skin seem rosy. 'You look like you're always out of doors. And you're so at home here, in this out-of-the-way little place. But I'm glad to see how *sensible* you are about the baby.'

Vanessa thought, amused, that only a woman could really translate that speech. In other words, I've deteriorated, my skin is weathered, my clothes and outlook provincial. And to cap it all, I don't give a damn about my baby. She almost laughed aloud. 'Thank you, Bea,' she said calmly, as if what her sister had said was the highest compliment.

And she had to admit that the latter charge came perilously near the truth: the memory of her thickening body, her discomfort and confinement, the dreadful pain, were still too much alive. She had been hard put to join in her father's transports over his first grandchild.

Vanessa glanced at her father, deep in conversation with Amas and Sam Dillon. She felt a deeper affection for him than ever; he reacted to Africa, and to Kimberley and the mine, like a young boy whose adventure stories had come alive. He already looked at least twenty years younger than he had when they arrived.

Although heaven knew they had had little rest; this was their fourth visit to the Kimberley Club in little more than a week. Beatrice was not an easy guest to amuse. She was already urging Vanessa to go to Cape Town for a shopping trip, having expressed horror at the sight of the Kimberley stores.

'You're very thoughtful,' Bea said sharply. Vanessa, bubbling with fresh mirth, reflected, which is Bea for 'rude'. 'What *do* you do for entertainment, Vanessa?'

'I'm fully occupied, believe me.'

Bea's great black gaze darted to Amas Holder. 'Well, of course, with a husband like *that* –' she gave an insinuating laugh. 'But I meant, what *else*, my dear?'

Vanessa was saved from replying by Sam Dillon, who had risen from his chair and was standing before Beatrice. 'May I have the honour, Miss Beatrice?'

'Why, of course, Mr Dillon.' Beatrice fluttered and rose to join Sam Dillon in a waltz.

Martin Stirling was talking to a British officer. Amas turned to Vanessa and took her hand. 'How are you bearing up?' He smiled.

'With difficulty,' she admitted. In a lower voice, so her father would not overhear, she added, 'I'm a prisoner again. Oh, Amas, I miss the mines so much.'

'I know. I miss *you* there. I wish to God she'd never come.' He watched the dancing couple. 'For more reasons than one.'

Vanessa followed the direction of his stare. Sam was looking down earnestly into Beatrice's upraised eyes, pressing her close to him in the dance. Poor Sam, Vanessa reflected. She recalled the way Sam had looked at her when she and Amas first arrived, his hungry gaze involuntarily devouring the lines of her body. Amas had often said Sam needed a 'good woman to love him', hinting that he'd had to make do with the mechanical attention of the women at the Digger's Rest. And Vanessa had not missed Sam's envious expression when he saw her with Amas. Now he seemed absolutely besotted with Bea.

'Yes,' Vanessa murmured to Amas. 'That would be a tragedy. Talk to him, Amas.'

'How can I?'

That was true enough. How could Amas tell his friend that Beatrice was little better than a rapacious whore? Vanessa had a gloomy conviction that nothing could save Sam Dillon.

Sam Dillon stared down, hypnotised, into the dark and gleaming eyes of Beatrice Stirling. It had taken all his nerve to cut in on that fellow Seton – class was class, Sam reflected gloomily, even here in Kimberley, and Anthony Seton's languid, uppercrust air, his smooth perfection, his dashing British Army uniform, were making quite an impression on the ladies.

And yet now . . . Sam took a quick, excited breath, struggling for something clever to say to Beatrice. Her gaze was still fixed on his, and he felt his heart hammering, the heat of excitement breaking out all over his back.

It was she who broke the silence. 'It's true, then,' she murmured, with a languorous smile.

'What's true, Miss Stirling?' he asked awkwardly, almost stammering.

'All the things I've read about you strong and silent men,' she responded so softly that he had to bend his head down to catch the words.

'And what have you read?' he queried with great effort, because her nearness was extremely disturbing; he could hardly get his breath.

'That strong and silent adventurers are very exciting,' she answered boldly, moving closer to him. His body throbbed and he could not think of a word in reply.

There was a seductive glitter in her great dark eyes. 'You are different from all these others, Sam Dillon.'

Indeed he was, Sam thought dolefully. Middle-aged and plain. And still she was comparing him favourably to all these younger, better looking, better educated men who were swarming around her. He could hardly credit it. She was so elegant, so lively; there was an aura about her none of the local women could even approach, a slightly naughty air that titillated him almost to madness. He made another supreme effort and spoke.

'How?' he demanded boldly.

'You are more of a man than anyone I have ever met,' she declared with an honesty and openness that touched his heart. He was overwhelmed with longing, so overwhelmed he was at a loss for words. In response he could only stare and stare at her, knowing his heart was in his eyes; he drew her even nearer, his whole self singing.

Only a week later Sam Dillon and Beatrice were married in Kimberley.

When Vanessa told Martin, he blurted out, 'Oh, my God, not *Dillon!*'

Amas and Vanessa exchanged a bewildered glance. There had never been anything snobbish about Stirling, yet now he looked horror-stricken.

'Come now, Martin,' Amas protested gently, 'you accepted a Holder in the family. Why not a Dillon?'

'You don't know what I mean at all. I may have destroyed a fine man, by bringing her here in the first place. I thought she might pair off with that idiot Seton.'

Vanessa heard him with astonishment. Whatever Martin Stirling's private opinion had been, he had never said such a thing before in all her memory. She was so confounded that she sank down numbly on the sofa.

'Get me a brandy, would you, Amas?' Stirling looked quite pale. Amas complied, apparently as surprised as Vanessa had been. Stirling took a hefty swallow, then said in a tired voice, 'There's something I must tell you, both of you. Something I've kept hidden for years, even from Bea. Although I suspect she must have guessed the truth; she'd have to, if she ever really looked in a mirror. And she does that with great frequency.' His narrow mouth twisted in the simile of a smile. 'She looks too much like me not to be my natural daughter.'

I should have known, Vanessa thought. I should have always known, from the very first. An adopted child never looks that much like an adoptive father.

'Her mother,' Stirling went on, 'was a woman as . . . warped as Bea. An indiscretion I'm not proud of. But suffice it to say I felt responsible – I *was* responsible – for her. Bea's mother . . . entertained a good number of men. She neglected the child completely. I arranged, shall we say, for the child to be taken from her and placed in a foundling home, where I "adopted" her. I thought in the proper environment, with the right care . . .' He shook his head. 'But she was different from other children, from the beginning. She was physically a woman, able to bear children, when she was only eleven. Bea would have been better off in Samoa, or somewhere like that, where she could have married. I've watched her all these years with dread, watched her become her very mother.'

He looked so desolate that Vanessa sat down beside him, putting her hand on his shoulder. 'Oh, my dear,' he said, 'you can imagine what *you* meant to me, in the face of all that, the miracle we thought could never happen.'

She nodded, raising her hand to caress his face.

'There are things I hate to reveal, even now.' Stirling put his hands over his face. His words were muffled when he added, 'There was a time, when she was only twelve years old . . .' His voice died away. Then he dropped his hands and concluded, in a dead voice, '. . . she tried to seduce me.'

'Oh, my God.' Vanessa felt nauseated.

'Forgive me,' Stirling said, 'I've upset you. I've shocked you. But

70

this is a burden I've carried for a long time. I've never told these things to a living soul.'

'No, you haven't shocked me, Father.' Vanessa glanced at Amas. He nodded almost imperceptibly. 'We've both known, for quite a while.'

Stirling studied them both and shook his head, as if to plead that they tell him nothing more.

'I thought that things would change,' Stirling muttered, 'that she might . . . grow out of it. A fruitless wish, a foolish hope, as it turned out. And now she has fastened on Sam Dillon.'

Vanessa repressed a shudder. 'Fastened'. It sounded like the sting of a bee piercing hapless skin. She leaned back against the sofa, drained and trembling.

'I think you ought to lie down,' Amas told her gently. 'You look done in.'

She was too tired to protest.

'Come on, Martin,' Amas said firmly. 'Let's go for a ride around the place. You haven't had a proper look at our "peaceable kingdom", as you call it.' He forced a smile.

Accepting Amas' kiss, Vanessa started into their bedroom. She heard Amas say to her father, 'Don't worry, Martin, Sam's a grown man. He'll be fine. He must take the responsibility for himself.'

'No, Amas,' Martin retorted. 'I brought her here. I'm the man who's destroyed your peaceable kingdom.'

Wide-eyed in the stuffy darkness of the bungalow, Sam Dillon raged in silence. One o'clock. And she still hadn't returned from the Kimberley Club which, in that early rising area, closed at eleven. Where was she? He had to get some sleep; he had to be on the site at seven and she knew it damned well. Sam shifted his heavy, naked body, seeking a position that would help him drowse off.

Some hope. He could not fall asleep unless she was there. He cursed himself now for not going with her. It didn't look right, in the first place, as they were so recently married. Bea told him she was meeting some women friends. Women friends! Not bloody likely, when nearly every woman in Kimberley looked on her with jealousy and suspicion. No wonder – she was dazzling.

Sam Dillon had never been easily awed, but he'd been just that when he met the noted Martin Stirling, astonished that Beatrice Stirling would even look at plain Sam Dillon. He knew his good points, but he was clear-eyed about his limitations. Sam was surprised at Beatrice's difference from Vanessa, exquisite Vanessa who was someone to be worshipped from afar.

Sam thought Amas Holder had everything – until the stupefaction of that first encounter with Beatrice Stirling. At the club she was always surrounded by single fellows, young British officers and the like; they absolutely swarmed around her, drawn by her dainty ways, the glitter in her dark, exciting eyes.

And nothing had prepared Sam for what happened only a week after they met. One night she had come to this very bungalow. And when, astounded, he had taken her hot-skinned, vital body, he was overcome with the miraculous knowledge that she loved him. It had to be so; otherwise that daughter of such a proud man would never had given herself to him.

What had been even more astonishing, what made Sam Dillon count himself the most fortunate of men, was that despite her innocence Bea was knowing in the ways of love. He could hardly credit it, yet it was true. After the empty years of the whores and the casual women, Bea's passion was a marvel he still could barely accept.

She told him, touchingly, how lonely she had always been; that she had not been able to help herself in coming to him. Sam's pride in his manhood, in the strong body he'd always taken for granted, swelled to bursting. This, then, Dillon concluded, was the same powerful feeling Vanessa must have brought to the blessed Amas. What wonderful women the Stirlings were, Sam told himself over and over again in the first mesmerised days.

And then, in only another week, she had actually consented to marry him. Sam's shining new hopes, his faith in the beneficence of fate, were vindicated. He was to know, every night, the ineffable glory of the release that only she could give him.

It seemed in no time at all that the dream began to die; she assumed a cool and teasing manner; she was full of imperious demands. In spite of the fact that he was running himself into exhaustion, she required to be entertained, escorted out almost nightly. She began flirting with every man she saw at the Kimberley Club, laughing at Sam when he protested. He was so terrified that she would become bored that he had even acceded to her order to be taken to the Digger's Rest. He smarted even now with chagrin to recall the contempt in other men's eyes. Worse, he suspected she was with other men.

Racked and tortured, he came to a grim conclusion – she was a devil, she was playing with him. She was no better than a whore.

Worse. A whore never lied, but just delivered the merchandise, inferior as it was. Yet Sam could not stop wanting her with a constant, desperate itch of lust. No woman had ever been so abandoned, so satisfying. The very coldness of her desires made her a thousand times more arousing than the others.

Sam's swollen body throbbed; he cursed and thrashed about in the bed again, vainly seeking rest, forgetfulness. He decided to get up and have a drink. She was destroying him. He hadn't been sleeping or eating enough, he was late on the job, making mistakes. And more and more he needed a drink to steady himself. If it went on like this Amas would be forced to find a better man to replace him. And Bea would leave him. He'd have nothing.

That cold fact helped him snap to his senses. That, and the comforting fire of the liquor in his belly. He drew a ragged sigh of relief. He'd sleep now; she'd soon be home and everything would come right again. His eyelids were growing heavy, his breath calm, when he heard a little scratching noise at the door, as if a big cat were clawing to be let in. It was Bea's signal that she was home.

Sam felt new anger. How dare she shame him like this, by coming home so late? He stood staring at the door; he'd be damned if he'd even open it for her. She scratched again with her long, pointed nails.

He remembered how they felt on his bare skin, rasping, arousing him to that damned wild wanting. He made a low sound like a sob. To hell with her, he'd make her wait a little longer. But the scratching went on, steadily. Then there was a silence, followed by a sharp, impatient rap.

Sam imagined the nails abrading his nude skin, his slackening body come to painful life. His loins drummed and vibrated; he fairly ached. There was no way he could delay longer, reproach her. The agonising tumescence of his flesh told him that, driving him, mocking him.

He strode to the door and opened it with a shaking hand. He expected an irritated attack but she entered smiling.

'Good morning,' she said, and in the dim reflection cast by the round moon he could see her pink tongue between sharp white teeth framed by thin red lips. The memory of that small tongue's skill made him tremble.

She was wearing a pale yellow dress and he made out her naked upper body through it clearly – the huge, sharppointed breasts so large for such a small, slender woman; the hint of narrow loins, black-shadowed whiteness. Her long, strangely lustreless black hair tumbled down about the great lobes of her breasts, a tendril curling around the aureola of one, erect nipples thrusting out the flimsy cloth.

'You . . . you came home like *this*?' he cried out. 'Where in hell have you *been*, Beatrice . . . what have you been doing?'

She only laughed softly and, parting the dress, let it slide over her shoulders and arms and slither to the floor. Then with enormous calm she stepped out of a thin petticoat and stood before him nude, leaning against the closed door, studying his face.

'What do you care?' she inquired in a lazy, challenging tone. 'I'm here now.'

His unwilling gaze devoured her from the oblique glimmer of her big black eyes to the moist, red mouth, the heavy breasts, the dark triangle of Aphrodite.

Her arms hung down on either side of the offered nakedness; she made a low, growling sound and leaned back, standing wide-legged on her naked feet.

Dillon grunted and lunged, grabbing her breasts, feeling their softness, squeezing them in his big hands until she cried out in an animal way, half-pain, half-delight, as he jerked her to him and thrust himself into her waiting, insinuating moisture. Her body tilted to his and he was lost in pounding frenzy, driving forward to that irreversible prize, that one titanic explosion while his mind screamed back to him, oh, God, like dynamite, a charge of dynamite when it blows, oh, Christ almighty; and he sank into that sweet and pillowed writhing, on to the . . . on, hearing dimly the drum of her naked haunches against the door, drumming and drumming . . .

Then his mind shouted, or maybe his throat, he was there, he was there, already there. . . .

He felt an incredible weakness, his body quaking all over, his quavering legs like those of a man in a seizure. He leaned on her for a moment, gasping, supporting her while his aching knuckles pressed against the door.

'Too soon. Much too soon, husband.' The clear, matter-of-fact intonation jarred him; he felt as if someone had struck him from sleep with hard blows to his head. 'Too soon,' she said in a quieter tone, and he felt her sharp-nailed fingers pierce the skin of his naked, sweaty back, climbing his muscular biceps, puncturing his flesh, but he was too drained, too weak to care; he could hardly feel pain anymore, he was so shaken and appeased.

The pointed fingernails were breaking the skin of his neck now,

74

slashing and scraping at his face. 'What . . .' he mumbled drunkenly.

She was pushing at his shoulders, pushing him down to his knees, her fingers biting into his face again, pulling it towards her lower body.

'Now . . . now . . . now . . .' she ordered coldly, the word beaten steadily out as rhythmic as a fist on a drum; with her relentless claws she drew his face into her, demanding.

He could feel those nails stinging, paining, never ceasing, sharp as the sting of a bee while he obeyed her command, caressing, caressing; his head pounded, his cheeks received the warm gush of his own flowing blood; she would not let go. He went on and on until he perceived her leap and shudder, heard her squeal with pleasure.

The cruel nails were withdrawn; her hands winced and slackened, shaking, and she gave one last terrible squealing cry that sounded like a dying boar.

Stunned with disbelief, Sam knew his own lust was renewed: he grabbed her by the hips and threw her down on the matted floor, listening to her head and body thud against the wood and rushes, the savage vibration of his own voice deep in his throat, falling astride her for the pounding drive once more. Now he didn't even feel the stinging lacerations on his face and arms and body.

There was no turning back; there never was. He was insane, and the madness would never end. Even when he was empty there was no peace for them. Aching, sick with his exhaustion, he dimly knew that at some moment in their mindless frenzy he had carried her to the bed again and, sooner than he could have imagined possible, was being teased to repeated performance.

She's a devil, he thought crazily, a demon who can never find the end of satisfaction. Yet he was so mesmerised, so crazed in her abandon, that he found his own flesh infected with her gnawing fever.

The night was fading before she would let him be. Slack and sore, his every muscle screaming with fatigue, Dillon looked at her face, her bedraggled hair. She was almost ugly now. And yet he knew he would always want her, want this . . . insanity, as long as he drew breath.

As long as he drew breath, Dillon repeated in melancholy silence. He put out his hand and touched her face. She received the touch impassively, staring out the window at the approaching dawn.

'Where were you, Bea?' he whispered.

75

She smiled with a gleam of sharp white teeth through swollen lips, stung with his constant, hungry kisses, her face abraded from his stubble. The huge black eyes were bright as ever, as if nothing had happened at all. He could hardly keep his own lids open.

'What do you care, Sam Dillon? It didn't keep you from your rutting.' He winced at the coarse expression.

With an impatient gesture she threw off his hand and, getting out of bed, walked to the bureau naked. She looked at herself in the mirror, as if she were alone in the room, and picked up a comb to run it through the snarls of her hair.

'Good God, I look like a wreck,' she muttered.

'Bea.' He got up and stumbled to her, standing behind her with his arms around her waist while she tried to comb her knotted tresses.

'What now?' she demanded. 'Have I married a Greek?'

He wanted desperately to hit her, to stop her foul mouth for good and all. But he reined in his ire, and said gently, 'Please, tell me where you were. You can't go on doing this to me. I'm your husband. Tell me, Bea.'

'Why, you simple fool.' She smashed the comb down and shook his arms away. He was flabbergasted; he stood with his arms dangling loose at his sides, watching her pace around the room.

'You damned simple fool, do you think I'm going to stay in this hole for the rest of my life? You must be crazy.' She flicked him with a scornful glance and laughed.

'But good God, you've married me . . .'

'Do you think I would have, if I could have brought a better man to heel? You were the quickest bull in the nearest pen.' She raised her swooping brows and grinned at him. 'I must say you have remarkable endurance, but you had a hell of a lot to learn.'

That was true. In just a few days she'd taught him things even the whores hadn't known.

'What in hell do you *think* I was doing, till one o'clock in the morning? Needlework with the women?'

He was so transfixed with agonising pain, inflamed with such a towering rage, that he feared he would kill her. All that warmth, that sweet, insinuating softness, was just the leaving of another man. Why, God in heaven, he had received it with his very . . . He began to shake, and an inchoate, bestial sound gathered deep in his throat, emerging from his mouth, which was trembling and ajar.

'Do you really think you're a better man than Tony?' she

76

demanded. She showed no fear at all, only a vast irritation.

'Tony . . .' Anthony Seton. That posturing, effete little bastard. Tony Seton. Involuntarily Sam's hands balled into fists.

'Yes, Tony Seton. I'll marry him yet. You'll see. And he'll take me out of this hole to England.'

Sam took a step towards her and grabbed her by the arms, holding her in a bruising grasp. 'I'll see you both in hell first. I'll kill you, Bea, I'll kill you both.'

She threw back her head and gave one short, cruel yelp of laughter. 'You . . . kill? Why, you weak-kneed fool, you can't even shoot an animal.'

It was not the first time that she had taunted him about his distaste for hunting. In one cold, startling instant his anger evaporated, and all of a sudden he felt too tired to say another word, too defeated to strike out at her.

Her face was triumphant. She knew she was safe. He loosened his hold and dropped his hands. With one last contemptuous look she undulated from the room and he heard the water running in the tub.

Like someone drugged he picked up his discarded clothes from a chair and put them on. Then he put on his stockings and his boots and walked slowly into the parlour. He poured a tumbler of whiskey and drained it without taking a breath. Putting the glass down, he opened a drawer in his desk and took out his pistol. He would not cringe now.

He thrust the pistol in his belt.

'While I draw breath . . .' he mumbled.

Sam walked quickly out the front door, heading for the clump of willows by the stream where quachas grazed peacefully. They usually accepted his presence without dismay. That might not be so this morning.

This morning he had drunk the very essence of his enemy. No hell to come could burn him like that knowledge.

Part II
The Blade

CHAPTER FIVE

'19 September 1899.'

Beginning her weekly letter to Martin Stirling, Vanessa Holder paused, staring at the date she had written.

Thirteen years had passed on wings, all those years since Sam had killed himself, with not even a gravestone here in Kimberley to mark him. The body had been shipped to Liverpool for burial with his family.

There had been no word of Bea in Cape Town or in America, not until Mitchell Farley came to teach the children. He told them he had met her in London with her husband, Anthony Seton. It made the world seem a tight little island, Vanessa reflected – Bea and Tony Seton, and their own children's tutor. When she and Amas had sent that advertisement to the *Times*, they'd never dreamed of such an eventuality.

The thoughts of Sam and Bea, of Farley and the children, recalled the problems Vanessa could never mention to her father.

And now in addition there was the Boer threat that preoccupied him so.

For nearly a quarter of a century the British had been clashing with the native Boers, the Dutch landowners who had lived here long before the European adventurers came, looking for diamonds and for gold. In 1877, the year before Amas arrived in South Africa, the British had annexed the Transvaal; the Boers rebelled and won a brief war against the British intruders and in 1881, when Amas had made his first great find, the Transvaal was given complete self-government subject to the 'suzerainty' of the British Crown.

But then in 1884, the year before Vanessa had arrived in Africa, the Transvaal government gained greater powers and British powers were sharply reduced. In return all European settlers, under the agreement between the Transvaal and Britain, had their civil rights protected and there were to be no more discriminatory taxes at the expense of the *uitlanders*, or non-Boers. A customs union was set up.

But then the British South Africa Company had come into being in 1889, and its interests ranged far beyond the mining of gold and diamonds. The function of the company, as Cecil Rhodes saw it, was to explore and settle the area north of the Cape Colony, thus containing the Transvaal and hindering its expansion. Anti-British feeling was deepening and widening.

Even now, Amas had said anxiously to Vanessa, he foresaw the imminent closing of overland routes through the Transvaal to British and Cape traders. And that would mean trouble.

It was this trend that aroused Martin Stirling's fears and was a constant refrain in his letters. In her preoccupation with her own small world, and resigned to helplessness in matters in which women were allowed no voice, Vanessa had taken an ostrich position for years, burying her head in the sand of the house and the mines, her family and her music. Amas had always been apolitical, having no quarrel with the Boers and detesting Rhodes, but the fact remained that the Holder mine was partially supported by British interests. As Americans, the Holders were *uitlanders*, it was true, but somewhere on the perimeter of things. Nevertheless, the British interests made the Holders pro-British in Boer eyes.

There was so much that had to be glossed over and hidden, Vanessa thought, that it was sometimes almost impossible to write to her father. But she must manage. She knew how much he depended on their correspondence. After all, as a woman she could feign a certain ignorance of politics – and yet she wondered if that would fool Martin Stirling, who was too aware of her sharp intelligence to accept such an evasion.

Well, there was always the mine, and now the chambering. She could always write him safely about that, and American news.

Vanessa took up her pen and started.

'Dear Father,

'Our tardy journals inform us with far less grace than you about what's going on over there. What a world it is away! It's hard to picture Riverside Drive packed with women on bicycles . . . and lead in the hems of their skirts.

'We relished your description of Diamond Jim and the great John L. Sullivan, but I must say the tailors' strike and the Irish riot sounded anything but gay in these so-called Gay Nineties.

'I look forward so much to receiving the new Stephen Crane book, which should be along any day now, as well as the Ward man's mail order catalogue. That sounds like a real curiosity. What a boon if there were an English one.'

Vanessa glanced over what she had written. It sounded stiff and false, like a letter to a stranger. And except for Amas she'd been closer to her father than to anyone in the world. But the habit of years was hard to break. It had been too long since she could be open with her father.

He'd blamed himself wholly for Sam's death, despite their every effort to dissuade him. Soon after the tragedy he'd gone back to New York. Vanessa wondered if he'd ever come back. Now, with the Boer matter hanging fire, she hated to pain him with any additional worry, even if there had been times when she'd desperately longed to open her heart to him, when she thought and suffered things she hadn't even been able to tell Amas.

Doggedly she went on with her letter.

'Do something for me. If you get a chance to hear Chadwick's symphonic sketches, please tell me what you think of the "Vagrom Ballad", the one based on hobo themes. You might know that would be dear to my heart; it reminds me of Amas' chequered past.'

With a small pang Vanessa stopped again. She stared out the window. Ranee was hanging fresh washing in the yard and from somewhere Vanessa could dimly hear the shrill voices of the children. She distinguished Lesley's indignant tones from the calmer sound of Martin and Kossee. Vanessa wondered vaguely what was going on, then purposefully stopped wondering. She had enough on her mind now.

The very mention of music reminded her of her own. She thought of what might have been if she'd stayed in New York.

That was something else she couldn't be open about. Her father was, after all, a man, blithely assuming that her true fulfilment came from Amas and the children. Certainly that was truer of Amas than the children. Nothing had ever tarnished the early magic between them. Their passion for each other was miraculously unabated; if anything, even stronger than it had been at the beginning.

But when it came to her music . . . or the children . . . and now, Mitchell Farley, Vanessa reflected darkly . . . she'd had to resort to evasions, euphemisms and downright lies to keep her father from knowing how she really felt.

Just once, just once she'd like to write to her father with utter frankness about everything.

Except the children.

Her father would be deeply shocked to know the truth. Even now Vanessa could not face telling him that the children were intruders on their Eden, or hint that Farley was the recent serpent. Vanessa smiled at her own extravagant thinking.

But she considered the children again and sobered. Something is lacking in me, she thought uneasily. I don't feel the way other women do about their children. Amas is all I need. The news that she was carrying Martin, right on the heels of Sam's suicide, had rocked Vanessa's world.

For nearly two months after Martin's birth Vanessa suffered enforced idleness under the stern and watchful eyes of Amas, the servants and the doctor. When her energies returned at last she gave the baby into the servants' keeping and went back to her music and the mines. She felt a secret, guilty elation when the children got old enough to go to school in Kimberley. However, all too soon she had to face the fact that the school was inadequate, that the children should have a tutor. And Mitchell Farley, that cool and rather disturbing young man from London, had been engaged.

This was not getting her letter written. She must go on while she still had the courage of her new-found frankness. She'd work up to it with something about the chambering.

Amas had recently introduced that method of mining; chamber levels were established from shafts at forty-foot vertical intervals. As successive 'blue' chambers were mined out, the overlying waste rocks dropped down. For safety the chambers, separated by thick back pillars, were so located that each level's back pillar was just over the chamber below it.

Chamber-mining was done by drilling and blasting vertical holes. To give them enough working space, the broken ground was lowered after each blast on hand-loaded carts in the parallel tunnels. As the chamber broke through into the level above, the overlying pillar was allowed to collapse into it. The workers kept on loading until the kimberlite ore was so diluted by waste rock that it was uneconomical to continue. Chambering had shown Amas that the kimberlite would break up of its own accord, and he was elated with the safer, more flexible method.

'But it cost the earth to develop,' Vanessa wrote to Martin 'and it needs a bigger crew. So I have a feeling that this will ultimately be a stepping-stone rather than a staying place. It's transformed the look of the Big Hole . . . you'd hardly recognise it now.'

Vanessa stopped writing a moment, then took the plunge, resuming, 'It's been too long since you have seen Kimberley, Father, since you've shared in our difficulties and triumphs. Surely now, after all this time, you might consider another visit. The old days are gone, with their sorrows, and the new ones are so exciting. You haven't even seen your grandson, except in photographs. And I miss you.

'I need you. There are certain matters I want so much to talk with you about.'

Vanessa put down her pen again. This was going to be more difficult than she'd anticipated. She would have to recopy the letter, omitting the last sentences. Why create anxiety in her father when she could not go on to explain what she meant . . . her gnawing restlessness, her new dissatisfaction and the suspicion that the mines, and even Amas, were not enough? She wanted to perform, needed to perform in a civilised city; it was maddening, after keeping up her music assiduously all these years, to continue with the polite little concerts she'd given in Kimberley and Cape Town.

What was more worrying, Amas seemed to attribute her restlessness not to the dilemma with her music but to Mitchell Farley. Nothing she could say or do could change his mind. He seemed to suspect that she was attracted to the young tutor, and nothing was farther from the truth. The notion of any man supplanting Amas was downright grotesque, especially the rather effete young Mitchell. The very qualities that Amas might imagine attracted her in the tutor were the very ones that attracted her least – his knowledge of music, his worldly smoothness and background of ease, his lean good looks only flattered Amas by comparison, making her husband seem stronger and more virile than ever.

Surprised by the chime of the clock, Vanessa realised how late it was. Mitchell had kept the children a long time. She heard his voice and theirs; they must be coming back to the main house now, from the annexe, where the schoolroom had been set up next to the guest quarters where Mitchell had his rooms.

Hearing them enter the rear of the house, Vanessa put her letter and writing materials away. She shut the secretary's leaf just as Mitchell Farley shepherded the children into the room.

All three were unusually subdued and Farley had a slightly pinched look around his handsome mouth and nose, a look he always had when he was annoyed about something. He always reminded Vanessa of Comus, the lord of misrule; a faint spite and rebelliousness slept below his surface calm, his Oxonian drawl. She glanced at him and his slanted black eyes tried to capture her roving look. But now she was examining the children's faces. Obviously something was up; Martin always ran to her for a quick, affectionate hug, and now he was hanging back, with a sullen expression in the lionlike eyes that were so like Amas'. He was Amas' very image except for his bright blond hair. Lesley looked indignant and put upon, which was not unusual for a girl with two boys for companions. Her sulky, pretty little face was blank, framed by tousled, bright gold hair. A very mature thirteen.

Lesley was no different from usual; she was affectionate only with Amas and patently worshipped Mitchell Farley. With Vanessa she was distant. Already she had something of her grandmother Hester's querulous ways and rigid turn of mind.

It was Kossee's small black face that disturbed Vanessa most. Customarily he was a merry simile of Sala. But today there was a shadow of hurt in his shining eyes and around his generous mouth. He greeted Vanessa and ran off to the kitchen regions, to look for Ranee.

'What's going on?' Vanessa asked calmly.

'We've had a bit of a dust-up,' Farley drawled, caressing Lesley's hair. He sat down on the sofa. Lesley followed him and sat beside him. Martin stayed where he was, tight-lipped, observing the others. His sturdy body, his stubborn posture were so reminiscent of his father's that Vanessa's heart turned over.

'What happened, Mitchell?' She gestured to Martin, who came to her and she put her arm around his shoulders.

Farley's oblique black regard swept Vanessa from head to foot in a bold, disturbing manner that annoyed her. He responded, 'Our Lesley, all of a sudden, has an aversion to studying with Kossee.'

Martin made an impatient sound. Vanessa stilled him with a touch. 'What's all this, Lesley?' She kept her voice neutral and gentle with an effort. This was not the first time that there had been problems between Kossee and Lesley, but it had never been quite this open before.

'He's a servant child, Mother.' Lesley stared at Vanessa defiantly from her pale blue eyes, and her scandalised, prissy piping was an eerie echo of Hester Stirling's very manner.

'That's bloody stupid!' Martin burst out.

Vanessa raised her brows and knelt down, turning her son to face her. 'Where did you get a word like that? Not from Mr Farley.'

'Hardly,' Farley agreed in his lazy drawl. 'I've spoken to Martin about his less . . . polite speech. I think that comes of hanging about the mine.'

'Damn right I "hang about" the mine! I'm going to be a miner, like my father!'

86

'Martin,' Vanessa warned him, repressing a chuckle. 'That's enough. The question now is this nonsense between Lesley and Kossee. I want to know exactly what happened.'

'I told Mr Farley what Gramma Stirling said, that's all,' Lesley answered indignantly.

Vanessa repressed her irritation – her mother and her daughter had been corresponding since Lesley was old enough to write letters, and Vanessa sometimes did not even know when Hester's letters arrived. She asked calmly, 'And what did Gramma Stirling say this time, Lesley?'

'That it's not proper for us to share a tutor with a servant child.' The girl's smug expression nearly caused Vanessa's temper to slip its moorings. If she were this great a snob, so soon, what would she be later? But after all, she was only a child; it wasn't her fault, but Hester's. And mine, Vanessa thought gloomily. I suppose if I were the kind of mother I ought to be, she wouldn't have turned to my mother as a substitute.

'Why don't you go on now and have your bath, Lesley?' Vanessa suggested in a tired, gentle voice. The child looked at her with surprise; obviously she'd expected another reaction.

'Very well, Mother.' Her lack of expression made Vanessa uneasy; there was something almost unnatural about it. Lesley went out with her mincing step.

'You, too, Martin.'

'Okay, Mother.' The cheerful, more open boy went out after his sister.

Vanessa turned to Farley. 'Look here, Mitchell, I want a straight answer. Have you been encouraging Lesley in these matters? I want to know.'

Farley's dark gaze swept her. 'Of course not.' After an instant, he resumed, 'Hasn't it ever occurred to you ... Vanessa,' he emphasized the name ever so slightly, 'how silly it is for me to keep calling you "Mrs Holder"?'

She heard the creak of a floorboard and turned, startled. Amas was standing on the threshold of the room, and his face was stormy. Oh, my God, she agonised. He'd heard that intimate, insinuating question of Farley's. Things had been awkward enough before, but this . . . Nothing like this had ever happened.

'Hello, darling.' She gave Amas a smile of welcome and hurried to embrace him, ignoring Mitchell Farley's presence. But she could sense Amas' stiffness. He did not return her hug with his usual strength and enthusiasm. 'How did it go today? Can I get you a drink?'

She realised in her nervousness that she was overdoing it a little. Amas glanced at her, his leonine gaze blank in his swarthy face. 'All right,' he said tonelessly. 'I'll get my drink.' He started to the sideboard. 'Farley?' His voice was tight and hard. 'Will you join me, or do you have one already?' The question was rhetorical, sarcastic; he'd seen at a glance that neither of them had one.

'No, thank you very much,' Farley said, rising. 'I'll be shoving off.' He went out without so much as a nod from Amas.

'What was all that about?' Amas demanded, facing Vanessa. She was shocked and hurt; his expression was angry, remote. And he hadn't even offered to pour her a glass of wine, something he would have unfailingly done on other evenings.

'What was what about?' she parried. 'Mitchell and I were talking about Lesley.'

One of Amas' sandy brows shot up. He took his drink to the couch and sat down heavily. 'Lesley? Is that why Farley said it was "silly" for him not to call you Vanessa?'

'Oh, Amas.' She went to him and took the glass from his hand, setting it gently on the table before him. Then she took his head in her hands and urged his face upward for her kiss. But his lips were hard and ungiving under hers, as stiff as his arms had been when she first embraced him. She sat down next to him and moved close, hoping he would relent and touch her. But he did not.

He picked up his glass again and took a swig of whiskey. 'I repeat, why is it "silly", Vanessa? Because things have reached such a point that formality between you is a charade? Is that it?'

She stared at him, speechless. The harshness of his query cut her to the heart. He'd never shown jealousy to this extent, never been quite so open in his dislike of Mitchell Farley, even if he had made no secret from the first that 'the fellow gave him a pain', while conceding his value as a tutor and the utter inadequacy of the Kimberley school. Vanessa felt a knot of heat in her throat, incipient moisture under her lids.

And then her hurt blossomed into a mighty indignation. 'How dare you?' she cried out. 'How dare you assume that there is . . . something between us, without hearing my side of it, without trusting me, after all these years?' Her voice was shaking so that questions came out with angry sobbing.

Something seemed to break in Amas. He slammed down his glass

88

on the table. 'Oh, my God, Vanessa,' he said in a choked voice. 'I'm sorry . . . I'm sorry. Forgive me.' He grabbed her in his embrace and stroked her head, pulling it down on his shoulder. 'How in hell could I say such things to you? I must be crazy – I *am* crazy.' He emitted a small, rueful laugh. 'So crazy about you, still, that when I heard that I wanted to kill him.'

'Believe me, my darling, he never, never said anything like that to me before, never gave any hint . . .' Uneasily Vanessa thought of the look in Farley's eyes when they were together, but she tried to dismiss the idea. 'If you had heard the answer I was about to give him, none of this would ever have happened.'

'And that answer was?' Amas was smiling at her now in the old way and she felt a warm flood of relief.

'. . . was that he had better watch his tongue, or look for another situation.' Vanessa's words were muffled against Amas. His big arms squeezed her more tightly. 'Oh, my love,' she sighed, 'please don't ever think these things. You are my life, the only thing in the world. You know that, don't you?'

With closed eyes, she was aware of his emphatic nod. 'Yes. Yes, Vanessa. And I thank whatever gods there may be for that.' He loosened his hold slightly and she looked up at his familiar, beloved face. His lionlike eyes had a sharp gleam. 'Nevertheless,' he added softly, 'I'm going to have a little chat with Mister Farley.'

At her restless movement, he chuckled, and said, 'That's all, Vanessa. Just a chat. I promise you. That nervy young bastard.' He held her for a moment in silence, then he murmured, 'At the same time, I can hardly blame him.'

He moved back, staring at her. 'Look at you.' He shook his head in wonder.

'Yes, look at me,' she twitted. 'I'm thirty-three years old.'

'And a thousand times more beautiful, more seductive than you were when I first laid eyes on you,' he told her softly. 'The years . . . no man feels like this after thirteen years – except about a woman like you, Vanessa.'

The gleam in his eyes was not vengeful now; she knew that light. It was the light of another fire, the one she had seen in his eyes on that long ago night of the ball, when he had stared at her down the corridor of ghostly marbles in her father's house.

And, submitting to his kiss, Vanessa felt that same wild, heated longing stab her body, racing through her veins with the speed of mercury ascending to a fever in the blood.

Speaking against her lips, he whispered, 'Let's let the children have their dinner without us, shall we?'

The nibbling murmur against the flesh of her mouth was maddeningly arousing. Without moving away, she murmured, 'That's a splendid idea. Will you give the order, or shall I?'

'To hell with the order.' He grinned. 'Listen.' They heard a mild clamour from the kitchen quarters. 'Sounds like the children are starving now. It'll be taken care of.'

The last fire of the sinking sun cast coral-coloured light over the sequestered bedroom through the jalousied windows. Watching Amas close the door, Vanessa sensed that the canny Sehoiya had once more intuitively recognised their need to be apart and had corralled the children in her expert way. Only a contented murmur could now be heard from the kitchen quarters.

Amas came slowly towards her; she gloried in him, exulted in the great, strong body and the weathered face below his vital thatch of straw coloured hair, familiar as her very breath and still as heart-quickening as it had been years before when she first stared into his tawny eyes.

This, she thought, is a magic given to so few – this never-fading brightness, the drumbeat of the pulses when the beloved is near. Three thousand nights and days or more she had looked at that face, heard the deep, growling strength of that voice; come into those arms again and kissed that mouth. And yet this moment, on this fiery evening, it was all new again for her, if anything more moving than the first ecstatic instant.

She felt her body's habitual warming, weakening, and something in the light of the room, which was like a rose on fire, with a more urgent force than ever, dismissed the intervening time. She was with him again in their cabin on the *Walmer Castle*, riding at anchor in port, and the setting sun was that, not of Kimberley but of the Caribbean.

Without a word Amas put one massive arm about her waist and drew her body near him. With one calloused hand he raised her face and lowered his mouth to hers, caressing the trembling flesh of her mouth with eager and half-open lips.

The wavering warmth of her flesh was heating, heating, turning into a barbaric hotness that lashed her, licking her skin.

And when he made a sound of urgent longing, deep in his throat, and began to reach for the buttons of her dress, she whispered, smiling, 'No. Not this time, my love. Let me. Let me.'

90

He looked at her half in question, half in eager wonder, as she swiftly unbuttoned his rough shirt, leaning into him to dart her questing tongue into the beating hollow at the base of his throat.

She felt him quake with excitement, felt his whole strong frame begin to quiver. He ran his hands over the breadth and length of her, saying hoarsely and softly, 'Vanessa, Vanessa, oh, my dear one.'

Raising her head for an instant from his chest, she murmured, 'It's been too long, much too long since . . . I truly loved you, *really* loved you.'

His fingers were wildly caressing her hair and her face, then descending to her vibrant breasts, tracing the inward curve of her waist, the outward swell of her still narrow but cloud-soft haunches, groaning softly in his mad arousal; but she only murmured low, half-teasing, tender wordless words, proceeding to undress him.

Amas stood on trembling legs while his clothes slid to the carpet and Vanessa, murmuring wildly, almost inaudibly still, with excruciating slowness let her clothed body glide downward, the soft cloth of her dress tickling, tantalising his hard, bare, glowing skin, until he cried out, 'Oh, God, my God, Vanessa.'

He was trying to pull her upward but, with a little laugh so soundless it was no more than an exhalation of the breath, she resisted, grasping his stalwart thighs with her surprisingly strong pianist's hands. She stroked his legs for a moment from the loins to the knees, and felt him quaver, weakening, giving himself up to his desire.

Vanessa's wandering, nibbling mouth found the centre of his yearning and as she relentlessly caressed his hard, vibrating skin, she heard a deeper cry escape from him, the very acme of his utmost need.

And suddenly his steely hands were biting into her shoulders, lifting her, forcing her upward to pull her to him until his demanding body was seeking her through the frail barrier of her clothes; he was frantically undoing her dress, pulling it from her shoulders, until it fell over her hips around her feet, and she was divesting herself of her underthings.

At last they stood naked and close and his hands were stroking her everywhere. Then, with a dancelike motion, still closer to her than her very heart, he was guiding her backward to the bed, lowering her swiftly onto its wide softness.

With another teasing, catlike sound, she slipped out from under him and putting her hands on his chest, urged him, pleading, to lie down.

'Oh, my love, I told you . . . it's been too long since I . . . I loved you just like this,' she whispered, and his eyes blazed down at her, a half-smile on his parted lips.

'Since we have loved like this,' he protested softly. He put his hands on her naked shoulders again, and with his fingers urged her about until both their quivering mouths could find the throbbing core of the other one's desire.

When his nibbling lips descended to her pounding centre, and his darting tongue had found the point of pulsing fire, a drumming sweetness started in her depths and spread its flaming honey in a slow-rayed pleasure tide, radiating, radiating outward from that single bud of raging wildness; as her own caressing, teasing lips began to bring him to the trembling height, the vortex of devastating pleasure, Vanessa felt her own flesh leap and drum; it seemed that every surface of her, to her blood and marrow, danced the leaping dance of that delight.

At almost the identical instant she knew the outburst of his final, titanic release, heard his outcry, her own flesh shuddered with that exquisite implosion; that sudden bursting inward, shooting its phosphorescent tendrils from her dazzled core outward everywhere in racing strands of light as fireworks wash a blackened sky.

And, floating downward from that high forgetfulness, Vanessa realised once more that this, this mysterious and unexplainable departure, was stronger still than all the uncertainties that had lately overwhelmed her. This fevered flight their bodies took together mocked and paled the small resentments, the silly anxieties, making her fears seem as unreal as the hobgoblins that frighten children.

Returning from that infinite, yet narrow space, she was aware now of her cheek resting on his massive leg, of his mouth murmuring against her own soft flesh. There were no words between them, only the inchoate sounds of wonder; then he was urging her with gentle hands to lie beside him. He gathered her to him, pressing her curly head to his chest again and again with tender pressure; she burrowed into the hollow of his arm, tasting the clean, sea-savoured moisture that dewed his chest, her whole self palpitating still, a faint tingle along her skin like the distant ringing of innumerable, minute gongs of brass, reverberant.

She stroked the damp, crisp hairs of his chest and ran her hand over his hard-tendoned belly. He trembled slightly, in recall, and planted quick, light kisses on her ruffled hair.

Vanessa rubbed her head against him and whispered, 'Do you still have doubts?'

His big arm tightened around her and he stroked her haunch. 'I never did. Not about you. Only about Farley.'

She sensed a certain tenseness in him, stabbed with sharp regret. Why had she brought up such a thing now, of all times?

'I'm sorry.'

'Sorry?' Amas turned his head, looking down at her, his expression relaxed and gentle. 'For what, my darling . . . making me happier than any man has a hope of being?' His smile fired her with new tenderness. She slid upwards in his hold and kissed the corner of his mouth.

'For bringing up such an unpleasant subject.'

He laughed softly. 'Nothing . . . nothing can bother me at a time like this.' He squeezed her arm. After a brief silence he added, 'I only wish I could tell you, Vanessa . . . tell you what these times are like for me.'

'But I know, Amas. I know.' She leaned over him and took his face in her hands, lowering her mouth to his for a long, sweet caress. She lay against him a moment while his fingers traced the shape of her. Then he encircled her body again with his arms.

'Vanessa.' There was something hesitant and reluctant in his tone.

'What is it?' She lifted her face from his chest and looked into his eyes.

'Speaking of unpleasant subjects . . .' He stopped. 'Here, love, lie down beside me again. I've got to tell you something, something I've been putting off.'

Wordless and apprehensive, she moved, but she was too anxious to lie down. She half-sat on the pillows, trying to read his face in the gathering dusk.

'It's Beatrice. She's here. She's back in Kimberley with Seton.'

'Oh, my God.' Vanessa's head sank back into the pillows. 'No, Amas. I can't bear it.'

'I'm not too happy about it either.' His tone was heavily ironic. Turning to survey him, Vanessa caught the look of old pain, old anger.

'Amas, Amas. Forgive me. It's so much worse for you, because of Sam.' She was deeply aware that under his calm exterior Amas still mourned Sam, and the years had not softened his bitterness. Vanessa put her hand on his cheek; he turned his head and kissed her palm.

'It's just as bad for you, Vanessa.' He studied her face, and with a calloused thumb caressed her brief nose and her half-parted mouth. Vanessa moved her face into his hand and rubbed his palm with her cheek.

Then she said, 'We've got to talk about this, Amas. We've got to face it.'

'Then you'd better not pet me like that.' He grinned. 'You have a way of distracting me from anything and everything.'

Ignoring that, she asked soberly, 'What are we going to do?' She lay back again on the pillows. 'Damn her, Amas. Damn her. What a revolting, grotesque situation this puts us in. My *sister*. And the whole world knows, or guesses, what happened.'

'Well, I hardly think you'll be giving her a dinner party.' Amas reached over and took her hand. 'We'll just put the best face on it we can. And hope.'

And hope, Vanessa added silently, that there won't be another disaster.

Mitchell Farley strolled out of the billiard room of the Kimberley Club, nodding to Cecil Rhodes. Peculiar fellow, that, with his buggy eyes; bit of a fire-eater. Before they'd turned around he'd have them in a damned war, a show that Mitchell Farley would gladly give a miss to. Very pally with the stiff-necked Lady Cecil, though. And the fellow had a point. Schoolmastering *wasn't* a job for a man. Maybe he ought to think about throwing in his lot with this fellow's company.

Farley glanced in the ballroom, catching sight of the Beauty waltzing with her big colonial clod. Farley swore under his breath. There must be some way to reach her; surely that great animal had no idea of the more subtle forms of love.

Just then there was a bit of a flurry at the entrance door. Farley saw a dark, sharp-featured woman coming in, a British officer behind her.

The woman caught sight of him and rushed forward with a brilliant smile on her pointed face. 'Why, Mitchell, my dear!' she cried out in her high, nasal tone.

Farley bowed over her hand and turning it insinuatingly in his,

94

kissed her with a lingering caress on the palm. Farley watched her reaction with some amusement. Absolutely instant. The bitch was never out of heat.

'Tony.' He nodded to Beatrice Seton's husband and awarded him a neutral smile, thinking what a poor stick the fellow was. Bea, of course, would choose just this kind of lap dog. Farley had to restrain himself from laughing out loud at the simile: lap dog was a capital expression, considering how Seton had gone along with the doings at that London club.

'How are you, Mitchell?' Tony Seton asked stiffly. Seton was a perfect toy soldier, in his trig uniform buttoned high at his uneasy neck, his brown centre-parted hair and moustache seeming painted on his ruddy face.

'Splendid, Tony, perfectly splendid.' Farley pumped Seton's hand. 'But how on earth did you persuade our bewitching Bea to abandon the pleasures of London?'

Farley shot a look at Bea; her large, dark eyes held a glint of anger. So that was it – her manoeuvres with Lord Dawlish's son hadn't paid off. She'd assumed after she slept with Dawlish he'd marry her. Some hope! Farley knew that if Dawlish had taken the bait, Bea would have left Tony like a shot. Mitchell Farley burned to know exactly what happened.

Seton's ruddy face turned livid with embarrassment.

'How naughty of you, Mitchell.' Beatrice fluttered her black fan and then quickly snapped it to and tapped Farley with it on his cheek. 'A good wife always goes where her husband is sent.'

Farley almost guffawed at that one; Bea's rapacious eyes were darting over his face, lingering on his mouth. Her little red tongue emerged for a second from between her moist red lips. Farley glanced over her swiftly; as usual she was dressed in the height of fashion. The bustle had been forgotten. Dresses had skin-tight bodices now, hugging the hips, with the skirts flaring out below the knees, more than suggesting the female form.

Bea's gown was very much in the mode – Farley prided himself on keeping up with these matters; it went down well with the women – but as he remembered her clothes were made with a difference. The bodice of her gown, striped horizontally with black and cloth-of-gold over a black skirt, was cut so deeply that one could almost see the sharp points of her breasts.

Farley was merely amused, and not aroused; he was too familiar with those contours, through several of his senses, to be thrilled. But the old Queen Bee herself, he judged, was champing at the bit. And didn't Seton know it.

'Your sister's here,' Farley said casually.

He enjoyed Bea's struggle to maintain a pleasant and neutral expression. 'Really?' She gave a tinkling little laugh that sounded like metallic bells. 'With my stunning brother-in-law, I take it. My sister always had a chaperone.'

Mitchell Farley caught Seton's chagrin. One really had to admire the bitch, Farley reflected. He'd heard the story from her; knowing Bea, most of it was a lie. Farley had gathered more than he'd been told. Poor old Seton seemed about to sink through the floor. Farley imagined his telling Bea that it 'wouldn't be quite the thing' to encounter the Holders, blood relatives or not. Still, Farley felt that reluctant admiration. No other woman in the world would have the face to carry this off, especially after London. Farley had a vivid picture of the Mask Club. Bea had always been the most outrageous woman there.

A French acquaintance had introduced Farley to the Mask, a private club whose doors its members unlocked with obscenely shaped keys. Everyone in the place wore masks, and little else, enjoying odd forms of pleasure in carefree anonymity. The first time Farley and Bea had met had been at the Mask; even he was astounded by the variety of her skills, the extent of her total depravity. At first, it seemed, Seton had not known of her membership. Then at last she'd sucked him in too. Farley remembered with something like pity Seton's reactions. Especially when Bea had brought the boy into it all. The kid was no more than thirteen, but the little beggar seemed to know as much as any of them and was totally unmoved by it all.

'Dear Amas,' Bea murmured, as she moved towards the ballroom between the two men. 'The *beau sauvage*.'

'Savage, yes, but I can hardly see the beautiful.' At once Farley regretted his snappish comment; he'd given himself away. Bea's black glance leaped to his face, and she smiled a most unpleasant smile.

'Why, Mitchell, you naughty boy! That sounds like the green-eyed monster raging.'

Farley cursed himself for his stupidity; the well-creamed cat wasn't in it, he thought, when it came to Bea's satisfied smile.

'Hardly,' he said lightly, and gave her arm a little squeeze. He could fairly feel the heat emanating from her skin. Well, let her think he was after her; he didn't give a damn. Anything to keep her mind off his passion for Vanessa. She'd use it against him if she could.

Beatrice swept on ahead into the ballroom.

Farley saw the Holders then, sitting at a table for two. Holder's face tightened. And the Beauty turned as pale as milk, but her proud head was still held high and her features were calm.

Forgetting everything else in that moment, Mitchell Farley devoured Vanessa Holder with his look. She was more exquisite than he had ever seen her before; the modest neckline of her shining blue-grey gown half-bared her creamy shoulders, merely hinted at the rich curves of her breasts. And the sombre colour made a glory of her burnished hair, the wide grey eyes, the pillowed mouth so indicative of passion restrained. That mouth, he thought, was as full of sweetness as honey in a honeycomb.

Other extravagant images of her hidden flesh came to Mitchell Farley. He knew nothing of love; he had never loved any woman – or man, for that matter – but he did know he wanted this woman as he'd never wanted anything in all his life. He would like to bare her body this instant and put his lips to her breasts.

Farley's flesh hardened and pounded. He would have that woman, by God. He'd have her yet, one way or another.

Brazenly Beatrice went forward, the hangdog Seton in her wake with Farley.

'Vanessa. It's been so long,' Beatrice cried out in a high, tinkling voice. 'Amas, my dear.'

Holder rose slowly, unsmiling. He inclined his head. 'Beatrice. Captain Seton.' With an even cooler intonation Holder acknowledged Mitchell Farley.

He noticed that Seton was looking at Vanessa with a kind of yearning, as if comparing her to Beatrice.

'It's been too long, Vanessa.' Bea gave her sister a bright, false smile. 'How sweet you look, still.'

Farley struggled between amusement and annoyance – Vanessa's expression, although apparently controlled, seemed to comment that it had not been long enough, and ironically registered the true meaning of Beatrice's remark. Looking 'sweet . . . still', it was clear to Farley, who knew both Bea and fashionable London, could be translated as 'You are just as dowdy as ever'. And Farley's admiration for Vanessa grew; she was amazingly astute, as well as gifted and beautiful.

'I trust we can join you,' Bea said before the others could say anything. She was already taking possession of a chair, attempting to draw it to the too small table until Seton intervened.

'I'm afraid this table won't accommodate us all, my dear,' he mumbled.

Vanessa was rising. 'I must apologise,' she said quietly. 'We were just about to leave. Amas gets up so early, and I am feeling quite tired.'

'I thought you were looking wan, Vanessa. You really should take better care of yourself.' Bea's observation was patently absurd, Farley thought. Surely even the dimwitted Seton could see that Vanessa fairly glowed, while Bea herself looked older than her years; her rouge stood out in livid patches on her cheeks.

'I shall, Bea, you may be sure.' Vanessa met her sister's eyes head on. She nodded to Seton and Farley. Then she took her husband's arm and they walked out of the ballroom. Farley stared after her graceful figure.

'Forget it, Mitchell.'

Bea's sharp voice broke in on his reverie. 'I beg your pardon?'

'Stop mooning, dear boy, and join us for a glass of champagne. She's not for the likes of you.' Bea laughed unpleasantly.

'I don't know what you mean,' Farley replied coolly.

'Oh, yes, you do.' Beatrice put an insinuating, hot hand on his. 'Come, come, join us.'

Even if it were the last thing he desired, Farley thought it politic to accept. The three sat down and Seton ordered their wine.

'Well, Bea, how are all our auld acquaintance in civilisation?' Farley took a malicious satisfaction in her faint look of chagrin.

Seton answered for her, 'Capital, old fellow. Capital. Gave us a splendid send-off, don't you know, before our exile.' Seton let out a nervous guffaw, shooting a glance at Bea.

'Tony's quite right, Mitchell. Our farewell parties were so glittering I could hardly bear to leave.' Bea's eyes had a desperate gaiety; her cheeks grew pinker and there were unattractive blotches of colour now on her neck and her generously exposed breasts. 'But *you*, my dear,' she took the offensive quickly, 'how are you bearing up in this wilderness, in *your* exile?'

Rotten bitch, Farley raged in silence. Her emphasis was so plain she might as well have said his banishment, might as well have shrieked the name of Herrold to the whole room. God, if she ever told Vanessa . . . Farley decided he'd better not offend Beatrice Seton.

He let his eyes pretend to caress her face. 'Tolerably,' he smiled.

'And I'm sure it will be greatly enhanced, now that you . . . and Tony,' he amended after a deliberate pause, 'have joined us.'

'You're too sweet,' Bea purred. 'But you can't fool me, dear boy. I saw you casting sheep's eyes at Vanessa.'

'Really, Bea.' Seton was deeply embarrassed.

'Our Queen Bee is full of fancies,' Farley said lightly. 'That's what makes her so charming.' He consulted his watch. 'By Jove, it's later than I thought. I must be getting along.' He got up.

'That's right. Oh, you poor dear. You have to get up with the sun these days – to educate the little Holders, and that black savage, too, I heard. How bizarre my dear sister is. And how *clever* . . . to choose a man so good with children.' Bea smiled brilliantly.

This was such an obvious reference to the Herrold mess that Farley knew he must get away at once. He was within an ace of hitting her and then that fool Seton would shoot him.

'You're so kind, as always, Bea.' Although his gorge rose as he did it, Farley took her hand and kissed it. Then he said goodnight to the pathetic Seton.

'I'll see you out, old fellow.'

Farley was surprised. This was a very friendly gesture from a man he'd cuckolded on numerous occasions. 'Of course.'

As they walked towards the entrance to the ballroom, Seton said to him in a low voice, 'Watch your step, Mitchell. Holder may not be as worldly as our set, you know. These colonial johnnies are positive barbarians.'

'You're a good fellow, Tony.' Farley was sincere. 'Under the circs, I might say, *jolly* good. Don't know why you bother.'

'Well, I can't fight the whole of London now, can I, old fellow?' Seton's eyes looked flat and dead.

'Why do you stick it, Tony?'

'She's into my skin and under it, Mitchell. I can't do without her, you see.'

Mitchell Farley stared at Tony Seton for a moment, then, wringing his hand, walked out.

Nodding to various acquaintances, he left the club and walked out into the night, trying to ignore the vista of what they laughingly called the town, where the only things that looked like buildings at all were the railroad depot and the offices of Cecil Rhodes.

It was a long hike back to the Holders' bungalow; generally Farley left much earlier so he might share an acquaintance's carriage or buggy. He smiled to himself. He'd had thousands of acquaintances but couldn't count a single friend.

Tonight he was glad of the walk; it would give him time to think, maybe cool him down a little when he was taken with the eternal fever of Vanessa. Mitchell Farley had never loved anyone in his life, but this was the closest he'd come. The woman was a perpetual preoccupation. When he did not see her he was haunted by thoughts of her waking, dreams of her in sleep.

Taking the road that led to the bungalow, Farley reflected, feeling sore: that big, rough bastard. That ignorant miner, with his hamlike hands, had the right to such a goddess. Farley imagined Holder's arrogant mouth on the white hidden globes of those breasts, saw the huge hands on Vanessa's naked, flowerlike skin, and his mind cried sacrilege, sacrilege. What could that clod know of the subtleties of arousal, the intricate and infinite ways of bringing the delicate components of the female body to a screaming delight?

By God, if he could have her once he'd be able to enslave her, just as he had so many others, men and women . . . Herrold's idiotic kid, for instance. Why in hell hadn't the boy kept his mouth shut; why did he have to be so damned indiscreet? If he hadn't kept coming to Farley's room they could have gone on enjoying each other indefinitely. In between the others, Farley amended with an ironic smile twitching at his mouth as he remembered the housemaid and the cook. What was the maid's name again? She'd been a succulent little piece, at first; but then her whining had become such a bore. No matter.

Farley dismissed the nameless girl and thought back to the first time he'd set eyes on Vanessa Holder.

The Earl of Herrold had made it quite clear to Farley that he had two alternatives – get out of England or stay and face prosecution under the law, total ruin. In desperation Farley had answered the advertisement in the *Times* and sailed for Cape Town with a glowing reference forged on Herrold's notepaper as additional insurance. He'd already mailed one to the Holders.

He pictured a family about as exciting as the stolid Boers, a husband who grunted and a broad, maternal wife. Therefore Farley's initial meeting with Vanessa Holder was a shock so great he fairly reeled. He'd once taken a knockout blow in a boxing match at his college, and had never forgotten the tremendous impact. It felt as if his head were being lifted off his neck, that his jaw had been struck with a medieval iron mace. And that's just what it had been to meet Vanessa Holder.

His early awe had soon become an itching lust that never let him be, a sharp resentment over the waste of her – she was wasted on Holder, wasted in Africa, with her beauty and gifts. But more than all else Farley was consumed by envy. He envied everything about Amas Holder. The great brute had everything that Farley longed for – money, position, size. And Vanessa.

Almost everything, Amas Holder did not have Farley's education, nor his subtlety, nor his way with women. Amas Holder did not have the slightest glimmer of his wife's talent. As if her beauty were not enough, Farley had been even more dazzled by her pianistic skills; he knew a good deal about music.

And, for a time, he had even thought that her music would be the means of bringing them together. Farley recalled with yearning those few and exquisite dusks, before the Brute came back sweating from that hole, when he had listened to Vanessa's playing; when, speaking of music with him, her wonderful grey eyes would light up, her low voice quiver with excitement.

It had all been going so swimmingly, in Farley's estimation. Then things began to happen, he didn't know quite what, or how. Suddenly Vanessa seemed more enamoured than ever of the Brute; and then there were the disagreements about the books and that blackamoor. Small things, but they had torn the fabric of Mitchell Farley's laboriously woven hopes and dreams.

He looked around him; the ground was rising sharply. Jove, he was almost there. He'd been so deep in thought the miles had slipped away.

It was then he saw a tall and massive man standing by the turning to the mines.

It was Holder.

With a certain apprehension Farley caught a grim look on Holder's face; the moonlight limned his features clear as day. When Holder saw him, he only nodded without speaking.

Farley came forward and called out with a rather uncertain calm, 'Good evening. You're up rather late.' He tried a half-smile.

Expressionless, Holder said as Farley came nearer, 'I've been wanting to talk to you.'

Oh, good Christ, Farley thought, turning hot and cold. The bastard's got wind of Herrold. 'You don't say,' he answered a bit unsteadily.

'Oh, yes, I *do* say.' A little smile twisted Holder's mouth. 'Shall we walk a ways?'

'Of course.' Even more uneasily, Farley noticed that Holder was leading him towards the mine. For a wild instant he wondered if the savage were going to throw him right down in the pit.

'There's an item I wanted to check on,' Holder said quietly. 'Thinking of it woke me right up. Then I figured you might be coming along soon and it seemed a good chance to . . . have a talk.'

It seemed to Farley that there was an almost sinister overtone in that, but he ridiculed himself. The thing was to keep calm. Surely they couldn't have found out, unless that bitch Beatrice . . . But no, she'd just arrived and obviously hadn't spoken to them before. Farley wondered what it could be.

He was walking beside Holder now on the rough, ascending path to the Big Hole. The other man, although Farley himself was tall enough, towered over him; his big frame seemed to dwarf others. It was perfectly intimidating, quite maddening.

'I wanted to say this to you in privacy, Farley. We're all a bit on top of each other back at the house sometimes.'

Farley felt a stronger apprehension.

'I'm not too happy with certain things,' Holder said bluntly in his growling voice. 'One is your influence over my daughter; the other's my wife.'

Farley's heart began to hammer. His wife. Now they were coming to it. But what did the great clod mean about his stupid daughter?

Holder paused and Farley paused with him.

'What, specifically, do you mean, Mr Holder? If you don't mind.' Farley could not keep the sharpness from his question.

'Specifically, Farley, the books you've given my daughter to read . . . and the constant insinuations to my wife.' The big American glared down at him, a further annoyance. It was galling to have one's accuser possess such intimidating physical features.

'I'll answer the last charge first,' Farley drawled. 'I don't know what you mean by insinuations. But my attentions to Mrs Holder have always seemed welcome . . . even quite desirable. It's obvious I fill a lack,' he went on rashly before he could stop himself, 'that she has felt too long.'

'What in hell do you mean by that?' Holder growled, and Farley knew he'd gone too far.

'I was referring to her lack of . . . intellectual companionship. A woman of her gifts must have felt that sorely, here in this . . . desolation.' Farley could sense the big man's growing ire but once again he seemed unable to restrain his comments; he'd held them in too many months, too long.

'I don't give a damn about "intellectual companionship", Farley.'
Holder's tone was dangerously quiet and there was a threatening
gleam in his wild-looking eyes. 'I'm talking about my wife as a
woman . . . being made love to by another man.'

Mitchell Farley was suddenly overtaken with an overpowering
feeling – something primitive and deep in him had been awakened
by this roustabout's challenging manner and belligerent air. 'Oh?'
Throwing discretion to the winds, he found himself using his most
elegant and maddening intonation, one that had enraged many
another. 'If it comes to that, Holder, you can be sure that you're no
match for me.'

He realised too late that this case was like no other; he had never
traded insults with a man of such fierceness and size, and fleetingly
he recalled Seton's warning that 'these colonial johnnies are perfect
barbarians'. Amas Holder grabbed him by his lapels, spinning him
around as if he were a toy.

Farley was no mean pugilist and had even won a boxing prize for
his college. But this brute's strength was incredible. Still in Holder's
bearlike grasp, Farley kicked out at his leg, but the bigger, older man
merely laughed with a kind of gleeful satisfaction as if he'd been
itching for this very confrontation, and evaded Farley's kick with an
ease that dismayed the Englishman.

Mitchell Farley tried to use his booted feet again to good advantage, but Holder shot his great knee upwards, catching Farley in the
groin. The stunning pain sent Farley crashing backward onto the
ground and, before he could take another breath, Amas Holder was
upon him, with those massive hands around his throat, choking his
life away. Farley could feel that crushing pressure on his windpipe
and momentarily it drained all the strength from his tensile legs.
This was it, he thought wildly in his terror; he was going West for
certain.

Then, with astonishing swiftness, the horrible pressure began to
ease; Holder was relaxing his grasp, the big body still pinning Farley
down, and Farley was nauseated by the aroma of that hated sweat.

'No, Farley. Not yet.' Holder's deep growl sounded like that of a
maddened animal, and he was panting. The hamlike hands still
pinned Farley's lighter body to the ground. 'I'm not that big a fool.
I'm not going to kill you and let them string me up. Get on your feet.
I'm going to give it to you.'

Farley made a weak attempt to knee Holder and failed, and then he
felt the first stunning blow to his jaw. He literally saw stars, in scarlet

103

flashes and in jagged silver white. The big man got up and stood over him; Farley saw his immensity outlined against the moonwashed dark.

'Get up, Farley.' A swift, hot rushing of adrenalin took Mitchell Farley; he struggled to his knees, shaking his head to clear it. He'd show this lumbering savage who the better man was.

As soon as he was on his feet, however, Holder was upon him, battering his head and body with quick punches. Farley, whose speed had always stood him in good stead, bobbed and wove, dancing backwards, his strength returning, and as Holder's fist shot out again, ducked and landed a sweet, satisfying blow to the side of the big head. Farley followed that by three swift lightning punches and sensed that he had taken the other by surprise.

Didn't know, did you, you bastard . . . didn't suspect that Mitchell Farley was this good? Astonished, Farley could hear the lucid questioning in his own head, even as he shot out his fist again, catching Holder on the point of his heavy jaw. It was a fine hit, and yet the other man only winced slightly, waded again into Farley.

Holder was like a rock, he thought dimly, enduring his quick, sharp blows like a monstrous megalith. He'd never bring him down. The Marquess of Queensberry rules weren't going to work here.

Farley brought up his knee; he'd made a bad mistake. Holder made a lightning grab at Farley's knee, throwing him backwards again. He landed with a thud on the sparse grass, realising with terror that he was almost on the edge of the Big Hole's yawning pit. Then Holder was down at once, upon him, and they were wrestling on the very rim.

With rising panic Mitchell Farley knew, once and for all, that he was no match for his bearlike adversary; he was going to go over, he was going to go over the side of the Hole, plummeting downward to strike against the chambers, dashing his very brains out hundreds of yards below. They were so close now his head was almost hanging over.

But desperately something cried out in him, protesting. *No*, he could hear the shout from his brain, *No. I won't die.*

And with a superhuman effort of his muscles and his will, Farley threw his whole body into the final try, shoving at Holder with a tendon-straining, grunting, teeth-gritting might that had come from nowhere to him, setting the bigger man off balance just long enough to catch him with a swift kick to the jaw. Holder let out an astonished sound; to Farley's horror the kick had not even felled him.

But it had slowed him down enough for Farley to leap beyond him to the comparative safety of the blessedly firm ground.

Holder was up again and after him, battering at his face with hammerlike blows, panting, like a man insane, 'Get out Farley, leave the Holders alone, I warn you,' and Farley now was utterly on the defensive, no longer trying to hit, only to ward off the steady and bone-jarring punches.

All of a sudden one connected to his chin and Mitchell Farley's head rang; his whole body seemed to rise with the blow and he had a dim sensation first of falling backwards, with the firework splatter of red and silver stars, then there was nothing but blackness.

Somewhere in his black dream he sensed a touch upon him, a clamping on his wrists, then a heaviness on his chest like a man's head leaning there. Farley had enough consciousness to judge that Holder must have been feeling his pulse, then listening to his heart.

Those drifting thoughts were too much effort . . . too much. Farley sank again into that utter, peaceful dark.

When he opened his eyes the sky was lightening.

He lay there thinking of what Holder had panted out in their combat, 'Leave the Holders alone'. Mitchell Farley knew he would leave their house, that very morning . . . but as to the future, he would never leave the Holders alone. Not until he'd got his own back, for good.

CHAPTER SEVEN

'All right, darling, this is the last one. You go on up. I've asked Ransom to take you home.'

The cable car had lifted Amas and Vanessa to the topmost chamber of the Big Hole.

'Let me wait.'

He frowned. 'I don't know how long I'll be. We've gone over this before. It's not like it was a few months ago. You know that, Vanessa.'

Indeed it was not, she agreed darkly. As recently as June the mine had been just like the old days – a place she had ridden to alone almost every day for the noonday meal, where she had moved about freely. Now, on this seventh day of October, they were each holding a rifle upright as they rode in the car. For weeks bands of Boer guerillas had been riding the hills, making unauthorised attacks on the mines.

Vanessa had been hard put to make Amas allow her to come to the mine at all. But now she could shoot as well as he, and thus far the Big Hole had been unmolested. Nevertheless Amas was never easy these days when she was there; it cast a shadow over their enjoyment of each other. And he was especially restless near sunset, the hour that seemed a favourite time for Boer attacks. That hour was approaching now.

'Please,' she said softly, touching his arm. 'I've got the gun. And the chamber's a natural hiding place.'

Amas hesitated, looking reluctant and annoyed. What she'd said was true: the topmost overhanging chamber was totally impregnable to firearms of any sort. This afternoon, however, the men were engaged in a particularly dangerous operation. Amas' frown deepened. 'Vanessa, you're damned if you do or you don't. You're wide open here, and you know we've got that back-up in the access tunnel that's got to be cleared out.' She made a face at him, forcing him to smile slightly. 'Lady, you're as hard as blue ground. What does it take to convince you?' He raiséd his hand and caressed her glowing cheek.

'Blasting,' she retorted. She knew that the stubbornness that sometimes irritated him was the very quality he most admired in her. They had grown even closer during these last weeks since Mitchell Farley disappeared that morning.

Amas sighed. 'All right, then. I hope I won't be long. But I'm telling you now, at the first hint . . . the very first glimmer of trouble, I want you out of that car. You know where to go. Go there and don't move until you see me.'

She nodded. Amas had instructed her in this before, countless times, drilling it into her by repetition. She was to step from the car onto the walkway next to the outer chute where the brown ground came spilling out into the supply car and stand with her back against the wall of the overhanging chamber. He had made her do it, several times, like a child being drilled, to be certain that she could do it quickly and without danger.

'I will. I know.'

He nodded, seeming a little more satisfied and, kissing her cheek, stepped out of the car easily onto the platform. She watched him disappear, rifle over his shoulder, into the recesses of the top chamber.

Vanessa cradled her rifle, reviewing the last two hectic weeks since the night at the Kimberley Club. That horrible night when they had encountered Bea again after all those years. Vanessa still shuddered to remember it, the reawakened agony and anger in Amas; the cowering Seton. Worst of all, the words and stares and attentions of Mitchell Farley.

She'd hoped he was gone, when he wandered off to the billiard room and was absent for such a protracted interval, but then he'd come back, with Seton and with Bea. Vanessa had felt the tension gathering, building in Amas; by the time he'd returned from the mine, where he had apparently gone to 'check on the ammunition', she was prepared for what she would see.

Amas dirty and bruised. His clothes torn, grim-faced and exhausted. She'd known what had happened, although he hadn't told her about it until the next morning when it was discovered that Farley was gone, bags, books and baggage.

Trickles of news about Bea and Farley had reached them, of course; Mitchell Farley was now working for Cecil Rhodes. And he was constantly in the company of the Setons. Amas and Vanessa were assiduously avoiding the Kimberley Club.

The children's schooling remained to be dealt with, but Martin and Kossee were gleeful over their unexpected holiday. It was Lesley who was the greatest worry. Lesley had lost her god, and it was clear she blamed this loss on Vanessa. To Lesley, Amas, like Mitchell Farley, could do no wrong.

A little smile twisted Vanessa's mouth; she was sadly amused by the injustice of it all. Her glance wandered idly over the Big Hole. Then a peculiar sound caught her attention; it came from the surface. The drum of many horses' hooves, the shouts of men, not welcoming but full of anger. She recognised the shouted words: the language of the Boers.

Boers. The dreaded word roared in her brain, the word she had begun to hate and dread with its connotation of 'wild boars' and other fearsome images. Her heart fluttered in her throat and sweat exploded on her back. Dear God, it was a Boer raid.

Vanessa could see them now, riding among the winches and wagons, infinitely more threatening somehow because they were wearing ordinary felt hats and rough suits of clothes, incongruous below the ammunition belts slung diagonally from one shoulder to the waistline under the other arm. She saw one, hardly more than a boy, aim his rifle at a native worker and fire. The shot cracked out like the snapping of a huge and deafening whip, stunning, horrible. The young Boer's expression did not change.

It had all happened so quickly that it must have been over in a second, Vanessa judged, although her paralysis seemed to have lasted for hours, but then everything seemed to occur at once – Amas was on the platform, shouting at her, taking the rifle from her grasp; his strong hands were around her, lifting her from the car to the platform outside the chute.

She heard him bellow to another man, 'Take it up!' He had his rifle at the ready; they were rising to the surface.

'Wait, wait!' she screamed. Amas gestured her back against the wall.

'Get inside!' he shouted. 'Get inside as soon as the ground stops spilling!'

'No, Amas, no!' Vanessa was shrieking. 'Let me come!'

But he was ignoring her utterly now, taking aim at the Boers gathering on the surface. Vanessa clung to the wall for support; she was quivering all over, shaking with such force that she thought her arms and legs would be shaken from her torso. Even her head was nodding, dancing grotesquely, like a broken puppet's; not with terror for herself, for she was perfectly sheltered by the overhanging chamber, but for Amas, vulnerable in the open car.

The sweat of fear blinded her, gushing from her brow into her stinging eyes; she rubbed the moisture away with her hand and felt an even sharper, deeper sting. The salt of her perspiration burned her eyeballs like scraping fire. She blinked. She must see, she must.

Focusing her dimmed, agonising sight she looked upward, and cried out aloud, unheard in the din and the babel, 'Thank God, thank God'. Amas was already sheltered in the cleft of a rock near the surface, standing solid and easy, firing at the invading Boers again and again.

At that instant he looked immortal, untouchable, and her swift thought was, I should have known, I did him insufficient honour. All that he had ever been and suffered had toughened him to whipcord, lent him this obdurate and unrelenting courage. Amas always knew what to do. Even now he was doing it.

Vanessa's quivering subsided. Now she felt a new, wild urge to be there with him. She could not cower here when her place, as it always had been, was at his side.

Then she saw that the man next to him had been hit; he fell backwards into the great pit. Vanessa covered her eyes for an instant, fighting the need to vomit. Then at once she looked up again. Amas was still firing, his booted foot firm on the fallen man's rifle, to keep it from going over the edge.

Vanessa took a deep, shuddering breath. She was going to go up somehow. She gauged that she could just reach a crevice beyond the platform of the chamber; her sturdy boots would give her purchase as they had before when, to Amas' mingled consternation and delight, she had made such a climb in the lower regions.

But that had been lower down, and now she was terribly high, almost at the surface. Hundreds of feet yawned below. The idea nauseated her and her courage almost failed her momentarily; but she had to be at his side. Cautiously, she went to the end of the platform and put out a booted foot into a crevice. With all her will, she threw herself into the shelter of the rock and started to climb.

Once, when her foot slipped, she was terrified at the faintness that washed over her, but she clung like a limpet and went on. Just a few steps more.

Then she was standing on the narrow plateau at Amas' side. He was so intent that at first he didn't even know who was standing beside him. But he had relinquished his foothold on the rifle and she bent with extreme caution, picked it up and aimed it at the surface.

Her bullet whistled past the very ear of a mounted Boer; he rocked from the deafening sound and almost slid from his saddle, giving one of the Holders' men the few seconds he needed to fire. The Boer crumpled and fell from the saddle, his horse escaping in terror.

Amas shouted, 'Good man', without looking at Vanessa. But when he paused to reload his rifle, a lightning side-glance told him who it was. Amas turned pale under his tanned skin. 'Good God. Vanessa.'

But already she was aiming again, firing. She knew that if she stopped for the fraction of an instant to consider, she would not be able to fire. She had never harmed a living thing in all her life, but now their own lives were in the balance. She could not afford to think, only to fire, reload and fire. A mysterious strength, a resolve as hard as the very diamond, had stiffened inside her, holding her upright and determined.

A shattering reverberation smote her ear; she was afraid she would be deafened by it. Amas reeled backwards, and she grabbed frantically at him so he would not go over. A terrible, shouting groan was torn from him in the instant of the backward reeling. He'd been hit.

She shrieked his name, but he forced out two words from his pain-stretched mouth, 'A graze'. He leaned forward for what seemed the space of a heartbeat, then choked out an order, 'Keep firing'. Blood was gushing from the torn sleeve of his shirt. He would bleed to death, she thought in panic, if she didn't do something.

'Kneel down!' she screamed. He gave her one worshipping look and obeyed. Vanessa ripped her own shirt from her body and tied it around his arm as tightly as she could manage.

She was astonished that even in his agony he could smile at her. Slowly and unsteadily he got back to his feet. He took her rifle from her and began to fire.

She knew then that his must have been empty and at once reloaded it, taking her former place at his side.

Dear God, would it never end? Her mind screamed at her repeatedly. The battle was still raging, the great pit echoed with the shouts and screams of men, the shrill, pleading whinnies of the terrified horses, the constant, deafening whang of rifle bullets until Vanessa's fear became fear, not of death, but of madness.

Then some time in that nightmare interval the shots became more random, the shouts more widely spaced, less deafening. The Boers were scattering.

They were going away.

Amas turned to her, trembling, his tanned face muddy from loss of blood. 'We've held it. We've held it, my love.' His eyes began to change; his eyelids fluttered and now she could see only the whites of his eyes. He was leaning against the rock, about to fall.

And then she was holding him with feverish desperation, screaming, screaming, for someone to raise the car.

'Really, my darling, it's all right.' Amas smiled at her from the bed, smoothing away the anxious lines on her forehead. 'I've been hit worse, in Brazil and Mexico . . .'

He had a hard time with 'Mexico', she noticed; the doctor had given him something for the pain and his speech had slurred and thickened.

'Oh, Amas,' she murmured, leaning forward from the chair to take his hand in hers and kiss it.

He smiled at her again, regarding her from under his heavy lids.

'Rest, darling. Go rest . . . get yourself cleaned up. You look like a raga . . . muggin.'

She had to laugh at his pronunciation of 'ragamuffin'. Heaven knows, it was true. She was streaked with perspiration and tears, smeared with his own blood; swallowed in the enormous shirt of a worker who had given it to her to cover herself. It hadn't occurred to her at all until now, in the mad whirl of events, the dizzying transition to the safety and clean quiet of the bungalow.

Amas' eyes were closed. He still had a smile on his face as he drifted into sleep.

She tiptoed from the bedroom into the bathroom, undressing, bathing hastily and putting on clean clothes. In moments she was back in the chair, resolved to sit there until he woke again, glorying in the wonder of their being alive and safe. Amas had been fortunate indeed; the bullet had only torn the flesh of his arm.

Vanessa knew she ought to see to the children. Lesley had been hysterical, Martin pale and dumb, when the men had brought Amas back to the house. But she couldn't, not just now. They were with Ranee and Sehoiya, whose calm presences would soothe them.

Not just now, she repeated in silence. She could not leave him yet. Just a few hours ago she might have lost him for ever, and now there didn't seem to be hours enough left in all of life to gaze upon his beloved face.

It was several hours before he wakened, telling her he was terribly thirsty but not hungry yet. Vanessa rushed to the hall and called out to Ranee to bring some lemonade.

Amas drank it in grateful gulps. When she was taking the glass from him, he grabbed weakly for her other hand and held it.

'I always knew,' he murmured, still heavy-eyed and speaking with the thickness of opiates, 'that you were not like any other woman. Today convinces me more than ever.'

She raised the hand that still held hers and spoke softly against his fingers. 'I had to be where you were.'

She noticed that his eyes looked a little clearer now; they were resuming their old sharp, bright expression. He stared at her, taking in her renewed freshness, her hair brushed to gleaming.

Then a shadow of pain crossed the lion-coloured stare. 'Vanessa, being where I am . . .' she felt a faint pressure from his hand on hers, 'is something we've got to talk about.'

'Not now. No serious matters now,' she protested. 'You've got to rest.'

111

He shook his head. 'We've got to talk about it now or I won't *get* any rest.' His speech was sharpening, becoming more lucid already and she marvelled at his vital strength. 'This wasn't just a raid today. This was one of the first battles of the war. It's here.'

'Oh, no. No, Amas.' Vanessa felt that faint, sickly heart-flutter again, a ringing in her ears, the dreaded start of weakness in her body.

'Yes, my darling.' Amas' face was tight and grim. He swallowed as if painfully and went on. 'You've got to leave. You've got to take the children and go away, to England or America. England's quicker. And you have relatives there, you told me.'

He hurried the speech, trying to make his voice neutral, obviously eager to stem any demur.

'No, Amas.' She struggled to keep her reply quiet and calm; now of all times she must not show anger or hurt or hysteria. She had to convince him. 'No,' she said again with that hard-won calm. 'We will send the children. I will not go.'

He half-sat up in the bed, with a look of alarm, until she restrained him gently with her hands. She sat down on the edge of the bed, keeping her hands on his chest, lightly but with firmness. 'Vanessa, you've got to listen to reason. I've given in to you before, so many times. This time I won't. You've got to understand that.'

'Then you *want* me to go?' Now she was having a difficult time restraining her deep hurt, the rising indignation. 'You want us to be apart?'

'*Want* us to!' He lay back against the pillows and closed his eyes. When he opened them she saw that they were shining with moisture. She had never before seen tears in his eyes. 'Good God, Vanessa, *want* us to . . .' He closed his eyes again and shook his head. It was as if he were simultaneously rejecting the idea of their apartness and reproaching her for her irrational stubbornness.

'Then don't condemn me to death,' she urged him in a low, vibrant tone, her hands sliding upward to stroke his face, to cradle his cheeks between her fingers.

'You could be condemned to death by staying, Vanessa.' It was clear that he was fighting his reaction to her touch. He was bending every effort of his will to remain stern, unmoving.

'I might,' she said in a purposely neutral tone. 'But if you send me away, I *will*. At least here, with you, I will have a chance. Without you I'll have none. What do you think it would be like for me, Amas,' she demanded, her voice climbing, 'not knowing . . . with you here,

112

away from me, a million miles away? If something . . . happened, it could be weeks before I knew. But it's not even that. It's being away from you, not having your arms around me in the night; not being able to see you, hear your voice . . .' She broke off with a sob and leaned against him, letting the bitter tears escape, shaking and sobbing against his body.

'If you send me away,' she said, muffled against him, 'I'll leave the ship and come back here alone. Do you want that, Amas? Before God, I'll do it. I'll do it, Amas. If you tie me hand and foot I'll find a way to get back here to you, I swear it. I will not go away to England or America. We will send the children. How can you suggest such a thing, if you love me?'

His arms tightened about her with a little of their customary strength; she had been so distracted that she hadn't even considered the wound. With an exclamation, she straightened. 'Oh, Amas, have I hurt your arm?'

'No, no,' he said dismissively. 'Vanessa, you must know how I love you. I love you more than my very life. If anything should happen to you, I couldn't live on. Don't you see?'

'I don't want to live on, for a day or a night, away from you,' she sobbed, hiding her face in her hands, bowed over with the intensity of an anguish that seemed to press down, press down on her like a great weight.

'Vanessa. Oh, God, Vanessa.' Amas stretched out his uninjured arm and pulled at her hands with his fingers, enticing her face from its hiding. 'Look at me.'

She raised her swollen eyes.

'You really meant that, didn't you?' he asked softly. She nodded, shuddering, wiping at her face with her fingers. 'You meant it – that you will not go.' She nodded again.

'Then you give me Hobson's choice.' He smiled at her sadly. 'On the one hand it makes me more fearful than I've ever been in my life. On the other,' his fierce gaze flicked over her, 'I can only bless you for it.'

He reached over and took her narrow wrist in his grasp. 'I should not be surprised. It's always been this way, hasn't it? We were always two of a kind. You were never like the others, in any way. I was convinced of that when I saw you coming to the ship that afternoon in New York . . .' his smile widened with sheer enjoyment, 'when Sala came back with you from Kimberley, bug-eyed, telling me that tale of the barber shop.'

Amas sobered. 'Vanessa.'

'Yes?'

'We've got to talk to the children now.'

'Now?' she protested. 'But why?'

His mouth was tight and grim. 'Because we've got to make the arrangements at once. They must leave on the very next ship. We have no time to lose. We've got to tell them now, tonight. Then you must write a note to the Bartleys – Mrs Bartley and the children will be sure to be going – and have Sala take it tonight.'

'I'll go myself,' she offered.

'No,' he said sharply. 'From now on you will go nowhere, Vanessa, without me. That is a condition I insist on. If you need anything from the town, Sala and the men will get it. Otherwise, I promise you, I *will* tie you hand and foot, and gag you and deliver you to that ship.'

There was something in his intonation that discouraged argument of any kind. She inclined her head submissively.

'Now, darling,' he said more gently, 'please go and bring the children to me.'

Vanessa went out and, calling Martin and Lesley, returned with them to the bedroom, her hand on Lesley's shoulder, Martin bringing up the rear.

'Oh, Father,' Lesley quavered, and rushed to the bed, about to throw herself upon Amas.

'Careful,' Vanessa cried out more sharply than she'd intended. 'Be careful of your father's arm.'

Lesley did not look at her, but the young face, so much like her own, froze at once with resentment. When had that strange hostility begun, Vanessa questioned sadly? Why did it have to be? Apparently she and her daughter were engaged in some kind of contest for Amas' affections, a situation with which Vanessa had never quite learned to deal.

Martin, as usual, stood by quietly. At twelve he already had so many of the characteristics of a man. Vanessa's heart warmed. Martin was so very much like Amas.

'That's all right,' Amas said softly. 'She'll be careful, won't you, honey?' He beamed at Lesley and she glowed.

'Of course I will, Mother,' she said in her cool, distant way. The child was in some respects a more feminine version of herself, Vanessa reflected. Lesley had never exhibited a mind of her own; she had an almost slavish tendency with men. Immediately Vanessa was stricken with self-reproach. It was a pretty cold way to think of one's own daughter, but she'd never been able to help herself somehow.

'Sit down.' Amas patted the bed and Lesley obeyed at once. 'Martin, come over here and sit on the other side. There's something I've got to tell you. Both of you. Something very important and serious.'

Martin strode across the room and perched on Amas' other side. Again Vanessa was struck by his odd maturity, his manliness. Perhaps, after all, she had not done her children an injustice through her benevolent neglect. Each of them seemed capable of surviving without her, surviving very well. And that would stand them in good stead in the future.

And Vanessa realised something else – they were about to send their children away, to a distant country, and all their mother was thinking about was her own reaction. Another small pang of guilt assailed Vanessa, but she tried to dismiss it. She had not been born for motherhood, as other women were, and there was no point at this stage of their lives in regretting it. She could only do the best she could for them.

Amas, intent on what he was about to say, seemed unaware of Vanessa's unease at the moment. He plunged in, 'We've got to send you to England. Soon.' Amas, Vanessa knew from long knowledge of him, believed that circuitous speech was far more cruel than bluntness, created more suspense and therefore greater pain. He had never used euphemisms to the children: people did not 'pass away'. They 'died'.

And likely he was right, Vanessa judged. Martin looked pale, and Lesley gasped. But this would afford them the chance to overcome their shock. 'Why?' Lesley asked with a break in her voice. 'Why, Father? How can you send me away from you?'

'Me', not 'us', Vanessa thought. My daughter is even more like me than I realised, was her wry conclusion.

'Because there is going to be a war. You have read about wars, in your history, and you know what can happen.'

Amas' inflection was matter-of-fact, arousing Vanessa's admiration, calculated to stem hysteria.

'Mother,' Martin said calmly, 'you are coming, too? Mr Farley said that in wars all women and children are sent away.'

Before Vanessa could answer, Amas intervened. 'Your mother is staying, Martin.'

Lesley turned and looked at Vanessa. 'Why, Mother? Why? If you're staying, then why can't I?'

Vanessa wished that she could say: because I know the marvel that you have not yet found . . . because children and parents can survive very well without each other, but lovers never. She groped for a reply. Again Amas rescued her, as he had done on so many occasions in the past.

'Because I *need* your mother . . . to help me, Lesley.' Vanessa's heart fluttered; there had hardly been an instant's pause between the two phrases, yet she had caught the wonder and longing in his first words.

'You mean because of the mine, Father . . . and the shooting,' Martin commented.

'Yes, Martin.' For the first time Amas' eyes met hers.

'But I can learn to shoot, too!' Lesley cried out, that whine resembling Hester Stirling's creeping into her cry.

'No, honey,' Amas said gently, stroking her hair. 'There just isn't time. For all practical purposes, the war began this afternoon.'

Martin interjected with triumph, 'You see, Lesley? I told you and told you. You should have learned to shoot with me and Kossee.' The boys had learned to shoot three years ago; both shrank from killing animals but were adept beyond their years at targets. 'I can shoot, Dad. So maybe we'd better send Lesley and I'll stay here.'

Vanessa wondered how Amas would handle that. It was a poser.

But he did not disappoint her. 'No, son. You have to take care of Lesley.'

'I don't *want* Martin to take care of me!' Lesley was sobbing. 'I want you to take care of me, Father.'

'Shhh, shhh.' Amas leaned over and kissed Lesley's head. 'You've got to be a grown-up girl and help us. Promise me, now.'

Lesley looked searchingly at him; he met her eyes earnestly, with a kind of pleading.

'You'll be able to go to school in England,' Vanessa cajoled. 'You can live with the Stirlings in London, see all sorts of wonderful things. And they'll probably take you to Paris to buy you some beautiful dresses.'

She had struck the proper chord. Lesley brightened a little. She had inherited Hester's overweening vanity. 'Oh, Mother.' Lesley smiled through her weeping.

'You see?' Amas looked heartened. But the boy was still unconvinced. 'We are going to ask the Bartleys to take you with them.'

'Oh, I say, that's jolly!' Martin liked the Bartley sons.

116

Vanessa could sense Amas' distaste for the British expression, an unhappy souvenir of Mitchell Farley, but he said evenly, 'All right, then. It won't be so bad for either of you, will it?' Vanessa admired her husband more than ever; he sounded as if he were suggesting a picnic. Amas grinned at them both and then he became serious again.

'I'm counting on you, Martin. You'll be representing me on this expedition. You'll be looking after Lesley the way I'll be looking after your mother.'

Amas looked at Vanessa again, as if to say, I must be mad to let you stay in this. Vanessa answered his glance squarely, nodding her head a trifle in the direction of Martin. The boy was standing up, now, very straight, and he was fairly bursting with the pride of his responsibility.

After that the children bombarded them with questions. Amas answered every one as Vanessa went out to write a note to the Bartleys.

The answer that Sala brought back that night was in the affirmative, but Seldon Bartley, addressing the family's reply to Amas, expressed the belief that Cecil Rhodes would have already made arrangements. The following morning the Holders discovered the confirmation of that; when Amas' foreman came to report to him, he revealed that passage had already been booked on the next outgoing train, which would leave for Cape Town the day after tomorrow.

The remaining days were a maelstrom of preparations which Vanessa, and at last the queenly Sehoiya, were forced to oversee. Amas fretted at his confinement to the bed, and only the pleadings of Vanessa kept him from getting up until the day of the departure. He was insistent on going to the Cape with the children; the doctor, who came to examine him the day after the shooting, threw up his hands and thundered, 'Go ahead, Holder. Go ahead. If you want to contract an infection, and lose your arm, go to the Cape. A one-armed man will be of great value to Kimberley when the going gets rough.'

Vanessa was deeply thankful for the man's crude comment; it saved the situation as nothing else could have done. Raging, Amas declared himself defeated.

The children's possessions were packed and repacked, several times; at first they could not be persuaded that certain items were better left behind. At last, however, everything was completed. The cable was sent to the Stirlings in London, Amas made out several large cheques, giving one to each of the children to carry on their persons and the largest to Mrs Bartley for safekeeping, together with a generous amount of cash.

'Good heavens, Amas, why so much?' Vanessa asked.

'There may be a bit of a problem with the mails,' he said quietly. She realised what a foolish question it had been; worse, realised that the 'problem with the mails' might symbolise catastrophic events, horrendous perils that she had never imagined in her inexperience.

And when she came upon him drafting a large cheque to his mother and re-reading his will, a copy of which was on deposit in a Cape Town bank, Vanessa knew exactly what they faced.

As the time for the children's departure grew closer, Vanessa was resigned to the fact that nothing could keep Amas from accompanying them to the Kimberley station. That morning the children's strapped luggage was set on the veranda. Vanessa found Amas and Lesley waiting, Amas pale and unsteady on his feet, Lesley very ladylike in her travelling clothes with traces of tears on her face.

Martin was nowhere to be found.

'Martin!' Amas shouted. 'Where is that boy?' he asked irritably.

'I'll find him,' Vanessa promised. 'Please, Amas, sit down.'

But he ignored her, pacing back and forth along the veranda, further irritated, she was aware, by the necessity of her doing something he would otherwise have done.

Vanessa heard the dogs' barking and the ostriches' peculiar cry. Of course, he was saying goodbye to the animals. She felt a scratching of soreness deep in her throat; the child loved them so.

She came upon him, hugging the dogs, speaking to the lingering ostriches that regarded Martin steadily with their great comical-looking eyes. Vanessa stopped. Martin was unaware of her presence.

'Goodbye, now,' he was saying, and his voice broke into a sob. 'If things get bad, you'll hide out, won't you?'

Vanessa regarded them with blurred eyes. 'Martin,' she called out softly, 'it's time.'

'Oh, Mother.' He came to her and threw his arms around her. 'You will take care of them. Promise me.'

'Of course I will. I will, Martin.' She fervently hoped that when the time came she could, would be allowed to. When humans were running for their lives, she was afraid that animals wouldn't be counting for much, even to the humane British who were apparently running this nightmare show.

Vanessa took a jagged breath and repeated, 'I will. But we've got to go now. They're waiting.'

'All right.' Martin squared his shoulders and walked back with her to the bungalow. He stopped short, staring. 'Where's Kossee?'

Kossee! Dear heaven, how could she have forgotten? But there had been so much to cope with – reining in Amas, overseeing the business details, getting the children ready, all those things in the face of her paralysing dread, her sharp anxieties – that it had never occurred to her that Kossee would go with them.

'Come here, Martin.' Amas held out his uninjured arm. 'Kossee is not going.'

'Not going!' Martin stared at Amas, shaking his head in disbelief. 'Not *going*!'

At that moment Kossee emerged from the bungalow with his parents and Sehoiya. Vanessa was struck anew by the boy's amazing resemblance to that regal woman. He held his cropped head high, and was smiling at Martin.

'This is my country, Martin. I must stay with her.'

Martin looked shamed by his outburst, by the unmanly break in his voice. Kossee had the bearing of a warrior; he was the grandson of a king.

Vanessa was touched by what she read in her son: Martin Holder must be no less. The boy cleared his throat and stuck out his hand.

'I understand, Kossee.'

'So long, Martin.' Now the other boy's voice wavered. They were trying so hard to be men, Vanessa thought, and new pain gripped her heart. But she could see Amas' pride in Martin. 'You'll be back in no time at all.'

CHAPTER EIGHT

Vanessa remembered Kossee's words with bitterness throughout October and in early November, during the fierce fighting at Dundee and Ladysmith, and near the end of November when Kimberley first fell under siege. Amas was doggedly trying still to run the mine; at any hour, she knew, that would become impossible. The bungalow was a fortress, with sandbags piled high around it.

At the first sign of gunfire, the ostriches had run away, and Vanessa could only be relieved. They would have sought safety in the far reaches of the veld, away from the fighting. It was all she could do now, remembering her vow to Martin, to restrain the unhappy dogs in a small quarter of the land; enough to know that Amas and the household were still uninjured. There was scant emotion to spare beyond her terror when Amas left the house, beyond the draining, shuddering thankfulness she felt when he came back whole at dusk.

As he had predicted, the mails no longer arrived. But Vanessa was too immersed in the matter of daily survival to give the children more than a random thought. They were out of this, they were safe. It was all that counted. She did suffer, though, for her father, and Amas' mother, who had no first-hand knowledge that she and Amas were still all right. Sending a cable was out of the question; only messages pertaining to the war were allowed to go out these days.

The first months of the war dragged on at a leaden pace – through Magersfontein, and Christmas at Pretoria. By then all the mines had been shut down. And Amas had volunteered, with other civilians, to fight in the defence of Kimberley which, by January, seemed imminent.

In the long, secluded days her music was the only thing that kept her from going quite mad. She returned to it with her old passion, with a vengeance, sometimes considering that even to do so, in itself, was mad. Nonetheless she went on in her obdurate way, hammering out the shimmering floods of scales, rendering the wistful phrases of Chopin, Bach's fountains of pulsating silver, as she heard the deadly thud of exploding shells from far away on Kimberley's dusty streets.

Then for a time there was quiet, a sinister, brooding quiet like the stillness of leaves presaging a titanic storm. And one miraculous morning in early February, no one seemed to know quite how, a bag of mail arrived in Kimberley on the train. One of their distant neighbours rode by, to tell them, in a state of high excitement. Amas and Sala, with their rifles at the ready, went in to the town to get the mail over Vanessa's protestations. Amas assured her that the area was quiet, for now, but she did not draw a deep breath until she heard them coming back.

Among a number of other letters for Amas, there were two from his mother. There was a letter from Vanessa's father and three from the London Stirlings.

Vanessa tore open her father's letter eagerly. He was well, but riddled with anxiety for their safety. She was gnawed with frustration; if only there were some way to let him know they were alive.

But it was a fruitless exercise. She turned to the Stirlings' correspondence. What with the difficulty and delay, the first letter was postmarked months before. Vanessa decided to read the letters in order.

She was struck by the total unreality of the scene which the earliest missive described – the children's introduction to their relatives' orderly and elegant house. The whole of London seemed to Vanessa like a city from a fairy tale. That first letter was the soul of cordiality, replete with warmth and reassurance. Diana Stirling, the letter said, absolutely adored her young cousins.

The second letter indicated that a month had elapsed, and the tone of it was very different. It appeared to Vanessa that a certain coolness had crept into Diana's references to Lesley, although she was still effusive over Martin. He was doing splendidly at school, her cousin wrote, and had made a number of friends. But in regard to Lesley Vanessa thought she could read veiled hints at problems; the problems seemed to concern Lesley's fourteen-year-old cousin Rupert, Diana's son.

Vanessa felt a palpable chill along her body. What was going on? Her cousin Diana was far too well-bred, essentially too kind-hearted, to come right out and say that Lesley had become unwelcome. But the implication was there, between the graceful lines. Yes, Diana was too gentle and polite to hint about the madness of Vanessa's choice in staying, either; obviously reluctant to add to their overwhelming dread by any overt statement. Nevertheless it was there, and Vanessa was too astute to miss it.

The third letter revealed that Martin had fallen in love with London and had expressed a desire to remain and finish school. 'But then, of course, he has told you that already in his own letter.'

Martin's letter plainly had been delayed or lost. She would have to wait for that. Diana made no mention of Lesley's writing to them; Vanessa wondered painfully what that signified, but worse, about the significance of Diana's not mentioning her at all except to say that she was 'well'.

Vanessa let the correspondence slide into her lap, a sensation of gloom overlying her constant tension. She decided she must not let Amas see the final letter; there was no earthly point in burdening him with that now.

She went into the kitchen quarters. 'Sehoiya, where is Sir?'

Sehoiya turned from her dinner preparation and answered in level tones, but with a glowering face, 'Sir has taken Sala with him into the town.' Her words were accusing. Vanessa repressed her indignation, wanting to reply that her husband was at peril as well as Sehoiya's son. But she reproached herself at once: this was, after all, a white man's war, no matter what affection existed among the household's members.

'Oh, Sehoiya, why?'

'I don't know,' the woman grumbled. 'Some men's business, of this war. Sir told Sala that the fighting is coming here, again.'

'Oh, my God.' Vanessa went to Sehoiya and put her arm around the old woman's shoulders. 'Men are mad, Sehoiya, mad, to do this thing.'

Sehoiya let out a sigh and the ghost of a smile twisted her full lips. 'Yes, Misses. It seems they must tear up, tear up, like little children tear up the house. Then we, the women . . .' her lips grimaced, 'must clean up after them.'

Vanessa looked at her for a moment, thinking how wise she was; she had summed up the whole insane history of conflict. The men destroy and the women wearily sweep up the debris. She left Sehoiya and went out to wait for Amas.

It seemed to her he would never come, but at last she heard the sound of hoofs and, almost weeping with relief, saw them riding up the path to the bungalow. One glance at Amas' set face told her the news was bad.

Without a greeting, even without his usual kiss, Amas started speaking as he dismounted. 'We've got to take shelter in the mine.'

'What's happened?'

'I got word that Kimberley will be under siege by the morning.' Amas came to her then and took her in his arms. Sala had already disappeared into the kitchen quuarters, and Vanessa heard him giving terse orders to Ranee and Sehoiya in regard to water and to food.

'Bring the least things that you can do with,' Amas said, releasing her, 'We will go as soon as everything is ready.'

Vanessa wasted no time. It was summer again; there was no need even for a jacket. All the same, she didn't know what it would be like, down in those clammy depths, so she packed a small bundle of clothes, tossing her jewellery into the bottom, with the last letter from her father, and a picture of Amas which she particularly treasured.

When she came back to the veranda the others were already there. She whistled for the dogs. The two of them came bounding to her eagerly.

'The dogs, Vanessa?' Amas looked at her questioningly. 'It would be far better to let them go. They were wild to begin with, you know, and would fare very well on the veld.'

'The ostriches are gone, already,' she replied, hearing her voice begin to tremble. 'I promised Martin, Amas.'

He frowned. Then he nodded curtly. 'Very well. Sala, tie up the dogs, please.'

Sala did so, with difficulty. The frisky creatures had never known a restraint, but finally they were tied. Ranee and Sehoiya were given charge of them; Amas, Vanessa, Kossee and Sala would have to keep their hands free to shoot, if need be, rifles already slung over their shoulders.

Amas crowded them all into the buggy and drove swiftly to the Big Hole. Already there were milling crowds of natives and civilians. To her horror, Vanessa recognised Mitchell Farley standing in the middle of them, shouting directions.

She looked at Amas. His face gave away nothing at all. 'Stay here a moment, please,' he said to Vanessa. Then he jumped down and strode towards Farley.

In the uproar she could hear nothing of what they were saying, and she could see only Mitchell Farley's face. Amas' back was towards her. They concluded their conversation swiftly, however, and Amas was striding back to the buggy.

'Come, darling.' He held out his hand to help her down and she leaped onto the turf. 'Sala, Ranee, Sehoiya.' Amas addressed them curtly. 'Stay close behind us.'

Vanessa did not want to ask him, because he seemed about to break with tension, but she knew that something was the matter.

Finally he said, 'Mitchell Farley has been appointed the representative of Rhodes. I reminded him that this is still the Holder mine. There's going to be a problem about the natives, and the dogs. Pay no attention. Do exactly what I tell you, Vanessa. I have picked the exact chamber I feel will be safest. We are going to stay rather high. I believe the danger from shells will be offset by staying somewhere less vulnerable to rockfall. Farther down there will always be that danger.'

She was too terrified even to speak; her breath was coming in shallow gasps. The picture he painted was beyond all horror, any peril she had imagined.

123

'We will make two trips in the car,' he said, in that same quick, hard tone. 'You and the dogs, Kossee and Sehoiya will go first; Sala and Ranee will follow after.'

'But Amas . . .' her voice was rising to a shriek, 'what about you? What about *you*?'

'I'll have to come later, Vanessa. There are things that all of us have to do on the surface. Sala cannot help; there is too great a resentment against the natives. Rhodes' – Amas' face was suffused with sudden anger – 'Rhodes is abandoning his men.'

'Dear heaven,' Vanessa breathed, too low for him to hear her. Abandoning them . . . oh, yes, this was a white man's war, for certain. The sweat of horror began to trickle down her back, tickle at her legs.

'We must hurry,' Amas insisted, pulling her along. When she was in the car with Sehoiya, Kossee and the dogs, a hostile group of men moved towards them. 'You're taking dogs . . . and natives?' one of them bellowed.

Amas levelled his rifle. 'This is the Holder mine; I am the owner. If you take one step more, I'll kill you.' The unarmed man stepped back, frightened, but his eyes glittered with hate.

Slowly the car descended to a middle chamber. Vanessa looked into the darkness. The tethered dogs sniffed and whined.

'Well, Sehoiya.' Vanessa fought to keep her voice from shaking. 'We'd better get busy and lay out the beds. This is going to be our home for a little while.'

The 'little while' became an interval of twenty-four agonising nights and days.

All that evening, from dusk to midnight, the great mine wheels rotated and counter-rotated on the headgear, as the lifts ascended and descended. Down the mine-shafts the scenes beggared description: Vanessa saw hundreds of women and children and babies huddled together in the mine galleries, packed so tight that they reminded her of the flapping bodies of fish on the deck of a fishing boat, something that she had seen in France that had sickened her.

Before another day had passed, Vanessa and Sehoiya had made room for a dozen women and their children. The sanitary arrangements of course were non-existent; there was hardly space to breathe. And Vanessa caught only random glimpses of Amas, who was fighting at the side of the Town Guardsmen on the surface.

But it was enough, enough to know that he was still whole, that by some miracle he was still uninjured.

124

After what seemed an eternity of ear-splitting explosions and screams and the perpetual, terrifying crash of falling rocks and debris, there was a sudden, deafening silence.

'What is it?' Vanessa cried. 'Is it over, is it over?'

'Oh, no, I'm afraid not. Listen,' the woman next to her said. Dumbfounded, Vanessa caught the toll of bells.

'It's Sunday,' the woman mumbled wearily. 'There's one thing you can say for the Boers – they're too pious to fight on Sundays. We'll have some rest till tomorrow.'

At long, long last, one afternoon, a weekday afternoon, there was a great blast and then that deafening and utter silence. Vanessa raised her head from her hands, believing she was dreaming. She had become so accustomed to the noise that the quiet was incomprehensible. But now there were triumphant shouts from the surface and dimly she made out the words, 'The cavalry is here! We see the cavalry!'

Vanessa crept to the mouth of the chamber, and looked up. In the milling throng at the surface was Amas, and he was shouting to her, shouting and waving.

Then the car's wheels were squeaking downward, and Amas was leaping into the chamber to grab Vanessa in his arms, careless of her sweaty skin and filthy clothes, of the salty taste of her mouth blending with the streaming perspiration and wild tears, kissing her and holding her.

In a dreamlike blur she realised she was on the surface again, that in the uproar Amas was shepherding them all together for the long trek home. The horse and the buggy had long since disappeared, Amas told her.

Her body and her limbs were so cramped from confinement, her eyes so starved for light, that it was heaven for Vanessa to stumble along the dusty path, blinking in the sun, letting the dogs go free and watching them bound wildly ahead, running around the struggling group with loud, abandoned barking, ecstatic with their freedom.

Vanessa could hardly comprehend the scenes that lay about them – the bloated bodies of dead horses, the fragments of shells, the random, shattered houses. Her gaze focused straight ahead, as she strained for the first sight of the white bungalow.

It was standing. It was standing still, although a portion of the roof over the guest wing had been hit and the end of the veranda.

Suddenly she was overcome with weakness and staggered. Amas, with a low exclamation, scooped her up in his arms and carried her the rest of the way.

'All right now?' he asked her softly when they were on the veranda.

'Yes. Oh, yes, Amas.' He set her down and she leaned against the jamb of the open door. There was a thick coat of red dust over everything but, incredibly, the first room seemed intact.

Her gaze darted to the corner. The piano. Yes, even the piano was still there, untouched, unscarred after all that mad, black interval of bursting dread and screaming horror. The same thick layer of reddish dust was all that marred its shining.

'Even the Boers,' Amas muttered, his voice slurred with exhaustion, 'have too much respect for music to do that.'

For the first time Vanessa noticed that ring of dirt around his mouth; in contrast, his white grin was more dazzling than ever.

'I'd better see if we still have water,' he said, and strode out.

And food, Vanessa recalled. They had buried a good supply of food in the earth of the shed near the garden. She went out. Sala was already digging, aided by Kossee.

Then she heard the rush of water in the tub, and it sounded like music. 'We do! We do!' Amas called out triumphantly. 'We still have water!'

Vanessa raised the skirt of her stained dress and began to dust the surface of the Steinway, and there was a loud, wild singing in her heart, a great thanksgiving. We are all alive and here, said the singing; there are incredible riches – a whole house, and food and water.

And any day now they would be able to send the cables, to Philadelphia and New York, the cables that would bear the message, we are alive.

The war raged on for two long years, but the fighting never threatened Kimberley so closely again. During the first month after the nightmare siege, Amas seemed at a loss. He was neither engaged in battle – he persisted in the deep belief that this was not his war, that the only fighting he would do would be to protect his own – nor working in the mine, which he would have to keep shut down for an indeterminate time; they could hardly work with shells exploding around them.

But then one day he told Vanessa that, shut down or not, he was going back to work in the mine. He and Sala and Kossee had expeditiously repaired the damage to the house, and he needed, he said, to breathe diamond dust again.

The fighting had moved away, to the borders of the Cape Colony;

armed with rifles, Amas, Sala and Kossee went to the mine. As the days went by some of Amas' native workers began to drift back, impelled by the emptiness and famine they had found when they had attempted to rejoin their scattered tribes. The men were thankful for employment, glad to return to the Holders' benign and protective circle.

During the siege of Kimberley Cecil Rhodes' native workers had been confined to a filthy, crowded compound, so they could not escape. Stricken by scurvy and other diseases, many of them died. Amas Holder, on the other hand, had told his men to go if they wished, admitting that there was nothing he could do for them during the dreaded siege; the white people, he told them frankly, would take the shelters and there would be no protection for them in Kimberley.

Amas did not have the heart to tell Vanessa all of this; if she learned of the misery of Rhodes' workers, it would not be from him. In any case she had never questioned him. There had been no time before. But now the natives had remembered, and were drifting back, grateful to Amas for giving them the choice of freedom.

And so the Holder mine resumed, in a bizarre and spotty fashion, its partial operation. Amas' British foreman had joined the civilians fighting at the side of the Army against the Boers near the Cape. Gradually Sala grew more and more conversant with the mining of diamonds, and Kossee as well found his pride increasing with his knowledge. In three months Amas conceded that it was safe enough for Vanessa to join them at the mine.

Kossee and Sala, delirious in their new status as men doing the work of men, no longer confined to house quarters, appointed three young native men who could shoot to guard the women at the house and engage in the gardening and care of the property.

Meanwhile the yawning pits of DeVries were empty and silent. The community looked askance at the money-grubbing Holders who could be risking their lives in their struggle to wrest another fortune from the ground with the help of so few. Amas and Vanessa, who had never cared much for the opinion of neighbours, went doggedly on, growing ever closer in their isolation from the others.

Vanessa felt an obscure guilt; she hardly missed the children at all. It was glorious to be alone with Amas again, heavenly not to have their privacy intruded on. They had received random letters from Martin Stirling and Ellen Holder, exulting that Amas and Vanessa were safe, that the children were far from danger.

127

Only two letters, in all this time, had arrived from Lesley. Both were addressed to Amas. He was angered by the omission of Vanessa's name from the envelope and, replying, signed his letter 'Your mother and father'. Vanessa coolly accepted the situation, almost dismayed at how little she was affected.

Letters from Martin were another matter, frequent as the mails allowed, often arriving in threes or fours, warm and confiding, full of glowing descriptions of London in the exciting new twentieth century. As Diana Stirling had written so long before, it was clear that Martin had fallen under the spell of the great, varied city.

Near the end of 1901 he wrote them that he wanted to stay on and continue school there. 'But with your permission,' he said in his letter, 'I would prefer not to go on to the University. I would like to work with diamonds in the market, and not in the field. I met a splendid German fellow who works at Dunkensreuter, the diamond firm. He thinks that when I'm sixteen I can get a post there. I want to do this very much, and I hope that you will let me stay.'

Amas and Vanessa granted him their permission, Vanessa with a poignant sense of loss. The affectionate and loving child, the one who looked like Amas, was fated to be far away, while the child who loved her not at all, for whom Vanessa herself had such shockingly ambiguous feelings, was bound to return.

That Lesley would come back was somehow a foregone conclusion. Diana Stirling's references to their daughter had become increasingly reticent and cool. Vanessa could sense that her cousin looked forward with great eagerness to the end of the war, and Lesley's departure.

But what disturbed Vanessa and Amas most of all were Diana's reports of encountering Beatrice Seton, and of her visits to the children. Diana had never approved of Bea, Vanessa recalled, even from the sisters' adolescence, when Bea and Vanessa had visited England. Now Diana's scarcely veiled animosity was stronger; without stating it she hinted at Bea's patent influence over Lesley.

Amas and Vanessa received this news with gloom, but Amas said reassuringly, 'The war will soon be over. Lesley will be back with us, where she belongs.'

Vanessa did not reply that she wondered, indeed, where Lesley did belong. It was obviously not in Africa, a place she had always seemed so eager to escape.

The war itself seemed far away and almost without reality for Vanessa Holder. She wondered if there had ever been such a strange conflict since the Middle Ages when, she had read somewhere, 'people used to stand on their porches and watch the fighting'.

Then finally, in the spring of 1902, the war came to an end. Cecil Rhodes did not live to see it; he had died of a heart attack the month before.

And Mitchell Farley, the Holders learned, was now a power with Rhodes' company, DeVries.

The mines stirred from their sleep; the great wheels rotated once more. Jubilant, preoccupied with the hiring of new crews, Amas Holder looked forward with a kind of absent-minded pleasure to his daughter's return.

Vanessa was ashamed to realise that she herself looked forward to the event with little enthusiasm, even a form of dread.

The girl had been a stranger to Vanessa from the day of her birth. Now she would soon be sixteen, a young woman. Lesley's correspondence had told them nothing. What she had experienced and felt, how deeply she had been drawn into Beatrice's web, her mother could only conjecture.

Part III
The Cleft

CHAPTER NINE

'There she blows.' Amas Holder pointed towards the crimson funnels of the *Dunottar Castle*, making her majestic way into the Cape Town port. 'She's a far cry from the *Walmer*.' He smiled down at Vanessa in the gloomy morning light.

'She is indeed.' Vanessa raised the pitch of her voice to make herself heard over the ship's horn and the wind, the vast confusion of the roiling pier. There were hundreds of British Army soldiers around them, now mustered out, waiting to be borne back to England on the ship that would bring Lesley in.

'Fourteen days,' Amas murmured. 'The *Dunottar*'s quite a flier.'

Vanessa nodded absently. The two great rivals, the Union and Castle Lines, had merged in 1900, and now the Union Castle's ships had set a record for speed. The colours were distinctive – the lavender-grey hull, with white; the vivid, black-topped funnels. But this was tea party conversation.

She knew that Amas was skirting around the subject they had been avoiding even while they had been discussing little else, the subject of their daughter. Amas was uneasy about Vanessa's uneasiness. Three years before, when she had sailed, Lesley had been a little girl. Now neither knew the Lesley who would be returning.

Even the weather was against them, Vanessa thought. On this sharp morning of African winter, the sky was thick and dense with clouds, the wind blew cold. It was not a happy omen.

With a final, hoarse, ear-shattering blast the ship slid into port.

'Where is she? I don't see her,' Amas said tensely, scanning the *Dunottar*'s crowded decks.

'Neither do I.' Vanessa could feel her tension build and coil, like a huge, hard spring. 'But wait . . . there . . . no, no, it couldn't be . . .'

It couldn't be Lesley, she repeated in desperate silence. Not that heavy-breasted figure in the too light, inappropriate clothes, not that face under the feathered hat.

'Where?' Amas demanded, straining to follow the direction of Vanessa's stare.

'There,' she said reluctantly, pointing. 'Between those two young men, amidships, on the middle deck.'

Amas shaded his eyes against the grey-white glare and looked. 'It is. It's Lesley.' Vanessa heard his unhappy wonderment. They could see their daughter clearly now; the sight was astonishing.

In spite of the weather Lesley was scantily clothed in a pale blue dress of the latest mode, and not in the quiet travelling clothes worn by the women around her. The dress was very snug in the bodice, frankly outlining large, ripe breasts, emphasising the swell of rounded and mature hips. But worst of all, below the feathered hat, the teasing young face was painted.

'What's the matter with her face?' Amas queried, raising his hand in an uncertain salute.

'She's painted,' Vanessa answered grimly.

'Good Lord! But surely Diana . . .'

'I have a feeling Diana had nothing to do with that. Or the clothes.' Vanessa looked at Amas. He was staring at Lesley with a helpless expression.

He mumbled, 'It's like that time when Bea . . .' He stopped abruptly.

Bea. Vanessa recalled her sister's ruffled yellow dress, when she had disembarked on that long ago afternoon. This was the creation of Beatrice Seton.

But there was no time now for gathering wool; Vanessa shook off her reflections. Lesley was disembarking. She minced down the gangplank in her high-heeled boots, emitting a shrill little laugh when her ankles wobbled, her thin heel caught in a plank. One of her young male companions held her elbow while she extricated herself.

Then she was hurrying towards them, her pale blue eyes aglow at the sight of Amas. 'Oh, Dad!' Ignoring Vanessa, Lesley rushed into Amas' arms and pressed herself full-length against him, planting fervent kisses on his face at the corner of his mouth. Her companions left in haste.

Amas flushed brick red. Holding Lesley a little away, he kissed her rouged cheek and mumbled, 'Welcome home.'

Lesley stared up into his eyes for an instant, then turned to Vanessa. 'Mother.' In contrast the greeting was rude and cold.

Guilt and resentment struggled in Vanessa, and the former won. I have never really been a mother to her, not from the very start, Vanessa thought. Only Amas showed her affection; only Amas has given her love. What else could I expect?

And, resolving to do her utmost to win the girl to her, Vanessa smiled and took Lesley in her arms. 'Lesley, Lesley. It's so good to have you back again.'

But the voluptuous young body was stiff in her embrace, and Vanessa felt a strange distaste when the thrusting breasts rolled and flattened against her own body.

'Let's get out of this,' Amas directed. 'Our carriage is right over there to take us to the train.'

Lesley nodded, the feathers on her hat dancing with the motion. She took Amas' arm and matched her steps to his, forcing Amas to pause and urge Vanessa forward with them after she'd been jostled backwards by the mob of oncoming passengers.

Amas put his arms protectively around the women, calling out sharply, 'Look out!' to a hurrying soldier.

The soldier stepped aside in embarrassment, touching his helmet to the women, his hungry gaze raking Lesley from head to toe.

'I'd better go ahead,' Amas shouted, 'and clear a path. Stay right behind me.'

He shoved ahead with Lesley and Vanessa in his wake. There was an instant of confusion, when the women fell back a little and someone passed between the mother and daughter.

Two young Army officers sighted Lesley. 'I say, girlie,' one of them shouted, 'are you coming or going?'

'Coming,' Lesley retorted.

Vanessa took her daughter's arm and said sharply, 'Lesley.'

One of the officers murmured to the other and they laughed.

Too late Amas realised that his wife and daughter were no longer at his heels. He turned about, with an anxious look, and sized up the situation. 'Lesley,' he said in a tone of command. 'Stay close to me, I told you.'

He glared at the two young men. Abashed they beat a hasty retreat. When Vanessa was walking at Amas' side again, he said to her in a low voice, 'When we get to the depot, take her in the washroom and make her wash her face.'

'With pleasure.'

Uneasily Vanessa wondered if Lesley had heard the exchange and gathered she had; the full painted lips looked sulky, and Lesley shot her a hostile glance.

When they were in the carriage, heading for the depot, Amas addressed Lesley with a horrible false cheer, 'Well, Lesley, how did you leave London?'

135

'Under a cloud, Father, under a cloud,' she retorted flippantly, and Vanessa's heart sank. It was going to be very difficult to deal with this hard young stranger.

Vanessa longed to slap her when she noticed the shock and consternation on Amas' kindly face.

'What do you mean?'

Lesley laughed her shrill, tinkling laugh that so inevitably reminded Vanessa of Hester Stirling. 'The weather was dreadful, Father, as it always is in London. That's what I meant.'

Amas looked very little reassured but he managed a smile. 'Do things seem changed?' He made another effort.

Lesley glanced at the streets of Cape Town with contempt. 'Hardly at all. The war didn't make an enormous difference, did it?'

The cool ambiguity of her comment, the affected British intonation, struck off a spark of anger in Vanessa. No difference, she raged in silence, remembering the Boer children who had died in concentration camps, the starving, bloated natives, the torn bodies of the horses. The women and children mashed together in the mines; the stench of their sweat and detritus. The awful silence of the veld, denuded of the fleeing, frightened quachas, the springboks and gazelles.

'It did to a great number,' Vanessa lashed out in a quivering voice, observing that Amas' mouth was drawn down at the corners, that he was restraining himself with obvious difficulty.

'There was terrible suffering, Lesley,' he said tightly. But then, making another patent try at lightening the conversation, he essayed a smile, and added, 'We mustn't talk about the war now. It's over. Let's talk about you, Lesley. What did you do with yourself in London? You never wrote us much about it. You had a tutor, you said.'

Lesley raised her pencilled brows. 'He wasn't a patch on Mitchell Farley. It was an awful bore . . . and so was cousin Diana. I'm glad to be back with you – both, Father,' she amended.

Amas apparently felt he could make no further effort at the moment to draw her out, and Vanessa was too subdued even to begin. She watched Amas settle back uneasily on the cushions opposite, drawing a little away from Lesley's pressing thigh. They rode the rest of the way to the depot in silence.

Handing them down, Amas said, 'The train won't leave for a half hour. We have plenty of time.' He gave Vanessa a significant look. She nodded imperceptibly.

'Why don't we go to the washroom and freshen up?' she asked Lesley with that same terrible false brightness she had heard from Amas.

Lesley dug into her little purse and brought out a mirror, scrutinising her face and pursing her lips as if she were alone in her bedroom. Vanessa frowned with vexation. 'Oh, I'm all right, Mother, you go ahead, and freshen yourself.'

Vanessa tried not to hear the feline implication, so like Bea's.

'Go with your mother, Lesley.' Amas was stern now, dropping all pretence. 'I want you to wash that . . . stuff off your face. You don't look nice with it on.'

A pale fire flashed in the blue, dark-lashed eyes. 'You're the only one who doesn't think so, Father.'

'Go with your mother, Lesley.' This time there was no mistaking Amas' order.

Lesley said nothing in reply. Sullenly she wheeled about and led the way to the washroom, walking so fast that Vanessa almost had to run to keep up.

'Lesley,' she said sharply. 'Wait for me.'

Lesley stopped abruptly, waiting, with her back to Vanessa.

'As I live and breathe.'

At the sound of the familiar drawl, Lesley wheeled. Mitchell Farley was strolling towards them.

'It couldn't be . . . it *couldn't* be our little Lesley! Not this beautiful young woman!'

Vanessa almost screamed in her frustration. Mitchell Farley here, now, on this already awkward occasion. She prayed that Amas had not seen him. Farley's insinuating voice was exactly as Vanessa remembered, but his appearance was far more impressive. Now he dressed and carried himself with the stateliness befitting a director of DeVries. He had gained in strength and weight; his formerly pale face was ruddy with good living. But the oblique black eyes, with their mischievous glitter that reminded Vanessa of Comus, the lord of misrule, were bright and insidious as ever.

Her gorge rose when she watched his effect upon Lesley. Her daughter fairly bridled, moistening her full, red lips with her small pink tongue, breathing deeply to minimise her waist and thrust out her breasts to his notice. Lesley made a chortling sound between a groan and a giggle. 'Oh, yes, it's little Lesley.'

'Not so little any more,' Farley commented lazily, letting his black, shining gaze caress first the girl's face, then her body.

137

'I don't have to call you "Mister Farley" any more, do I?' Lesley asked huskily, blinking her blue eyes in a slow, coy fashion. Good God, Vanessa raged in silence, she's acting like . . . a whore.

'Indeed not.' Farley grinned in his devilish way. 'I hope you'll let me show you the new Cape Town. How long will you be here?'

'We're taking the next train,' Vanessa snapped.

'Why, Mrs Holder.' Farley's black brows swooped upward. 'Forgive me. I didn't see you.' His glance at Lesley seemed to say, 'I was so preoccupied with this lovely lady.'

It was a clumsy, patent lie; Vanessa had seen him stiffen for an instant when he caught sight of her, but the naive Lesley appeared to take his remark at face value. Her pale eyes glinted with coquettish satisfaction as she studied Farley and then Vanessa. Her mother wondered what that examination meant, just exactly what Beatrice had told Lesley during the years in England. Had she hinted that Mitchell Farley was in love with her sister? There was so much that Vanessa still didn't know. The idea chilled her.

Then Farley voiced almost the words Vanessa had so eerily intuited. 'I was just so . . . overpowered by the change in our Lesley, you see.' Once again Farley's black eyes met Vanessa's, full of the old yearning and admiration.

It was sad, she thought, to see Lesley simpering and bridling like this. They must get away.

'She has changed greatly.' Vanessa's reply was neutral, ambiguous. Farley grinned more widely. Vanessa damned his almost feminine agility at reading between her words.

'I'm afraid you must forgive us,' she said coolly. 'The train will be leaving soon.'

'Oh, but Mother,' Lesley protested. 'Father said we have lots of time.'

'She's absolutely right. I'm taking the very same train, and I dare not miss it. I would arouse the ire of the whole board of DeVries.'

This was even worse. Vanessa did not relish a meeting between Amas and Farley. Lesley, to her deep annoyance, looked quite impressed. 'You're with DeVries now, Mr – Mitchell?'

'Only one of their very junior directors.' He tossed it off with elegant carelessness, irritating Vanessa beyond measure.

'May I wait for you ladies? When you've come back from the, er, cloakroom, I'll escort you to the train. There's a very rough element in the depot these days.'

His oblique criticism of Amas' failure to escort them – he must know damned well that Vanessa would not have come to Cape Town alone – annoyed Vanessa more than anything else.

'My husband is waiting for us at the train,' she said coldly. 'It's not necessary.'

'Please. I insist.' Giving up, Vanessa took Lesley's arm, fairly pulling her into the women's retiring room.

'Lesley, I want you to wash your face,' she said quietly.

'Why were you so rude to Mitchell, Mother? Is it because you feel awkward?' Lesley faced her belligerently.

Waiting for a woman to smooth her hair and resume her hat, Vanessa faced the mirror and brushed at her own face with a handkerchief, removing a mythical flake of soot. When the woman had gone out, Vanessa demanded, 'What do you mean by that?'

'Never mind, Mother, Aunt Bea told me everything.'

Vanessa saw her own skin change colour. The matter of Lesley's face paint was for the moment forgotten. 'I don't know what "everything" is, Lesley,' she contrived to answer with a measure of calm. 'But whatever it is, we shall not discuss it in a public place. Now,' she thrust her handkerchief at Leslie, 'wipe off that rouge and lip pomade. Right now. And take the stuff off your eyes. This minute.'

Her tone was apparently effective. The sullen girl obeyed.

'That's much, much better,' Vanessa said gently, smiling. 'You're much too pretty to hide behind all that. You have no idea how much prettier you look now.'

'I look like a scarecrow.' Lesley's tone threatened imminent tears. 'A lot of women in London, of perfectly good position, paint their faces now.'

'Not "women" of sixteen, Lesley,' Vanessa retorted drily. 'And this is Cape Town, not London.'

'Don't remind me,' Lesley shot back. Gathering up her reticule she flounced out of the retiring room, again forcing Vanessa to quicken her step to keep up.

The immovable Farley was still waiting, and he offered his arm to Lesley, teasing her, 'How pale you've suddenly become. I hope our air doesn't disagree with you after the pleasures of London.'

Lesley bit her lip, shooting a resentful glance at Vanessa, who walked on silently at her side without another word to Mitchell Farley.

She was thankful that when they came to the train, Farley had the sense to make himself scarce; even more thankful for the fact that he had a seat in another car.

This had surely not been an auspicious beginning.

Even less auspicious were Lesley's constant complaints about the train and the long, monotonous journey, far shorter than Vanessa's first trip had been but still not to be compared, Lesley commented, with the splendours of European transportation.

Lesley averted her eyes from most of the dusty jumble of Kimberley, more motley than ever in its stage of rebuilding, expressing interest only in the two-storeyed splendour, the columned verandas, of the offices of DeVries. Amas did not even glimpse Farley until the passengers descended to the Kimberley depot – Farley had, to Vanessa's joyful relief, avoided the dining car at the hour the Holders dined, apparently not leaving his compartment.

But, catching sight of him, Amas looked like a thundercloud. 'The world of diamonds is a small one, isn't it?' he muttered to Vanessa, assiduously avoiding the other man. Through some good fortune he hadn't seen Lesley's smile, her yearning glances at the Englishman. Amas was intent on the bestowal of Lesley's copious baggage in the cart which would follow their buggy, too busy calling out to Sala and Kossee, 'Here she is at last. Lesley's home.'

Sala greeted Lesley warmly, with deep respect, but the lean young Kossee, who in the last months had shot up like a sap-filled tree, was abashed at Lesley's new, strange beauty. He was barely able to speak.

When Vanessa caught the flirtatious look that Lesley absently awarded to Kossee, the coldness with which she treated Sala, Vanessa's heart sank lower. Matters did not improve when they reached the bungalow and Lesley spoke to the gentle Ranee, the queenly Sehoiya in an imperious fashion. It seemed to Vanessa that Lesley had hardly set foot on African soil before new difficulties were crowding upon them.

The next day Vanessa got up at the usual hour to go with Amas to the mines. She asked Ranee not to disturb Lesley, who would likely sleep quite late, tired out as she was by her journey.

At sunset when she came back to the bungalow with Amas, Vanessa was dismayed to see that Lesley was nowhere in evidence. When questioned, a glowering Sehoiya told Vanessa that 'the young Misses' had required Sala to drive her into town that forenoon, and had taken Ranee with her. They had not come back. The report was heavy with the implication that Ranee had not been available to prepare dinner, which was now her duty, not the ageing Sehoiya's.

140

Vanessa answered Sehoiya as calmly as she could, trying to make light of it.

'The young Misses,' Sehoiya volunteered, 'said there were certain things she must buy from the stores.'

That seemed odd, for someone who had just arrived from London. Vanessa considered uneasily the fact that Mitchell Farley was in town on business for DeVries, but she made no mention of that to Amas at dinner. At least, she reflected, Lesley had had the good sense to take Ranee as a chaperone of sorts.

The moon was high when the two women heard the squeak and rattle of the buggy on the winding path to the bungalow. Vanessa was reading in the living room; Amas had gone out to the stable to talk to Kossee about the horses.

Vanessa put down her book and went out to the veranda. A worried-looking Sala was handing Lesley and Ranee down. 'We are very late, Misses,' he said. 'I ask your forgiveness.'

'That's all right, Sala,' she answered easily, having a strong suspicion, although Sala would never have said so, that it was not his doing. Lesley came regally up the path followed by Ranee, who was laden with bundles.

'Lesley,' Vanessa requested softly, 'why don't you give Ranee a hand?'

'What for?' Lesley stared at Vanessa. 'That's why I took her to town.' She spoke of Ranee as if the woman were a donkey, and Vanessa saw by the bright moonlight that Lesley's face was livid again with paint.

'Lesley,' Vanessa reproved angrily. 'Let me help you, Ranee.' Sala had gone to put the buggy away and take care of the horse. Vanessa relieved Ranee of some of the parcels and followed her into Lesley's room, where the native placed the bundles on a table, Vanessa tossing her burden on the bed. 'Thank you, Ranee,' she said, with a significant glance at Lesley. Ranee went out.

Lesley, ignoring Vanessa, went to the glass to examine her face. She calmly smoothed her hair.

Vanessa sat down on the bed. 'Lesley,' she began in a gently inquiring voice, 'why are you so late?'

'Because I had a lot of things to do, Mother. And then I had dinner with Mitchell at the club.'

Dear God, it was beginning already. 'And the servants? Did they get their dinner, too?'

'Really, Mother, how should I know? That's hardly any concern

141

of mine.' Lesley laughed, unfastening her dress. As she raised it over her head, Vanessa was once more surprised at the maturity of that young body. Lesley went to the clothes-press and took out a dressing gown made of heavy satin. She belted it around her narrow waist; its neckline formed a very deep vee over her heavy breasts.

'I'm surprised that you are so concerned over the servants, when . . .'

'You cannot treat Ranee as if she were a beast of burden, Lesley,' Vanessa broke in.

'. . . when,' Lesley resumed calmly, as if Vanessa had not spoken, 'it seems to me that the main offence is my dining with your lover.'

Vanessa took a gasping breath, too stunned at first to answer. Then she repeated, 'My *lover*.'

Lesley was at the glass again, taking down her hair. She picked up her hairbrush and began to brush her pale, shining hair with rhythmic, slow strokes, counting under her breath as she replied to Vanessa. 'Bea told me everything, you see.'

Struggling to overcome her horror and indignation, which threatened to render her speechless, Vanessa said, 'You made that remark before, Lesley. I want to know what it means.'

Without interrupting the tempo of her brushing, Lesley retorted, 'I'll be more than glad to tell you. Diana of course tried to keep me away from Aunt Bea, the whole time I was in London. Naturally. Because she didn't want me to hear what Bea had to say.'

'*What* did Bea have to say?' In her agitation Vanessa heard herself fairly shrieking. She got hold of herself and repeated, more quietly, 'What did Bea have to say to you, Lesley?'

'A great many things. One, that you took my father away from her, years ago, in New York . . . and, not content with that, you fell in love with Mitchell. He confirmed that to me, tonight.' Lesley threw down her brush and wheeled to face her mother, her pallid blue eyes glowing with anger. 'Bea *told* me you'd be jealous of me, just as you were always jealous of her. She said you would probably write to Diana and ask her to keep me away from Bea. You always hated her, didn't you, Mother, from the time you were little girls? Because she had all the beaux . . . and all you ever were able to do was play the piano. Until father came along; then you had to take him away from Aunt Bea. And then you couldn't even let her have Mr Dillon. She told me when he knew he was going to be fired from the mine, it drove him to shoot himself.' Lesley was trembling, her voice high, hysterical.

'Dear God! Stop it, Lesley. Stop it! None of this is true, none of it.' Vanessa got up and went to her daughter, taking her by the shoulders, shaking her, trying to shake some sense into that warped young consciousness. 'It's all a lie,' Vanessa pleaded with her in a low, urgent voice, dropping her hands from the girl's shoulders.

Lesley's palm shot out and slapped Vanessa, hard, on her face.

With the sharp blow something seemed to break, to melt inside Vanessa. She began to cry; deep, tearing sobs racked her body. She sank blindly down onto the bed. 'Lesley. Oh, Lesley. None of what you've been told is true. You've got to listen to me. Bea lied to you. So did Mitchell Farley.'

Lesley's eyes were flat; the child seemed impervious.

Suddenly the burden of her long-repressed guilt fell with its full weight on Vanessa Holder. Why should Lesley believe her, after all . . . why should she trust her? She had never been a proper mother to her since the child was born. Painfully Vanessa remembered turning her over to Ranee for nursing and care, the continual battle, as the baby Lesley grew to childhood, not to compare her to the foolish Hester.

Then, through her own selfishness, sending the girl to England at that delicate time of adolescence when the teetering scales of development could waver one way or the other. Whatever Hester had been to Vanessa, she had never abandoned her. She is my own creation, Vanessa reflected in her black awareness.

'You're crying now, Mother,' Lesley said with the terrible cruelty of the young. 'You didn't cry when I went to England. Did you while I was there, while the other girls were looking at me strangely, wondering why you weren't with me, as their mothers were?'

And Vanessa sensed the pain below her daughter's malice, heard it without resentment now, thinking again, she is what I made her.

'Please, Lesley,' she began with tortuous slowness. 'Please, let's . . . try to make peace. I'm your mother, Lesley. I love you.' With the saying of it Lesley knew what a sad lie that was. 'At least listen to me. You listened to Bea, and she lied to you. Let me tell you how it really was.'

Under the disfiguring cosmetics her daughter's face was pathetically childish, but her expression was still obdurate.

'Lesley, things were almost diametrically opposite to what Bea told you. You've got to believe me. When I met your father in New York,' Vanessa rushed on, to stem interruption, 'we fell in love with each other almost at once. Bea was . . . smitten with him, and made advances to him herself, which he rebuffed. She even went to his hotel.'

'I don't believe you,' Lesley retorted angrily.

'Be that as it may, I'm going to tell you anyway.' Vanessa was heartened to hear her own voice grow firmer, gain strength as she went on. 'Bea herself drove Sam Dillon to suicide. She was having an affair with Tony Seton . . . and, we all believed, with others. She didn't have the slightest interest in you, Lesley, ever. Except to use you in the battle between herself and me. She has never forgiven your father for not . . . wanting her.'

Ignoring the rest, Lesley lashed out, 'And I suppose you *do* have an interest in me?'

'Lesley.' Vanessa went to her daughter and put her arms around the resistant young body. 'At least we can be friends,' she suggested softly. 'If you . . . hate me so much, why did you come back to Kimberley? We allowed Martin to stay. If you had asked . . .'

'Because no one else would have me!' Lesley blurted, on the edge of tears. Vanessa could feel her tremble and tightened her grasp.

'What do you mean?'

'Diana couldn't wait to be rid of me, because of . . .' She stopped short.

'Because of what?'

'Nothing.' Vanessa wondered if it had to do with Lesley's young cousin Rupert, but decided not to press her. At least she was being open, more open than Vanessa had hoped for. 'Bea would have asked me, but Captain Seton didn't want me.'

Vanessa was sceptical: Bea had never paid the least attention to Anthony Seton's wishes, or anyone else's for that matter. Likely she was not eager to expose her husband to the attractions of a nubile young girl. However, Vanessa let it pass.

'Otherwise, you would have stayed?' she asked sadly.

Lesley drew back, avoiding her eyes. Then she said, 'Yes. But now I'm glad I didn't. Otherwise I would never have found Mitchell again.'

One moment the girl was a reticent, resentful young woman and the next a rash, frank child, too old and too young at once. Vanessa was touched by her vulnerable air.

'Lesley, Mitchell Farley is at least ten years older than you, he's . . . don't you see, a young girl can't go on pursuing a man like that? It can only end in trouble.'

Lesley smiled, and it was not a pleasant sight.

'When you were explaining things to me, you didn't give me an explanation about Mitchell. The fact is, he was your lover, wasn't he . . . and just got tired of you?'

'That's untrue. That's outrageous, Lesley,' Vanessa said angrily.

'That's the point of all of this, isn't it, Mother? You just can't bear to think of us together. Well, I love him . . . I love him already. And I think he's falling in love with me. Nothing you do or say can keep us apart.'

Vanessa opened her mouth to reply, but she was overcome with a cold feeling of defeat. She would never be able to convince her daughter of what Mitchell Farley was. But there was one thing she could, and would do. She would keep Lesley from ruining her life, if she had to tie her to the bedpost, Vanessa decided coldly. Even if it meant sending her back to England, away to school. Perhaps that was the only solution.

'We'll see about that,' she said calmly. 'I imagine your father will have something to say.'

'Father is only a man,' Lesley replied in a silky voice, 'just as Grandfather was, according to Bea.'

The soft words were like successive blows; Vanessa reeled, a chill of horror prickling her skin like the nails of icy fingers. She remembered vividly what Martin Stirling had told them after Sam Dillon had eloped with Bea. What nightmare version of the truth had Bea given to this confused and precocious child?

Just now she couldn't bear to know, even if she suspected. And Lesley could sense that, Vanessa knew, was triumphing in it. It was so hard to love this girl, no matter how valiantly she tried. It was almost like having Beatrice back again.

'I don't want to hear any more, Lesley. Not tonight.' Without saying anything else she went out of the room, realising she had made a glaring tactical error. She should have stayed, should have demanded to know what the teasing statement signified. But now she was drained, exhausted, and feeling totally incompetent and defeated.

Amas was already in bed when Vanessa entered their room. At the first sight of her face, he said, 'It didn't go well, I take it.'

Vanessa shook her head wearily and went behind the screen to undress.

'Where was she all that time?'

She hesitated, dreading to tell Amas the truth. But it was unfair not to, perhaps it would be fatal to hesitate. 'I'll tell you in a moment.'

145

Quickly she put on her nightgown and, smoothing her hair, emerged from behind the screen.

'Please, Amas, don't . . .' She held up one hand, beseechingly, and went towards the bed. Pulling back the coverlet, she lay down beside him. 'She went to see Mitchell Farley.'

Amas tensed, flushing, his skin darkening by the faint golden light. 'Farley . . . Farley. That bastard. First he tries to seduce my wife, and then my daughter. I'll . . .'

'Amas,' Vanessa said sharply. 'Lesley went to *see* him. He took her to dinner at the Kimberley Club. That's all.'

'That's *all*?' He twisted around to stare at her, his motion swirling and roiling the sheets; a hem flicked her cheek and involuntarily she gave a little cry, disproportionate to the feathery blow of the cambric.

'Please.'

He subsided onto the pillows for an instant with an exasperated exhalation. Then he snapped, 'How do you *know* that was all, Vanessa?'

She could not prevent a hot little crawling of resentment and irritation. He had not even asked her what they had talked about; he was concerned only with the dubious chastity of his daughter. At once Vanessa was dismayed by her own estimate – *dubious*. But that was just what it was; she felt that strongly.

'The event was not my doing,' she answered brusquely.

He reached over and took her hand. 'Of course it wasn't. I'm sorry.'

'In some ways, Amas, the dinner with Mitchell Farley is the least of our worries.' And she repeated to him what Lesley had said to her, told him of the whole conversation. She concluded gloomily, 'I don't think I handled it too well.'

Looking at him she was saddened by his expression of anxiety and hurt. 'Not . . . perfectly, perhaps,' he conceded in a cautious, gentle manner. 'But I'm sure a good deal better than anyone else would have.' His reassurance, while welcome, sounded false to her, and he did not look at her directly, but stared straight ahead.

'I think,' he said slowly, 'that I am going to have another little chat with Mr Farley.'

Vanessa was overcome with dread. But she strove to keep her voice light and calm. 'Not like the other one, I trust.'

'No. No, I promise you. I'll behave this time.' He smiled at her.

'Amas . . . she is only a child. Perhaps we're making too much of this.'

'She's no child,' he replied in a decided fashion. 'Not any more, Vanessa.'

She was disturbed by the faint dart of jealousy that pierced her; she recalled the blooming body with the heavy breasts, the flowerlike skin emerging from behind the washed-away paints, the full and sensuous mouth. Good heavens, she thought, when I was only sixteen . . . Vanessa tried to dismiss the comparison.

'Amas . . .'

'Yes?' She imagined his reply was a little absent, the touch upon her hand perfunctory. He was still intent on his own thoughts, probably the coming conference with Mitchell Farley. Probably. Or was it something else, she wondered, still with that dismaying itch of jealousy? 'What is it? What were you about to say?'

She hadn't imagined it. His question was almost impatient.

'Do you think this is all my fault?' she pleaded. 'Because I have never been able to be a . . . real mother?'

'Of course it isn't,' he said firmly, and this time his pressure on her hand was strong and consoling. 'It's the war,' he murmured vaguely. 'And that rotten, decadent Farley.' Somehow she felt he wasn't answering her question. 'We are what we are, Vanessa.'

In other words, she judged in resentful silence, Vanessa Holder was capable of a good number of things – of coaxing magical sounds from a piano's keys, of defiance, endurance, shrewdness and love. Capable of throwing away the world for the love of one man. But not of being a mother. That was in his answer.

'And I love everything you are,' he added, softly, moving to her to take her in his embrace. 'It was not your fault, or mine, that the war came . . . that Beatrice happened to be in London, and that Lesley came under her influence. Believe me, I am going to have a talk with Lesley, too, as well as Mitchell Farley. I heard the two of you in her room, but I didn't want to interrupt by coming in. I thought it best for you to talk with her.'

'And a royal mess I made of it,' she said despondently.

'Stop that. I told you. We are what we are. We do what we can. And Vanessa, you do almost everything superlatively well.'

Almost.

His unrelenting honesty would not let him say that she was anything but a failure as a mother.

'Vanessa . . .' He was smiling at her now, caressing her, and his mouth lowered to hers for a long, sweet kiss.

She was shamed now, mortified that she had been jealous of their

147

own child; it was an emotion too shaming to admit even to herself.

Surely Amas would be able to bring Lesley to her senses, to command cooperation from Mitchell Farley. Amas Holder had never failed at anything, she thought, exultant, as she melted into his embrace.

CHAPTER TEN

Amas Holder strode through the porticoed entrance of the imposing, turreted building that housed DeVries.

'Mr Farley, please,' he said to the man on duty. 'Amas Holder.'

The name brought the man to respectful attention. Calling out to another clerk to relieve him, he personally escorted Amas to Farley's office on the second floor.

Mitchell Farley was seated behind a heavy desk in an absurdly elegant room according to Amas' standards. Had his mission been less serious he would have laughed aloud. Farley's clothes, too, in contrast to his own rough gear, were dandyish. He realised the renewed force of his dislike for this effete bastard.

Farley rose, smiling, his slanted black eyes surveying Amas with critical amusement. 'Well, Holder,' he drawled, 'this is a pleasant surprise. Have you come to sell out to DeVries at last?' He held out his soft-looking hand.

Amas ignored the hand. Smothering an obscene retort, he replied, 'Not likely. I've come to talk to you about my daughter.'

'Now that's a pleasant topic, Holder.' Amas came within an ace of hitting him. Farley sat down again and settled back comfortably in his chair. 'Sit down, sit down, why don't you?'

'No, thanks. I won't be here long enough for that. It's very simple. I'm warning you to stay away from my child.' Amas found it was more difficult than he'd expected to contain his belligerence.

'Good heavens, Holder.' Farley smiled. 'You once hired me to be with her. And she is hardly a child. She is a very charming young lady who sought *me* out, let me emphasize; it was not the reverse . . . and I only did the polite, by taking the young lady to dinner.'

A rude word exploded from Amas.

' "The polite", Farley? My daughter fancies herself in love with you. That's a good deal of "politeness".' Amas leaned threateningly over the shining desk, glaring at the other man.

There was a flicker of apprehension in the dark eyes but the smooth face was determinedly unreadable.

'Come now, Holder. Surely you do not hold me responsible for a young girl's fancies? That is the rankest injustice.' Mitchell Farley smiled.

The smile maddened Amas. 'Directly responsible. I'm through parrying with you, man. Just stay away from her. You've been warned.'

'Or . . . what, Holder?' Farley met his eyes in a challenging way. 'Are you threatening me?'

'Damned straight.'

Before the other man could say anything, Amas turned on his heel and stormed out of Farley's sanctum.

Striding along the dusty thoroughfares of Kimberley, Amas reproached himself for his indiscretion. He had really meant to hold onto his temper. Now it would be all over Kimberley by nightfall. But to hell with it; the bastard couldn't be allowed to seduce his own daughter, an innocent young girl.

Amas mounted his horse and headed towards the Big Hole thinking of his last interview with Lesley.

Of course he believed Vanessa; she was incapable of a lie. And yet it seemed difficult to reconcile her account of the conversation with Lesley with the one he'd had with his daughter. She was a wistful child, beneath all that surface attempt at sophistication, avid for the love Amas and Vanessa had failed to give her at a very critical time of her life. He was stung, recalling Leslie's face, the trembling young voice. So pretty, he thought, and so misguided. A positive sitting duck for that smooth, immoral bastard. And so much like Vanessa, in many ways.

In some ways – and he felt a strange little twinge of guilt for thinking it – more feminine, because Lesley had none of Vanessa's independence. Where Vanessa had that air of stern passion, which indeed aroused him strongly, gave her a quality of elusiveness that would titillate him forever, Lesley was soft and dependent. There would never be the slightest question in Amas' mind as to Lesley's ambitions. They would always centre around a man.

Amas smiled to himself. Then he thought, but he must be a worthier man than that effete contriver.

He was so lost in reflection that it was several moments before he realised someone was calling his name, and it had the sound of repetition. Amas looked around.

It was his old acquaintance, Aaron Ledbetter, proprietor of the Digger's Rest saloon. 'Say there, Holder!' Ledbetter strolled towards him with his shambling, bearlike gait, his grin merely hinted at behind his shaggy beard, an amiable light in the small, shrewd eyes obscured by overhanging brows. 'You were in a brown study. You must have heard the news already, then. Already plotting to take over?'

Amas grinned back and, leaning over in the saddle, grasped Ledbetter's hand. He hadn't been a customer of Ledbetter's for many years now, apart from an occasional quick drink. But they constantly ran into each other in the street. Amas had always liked the fellow. 'Whoa! I was thinking about my family. The problems of a father.'

'I wouldn't know.' Ledbetter was a confirmed bachelor.

'What did you mean, "plotting", Aaron? Take over what?'

Ledbetter shifted his tobacco-plug to the other cheek and drawled, 'Where've you been this morning, Amas? The Pretoria mine. The boys have been jawing about it all the morning. You married men miss all the news,' he twitted. 'But like I always say, if I had your luck, I wouldn't be single.'

Amas smiled absently, hearing the oft-repeated phrase, and reiterated, 'What's up with the Pretoria mine? This is something new.'

'Damned straight it's new. New as last week. Word just came on the wires to Kimberley this morning.' Aaron Ledbetter chuckled. 'Mark my word, DeVries is going to lose out on this; they're still jawing about it right now. If you get a move on, you can get it first. I'm here to tell you, it won't be five years before that mine in Pretoria does as good as DeVries. They're saying there's a few million carats out there.'

The saloon keeper could not conceal his delight. A rebellious and independent Australian, Ledbetter had always hated Cecil Rhodes and his company, always pulled for Amas. In the early days he'd even invested some in the Holder mines, and realised a substantial profit.

'Get yourself over to the post office, boy. They know all about it. Then, if I were you, I'd get my tail to Pretoria.'

'Thanks, Aaron. I'm going to do just that.'

Amas turned his horse and cantered towards the post office, feeling that old excitement begin. A new mine – a new world to conquer. It was like a fire in his blood, and he felt like a kid again.

Then all the ramifications of the discovery burst upon him in all their glory. In five years, Aaron had predicted, the mine would 'do as good as DeVries'. That was one in the eye for Farley, Amas thought, mirth bubbling up inside him. Maybe that was one reason Farley looked so funny today when Amas first walked into the office.

Amas Holder was so exhilarated he almost laughed out loud as he dismounted and walked into the post office to get the whole story.

Used to the old established mines of Kimberley, Vanessa was struck by the primitive bareness of the crude mine in Pretoria. It was little more than a towering mound of rocky earth, like the residence of some lost, savage cliff-dwelling tribe, looming over a scooped out pit of dust where horse-drawn carts lumbered to and fro.

Standing on that eminence she shaded her eyes and turned to survey Amas in earnest conversation with the banty Irishman who had discovered the mine. The lonely prospector had found a three-carat diamond on a nearby farm and had seen a *kopje*, a hill, like the ones he'd seen in Kimberley. The *kopje* was the mouth of a pipe to what was now the mine.

Vanessa saw the men gesticulating. And then they were shaking hands. Amas gave her a triumphant wave and she hurried towards him. The Irishman was walking away with slow steps. Amas stood grinning in the brilliant sun and she warmed to his elation. 'It's ours!' he shouted, closing the distance between them with a few long strides. He took her in his arms. 'It's ours, Vanessa. I named a price that Harrigan couldn't turn down. This is going to be the biggest thing since Kimberley.'

She hadn't seen him so excited in years, not since before the war, when they had made their last spectacular find in the Big Hole. With all her heart she wished they were alone, that Lesley had not come with them. Otherwise she could stay here, with him, in the shack, and be on hand for the first great treasure hunt.

'Now, I've got to talk to that fellow about selling the farm. It won't be easy; he's already been driven off two by other mines. But maybe you can help me to convince him.' Amas laughed, as carefree as a boy, apparently forgetful of the matters that weighed so heavily upon Vanessa – the intrusion of Lesley on this fresh paradise, the burden of her daughter's resentful company.

But she managed a bright smile, and said, 'Of course I'll come.'

In the carriage he said, 'Afterwards, darling, I suppose you'd better get back to Jo'burg.' He used the localism for Johannesburg, the teeming city fifty miles away through which they'd passed on the day-long journey northward from Kimberley, the wearisome trip that took nearly as long as reaching Kimberley from the Cape. 'We've left Lesley alone long enough.'

A trifle sharply, Vanessa retorted, 'At her insistence, Amas. She was quite tired out from the trip, she said. Which she didn't want to make in the first place.'

'I know that.' His reply was somewhat cool, but then he seemed to relent. He took her hand. 'I'm sorry it has to be this way, Vanessa. I know you want to be on hand, but I don't know what else we can do.'

'We could make her come here, make her obey, as a child should.' Vanessa could not prevent the snappish reply.

'I am not her warden,' he countered in a hard voice. Vanessa felt the tears gathering in a knot in her throat; it was the nearest they had ever come to a quarrel.

'But you are her father.' She heard her voice quiver.

Amas stopped the carriage. 'Vanessa, Vanessa. I'm sorry.' Holding the reins in one big hand, he put his other arm around her and kissed her. 'I'm sorry I snapped at you. But you know it has to be this way – I can't imagine Lesley in a shack.'

Somehow the rueful remark took all the joy from the embrace. In resentful silence she leaned back as he resumed the journey.

As he had predicted, the Boer farmer was not in a mood to talk of selling. He told them angrily that the farm would be sold after he was dead, and not an hour before.

Dejected, Amas drove Vanessa to the train. 'You're sure you'll be all right alone?' he asked, but the question seemed perfunctory to her. She was still feeling raw over his exaggerated concern for Lesley, and what she considered his inferior concern for her.

'Of course I will. It's a very brief journey, Amas. Get going, now. You know there's still a lot to see to.'

He nodded, his eyes already blank with distraction. After a hasty kiss, he put her on the train, where she quickly found a seat and watched him driving off.

When she got back to the hotel in Johannesburg she found the note from Lesley. The girl, and all her possessions, were gone.

Vanessa felt weak-kneed; she sank down on the bed with the note still clutched in her hand. She almost knew what it would say before she opened it.

At last with great reluctance she unfolded it and read, 'I have gone

152

back to Cape Town. Mitchell and I are going to be married. There is no way you can stop me.' The note was signed simply, 'Lesley', without any form of apology or affection.

Vanessa stared at the few curt phrases then crumpled the note in her hand. She had made light of Amas' apprehensions and all the time he'd been right.

And she had guessed nothing, done nothing.

But there was still something she could do now. Vanessa smoothed the note and put it on the table, snatching up the key to their set of rooms. Still trembling, with a queasy feeling in her stomach, Vanessa locked the door hastily and ran down the stairs to the desk.

She dreaded the interview with the Afrikaaner there – he was apparently a Boer, and still exhibited great hostility, under a veneer of ingratiating manners, towards the *uitlanders*. However, this was no time for hesitation. Vanessa approached the man with a tentative smile.

'I wonder if you could help me, please?'

The man regarded her coldly with his small blue eyes, an artificial smile pasted on his lips. 'Possibly, my *vrouw*.'

How she detested this man. 'Could you tell me, please, when the last train left for Kimberley?'

'Surely, *vrouw*, you mean the *next* train?' His eyebrows mocked her, as if to say, how foolish they are, these women.

'I mean the last train,' she snapped.

'Are you referring to a train for passengers, or a train for *vracht*, freight?'

'A passenger train,' she said, almost in tears.

'Ah . . . that left than an hour ago.' Seeing her face fall, the man appeared to delight in her dismay. 'Now, the *next* train, for *vracht*, will be leaving . . .'

Vanessa turned away without thanks, unable to stand the sight of his almost evil grin, and retraced her steps. The war, it seemed, would not really be over for a long, long time.

Back in the room she threw herself into a chair with a sensation of overpowering gloom. There was little point now in going to the depot, since the train was long departed. She wished desperately for Amas' return.

The hours were endless; she tried to distract herself with a book, but it was no good, and she was too low-spirited to go down to dinner.

153

At last she heard his light knock and rushed to the door.

As soon as he saw her face, Amas asked, 'What is it? Something's wrong. Where's Lesley?'

In answer Vanessa went to the table and got the note, handing it to him. His face darkened with worry and anger.

'God damn it, I knew it. I knew it,' he muttered, balling up the note in his fist and tossing it on the floor. 'We should have watched her more closely, Vanessa.'

He had still not embraced her, nor given her any sign of welcoming. She knew he meant '*You* should have watched her'. Overriding her pained resentment was another emotion, one so faint it was barely recognisable – a shamed relief that Lesley was gone, with her disruptive influence on their lives.

'If she is so determined to be married,' she responded in a defensive way, 'how can we stop her? You yourself said that you are not her "warden", Amas.'

'I said too damned many things.' His face was still like a thundercloud. 'And we only know that *Lesley* intends to be married; we have no guarantee of the good faith of Mitchell Farley. We'd better get started at once. I'm going to Cape Town.'

'And the mine?' she asked weakly, knowing it was useless to protest.

'That is hardly the great question now.' His voice was cold. 'In any event, I was about to tell you we can leave, anyway. Nothing further can be done until we can buy that farm, which is not foreseeable at the moment.'

She did not answer for an instant. He studied her and, apparently seeing the pain on her face, took her in his arms. 'I'm sorry, my darling. I'm sorry I sounded so angry at you. None of this is your fault, or mine, really. I lay it all at Farley's door. And he is going to answer to me, I promise you.'

During Martin Holder's early months in London, although he never wrote it outright to his parents, he had been fairly longing for home. That first chill, grey November had sapped his spirits; then he endured the lonely Christmas holiday. After that, when he was enrolled in the country preparatory school by Diana, everything had gone a little better, even if it seemed to him he'd never be really warm again.

Accustomed to the long veld and the wider, taller skies of Africa, Martin had at least found consolation in the country space and was out of doors as often as he could manage. The outside life back home, where he had clambered up and down the walls of the Big Hole like a monkey, and wrestled and run so many hours with Kossee, had toughened him beyond the other fellows in his form. The seniors' ragging and hazing left him unmoved and undismayed; in no time at all he was a relentless player of rugger, excelled in boxing and became greatly respected for these achievements.

Mitchell Farley's tutoring had brought him to the level of the better scholars, therefore the academic side of his schooling presented no difficulties.

The greatest thing was his constant dragging ache for Kimberley, for the dogs and ostriches, and for Kossee, his constant companion. The fellows at school all seemed to think the blacks were little more than screaming savages, painted, feathered and bespeared, in a perpetual state of uprising. But beyond correcting some of the boys' more absurd statements, Martin did not bother to enlighten them much. He sensed that they would never really understand; that he himself was something of an oddity, having actually been born 'out in the colonies', and living there so much of his life.

The war, which to the other boys was a matter of passionate interest, seemed quite unreal to Martin Holder, aside from a natural apprehension about his parents' and Kossee's safety. During the terrible siege, however, Martin followed the news with total intentness. He was not a prayerful person, but during that black time he prayed every night, in secret, for the lives of those he had been forced to leave.

Of the two, he missed his father most; they had always been such good companions. Amas Holder stood head and shoulders, in every way, above the fathers of his companions. Martin's mother, on the other hand, had never seemed like a mother at all, certainly unlike the plump, well-upholstered and twittering matrons who visited their sons at the school. Martin's mother had been at once a jolly chum and a distant goddess; thinking of that, Martin reflected on the marvellous strangeness of it. He remembered vividly how she looked in her divided skirt and helmet, riding to the mines with his father; the times she had frolicked with him and Kossee, practically like another boy. And then those times he would come upon her, playing the piano, sitting upright and graceful at the keyboard, with the lamplight glimmering on her golden hair. Then she had been a goddess, like that Rossetti poem about the 'blessed damozel', which Martin secretly loved, even if he twitted the English master with the other fellows.

Yes, Martin's mother, whom he loved dearly but had never

understood at all, was nothing like the others. Martin proudly displayed pictures of his mother and father in his room, none of Lesley – he confided that his sister was an 'awful wet', and since the other fellows had sisters, too, they fervently agreed – and the boys remarked that she was 'smashingly beautiful'. When one had made an impudent remark about the brevity of his mother's hair, however, Martin had thrashed him soundly. Thereafter the boy treated her image with greater respect.

School wasn't bad, but when the spring hols came, Martin was not sorry to return to London for a time. Spring was better, although still quite cold, and Martin began to fall under the spell of its swift variety, to enjoy some of London's alien splendours, the Guard and the Tower and the plays.

That summer he encountered the decisive factor, the real turning-point in his life's direction. With his friend Wertheimer from school, with whom he felt a particular kinship – Wertheimer was a rich Jew, Martin a rich colonial, so both were outsiders in a way – Martin visited the London offices of Dunkensreuter, managed by Wertheimer's uncle. There Martin met Wertheimer's older cousin, from Berlin, and his old excitement over that familiar pebble, the diamond, was reawakened in an utterly new form.

Watching the sorting, Martin had impressed Wertheimer and his cousin with his amazing sense of value; Martin Holder seemed to have a natural genius for sorting and evaluating that glimmering treasure which his father mined.

'A busman's holiday for you, isn't it, Holder?' Wertheimer joked with Martin.

'In a way,' Martin admitted and, with a kind of certainty beyond rudeness or impudence, said to the seasoned sorter, 'Not those, sir. I think you'll find they belong there.' He indicated the trough of less valuable stones.

'Jehoshaphat, boy, I haven't even weighed them or examined them yet.' The sorter looked at Martin irritably. However, when he had concluded those operations, he said to Wertheimer's cousin, 'The boy's right, you know. You have quite an eye, young man.' The sorter twinkled at Martin.

'Say, maybe you should go into business with us, Martin,' Wertheimer remarked, half in jest.

His cousin, however, did not smile. 'Perhaps you really should,' he said seriously to Martin Holder.

It seemed a dazzling idea to Martin – to work with the commodity he knew so well and loved, in the setting of this great, thrilling metropolis. He was not enamoured of the idea of going on to the University; Wertheimer wasn't going, rich as his family was. He was going to quit school when he reached sixteen and go into the business. Why, indeed, shouldn't Martin follow suit? He would write to his mother and father, sound them out. After all, his father hadn't even gone to prep school, and he was one of the smartest men Martin had ever known. Martin had a feeling Amas Holder would not stand in his way.

Amas didn't, and joyfully Martin looked forward to the day when he would be free of what seemed to him the childish atmosphere of the school, with its silly pranks and rigid discipline, its rotten food and baby curfews, to pursue the life of a man.

The only drawback was, he'd still miss the folks and Africa. But even that ache had eased; as time went on, with new delights and discoveries, it was easing more, practically disappearing. And of course he would always go back to visit.

For now there was the excitement of the majestic city. And it wouldn't be long, Martin reflected, before he and Wertheimer would really be men, old enough to share a flat and move away from home. That brought to mind a whole new mystery and excitement – the matter of women. Martin couldn't fool Wertheimer as he had tried to fool the other fellows. And his friend in turn could not fool Martin. Neither of them really knew yet what it was like, to . . . associate with a woman. But that, too, would come soon, with the other delights of the promising future.

Meanwhile, by the year of 1902, Martin Holder was tall and stalwart for a fifteen-year-old. He looked a good deal older, as his friend could attest when the two were going to a matinée, strolling along Piccadilly, and Martin was frequently accosted by young ladies with brightly painted faces offering numerous diversions. Martin sometimes wanted to accept the offers, but the more worldly Wertheimer warned him about the possibility of diseases and trouble with the police since the boys were under-age.

Martin's Aunt Diana often told him that he was becoming very handsome and was 'the image' of his father's picture. Already Martin stood nearly six feet tall, sinewy and broad-shouldered as a result of his participation in sports and the native toughness he had inherited from Amas Holder and developed in the freer vastness of South Africa. The first time Martin tried to shave the few light hairs on his jutting chin he studied himself in the glass – he did, certainly, have the same ferocious brown eyes his father had, which his mother always said looked like a lion's, and likewise the mane of hair, thick and springing. Martin got the picture of his father and put it up to the glass beside his own image. Yes, by Jove, they looked like brothers.

The knowledge made Martin very proud, because there was no man he admired as much as he admired his father. Therefore he was even more pleased when his cousin suggested that he visit a professional photographer, a delineator of society on a small West End side street, to have new pictures taken to send to his parents.

On that day in June 1902, Martin had completed his appointment and was leaving the studio. He took a deep, grateful breath of the mild air, smiling to think of Wertheimer's wry comment, 'the day we have summer in England'. Martin was always amused to hear Londoners complain that it was eighty in the shade, remembering the scorching summers on the veld.

However, the pale sun felt good on his shoulders, and Martin was proud of his appearance, as fine as any Mayfair dandy's, as he strolled along. He thought of the pictures with anticipation, and the pleasure they would bring his parents. He wondered how Lesley was getting along in Africa, but he did not linger long on that.

He and his sister had grown poles apart; in the last three years she had become more alien to him than ever, incomprehensible and querulous, forever quarrelling with their good-natured cousin, unable or unwilling to talk with Martin about anything but fashions and young men.

No, he did not want to think of Lesley right now, when he was feeling so grand. It had been too bloody awful when they caught her with Rupert in his room that night.

Throwing his shoulders back, holding his head high, Martin strolled forward, determinedly concentrating on the happy future and the work he was to do next year.

'Good Lord! It couldn't be!'

In his absent-mindedness, Martin had almost collided with an elaborately dressed lady bearing a ruffled parasol the colour of a bright rose. Startled and chagrined, he stammered, 'Oh, I say, I beg your pardon.' He touched his hat.

Then he recognised her. It was his Aunt Bea. It must have been two years since he'd seen her, although certainly he'd heard enough of her around Diana's house. His cousins mentioned Bea in freezing tones.

158

'Good God,' she said. Martin was shocked. Ladies did not generally use the Deity's name in this free fashion. 'You're Amas to the life, Martin Holder. Amas younger and all togged out so splendidly.'

Martin did not know how to answer. This was awfully awkward. He couldn't even say 'It's been a long time', without recalling the unmentionable truth – that Beatrice Seton was unwelcome at the house of her cousin-in-law Diana. But he offered, 'It's . . . nice to see you, Aunt Bea.'

She looked amazingly young and pretty; the rose-coloured shelter cast a flattering light on her skin and made her large dark eyes glow. She wore a pert hat of palest grey trimmed with flowers the colour of her parasol and a tight-fitting matching dress that exposed a good deal of her . . . chest, Martin reflected. He swallowed. She really looked unusually nice, he thought.

Bea smiled up at him. 'You must take pity on your old auntie, you big, handsome darling.' She fluttered her lashes. 'I only live a step from here. You absolutely must come to tea and give me all the news from home.'

She really wasn't so awful, Martin thought. He wondered why Diana disliked her so. 'Why, yes, of course,' he consented, the habit of respect and obedience still strong in him.

'Do give me your arm, dear boy,' she commanded gently. 'I've been rushing about and am utterly done in.'

He obeyed. She leaned rather heavily against him and he felt her heavy breast roll against his biceps. Horrified, he felt a kind of livening, a stirring in the area of his loins. This was his aunt, and he had no business to feel that way. Yet in so many ways she was practically a stranger, a mysterious person whispered about, disapproved of, and that gave her an aura none of his other female relatives had.

His unreined thoughts allowed him to marvel that the neighbouring breast felt so . . . plainly exposed. He'd thought that all women wore some kind of corset thing that would make them feel stiff and . . . hidden. Of course, when he'd danced with girls, it was always about a foot away. Why, he'd never even kissed one, much less held her close.

'You are so silent, my dear,' Bea murmured, glancing up into his face. Martin could sense the heat of confusion and shame darkening his cheeks. She leaned more heavily on him and once more he felt that staggering dart of hotness from his arm, shooting towards his loins; with even greater dismay he realised the painful ascension of his aroused flesh.

It was a relief to hear her say, 'Here we are.' He must not go on with such thoughts. It was wrong; it was horrible. They were climbing the steps of a trim Georgian house.

'Is, er . . . my uncle at home?' Martin queried and heard his voice crack. Damn it all, he sounded like a little kid.

'I'm afraid not, my dear Martin. You will have to make do with me today,' Bea said softly, unlocking the door and standing aside for him to enter. He realised that she had not rung the bell for a servant to open to them.

He stepped into the dim hall, smelling flowers and the musky scent of her perfume. 'It's the servants' day out,' Bea added. 'So I fear, also, that you will have to put up with my amateurish service.' She gave a small tinkling laugh, and Martin felt even more uncomfortable. The look in her great black eyes, the moistening of her red, half-parted lips reminded him of things that had little to do with aunts.

'Here, my dear, let me have your things.' Recalled to politeness, he snatched off his hat. She took it from him, and their fingers brushed. 'Take off your coat, Martin. Make yourself comfortable, darling.'

She helped him remove his jacket and hung it away in a closet, where she put his hat on a shelf. Then she turned back to him, breathing, 'Let me look at you. Why, you've grown into such a *man*.' Her dark gaze held his, and he could see puzzling things in its depths. 'You are the spitting image of Amas,' she added in a throaty tone.

That pleased him inordinately, but he was startled when she suddenly traced the breadth of his shoulders with her hands, and ran her fingers down his hard arms. 'My, my, so *strong*.'

He shivered.

'Are you chilly, Martin?' She smiled at him and once again fluttered her thick darkened lashes.

'Not at all,' he muttered, sharply aware of her perfumed smell, exotic as a Far Eastern bazaar, and something else – some hot, moist aroma that inevitably aroused in him the imagined scenes of golden flesh and writhing, barely veiled bodies of strange, exciting women.

'Well!' she said with sudden brightness, dropping her hands. 'Let's have tea. Or shall we be naughty and take something stronger? After all, it is nearly five o'clock in the afternoon.' She grinned in a conspiratorial fashion.

'Why not?' he retorted in an imitation of the worldly Wertheimer. He'd never had much to drink beyond a glass of wine at dinner and this was all very titillating.

'Splendid!' She divested herself of her hat and went to a handsome cabinet in the corner of the sitting room. Following her, Martin reflected that it was a jolly room, not at all like his cousin's, filled with low divans and great pillows tossed in various corners.

'What do you think of my little Bohemia?' she asked lightly, pouring out two glasses of sherry.

He recognised at once the reference to the opera, and ventured, 'You make a charming Mimi, Aunt Bea.'

Coming to him, holding out his glass, she seemed to glow. 'How clever of you . . . young Rodolfo.'

He took his glass from her fingers and they touched glasses. Then, as she continued to stare into his eyes, Martin realised what it meant when she called him by that name. Rodolfo, the lover of Mimi. He couldn't believe he had heard aright, couldn't credit what was happening. This woman was his aunt, the sister of his own mother. Aunts and nephews didn't talk to each other like this, look at each other like this.

And yet they were doing so, at this very moment. Incredulous and shamed, Martin felt that relentless stirring of his flesh, that hotness in his very vitals. He tried to will both away; surely she had meant nothing by it except a joke, a silly pleasantry. He made a valiant effort to control his runaway sensations.

'Come, sit down, my dear.' She took his hand with her free one, leading him to one of the dimly lit corners of cushions. 'Relax yourself on the Baghdad couch,' she ordered coyly.

Martin sank down awkwardly, setting his glass on an uncarpeted portion of the floor. With surprising grace Bea coiled herself down beside him, her ruffled skirt sliding upward to expose a generous portion of her shapely, pink-stockinged leg. That hot, sweet, insinuating scent was very strong from her.

'Do you know what I'm going to do?' she asked in a whimsical tone. 'I'm going to slip off my shoes, and be really comfy. Why don't you, Martin?'

He watched her unfasten one of her patent leather boots, then the other, and toss them away. 'All right. Sure,' he agreed, and took off his own shoes. He felt peculiarly naked and strange without them.

'It's nice to wiggle your toes, isn't it?' She suited the action to the word; he saw that her toenails were painted; they shone under the thin stockings. For some reason that excited him unduly; suddenly he remembered a forbidden book he and Wertheimer had read, about a woman putting rouge on her nipples. The heated stirring of his flesh was painfully obvious now to Martin; he could no longer control it at all.

161

He saw her bright black eyes descending to the centre of him; the dark eyes sparked and a slow smile trembled on her moist red mouth.

'Ah, poor boy, dear boy,' she whispered, and then her hands were upon him, caressing him through the fabric of his trousers. She was, good Lord, she was doing to him what he had done to himself, in the shamed dark, for the last two years, and he was quivering at the wonder of it, wishing she would go on and on, not caring at all now who they were or where they were or anything but that it should not cease.

And she was murmuring wordlessly now; still stroking him, she leaned forward and opened her lips over his mouth, until she seemed to be devouring him, and it was wonderful. He shook and shook, his heart thudding with such force and loudness he knew it was going to jump right through his shirt, right out of his body; she was kissing him, kissing him hungrily and leisurely and long.

Then she took her mouth away with that same excruciating leisure, whispering, 'Don't move, dear boy, poor boy, poor Martin,' pressing her heavy breasts, now about to spill from their bodice, for an instant against his startled mouth until he felt like a coddled infant being pressed against its mother's softness. Soon, he knew, he would fairly explode. Then she was kneeling, undoing her gown, and it fell away. She rose and stepped out of it.

Astounded, he saw that she had been wearing nothing at all below the gown except for a kind of lacy pink harness that was attached to her rosy stockings. She stood there smiling down at him, standing on parted legs and he stared, wondering, at the patch of mysterious darkness on the white skin below the frivolous, ruffled, rosy harness.

Trembling, Martin stared and stared, devouring the sight of that mystery. This, then, was what it was like, he marvelled; that was the centre of all that wild grandeur men boasted of and the forbidden pages hymned.

She knelt again, slowly, whispering again, 'Don't move, my poor hungry boy.' Somehow then she had unfastened his clothes and he was snatching at them, to rid himself of them, and she was urging him gently to lie back again upon the cushions. He sank trembling into their insinuating softness, drowning backwards.

With utter disbelief, not sure if he were dreaming or awake, he was aware that she was lowering her face, lowering it onto the centre of his beating body, and her lips were nibbling, nibbling and caressing him in a manner he had never even thought of in his most abandoned fancies. His body leapt and writhed and he reflected dimly, almost

162

insanely in his wondering frenzy; it is like the drawing of poison, poison from a throbbing wound; and his drumming need, now, was like the pounding hooves of runaway stallions, there was no reining of them now, no ability or desire to control or slow these racing, screaming beasts; he found that she had thrown herself full length upon him and was urging him to her, demanding the shattering entrance.

And he was leaping upward, strongly, riding onward, his fevered flesh enclosed now in an alien, pulsing throb of soft, moistened silk; he was assaulted with pillowed satin, rising and sinking at once into many small nibbling mouths of sweet, cool fire. Then all at once he was approaching a sensation so all-encompassing, so marvellous, so utterly pleasurable that he feared the very imminence of death with his brain stopped, his heart not beating; he was there, and there was a mighty blow to him, a rush of releasing, and he heard a man's voice sobbing, crying out, a woman shrieking.

Come to a form of quavering sense Martin knew the man's voice was his, the woman's – Bea's.

Everything after that was as hazy as dreaming; dimly he took another glass of wine from her fingers, and drank. And he knew, somehow, that again they were coming together in that wild converse, to reach again that longed-for, throbbing height; and yet again.

At last the long delirium seemed to ebb; the light through the curtained windows had fled.

Martin lay with his face against Bea's smooth breast, murmuring, 'I don't want to move. I want to stay here for ever. But I've got to go. I was supposed to be home hours and hours ago.'

Bea chuckled, stroking his bare body. 'You don't have to go at all. I will telephone to Diana and tell her that my nephew is staying for dinner with us and then will visit overnight.'

' "Us?" ' Martin repeated, smiling, with closed eyes. 'Where is my uncle?'

'In Paris, dear heart, where he will not trouble us,' Bea murmured, grazing his skin with her mouth until he tingled. 'Ah, my dear, do you realise how many times . . .? Youth is really the most marvellous quality there is, you know.'

Martin felt at once immensely lazy and terribly manly and strong. Now he was truly a man of the world. Already with a more practised touch he found himself caressing her. His aunt.

Realisation washed him coldly. He had made love to his own aunt. It was a great and terrible sin. He must go, go now.

163

And yet, when she leaned into him again and rubbed her softness insinuatingly over his hardness, Martin knew he would not go. And no matter how great a sin it was, he could not forego such a shattering pleasure, such an indescribable delight; knew that he would come back to this house again, and yet again.

CHAPTER ELEVEN

'A young lady?' Mitchell Farley frowned with annoyance over his littered desk in the Cape Town offices of DeVries, wondering who the hell it could be. Hardly one of the girls from Madame Lafrege's; they rarely even came out in daylight. And the kid was supposed to be in Pretoria. 'Well, what's her name?' he demanded irascibly.

This idiot's description offered no clue; in the primitive Cape there were no distinctions. Respectable women and whores alike were called 'young ladies'.

'What does she want?' Farley pursued.

Harper, the clerk, looked nervous. Farley was an impatient employer. 'I could not ascertain what she wanted, sir. And she would not give a name.'

Farley made an exasperated sound. 'Very well, very well, Harper. Show her in, then.'

The fellow went away and in a moment there was another timid knock at the door.

'Come *in*,' Farley growled. A tense Harper appeared, holding the door open for a bedraggled Lesley Holder.

'Good Lord. Les!' Farley stared at the kid. She looked as though she'd been dragged through a hedge, very mousy without all her war paint. 'Well, come in, come in, now that you're here. That'll do, Harper.'

The clerk fled, closing the door with extreme gentleness.

'Oh, Mitchell, Mitchell!' Lesley dropped her reticule on the carpet and rushed to Farley, throwing herself against him. He put his

164

hands on her trembling shoulders, holding her a little way away. Her hair smelt like cinders, and to his great distaste she was perspiring. 'Mitchell! At last!' she breathed in a novelistic fashion, trying to snuggle close to him.

'Now, now,' he said soothingly, pushing her away with an expert motion, urging her into a chair. 'What is all this? Where are your parents?'

She stared at him with her pale eyes, her soft, silly mouth all aquiver. He marvelled that anyone with Vanessa's features could look so little like her; the girl had all the appeal of a sheep. 'What do they matter?' she quavered. 'Aren't you glad to see me?'

'Well, of course, Lesley. Of course I am. But you catch me in the midst of a very busy morning.' Farley smiled at her, indicating the piles of papers on his desk. 'I thought you were in Pretoria. Now, I take it, you just got off the train.'

'How did you know that?' Her eyes widened.

What a perfect fool she was. 'Because the train from Kimberley arrived a little while ago,' he explained with great patience in the tone he used to use with her when he was her tutor. 'And you are carrying a bag.' He did not add that she was obviously travel-stained and sweaty as a roustabout.

She had the grace to look chagrined. 'Of course.' She grinned at him; unwillingly he was struck by her faint resemblance then to Vanessa.

'Lesley,' he inquired in the same patient tone, 'where are your parents?'

'They're still in Pretoria. I ran away. Oh, Mitchell, aren't you glad to see me?'

If the little bitch whined like that again he would be hard put not to slap her face.

Ignoring the last question, he murmured, 'You shouldn't have done that, Lesley. Your father will come after you, and he will no doubt shoot me.'

A look of terror flared in her pallid eyes. 'Oh, no! No, Mitchell. He couldn't – he wouldn't. Not after we're married. You will marry me, won't you? You told me you . . . loved me.'

Farley almost laughed aloud. Marry that stupid little fool. He'd as soon marry the dressmaker, or one of the whores. But he restrained his mirth. This was a hell of a note, indeed.

She was examining him anxiously, leaning forward in the chair. 'You do want to marry me, don't you, Mitchell?'

Good God, she had no pride, no manners whatsoever. But then it struck him: what a splendid way this would be to get back at Holder. Marry his lamb and make her miserable. And there could be money in it; Holder would beyond any doubt try to buy him off. Yes, there might be money in it. It was an amusing idea, after all.

'Of course I do, darling,' he said in a silky voice. 'But don't you see – I can't have my future wife rushing into the office in this improper way? Such things cause talk, Lesley. Now, be a good girl and let me put you into a carriage. Then, when I come for you, you'll be all rested and pretty, and we'll go find a parson. And I'll have to buy a ring, you know.'

'Oh, Mitchell, Mitchell!' She got up from the chair and rushed around the desk, catching her hip on its sharp corner, throwing herself upon him to smother him with sticky kisses. His gorge rose. Why did all of them have that unclean smell? A sudden image of young Jeffrey Herrold assailed him. The boy had been foolish, indiscreet, and an utter nuisance, but Farley yearned at that moment for the fresh, clean scent of the boy's smooth body. This girl's nearness left him queasy. 'Aren't you going to kiss me?'

Farley was disgusted with her abject manner.

'Of course I am, darling.' He steeled himself and, rising, took her in his arms to give her a long and thorough kiss. 'Now you must run along. I have a great deal, a very great deal to do before we meet again this evening.'

She nodded submissively. He picked up her reticule and escorted her down to the street. When he had handed her into a public carriage, he asked, 'Do you have enough money?'

'Oh, yes, plenty. I took . . .' She paused, flushing.

Farley laughed. 'I see. I see.' She wasn't quite so much a fool as he'd thought. This was going to be amusing. 'All right, love, you go along. I'll see you about four at the hotel.'

When he got back to the office he summoned Harper. 'I'll be away for a while this afternoon; I have several outside errands. Hold down the fort.'

'Oh, I will, sir. I will.' The boy looked pleased and flattered; his employer seldom spoke to him in such a genial way.

Mitchell Farley put on his jacket and hat and strolled out again. His first stop was the jeweller's, where he resolved to spend as little as possible on the ring. If things went well, he wouldn't need it, anyway. He bought the thinnest gold band in stock and then enjoyed a long, substantial lunch with several glasses of wine in the dining room of Government House, where he was a welcome guest.

After lunch he made arrangements for the ceremony: it would take place at six in the office of the official empowered to perform weddings. He had a difficult time responding suitably when the man congratulated him fervently, pumping his hand. Perhaps he'd been a bit precipitate. But surely Holder would show up that afternoon; even now he might be waiting in Farley's office.

However, there was no sign of him when Farley returned. Why the hell hadn't he waited? He could have put it off for a day or two. But it really didn't signify; he'd be worth more as a husband than a suitor. The thing could always be annulled. Farley did not have the slightest intention of bedding the little fool, so she would still be *intacta*. If any protégé of old Bea's *could* be *intacta*, Farley mused, grinning, beyond the age of nine.

He began to feel better and threw himself with renewed energy into his work. He was so involved that he didn't realise it was five o'clock until Harper happened to mention it.

Farley put on his hat and coat again and hurried to the hotel. Ascertaining Lesley's room, he rushed to it and found her in tears. 'I thought you had changed your mind,' she sobbed. Her wet nose and red-rimmed eyes were revolting, but he soothed her as best he could, suggesting she wash her face and get herself ready for the big moment.

Ecstatic, she obeyed and emerged in full war paint again. Her dress was fairly decent, he admitted, then he remembered that he had not bought her any flowers. He told her he would obtain some on the way.

The ceremony was brief and businesslike, with witnesses brought in from another office, but apparently to Lesley it was wonderful, because her pale eyes were on fire and her skin was fairly incandescent. Farley got a perverse enjoyment out of playing the devoted groom, a tongue-in-cheek pleasure from their bridal dinner in the private room he'd engaged. He plied Lesley with so much champagne that when the time came to go upstairs her speech was slurred and her feet unsteady.

This was going to be even easier than he'd expected.

In the bridal chamber she was overcome with dizziness and gently he urged her to lie down. 'My dress, my dress,' she mumbled, protesting.

'It's all right, Lesley,' he reassured her, watching her lids grow heavier. In no time at all she was snoring.

Mitchell Farley glanced at his watch. Still only nine, the shank of the evening. He grinned at the sprawling figure on the bed. He'd just pop off home now and have a bath and shave, then go on to Françoise Lafrege's.

That canny old frog, who boasted that she offered everything for all possible tastes, had informed him that an enchanting new boy had been imported recently from England. It was going to be a perfectly splendid night.

The boy did not disappoint him. Neither did Holder, who appeared at ten the next morning as Farley was nursing his head over numerous cups of coffee at his desk.

But Farley hadn't counted on his bringing Vanessa with him, and he was dismayed to face her with his bleary eyes and somewhat ruffled appearance.

When she preceded Holder into his office, Farley wished fervently that he had changed his clothes. As always the sight of her beautiful face, her queenly deportment, left him bedazzled, feeling like a boy. She was the only woman on earth who could have . . .

'Where is my daughter, Farley?' Holder demanded without preamble.

'Amas . . .' Vanessa murmured.

Farley scrambled to his feet. 'Mrs Holder. Please, sit down.' He pulled a chair away from the desk and made a gallant gesture. His nostrils quivered; she smelled of hyacinths, and her skin, in the harsh morning light, was pure as water.

'Thank you,' she said in a low voice, meeting his stare with blank grey eyes.

Holder's rough face darkened. 'Where is Lesley, Farley? She left us a note in Pretoria telling us that she intended to marry you. Is this true? Where are you hiding her?'

'Amas,' Vanessa Holder repeated quietly. 'Please, let's discuss this in a rational manner.' To Farley she said coolly, 'I assume you have seen her, Mitchell.'

'We were married last night.'

Farley studied the effect of that statement on them: Vanessa had a look of odd relief, Holder was outraged.

'Good God!' he exploded. 'You've *married* that innocent child!'

'Hardly a child any more,' Farley protested, smiling. 'Lesley has a mind of her own, you know. Come now, Holder, I'm your son-in-law now. Let's shake on it like civilised men.'

168

'I will never recognise you as my son-in-law,' Holder growled. 'Mitchell Farley . . . my son-in-law!'

Ah, good, Farley thought. Here it comes. This is my opportunity. 'Do you propose to separate us, Holder? What did you have in mind?'

But he did not receive the answer he expected. Apparently the hint went right over the barbarian's head.

'What can I do about it?' Holder snapped. 'It's done – you're married to my daughter.'

Farley shot a glance at Vanessa; her expression of anxiety was easing. Maybe she'd expected the fellow to shoot him, and seemed to be thanking her stars that he was calming down.

However, he said softly, 'She is under-age. I am aware of that. I feared you might take steps to have the marriage annulled.'

'Then you "feared" wrong, Farley. If my daughter has been misguided enough to marry someone like you, I'm going to let her lie in the bed she's made.'

Vanessa was astonished. 'But Amas . . .'

He ignored her. 'I came here to find out if you had dishonoured my daughter. Apparently you haven't,' he added with reluctance, as if he were sorry to give Farley any credit at all. 'You've married her. Or so you say. Are you in possession of the certificate?' he asked with sudden suspicion.

'As it so happens, I am.' Farley reached into his pocket and took out the document, handing it to Holder. The man scanned it and showed it to Vanessa. Her great lovely eyes were still expressionless.

'We want to see Lesley,' she said. 'Where is she, Mitchell?'

'In the bridal suite at the hotel.' Damn it all, this wasn't going the way he'd planned. Holder should be offering him a fortune by now. What on earth had happened?

'We will go and see her then, Mitchell.' She handed him the certificate.

'You will go, Vanessa. I do not want to see her, ever again.' She paled at Holder's angry declaration. This was a fine kettle of fish.

Vanessa looked deeply embarrassed. 'Amas, perhaps we had better not . . . discuss this now.'

'Let's go, Vanessa,' Holder growled. She rose at once. Holder stormed to the door and held it open for her. He did not echo her murmured farewell.

After the door slammed to, Farley sank down in his chair.

What a rotten mess it all was. Now he was stuck with the idiotic girl. Well, he wasn't going to give up. There would have to be something

169

in it for him, some time. Maybe Vanessa could talk Holder around. He'd see the girl eventually, Farley assured himself. And when he found out how wretched she was, then he'd offer Farley plenty to divorce her.

And wretched she was going to be. Farley would see to that. He would get off on the right foot by not hurrying home tonight.

Therefore it was nearly ten when he got to the hotel. Bracing himself for Lesley's reproaches and tears about his disappearance the night before, their very wedding night, Farley was surprised to see her looking wistful but calm. She looked almost nice, as a matter of fact, in her soft teagown of a blue that enhanced her dull eyes and her hair glowing with youth.

Instead of questioning his lateness, Lesley to his deeper surprise held out her arms to Farley.

'You were angry with me,' she said in a soft, little-girl's voice. 'And you should be.'

This was a turn-around, indeed. 'Angry with you, Lesley? Why should I be?'

'You see – you're not even kissing me. Your bride of only two days . . . and a very wasted night.' She twinkled at him coquettishly, rubbing herself against him. The feel of her bovine breasts was extremely unpleasant to him. 'I had too much champagne,' she confessed, 'and that was very silly of me. To think of spending our wedding night asleep. Then when I woke up you had already left for the office.'

He was so amused at her misinterpretation of the incident that he nearly laughed.

But apparently, taking his hesitation for a reluctance to make up, Lesley cajoled, 'Please, my darling. Say you're not angry. Come, I've had a lovely supper laid out for us . . . see?'

She took him by the hand and led him to a table laden with covered dishes, goblets, a bottle of white wine and a coffee service. 'Say you're not angry with your Lesley.'

'I'm not angry, Lesley. Only vastly amused.' He lifted one of the covers from the dishes and examined the food with a critical air.

'Amused?' she repeated, goggling at him.

'Chicken, Lesley? How imaginative.' He picked up the bottle of wine and looked for the year. He might have known. A bad one.

'Don't you like it?' she asked anxiously. 'I got the right wine to go with it, Mitchell. I thought you'd like it.' She seemed on the verge of weeping. Oh, God. But he couldn't stop himself now; he wanted to

170

lash out at her, wanted to see her silly face crumple and break. He wanted to hurt her because she wasn't Vanessa . . . or even Jeffrey.

'This wine is swill,' he said brutally, 'and will probably taste like vinegar. And above all foods I detest chicken with the greatest passion.'

Her face was crumpling now into a kind of unattractive sponge of misery. 'I didn't know.'

'And for dessert, Lesley? What did you order – apple pie?' Before he lifted the cover he knew he'd guessed correctly. She looked very downcast.

'Almost everybody likes that,' she mumbled; a tear ran down her face, carrying with it a streak of black paint. 'The hotel doesn't have a . . . large selection,' she said defensively.

'Go fix your face,' he snapped, pouring a cup of coffee from the pot. Sobbing, she fled from the room.

Even the coffee, Mitchell concluded with disgust, tasted foul. He wasn't going to waste any more time here; he wanted another night with Christopher. The boy was enchanting, with his white skin and red hair and eyes as azure as aquamarines; his young skin felt like satin. Farley shouldn't have wasted all those hours on the card game. He would leave now.

But no. First he would have the pleasure of telling of that young cow . . . and ask her if her parents had been here today. Of course. It would add an excruciating edge of enjoyment to his anticipated pleasure.

She came back promptly, trying to smile. He'd been wrong in his estimate: she was not a heifer, she was like a little crawling cur dog, an abject bitch. 'I'm sorry I ordered the wrong thing,' she said in a doleful voice, angering him even more. Any creature with spirit would have tossed the dinner at his head. 'Tell me exactly what you want and I'll order it right away.'

'If you had any sense at all,' he retorted contemptuously, 'you'd realise I've dined by now.' He decided not to mention right at this moment that he was going out again; he couldn't have her clinging to his ankles until he'd found out what he wanted to know, then said what he wanted to say.

'Mitchell, why . . .'

He cut her off. 'Your parents came to see me today. Were they here?'

'Yes. I told the man I didn't want to see them,' Lesley answered sullenly.

'That was not a very bright thing to do.'

'How could I see them?' she flared, showing the first sign of spirit that evening. 'All they would do is tell me I shouldn't have married you.'

'Indeed you shouldn't, my dear.' He took another swallow of the loathsome coffee and made a sound of displeasure. 'I don't really care for women, you see.'

Her astonishment was highly diverting.

'But what . . . what do you mean, Mitchell? Why did you marry me?' She held out her arms in an awkward gesture.

'For sheer revenge, my dear . . . and because you look a little bit like your mother.' He set down his coffee cup, smiling at her. Then he consulted his watch. 'I'd really better be going now.'

'*Going*?' she repeated stupidly, and her mouth fell open in sheer amazement.

'I have an appointment . . . at Madame Lafrege's. Do you know what that is?'

She shook her head, the tears beginning to gather again in those vapid sheep's eyes.

'A whore house, my dear Lesley, full of exquisite pleasures.'

Slack-jawed, she continued to stand there, staring at him, and he glanced contemptuously at her naive face with its woeful eyes, the crude young body in the thin gown, displaying its heavy treasures with such unsubtlety in the garish light.

'Goodnight, my dear,' he said silkily and went out before she could let out the calflike, bellowing sobs he'd heard before.

Mitchell Farley ran lightly down the stairs, savouring the sweetness of his revenge against the mighty Amas Holder. It had been almost as satisfying as cutting her thick skin with a whip, to lash out at her with brutal words. He would return to her every night, at about this time, if only to torture her.

The honeyed heat of his malice fired his veins, titillating his lust for the boy. He would tell Christopher about it tonight, and make him laugh. All that would make it more marvellous than ever.

It was exactly as he'd predicted. Afterwards he went back to his own house and snatched a few hours' sleep. He woke in high spirits and went to the office to plunge into the day with relish. That evening he dined long, and rather too well, with his cronies. His head was fuddled when he decided to pay a call on his little bride.

Farley was smiling to himself when he went into the suite, his vision a trifle blurred. She was not in the sitting room; there was no offensive meal on the table in the corner. The lights were very dim.

He called out her name, but there was no answer. He went into the bedroom and looking at the figure on the bed, fairly reeled with shock.

He must be very drunk indeed . . . or perhaps he was asleep and dreaming. Vanessa Holder was lying on the bed, a faint light glowing on her brief golden hair; her eyes were shut and the long, gilded lashes lay fanned out on her sun-touched cheeks. Her generous breasts thrust up the coverlet and her mouth . . . there was something odd about her mouth.

Here she was, he reflected hazily, the only woman who could ever give him his manhood. And he hastily began to throw off his clothes. He felt dizzy, almost insane. How could this be?

Don't question it, he warned himself, don't pause for an instant. And naked he strode towards the bed and threw himself upon her.

'Vanessa, Vanessa,' he cried out in a voice he barely recognised as his own, so passionate was it, and young again, beseeching.

Pressing himself upon her, he ran his fingers through the short gilded hair; dismayed, he saw that the small curls did not spring back into their silken arcs but instead fell into limp hanks under his touch.

'Oh, Mitchell, Mitchell . . . at last, at last.' He heard Lesley's thin voice, her whining intonation, and snatched his hands away from her hair as if it could burn him.

He raised himself and rested on his haunches, looking down at the empty blue eyes, now open wide, the sheeplike face. He must have been mad to mistake this idiot for that goddess, that longed-for dream. But for that moment the resemblance had been so strong . . . she had cut her hair, done something to her skin with paint to darken it, even thickened her brows. Good God.

'Oh, Mitchell, my darling Mitchell,' Lesley repeated, holding out her arms. Still in the heat of his arousal, Farley abruptly threw himself upon her; he would have his satisfaction, by God, some kind of satisfaction with this heifer. It had gone too far now, anyway; to turn back now would be absolutely painful.

He threw back the covers and shoved the nightgown upward from the chunky little body. Thrusting cruelly and fast, he emptied himself into her, ignoring her cries of pain.

When it was over, he heaved himself from her and lay at her side, staring upwards.

She was crying quietly.

'Shut up,' he ordered. When she continued to weep, he said more loudly, 'Shut up.' The mewling cry went on.

Farley raised his hand and delivered a stinging slap to her face. She gasped once and was silent. Rolling over with her back to him, Lesley covered her face with her hands.

'What kind of charade is this, anyway?' he demanded 'Did you really think you could compete with her, you little idiot?'

He could hear her sobs begin again.

'Why did you do such a stupid thing?'

'I wanted to be like her,' Lesley finally answered in a muffled, tear-thickened voice. 'Because you . . . love her.' The last words seemed torn from her throat in positive agony.

'Damned right I love your mother, Lesley. I always have, I always will.' He was disconcerted now to feel his lust renewing; his palm striking her face, her pained confession, her sobbing, trembling body were very titillating. He could sense even now the urgency of his need. That had been a most unsatisfactory exercise; there was only one way he could truly be appeased. The thought of her sure reluctance excited him even more, almost to the point of frenzy.

'Now, Lesley,' he murmured, his voice tight with the quickening of his desire, 'you are going to do me a little favour . . . something your Aunt Bea does magnificently, by the way.'

Lesley turned over, staring at him. Her face was more foolish than ever with apprehension. 'What . . . what are you talking about? You . . . you . . . and Bea?' Her voice squeaked, and he laughed at the sound of it.

'Oh, yes,' he smiled, pushing her flat on the bed. 'Bea and I have a good deal in common – we are both so fond of boys.'

Lesley was still staring at him, dumbfounded. Then she tried to put her hands over her face again.

'Get your hands down,' he snapped, grasping her wrists, pulling her arms down to her sides. 'Now listen to what I want you to do.' He knelt above her, giving her curt directions.

She shook her head from side to side. 'No, oh, no, Mitchell.'

'Oh, yes, Lesley.' He grabbed her head and squeezed it. 'Otherwise I will squeeze your head like a melon, my dear, and your negligible brains will spill out of your skull.'

Her eyes were transfixed with horror; he could almost smell her fear, and it sharpened his lust to an unbearable degree.

'Now,' he ordered. She obeyed him. As she attempted to do his bidding in her fumbling way, he constantly corrected her efforts, angrily repeating himself over and over.

At last, despite her incompetence, Farley reached a kind of release and fell down at her side.

'That wasn't very good, Lesley. But you'll learn in time.' He was too sleepy now to say more.

A sudden darkness, a black silence swallowed up her wracking sobs.

Driving with Amas towards the farm of Joachim Ryn, Vanessa reviewed the last unhappy weeks since their disastrous visit to the Cape. It had taken all her powers of persuasion to convince Amas they must call on Lesley. Then, when the girl had refused to see them, Amas had turned on his heel and stormed out of the hotel, compelling Vanessa to follow. He was doggedly silent on the journey back to Kimberley; none of Vanessa's attempts at reasoning with him had come to anything.

Always, now, Vanessa bore the burden of her guilt: she had driven her child away to that horrendous union. Vanessa doubted that Farley had changed to such an extent that he would marry her daughter for love. Everything pointed to the suspicion that he was still infatuated with Vanessa. She was convinced that Mitchell Farley had married Lesley as a kind of punishment for Amas Holder. Nonetheless Vanessa wrote her daughter several letters, begging her to communicate with her parents. She had received no answer at all.

With a queer soreness around her heart Vanessa noticed that Amas acted more like a rejected lover than an indignant father. He stubbornly refused to discuss the matter in any way.

Then, only two weeks after Lesley's marriage, the letter from Margit Ryn had come. It told them, in Miss Ryn's precise and rather elderly hand, that her father, Joachim Ryn, was dead; that she and her niece, Anjanette, were not only willing but eager to discuss the sale of the farm which was the last impediment to the development of the Premier mine in Pretoria.

Amas was momentarily distracted from his gloom over Lesley, and his elation was infectious. Now they both could journey to Pretoria and see the beginnings of the great new endeavour without interference. In spite of her perpetual worry, and the constant nag of guilt, Vanessa could not resist the carefree sensations that buoyed her, the feeling of holiday. For now at least the old order of things had been restored. And she sensed the same emotions in Amas; he was newly tender with her, almost as excited as a boy.

Now they waited for admission, sharing the same anticipatory delight.

The woman who opened the door was not, to Vanessa's surprise, dressed in mourning, but in a sombre brown dress with white collar and cuffs. She had a careworn face, an expression of deep resignation. Her hair was severely coifed, a dreary grey-threaded brown, and she might have been anywhere between thirty and fifty years of age. But her smile was kindly and welcoming. 'Come in,' she said. 'I am Margit Ryn.'

When they entered the spotless sitting room a striking girl was setting out tea on a rough but polished table. She was dressed quietly in an almost black dark blue; her hair was so pale a blonde it looked quite silver. Her petal-like skin was flushed with exertion and, Vanessa concluded, shyness.

'My niece, Anjanette Ryn,' Margit said. 'Mr and Mrs Amas Holder.' The girl offered her hand to Vanessa, bowing her head slightly to Amas.

She looked no more than fifteen or sixteen; her body was childishly slender and her manners self-effacing. But there was a strange grace, almost a wisdom about her, Vanessa reflected, answering her sweet smile. Vanessa saw then that the girl was not as beautiful as she had at first appeared, only so striking that she had seemed so. She had oddly shaped, long-lidded eyes of such pallor that they, too, looked silvery like her hair. What impressed Vanessa most was her dignity, her strong emanation of a quality both intelligent and serene.

Margit urged them to be seated and plied them with tea and cakes. Then, when the Holders had declined a second cup, Margit Ryn said abruptly, 'You have not journeyed for more than a day for a cup of tea. Mr Holder, my niece and I are extremely anxious to be rid of this farm, and to move as soon as possible to Johannesburg. My niece, Anjanette,' she added with a smile at the girl, 'wants more than anything to complete her education and to teach at a school.'

Amas and Vanessa murmured politely and Amas, as abruptly as Margit had spoken, named an offer. It was a figure so generous that both the woman and the girl looked overjoyed.

'Done,' Margit Ryn said succinctly. Vanessa thought, these are two remarkable women. There had been none of the circuitous talk, the superfluous flutter, that one generally associated with women transacting business. Vanessa surmised that Amas shared her opinion.

'I have the papers ready,' the ever surprising Margit said. 'We have but to affix our names and state the amount. An attorney in Johannesburg has gone over these documents with me.'

'Before the settling of the amount?' Amas inquired, raising his brows.

'Mr Holder, let me speak plainly. This farm has been not a home, but a veritable prison to myself and to my niece, all these years. We do not wear black because my father, I am pained to say, was not a man to mourn.'

Vanessa liked both the women more and more; recalling the tyrannical and unpleasant Joachim Ryn, she could well believe it. And she respected Margit for her refusal to exhibit hypocritical grief.

Seeing Anjanette's struggle with the heavy tray, Vanessa realised for the first time that there were no servants in evidence. 'Please,' she said, 'let me help you. Do these go in the kitchen?' She took a few items off the tray.

The girl appeared scandalised. 'Oh, you must not do this.'

'Nonsense,' Vanessa said. 'Now, where is the kitchen?' She grinned at the girl to soften the apparent curtness of the question.

'I will show you.' Anjanette returned her smile and Vanessa was struck with its genuine sweetness. The girl was patently childlike and untouched, and yet she was imbued with a poise and calm beyond her years.

Vanessa could hear Amas in intent conversation with Margit Ryn as she helped Anjanette with her tasks, amused at her own offer. She hadn't washed a dish in her entire life.

'You are very kind, Mrs Holder,' Anjanette said. In a sudden burst of shy confiding, she added, 'Oh, Mrs Holder, you don't know what you have done for us! I have wanted so long to be free . . . to live in Johannesburg, to teach. We have been so lonely here.'

'I'm glad,' Vanessa murmured, imagining what her life must have been before.

When they were leaving, Vanessa remarked to Amas, 'We have made the heirs of Ryn very happy, it seems.'

He nodded in absent agreement; she could tell he was already planning the next steps he would take.

'The niece,' Vanessa said, 'is a lovely girl. If only . . .' She stopped, chagrined. She had been about to say, 'If only our daughter were like her.' But, glancing at Amas, she knew that the same idea had occurred to him.

CHAPTER TWELVE

Lesley Holder Farley shifted her heavy body in the hateful bed, trying to find a comfortable position. She closed her eyes to shut out the room, the bedroom in Mitchell Farley's house, where they had moved a month after the marriage. She had never thought of the house as theirs, but only as Mitchell Farley's.

There was little evidence of her occupancy. She could, she supposed, have changed that. But all she'd wanted for the past eight months was to die.

Lesley smiled grimly to recall her feelings after that first nightmare encounter, that brutal converse that had left her with this great stone in her body. She'd actually thought then that no greater horror could follow; how naive that Lesley had been.

That night had been nothing compared to what came after – the dreadful sickness of her early pregnancy, the shock of the genial doctor who had given her the news when he saw her burst into wild weeping. The contemptuous comments of Mitchell, then the new horror, that other manner of assault that left her even more degraded and sore. She had tried to muffle her screams in the night, but often she could not contain them; when they were torn from her, however, Mitchell would slap her again, so she had learned to be silent.

Sometimes it was so awful she almost wished she were back at the bungalow in Kimberley. And then she would remember that it was her cold, hypocritical mother whom Mitchell had always loved, and her hatred burned anew. It was the only thing now that sustained her. She would not deign to answer her mother's innumerable letters, signed 'Your parents', when all the time Lesley knew the letters were only from her. She had written to her father and never received a reply. Perhaps Mitchell had intercepted the letters; she no longer wondered, or cared. All there was now was the perpetual discomfort; she longed to rid her body of its awful burden, then to die as she had tried to do three times before, before they had taken away the laudanum.

But there was a good supply now, hidden away, for the hour when she could no longer bear to draw another breath. Meanwhile there was the diary, with the story of the horrors. Lesley's mouth stretched into a dry, insane grin. After she was gone, that would make them sit up and take notice. When her mother and father read it, they would die of guilt and shame. It would be good to take that realisation with her.

Lesley listened to the ticking of the clock. It was very late, and of course Mitchell hadn't come home yet. As her body thickened, his return home had become later and later; sometimes he didn't come at all.

If only there were someone. The little maid, Elizabeth, was kind but stupid, so stupid that she could never understand half of what Lesley said to her. Lesley longed for London, remembering the glittering rush of Piccadilly Circus, the shining shops along Bond Street . . . the plays, the restaurants, the gaiety, the lovely dresses. It was all something she had experienced in a dream, long ago; perhaps it had never existed.

Suddenly she was wracked with a series of shooting pains. Dear God, dear God, it was time, and she was alone.

She cried out in terror. Almost at once the door opened and she saw the frightened face of the little maid, Elizabeth, and her foolish, staring eyes.

'The doctor,' Lesley managed to gasp.

'I'll go at once, Mrs Farley,' Elizabeth shrieked, and slammed the door.

What succeeded was lost in a haze of paralysing terror, unendurable pain; Lesley heard a woman screaming horribly, and then, long, long afterwards, the sound of hurrying footsteps. On the edge of consciousness she was vaguely aware of a deep, soothing voice, of firm hands.

But always, never ceasing, overpowering, was the indescribable pain, an agony that made the other horrors pale by comparison; it seared and stabbed and pounded, unremitting, and Lesley knew at last her body would be ripped asunder. The only desire she would ever know again was the wish for the ending of the pain.

And then, at last, some time in that ordeal that had no boundaries and no time, the pain was gone. Her body felt weak and light, weaker than water; there was only a sharp soreness between her legs. She must not move.

A murmur drifted to her from somewhere, 'There, there, now. That's better. The baby is fine, Mrs Farley. Drink this.'

Dimly she saw the glass near her lips. She made a sound of protest, shaking her head.

'Very well, it'll be all right. I think you'll sleep now, anyway. Just sleep.'

It was the doctor.

Lesley sank back, closing her eyes. She heard him go out, heard lighter footsteps following. She was alone now.

Then there was another sound, a squalling cry like the sound of a cat. The baby.

She would never look at it, never. She would not endure a lifetime of seeing its face, that hateful reminder of her degradation and her pain, the disillusion that had made all life untenable.

Raising herself with a terrible effort, almost shrieking with the pain, Lesley leaned over, fumbling under the mattress. For an instant she was convinced that she would fall. But she must hold on, she must.

Finally, with a last powerful attempt, with a force that made something break inside her, she retrieved the bottle of laudanum, filled almost to the cap with the precious liquid she had so painstakingly preserved and, weeping, lay back on the pillows. There must be one more effort.

She reached out for the glass on the table, almost beyond her grasp. There: now she had it. Cautiously she curved her weakened fingers around the glass and brought it towards her.

She opened the bottle and poured the drug into the glass. Then without hesitation she drained it, to the very bottom.

Almost at once she felt the sweetness of sleep steal over her; her arms and legs were growing heavier and heavier, and there was no feeling now in her legs at all.

Lesley's fingers relaxed; the glass fell from her hand and rolled off the bed, striking the carpet with a muffled thud.

But that sound, like any other sound at all, did not reach Lesley Farley now.

When Mitchell Farley stole into his house it was practically dawn. He was amazed to see the little maid sprawled out on the couch in the sitting room, asleep and snoring rhythmically.

Puzzled and annoyed, he shook her awake. 'What's this? Don't you have a room . . . what are you doing here?'

The girl sat up, hastily pulling down her skirt, trying to throw off her drowsiness. 'Oh, sir! Sir,' she began to sob, 'the baby's come . . . but the mistress, the mistress . . .'

'What, girl? The mistress what?' he demanded, taking her by the shoulders and shaking her again until her head bobbed like a broken doll's.

'The mistress has died, sir.' The girl screwed up her plain face and tears spouted from her eyes.

'Died.' Farley sank down in the chair opposite. 'But what . . . what happened? Did she die in childbirth?'

'Oh, no, Mr Farley. The doctor said it was an over . . . an over . . . from drinking too much of the drug. They took her . . . took her away a long time ago. The doctor couldn't find you.'

That was no surprise. Lately he had rented a little room away from Françoise's house where he could meet Christopher without fear of detection, Françoise being so notorious.

The girl ran out of the room, still sobbing.

And the full import of the news struck Mitchell Farley. God in heaven, now he'd be blamed. Not by the police, because he had patently been absent from the scene, but by that bastard Holder. When Holder found out, he'd hunt Farley down like a wild animal and shoot him dead. That was certain.

Damn that mewling moron, he raged in silence, clenching his fists. She'd ruined everything now. He'd have to leave DeVries, of course, put a continent between himself and Holder.

Oh, why had he ever got into this mess in the first place? Why hadn't he made her get rid of the brat at the very beginning? Because he'd been so besotted, so bemused with Christopher, that he hadn't been able to think of anything else. He'd let everything slide.

He thanked his lucky stars that at least he'd done away with Lesley's letters to Holder. God knows what she would ultimately have told him.

Farley hesitated. To throw up everything he had worked for, toadied and sweated for – it was not to be borne, God damn it. It was not to be borne. Maybe, even now . . .

No. It was no good. He'd never be safe again as long as he was in Africa. And a ship was leaving for England this very day. He'd damned well better be on it.

He got up and rushed into his bedroom, glad that it was separate from Lesley's. The last thing he needed now was to look at the sordid locale of that fool's end.

In the midst of throwing clothes into a grip, Farley jumped nervously to hear a soft, steady knocking on his door. 'Who is it?' he called out tensely.

The door opened and a broad, glowering woman dressed in a nurse's uniform entered the room. She was carrying a small, red-faced bundle. The bundle waved its tiny fists.

God, the thing was no bigger or more comely than a rat, he thought. He closed the bulging grip.

'Misterr Farrrley,' the nurse began sternly, in a rough Scottish burr, 'I hae come to show ye yerr daughterrr.' It was plain from the malice in her squinty eyes that she thought him a perfect scoundrel.

'Get out of my way,' he ordered tersely. Hoisting the suitcase he thrust himself past her and hurried out of the house, aware that she was staring after him, shocked to utter speechlessness.

'Vanessa!' She heard Amas' excited call and turned cautiously, clinging to a cleft of rock on a ledge about twenty feet above the primitive pit, where she'd been working with some of the diggers.

Amas was gesticulating wildly to her from the floor, a wide grin on his face. 'Come here! Look what we have!'

She made her way slowly down the side – the grade was not steep. The Premier mine was a soup-plate compared to the dizzying depths of the Big Hole, and yet they had discovered in these last nine months more than a hundred thousand carats in diamonds.

Reaching the floor, Vanessa hurried to cover the distance between them.

The Premier was almost unrecognisable now; Amas had imported a good deal of equipment from Kimberley, but the vast network of cables and cars was not required in the shallower Premier. That very fact – that this mine was more accessible, more conducive to a very personal participation – was probably what had aroused their deep excitement.

The Big Hole still produced at a steady pace, and they had divided their time between Kimberley and Pretoria. But it was here that their real interest lay. Amas always said it took him back to the old days, working the Premier. And worked they had, like navvies, not only for the satisfaction of the find but to try and lay to rest some of the guilt and sorrow associated with the long silence of Lesley.

'Eureka!' Amas called out as she approached him. He was kneeling on the ground in the midst of a knot of workers. 'Round crystals, Vanessa. We've got to have five thousand carats right here, in this one pile!'

Exclaiming, she knelt down beside him; he handed her one of the rough diamonds, gleaming dully in its shell of golden brown kimberlite. She weighed it thoughtfully in her hand. 'I make this . . . about five hundred carats,' she said thoughtfully.

'You're getting better all the time,' he congratulated her. 'That's almost exactly what I make it.'

She could feel his pride in her, his jubilation. The thrill of the find was like a fever that possessed them both eternally. Already, when she looked at the faint gleam of the stone, nested like a precious egg in its surrounding kimberlite, Vanessa could see it cut and polished, faceted, glittering with that cold silver fire that nothing could extinguish, that confounding glimmer like a distant star in miniature, held in the human hand.

'And round,' she marvelled. The best-formed crystals, with their rounded shapes and smoother surfaces, were stronger than the flat ones, which also contained more impurities and were far less sure in the cutting.

'Yes. These are the first,' Amas gloated. 'It's a good day, Vanessa. A landmark day.' He grinned companionably at her. 'All right, boys, let's clean these off a bit and get them to the sorting shed.'

Vanessa lent a hand, careless of the blazing sun that heated her helmet, the eye-stinging, throat-catching dust of the floor.

They had almost finished when Amas' surface manager, Hogan, bellowed out to them from the top.

'Something's up,' Amas muttered. 'Are you ready for the climb?'

'Surely.' They left the men completing the task and made the brief, comparatively easy climb to the surface. Amas held out his hand to Vanessa, helping her for the last few steps and greeted Hogan. 'At least five thousand carats down there, Johnny.'

Straightening, dusting off her divided skirt, Vanessa was puzzled at Hogan's demeanour. Although he said quietly, 'That's fine, sir', his face showed no answering enthusiasm. It was peculiarly stiff and solemn, as if a smile would make the features crack.

Hogan slowly held out a yellow envelope. 'Telegram for you, sir, from Kimberley, from your native foreman . . .' Hogan cut off his words and bit his lip.

All of them were well aware that in the small world of Pretoria there were few secrets in telegrams; they were so rare that at some point the sender, messenger, telegrapher and recipient were all aware of the message.

'Come now, Johnny, what's it about?' Amas grinned. 'You already know it's from Sala.' He took the envelope from Hogan.

'I . . . I'm not sure, sir.' Hogan touched his hat to Vanessa and hurried off.

Frowning, Amas ripped open the envelope and unfolded the yellow paper. Vanessa watched him wince and grow muddy below his tan. He seemed to reel backward on his feet.

'What is it, what *is* it?' she cried, trying to snatch the telegram from him. He held it away from her, grasping her wrist.

'Sit down, Vanessa,' he said with a hollow terseness, an awful flatness of intonation. 'Sit right down on the ground here.'

Wonderingly she obeyed, sinking to her knees on the dusty earth. He stood still, but he was beginning to shake all over. Finally he handed her the yellow fragment of paper.

The letters danced in front of her eyes in the blinding sunlight; she caught Lesley's name. She read it again. Something about Mrs Lesley Farley. At last the message penetrated. 'We regret to advise that your daughter, Mrs Lesley Farley, has died of an overdose of laudanum.' The origin was Cape Town and dimly, as she tried to blink away her gathering tears compounded by the sting of perspiration, Vanessa made out the name of the Cape Town Constabulary.

It had not come from Sala then, but had been forwarded by him from Kimberley, she thought stupidly, clinging to the absurd detail in a last desperate effort to evade the full import of the wire.

'No, no,' she mumbled, shaking her head. 'Lesley . . . dead? It's . . . a mistake, Amas. A mistake.' With equal desperation she tried to believe that.

But Amas was trembling so now that she feared he would fall. She struggled to her feet and put her arms around his waist, feeling the horrible quiver in this rocklike man who had never been undone, in her presence, in all the years they had been together.

He did not encircle her in his arms, as he would customarily have done, but stood quaking with his hands hanging limply at his sides, saying over and over, 'I have killed our daughter, Vanessa. I have killed her.'

'No, Amas, no!' she cried out. 'Lesley . . . killed herself.' She forced the words out but with the saying of them came the whole dread realisation – their child, after so few years of life, so little known to either of them, was dead. Vanessa's pent-up tears broke forth, and gushed in a small hot river down her cheeks.

'No,' she repeated, 'don't say that, Amas.'

Obdurately in a strange, blank voice, he reiterated, 'I have killed her. I didn't even want to go to see her, that day at the Cape. You wrote to her, all the time. You tried. After a few tries I gave up, and sent her to her death.' The flatness of his voice cracked then, and he gave a rending sob.

It was horrible. Horrible to hear that strong voice break, that unbearable sob wrenched from the strong depths like a heart torn from a living body; the sob of a strong man, she reflected with pity, was the sign of an agony far greater than a woman's, with her facile and comforting tears.

Now all her thoughts were of him; in that moment she was almost able to forget the source of his pounding misery.

'Come,' she said softly, 'come, Amas.' She took his arm, urging him away from the blistering rise. 'We must go back to the house, at once. At once, Amas.'

All of a sudden he seemed to shake off his stunned lethargy. 'Yes,' he replied in a voice that was more familiar to her. 'Yes. We must go to the Cape at once.'

They made their way with stumbling steps back to the small house they occupied in Pretoria and in utter silence prepared themselves for the journey.

Vanessa was frightened at Amas' demeanour during the wearisome, two-day trip by train. He ate almost nothing and at night lay stiffly awake beside her in their compartment, as she herself vainly sought sleep, testing one miserable position after another without relief.

By the time they disembarked at the loud, busy depot in Cape Town, Amas seemed to have shed ten pounds of weight. His face looked caved in and there were dark circles about his bitter eyes.

'I'll go to the . . . the Constabulary office now,' Amas said in a horribly dead, even tone. She knew he could not say the other word, so cold and desolate and practical. 'I'll go there alone, Vanessa. You should not come with me. I'll see you to the hotel. We will have to stay the night before we take . . . before we begin the return journey. You must have some rest.'

He himself was swaying on his feet with physical and mental exhaustion, she could see.

'No, Amas. I'll go with you. We will do everything together.'

Amas was obviously too fatigued to argue. Defeated, he signalled for a carriage that took them to the offices of the Constabulary. There after a wearisome wait during which Vanessa was afraid she would lose consciousness, they were finally received by a sympathetic official who pressed coffee upon them and told them gently what had happened.

Afterwards there was another grim journey to the hospital, where Lesley's body lay in a cryptlike area of the cellar.

Trembling and sick, Vanessa said, 'I must go to the house now,' clutching at the scribbled address to which they had sent so many unanswered letters.

185

'You said we would do everything together,' he reminded her with the barest hint of his familiar spirit. She almost wept again over her joy at this tiny flicker of hopefulness, but instead she managed a slight smile. 'You're right. We'll go together.'

In the carriage again he said, as if it had just struck him for the first time, 'And Farley is gone. Gone right away, no one knows where. It is fortunate for him he has.'

The implacable hatred in his comment made Vanessa shiver, and she thanked whatever fortune there was that it was so. To see Amas confront Mitchell Farley, in the midst of this ordeal, would be far more than she could ever bear.

A dour-looking Scottish woman in nurse's uniform opened the door to their ring. 'I am Nurse McKenzie. You will no doubt be Mr and Mrs Holder, the parents of that poor lady.'

They both nodded at once, dumbly, so stricken they could not reply. Nurse McKenzie at once took over and ordered them in her gruff, kindly way to sit down and take tea. 'Afterrr such a jourrney,' she said sternly, 'ye must tak' nourrrishment. Do it now. I shall fetch the poor bairn.'

A baby. Lesley had had a child. Vanessa, like an automaton, poured out the strong, reviving tea and gave a cup to Amas. Neither of them could touch any of the toast or cakes on the laden tray, but the tea helped a good deal. Vanessa was relieved to notice that Amas was looking a little better. He drained one cup of tea and quickly asked for another.

In a moment or two the nurse was back, holding the baby in her arms. 'Your grand-daughterrr,' Nurse McKenzie announced. She came to Vanessa and carefully placed the baby on her lap.

Vanessa, awkward with the unaccustomed burden, stared down into the baby's face. She was all that remained to them now of Lesley. Quick moisture blurred Vanessa's sight.

'Why, Amas,' she said brokenly, 'she already has your colour of hair.' It was true; the negligible fuzz on the baby's unsteady head was exactly the shade of Amas' mane. She tightened her hold on the baby.

Amas put down his cup gently and rose, coming to stand by Vanessa's side, staring down fascinated at the baby.

'Has she . . . has she been named?' he asked the nurse.

'Her poor mother, rest her soul, died before she could give the child a name. I have named her for the time being. I call her Megan.' A suspicion of a smile twinkled in the nurse's stern eyes. 'It is a

186

Celtic name meaning "the strong". I thought the mite would be in need of such an omen, to lend her the force and will that . . .'

The woman stopped, dismayed. It was apparent to Vanessa that she was about to say, 'the force and will that her mother never had.'

'I do beg your parrdon,' the nurse said, abashed.

'It's all right, Miss McKenzie,' Vanessa said gently. 'You are very kind. And it is a lovely name, isn't it, Amas?' She smiled at him and he nodded absently. 'I think we will call her Megan, too, Miss McKenzie. Thank you.'

The broad, maternal woman looked extremely gratified. 'Well, now,' she said briskly. 'I suppose my job is done. She is safe with her grandparents now.'

Grandparents, Vanessa repeated in silent wonder. She was a grandmother at the age of thirty-six. It was grotesque. She was not really ready for this. And then immediately she was shamed by the irrelevant, frivolous idea. Megan was all that remained to them of Lesley, Vanessa repeated to herself once more.

'As to the other matters,' Miss McKenzie went on, 'I suppose this is not the best time to discuss them . . .' She looked at both of them in an embarrassed way.

'We have to discuss everything, Miss McKenzie. You have already performed above and beyond the call of duty in this affair,' Amas asserted. 'And we will be returning to Kimberley tomorrow. I think we must talk about everything now. First, your fees. Were you, er, paid by . . . Mr Farley?'

'No, sir. It pains me to tell you that . . . that the father of the baby dashed out of this verrry house on the day that . . . Mrs Holder passed, with neverrr a look at his own child or a fare-ye-well, leaving everything as it lay. Leaving it all to us.' Nurse McKenzie looked surprised for an instant at their lack of surprise.

Then she queried, 'I take it, then, that the fatherrr was not unknown to you?'

It was so circumspectly put that for the first time in days Vanessa positively grinned.

Amas answered drily, 'Not unknown at all, Miss McKenzie.' After a pause he went on, 'Let me assure you that we will be more than happy to compensate you for all your trouble and your care.' She seemed about to protest but he said insistently, 'The kind of care that was far more than you were *required* to give.'

Heartened, Vanessa watched Amas smile faintly at the nurse. Perhaps it was because the worst ordeal had passed; perhaps it was his preoccupation with the baby, with new things to be done, that calmed him. Whatever it was, Vanessa was thankful for it. She herself was already thinking of the things that must be bought for the baby. It was good to be occupied by these practical and urgent matters; they helped so much to still her gnawing grief.

While Amas settled with Miss McKenzie, Vanessa went to Lesley's room to which the nurse had given her directions. A soft sob escaped from her as she surveyed Lesley's pitifully few possessions, packed in two small grips and a couple of neatly tied boxes.

Grateful to the nurse for overseeing this sad task, Vanessa was relieved that she would not have to handle those possessions now. She would arrange for their shipment back to Kimberley after they had got to the hotel. The neat bed, with its pristine coverings, she assiduously avoided looking at. That must be the bed where Lesley had died.

Straightening her shoulders, Vanessa went back to the sitting room and took the small bundle of Megan Farley from the arms of Nurse McKenzie.

From now on, she resolved, she would be with Megan always; the child would go with her everywhere. This was her second lease on motherhood, her second chance to atone for all that she had failed to do for her lost daughter.

Leslie Holder Farley was buried in the family burying ground near the Kimberley bungalow, the ground whose first occupant had been the loyal Sehoiya. The old servant had died peacefully in her sleep the year before.

There had not been enough time, of course, for Martin to make the journey from England. As month succeeded month, Vanessa found that the hard rock of grief in her breast was melting, that Amas, too, was becoming healed.

For a time that painful soreness in her breast had seemed to be, not a rock, but a malignant growth that would increase in size, over the continuing weeks of sadness, and devour her. When at last she realised that this was not so, she breathed a prayer of thanksgiving and began to live again.

Megan and Martin now were the names she said over and over to Amas, and he to her. 'We still have Megan and Martin,' Vanessa would say, and he would smile, if a little sadly, and say it back to her like a kind of litany.

Martin's letters from London fairly sang with vitality and enthusiasm. He was working for Wertheimer's cousin now and apparently making great progress. Even at his age Martin had already become a highly expert diamond sorter, and his employers had even adopted some of his suggestions for improvements in the office's operations. 'Mr Wertheimer told me,' Martin wrote them proudly, 'that I am a "phenomenon". I knew you and Dad would want to know.'

Amas fairly burst with pride, reading the letter.

He was returning to his old self, day by day. Once he confided to Vanessa, after one of their habitual visits to Pretoria, 'You know, when we first got that . . . telegram, all I could think of was how we were grovelling in the dirt, like children, playing with pebbles, while our daughter lay dead. And then, when I realised the anodyne that work has been for us, I knew I had been thinking like a fool, Vanessa.'

'Not like a fool, Amas; unable to think in that . . . that unspeakable agony.'

He took her hand. 'You've been wonderful through all this, Vanessa. Wonderful with the baby.'

She replied frankly, 'Not wonderful at all, Amas. The baby, like the mines, has been my distraction. What I do for her is also for my own well-being . . . and it is also my atonement.'

He was silent, studying her. Then he said, 'You are atoning too much, Vanessa.' He grinned. 'You are not now and never have been a mother. You know perfectly well Ranee can manage Megan as well as you, if not better. You are neglecting your *own* work, you know.'

'Not you, I trust,' she retorted.

'Never. Never me,' he said tenderly, taking her in his arms. In truth the tragedy had brought them closer than ever together, and their lovemaking, she reflected happily, was an absolute 'disgrace', as Amas humorously put it, 'for grandparents'.

'What, then?' she demanded, almost knowing the answer before he made it.

'Your music, Vanessa. You haven't touched the piano for months. Think of all that wasted time in Pretoria. I must have told you a dozen times that we could buy a piano in Jo'burg and have it sent there.'

'That's such an extravagance,' she said weakly. 'And the house is so small . . .'

'The house *was* small,' he corrected. 'We've had the annexe now for six months. If you must pursue so relentlessly this new mother role . . .' he grinned, 'think of it this way. You are depriving Megan.

Have you forgotten all Martin's letters, over the years? How he missed the music he remembered? You surrounded the children with music, with constant beauty. Do you want Megan to grow up into an absolute barbarian?'

'Such language, Mr Holder. You sound like my mother. With us for grandparents what else could Megan be?'

He did not respond to her laughter. 'I mean it, Vanessa. It's time you got down to business.'

After he'd gone she thought about it. What he'd said was perfectly true. The Big Hole, these days, was such a huge and complex operation that her personal involvement, except in certain administrative areas, was needless and absurd.

Depriving Megan. That perhaps was what drove the argument most surely home, she thought, amused.

And that very day she returned to her piano, limbering her fingers, grinding out again the relentless exercise of scales. Late that afternoon she played a lullaby for Ranee and Megan.

To Vanessa's utter delight, the eight-month-old baby gurgled and clapped her hands in imitation of Ranee. There was a gleam of pleasure, Vanessa could almost swear, in the wide, tawny eyes that were a lighter version of the lioncoloured ones of Amas Holder.

It was Megan's first birthday in that month of June, 1903, when Vanessa realised she had left poor Lesley's possessions untouched in the box room of the annexe.

For the first six months the idea had been too painful; for the last, caught up in the business of living, Vanessa had simply forgotten day after day.

But this morning it occurred to her, and it was a task that must be faced. To leave the things there unattended was in a way to forget her daughter. And there might be little things she had obtained for the baby that were meant for use, that some day Megan would treasure.

So she hurried to the annexe and into the musty boxroom before she could change her mind. There was plenty of time left before Megan's little party that afternoon. Vanessa smiled, thinking of Martin's gifts, a lovely baby dress and soft toys carefully posted to arrive in good time.

But the heat in the boxroom was intense; she opened a window and gratefully breathed the somewhat cooler, far fresher air of the African winter. Finding the boxes and the cases, she attacked the grips first.

She unfolded Lesley's pathetic finery, marvelling sadly at the childishness of her taste. How young she'd been; how misguided. The other case yielded up much of the same. Vanessa gently laid the clothes aside; she would send the more modest dresses off to the local missionaries who were always soliciting clothes. What she would do with the others she could not imagine, already depressed with the task she had set for herself.

But with stern resolution and renewed energy, she patted her moist face with her handkerchief and then untied the string of the first box.

The first sight that greeted her was a miniature of Mitchell Farley. Vanessa turned almost sick, observing those smug features.

Under the miniature, which she cast aside with an impatient gesture, was a tiny velvet box on top of a pile of infant's clothes. Vanessa opened it. She found a fragile golden chain, so frail it looked almost like joined golden hairs, a minuscule diamond pendant attached to it.

Vanessa took a sobbing breath – Lesley's baby chain, that Amas had had made for her when she was only three. Vanessa would not have expected her to keep it, to take it with her on all her hectic journeys. But she had, and no doubt she intended it for the baby. Vanessa shut the box and put it carefully aside, examining the clothes.

Lesley had cared, then, she reflected, cared enough about the baby to prepare, before the onset of that terrible madness that made her take her own life, to collect these things.

But what . . . what on earth or under heaven, she asked herself as she had so often before, led her daughter to that dreadful action? Perhaps the answer would be here.

It was when she had emptied the second box that she found it – a small leather-covered diary. Vanessa sat on a disreputable, discarded chair and began to read.

At first it seemed too incredible to be true. She could not believe what she was reading, not at all. But then she read on with a horrible fascination, scanning rapidly, turning page after page, learning the truth of her daughter's tragic marriage to Mitchell Farley; queasily forming the picture of his cruelties and abominations, the indignities he had inflicted on her daughter's body, his hideous boasts.

And all of Vanessa's banished guilt, the pain that had quieted for a time, came flooding back to drown her with their black and awful power. Holding the book in her hands, she rocked back and forth on

191

the chair, too hurt even to cry out, her self-reproach escaping in the form of wordless groans.

How long she was flailed thus she did not know; but finally she realised that the sun had moved, the room dimming as this side of the house always did at a certain time of day and she knew that a great deal of time had passed. She straightened in the chair, her back aching from her long-held, crouched position and drew a sobbing breath.

The worst was over, but she was left with a dark, cold sense of self-hate that had settled in her to stay. Only she had condemned her child to that hellish torture, and the knowledge of that would gnaw at her until the day she died.

But she was resolved of one thing: Amas must never know. This was one secret she would keep from him beyond her dying breath, even if heretofore she had never hidden the slightest thing from him, ultimately telling him even the shameful thoughts she'd had that day long ago about how trapped the children made her feel, that day she was writing to her father, when Amas told her Bea was coming back again. No, this would remain hidden – for ever.

The pain of it would almost kill him, she knew. What was worse, his undying hatred for Mitchell Farley would be so inflamed by this additional evidence of Farley's meanness that Amas would lose his mind altogether . . . he would make it his life's ambition, in his implacable way, to find Farley and kill him with his own hands.

And all this, her mind cried out to her, could have been averted. I could have gone to Cape Town, I could have persisted. I could have saved her.

Then she thought in panic, I must burn the diary, burn it at once. What if Amas found her here now? Amas must never be allowed to read that nightmare account. Yes, she was convinced he would kill Farley and their lives would fall into utter ruin. He would be imprisoned, snatched from her and that would be worse than death because at least in death there might be peace.

Clear-sightedly she thought, even now I am thinking of myself, my life, our lives. And something answered, in that strange and ghostly moment of debate, why not?

Those who are still alive must cling to life and glory in it. Vanessa Holder had always valued life as she had not been able to teach her own child to do. And so did Amas. . . . and, praise heaven, Martin.

'In your eye, Death.' Vanessa said it aloud, feeling defiant and renewed. Neither Amas nor Martin nor Megan – above all, Megan

192

– nor anyone else on earth would ever know the true shame of Lesley Holder Farley.

Vanessa hurried to the kitchen and snatched up a box of matches; Ranee was in the yard and did not see. Concealing the diary in a fold of her skirt, Vanessa went to a far edge of the garden and set the book with the miniature inside, alight.

Seeing them burn, she said again soundlessly, 'In your damned eye, Mr Death.' She waited until the book was utterly consumed and then stamped on the ashes, mingling them with the fresh-smelling earth. It was a ritual for Lesley . . . and for the continuing battle they all must wage for their breath. She thought, every stroke of my brush against my hair, to keep its shine; every caress of my hand on Amas' body; every note of music, every kiss on Megan's face and every diamond we wrest from the earth is a denial of her death.

Consoled and heartened, Vanessa hurried off to prepare for the party.

Part IV
The Faceting

CHAPTER THIRTEEN

'No, Megan! Come back to Granna!'

The intractable six-year-old paid no attention to Vanessa's command; she was climbing the lower elevation of the Premier just like a monkey, her small feet in their rough shoes sure in the clefts of rock; her reedy little legs and arms, darkened by the sun, exhibited a startling grace.

In the midst of her annoyance and anxiety, Vanessa Holder was obliged to smile. Megan's strong and stubborn will was at once a source of concern and pride. In some ways the child reminded Vanessa so much of herself at that age – independent, tomboyish and obdurate – that it was hard to be severe with her. In fact, it was almost impossible, and Vanessa had spoiled her outrageously.

And this was the result, she concluded grimly. A possible broken neck.

'Megan!' she called again, more sharply. Vanessa's heart was in her mouth. The child was climbing steadily. Amas was with a group of diggers on the other side of the Premier's dusty bowl. A nearby worker paused in his digging and called out, 'Need any help, Mrs Holder?'

'No, I'll get her.' Exasperated, Vanessa clambered up after Megan – for an adult the climb was of no great consequence – and grabbed her hard around her narrow middle, feeling the astonishing play of her tensile muscles.

'Ah, Granna,' Megan said disgustedly, 'I'm all right.' She had been talking since she was two years old and her speech was unusually mature, even if she clung to the old names, 'Granna' for Vanessa and 'Ampus', her early approximation of 'Amas'.

'You can't carry me all the way down, Granna,' Megan added astutely. 'I'm not a baby. I can get down again.'

'All right,' Vanessa conceded with some reluctance. 'But let me hold you, Megan.'

Resignedly the child submitted to Vanessa's guidance as they slowly descended. Her manner, Vanessa noticed with amusement, was almost that of a patient adult conceding to the wishes of an unreasonable child.

Ever since she was three years old, Megan had had that peculiar air of an 'old child', some fey creature possessed of knowledge not shared by ordinary mortals, and her likeness to a displaced spirit of the air was still strong. Vanessa sometimes imagined that she could feel vestigial wings on the child's sharp shoulder blades and Amas laughed at that fancy. But he, like Vanessa, was astounded by Megan's utter fearlessness of heights, her unusual agility.

She might, Vanessa told him, become a dancer or something related that would satisfy her need for constant motion, utilise that most remarkable grace. In that regard, Vanessa already foresaw the need to educate the child in a wider horizon than those of Kimberley and Cape Town. The horizon of Africa, Vanessa said drily, was physically vast but aesthetically so narrow.

But not yet, not yet, she protested silently now, observing Megan with a queer little tug at her heart. She could not bear to part with this fairylike thing for a while, because she had grown to love her so much.

Safely on the floor again, Vanessa scolded, 'I thought you were enjoying yourself, helping me with the diamonds.'

'I like them, Granna,' Megan explained in her serious fashion, 'but I got tired of it.'

She grinned up at Vanessa. Her grandmother's annoyance dissipated with the observance of the wonderful golden eyes in the impish face, the resilient body in its dusty boy's clothes and the radiance of auburn in the ruffled, gold-brown hair.

Vanessa had remarked to Amas that Megan had been well-named; she looked like a Celtic changeling. And from where, Vanessa had demanded, had she got that touch of red in her hair? Perhaps she was a true changeling after all. The more matter-of-fact Amas said calmly that his own mother, Ellen Holder, had had a touch of auburn in her own hair when young, and thought no more of it.

As for Megan's getting 'tired' of her diversion, that was habitual. She seemed to require constant variety and change, and once more Vanessa was assailed by the gloomy conviction that the child belonged in a city and not on the veld.

'Why are you looking like that?' Megan demanded abruptly, noticing Vanessa's absent-mindedness.

'Oh, no reason.' It had become her habit to answer Megan almost as she would a peer, which had, doubtless, contributed to the child's precocity.

'Come on,' she said briskly. 'Aren't you going to help me sort the diamonds?'

'Yes, Granna.' Megan's tone was bored. She stretched out her small arms with a birdlike motion and looked up towards the surface, her strong golden eyes barely squinting in the winter sun.

'Oh, look!' She pointed in excitement. 'There are two Ampus.'

'What on earth are you talking about?' Vanessa followed the direction of Megan's stare. She blinked, narrowing her eyes against the sun. A tall, strong figure stood outlined against the sky, waving at them.

Good heavens, the child was right. It was like two of Amas – the original knelt down there on the floor with the workers, the other stood above them, waving.

Vanessa's heart gave a mighty jolt.

'Martin!' she cried out, returning his wave. 'Oh, Martin!'

The tall young man tossed his grip on the ground and began to make the descent. As he came nearer, Vanessa could make out his face more clearly, and it was astonishing how much he resembled Amas. He was descending quickly, careless of the dust already thickening on his elegant city clothes, and then he was running towards Vanessa to take her in his arms.

'Martin, oh, Martin.' Vanessa was so overpowered she could say only his name, again and again.

At last she was able to say, 'You can't know what it means to see you, especially now, that . . .' Vanessa paused, stricken again with the old pain.

'. . . that Lesley's gone,' he finished sadly. 'I still can't believe it, Mother. I can't believe what happened.'

'I never will.'

'Let me look at you.' She heard the strong English inflection as he stepped back, holding both her hands, looking her up and down, smiling widely, some of his sadness lifting. 'I knew it. I knew you would be as beautiful as you ever were.'

'I can't believe it!' Vanessa cried out. 'I still can't believe it. Why didn't you let us know?'

'I wanted to save you a two-day train trip to the Cape.' He chuckled. 'Which you assuredly would have made, a great waste of energy and time. And money, from the looks of things here. Besides, I wanted to look up Kossee in Kimberley.' His brown, excited gaze took in the busy floor. 'There's Dad!'

Vanessa was still holding his hands.

'And who's this?' Martin inquired, smiling down at the fascinated Megan, who could not take her eyes off this apparition. 'Could this be Megan?'

199

'Oh, yes,' Megan said demurely, holding out her small hand.

'That won't do at all!' Martin objected and scooped her up in his strong arms, planting quick, light kisses on the child's delighted face. 'Not for your Uncle Martin. I've brought you all kinds of things from London.'

'Oh! What? What, Uncle Martin? Let me see?' Megan wriggled with excitement in his grasp.

He laughed. 'A natural girl, I see. Well, the things are in my suitcase way up there. We'll get it soon.'

'I'll go up and get it!' Megan offered, grinning.

'Indeed you will not,' Martin countered. 'I saw that performance before. You're some climber.'

Vanessa was so enchanted by the exchange she had totally forgotten Amas. But she had not counted on his sharp eyes; he was already striding towards them, a big grin on his weathered face.

'Martin!' Amas hugged the tall boy to him; they were almost of a height. He clapped Martin hard on his muscular shoulder. 'This is great . . . this is wonderful!'

'I wanted to surprise you,' Martin repeated to Amas, forestalling the inevitable query. 'When can I start digging?'

'Tomorrow,' Amas retorted. 'The rest of this day we'll spend in celebration.'

The remainder of the afternoon was a happy, hectic blur – their ascent to the surface, with Megan safely in Martin's guiding arms; the journey back to the house, and a hilarious family dinner, when everyone seemed to chatter at once, and there were a hundred questions asked of Martin and numerous questions from him about the mines and Megan, Vanessa's music and the Kimberley people. Martin explained that he hadn't stopped there, in his eagerness to get to Pretoria.

Megan, who had clung to her uncle like a limpet all the afternoon and evening, persuaded to let him go only long enough to get into more comfortable clothes, had been on her very best behaviour. Beyond commenting that Martin was just like Ampus, 'but smooth' – which brought general laughter about Amas' seamed façade – the child had been very quiet.

However her patience reached an end after dinner, and she reminded Martin urgently of the 'things from London'.

'Megan!' Vanessa said gently. 'That's not very nice.'

Martin put his hands to his head. 'I'd totally forgotten. Of *course* it's nice. Come on, Megan. Help me bring in the presents.' She willingly obeyed.

He had brought gifts for them all – a handsome Morocco toilet kit for Amas, an exquisite dressing gown for Vanessa and, for Megan, a fluffy white lace dress, an elaborate doll and a minuscule gold bangle bracelet set with seed pearls, her birthstone. Megan squealed with pleasure over her presents; she showed the greatest excitement, however, over the bracelet. Clasping it on her wrist, she declared that she would never take it off again. In their happy preoccupation, no one seemed to notice that she ignored the doll.

'You are very generous, son,' Amas said. 'But you went a little overboard, I think. You've spent a fortune.'

'Oh, well,' Martin said lightly. 'I'm the fair-haired boy at the office now. I've had two rises since I wrote you last.'

His delighted parents made noises of congratulation and then Martin, a little embarrassed, insisted that Vanessa play for him.

It was a wonderful evening that went on so long Megan fell asleep on the sofa and had to be carried to bed.

Later, when Amas and Vanessa were in their room, she sighed with happiness. 'Oh, Amas, it's so good to have him home for a while.'

Amas smiled at her from the bed. 'It certainly is. He's a man now, a real man.'

'Amas . . .' she began shyly as she got into bed beside him. 'Did it strike you that Martin was a little . . . reticent about certain things?'

'What do you mean? It seemed to me he never stopped talking.'

Vanessa reached over and stroked Amas' arm. He made a sound of pleasure.

'Oh, not about the office, and his work, or Diana and London, and all that. He seemed to be . . . so secretive about his social life.'

'Oh, *well*, darling.' Amas chuckled. 'There are some things a boy doesn't discuss with his mother.'

'Not that, Amas. Of course the boy is, shall we say, discovering life. I meant something beyond that, something he seems to be keeping from us.' Vanessa did not know herself exactly what she meant; but it was *something*, she was convinced.

'Perhaps he's met a special young lady,' Amas offered, 'and he's working up the courage to tell us about it, because he knows damned well he's far too young to get serious at this point. As he *is*,' Amas added firmly.

'Are you sure? He's very mature for nineteen, Amas. Just as you were at twenty-four,' she reminded him, grinning.

'But I *was* twenty-four, Vanessa,' he countered gently. He kissed her nose. 'Now go to sleep. Tomorrow is going to be a very busy day.'

She moved into his embrace but lay wakeful after she heard his rhythmic breathing, still wondering what it was that was eluding her.

They had been overjoyed to learn that Martin was 'at liberty' for a whole month from Dunkensreuter and began to make numerous plans.

Martin good-naturedly agreed, but he seemed to be quite happy to stay, for the time being, in Pretoria, and the very next morning over Amas' protests rose early with them to go to the mines. In the days that followed both Amas and Vanessa were impressed with the boy's uncanny instinct for the find, his almost eerie ability to value a stone after a glance at it, hefting it in his tensile, long-fingered hand.

On the fourth morning after Martin's arrival, he was working with the diggers supervised by Amas when an exclamation escaped him. 'Dad!' he called out sharply. 'Look . . . I think we've really got something here.'

And, wonderingly, Martin Holder unearthed the biggest rough diamond he'd ever even imagined. He rubbed his eyes and blinked away his sweat.

Amas was at his side in a moment and together they lifted the massive block of kimberlite, stricken dumb by the sight of that nested object, gleaming dully – the stone itself was at least four inches long.

'This has got to be the biggest diamond in the world,' Martin said shakily, weighing it in his trembling hands.

'I wouldn't be surprised at all.' Amas' own rough whisper betrayed an excitement equal to Martin's. 'Good Lord, there must be three thousand carats there, boy.'

'That's what I figure it, Dad.' The two men, on their knees, stared at each other. And then the full realisation of their discovery burst upon them. They gave a simultaneous whoop of delirious joy and, rising, began to do a kind of giddy dance, like a Highland fling, with their hands on each other's shoulders.

Attracted by the spectacle, Vanessa came running to them, hand in hand with Megan.

'Vanessa, Vanessa!' Amas' eyes were blazing, and he looked drunk with excitement. 'We've found it – we've found the biggest damned diamond in the world . . . and it'll bring something near a million dollars!'

She shrieked with pleasure, and then the four joined hands and did a wild, abandoned dance together, around and around the enormous diamond that lay gleaming in the morning sun.

All work was suspended for the day, and all at once there were a thousand things to be taken care of – a safe place must be found for the stone; they must notify a reputable exchange. It seemed a foregone conclusion that that dealer would be Dunkensreuter. Amas declared that they would name it the 'Martin Diamond', with Vanessa's fervent agreement; Martin was fairly insane with the event, driven by an almost maniacal energy that made him babble.

He must cable Dunkensreuter at once, he declared, and it was decided that someone must therefore make the trip to Jo'burg; cable facilities were not available in Pretoria.

'I'll go, Dad.'

'I'll go with you,' Amas offered.

'No, Dad, no! You're forgetting. We can't leave Mother alone with that thing.'

Amas merely laughed at this evidence of his thrill-scattered judgment. 'You're right, you're absolutely right,' he admitted, not at all chagrined. 'Go, go.'

Martin hurried away and called out to one of the men to drive him to the train, obviously too excited even to give a thought to the fact that he was dressed in dirty, sweat-stained clothes as disreputable as a roustabout's.

The thought of his gear did not once occur to Martin Holder until he came barrelling out of the cable office in Jo'burg and collided with a daintily dressed young woman. A misting rain had begun to fall, and already the streets of Johannesburg were forming into mud.

The young woman, losing her balance, was about to fall backwards into the street when Martin grabbed at her with a bruising hold on her slender waist and pulled her upright again.

'Good God!' he exclaimed involuntarily. 'Oh, my God, I *do* beg your pardon.'

Cursing his clumsiness and inattention, Martin stared into her indignant, long-lidded eyes. He took a quick, gasping breath; he had never seen such eyes in all his days. They were so pale a blue they were practically silver, and glittered against the pink and white skin of her face, which reminded him of a new apple blossom. A faint and delicious fragrance, also reminiscent of that flower, emanated from her dainty person.

Below her saucy little hat, now knocked awry with the force of her tumble, there was a glimmering foam of pale gold hair; like her eyes, it looked almost silver, and Martin thought with dismay, I nearly knocked this unearthly, beautiful creature down.

He repeated, stammering, 'I say, I can't tell you how awful I feel, banging into you like that. Please tell me you're not hurt. I really . . .' Even more dismayed, he looked down at her clothes. The skirt of her lilac coloured dress was spattered liberally with disfiguring mud, the hem almost black with it.

He tightened his grasp on her waist. 'You must let me take you to a . . . doctor, miss. And I insist on paying for the ruin to your clothes.'

'Please,' she said at last, her strangely serene gaze taking in his raffish appearance with a calm distaste that pained him. Her voice was low and pleasing, with a hint of Boer, and she was amazingly unruffled, he thought, considering what had just happened.

Matter-of-factly the frail young woman raised her white hands and straightened her hat. 'It is of no moment,' she told him primly. 'Now, please,' she glanced down at his hands still on her waist, 'you had better let me go.'

Martin dropped his hands at once with a new flood of apology, concluding. 'You really must let me do *something*. I've acted like a perfect boor.'

'I would say you're an Englishman, not a Boer,' she retorted unsmiling but with a flash of amusement in her enchanting eyes.

Delighted with her quickness and her astonishing poise, Martin felt the sudden hammering of his heart. This was the most exquisite, the most delightful woman he'd ever had the good fortune to see. She must not be allowed to escape him. Then, conscious of her rather critical glance, he realised what he looked like and cursed himself even more roundly for coming to Jo'burg like this. Oh, why in hell hadn't he thought to change his clothes?

'You must excuse my appearance, miss. You see, I . . .'

'Forgive me, sir. I must go back to my children now.'

Her *children*! Martin's heart sank to the soles of his muddy boots. 'Your children?' he repeated dolefully.

'Over there.' She nodded and he looked. At least fifteen small children, girls and boys, were standing quietly together beside a capacious carriage across the way. All were staring unblinkingly at the beautiful young woman and at Martin.

'All those?' he asked, his incredulity so great that the question came out as a hoarse whisper.

The beautiful young silver woman laughed, and her laughter had an exceedingly pleasant sound. 'They are the children in my class.' She enlightened him. 'I am a teacher.' A smile at last broke forth and he was struck by its sweetness, by the dazzling perfection of her small white teeth.

His relief was so overpowering that a cold sweat broke out on his back. 'I see,' he murmured. She wasn't married. She wasn't married. He suddenly realised that if she had been he would have felt like cutting his throat, and the idea was astounding. 'Well, then, er . . . how should we go about this?'

'Go about what?'

Her eyes were twinkling now.

'Well, I think you ought to allow me to take you to a doctor,' he said more firmly. 'I might have . . . injured you in some way. And really, you must let me pay you for your dress.'

He reached into his trouser-pocket for money.

'Ah, no, please,' she protested, and a faint flush dyed her satiny cheeks. 'You couldn't . . .'

Suddenly he realised what she was trying so delicately to say. She thought he couldn't afford it. Laughter began to boil in Martin Holder; he had just cabled London about the discovery of a million-dollar diamond. And this angel thought he couldn't afford to pay for her dress.

'Look here,' he said, the laugh threatening to escape, 'I can afford to compensate you, miss. Really I can.'

Doubtfully she glanced at his awful gear again and then politely away. 'It is not necessary at all, I assure you. Now, if you'll excuse me, I must get back to my children.'

'I'll go with you,' he said boldly. 'Then, after we, er . . . dispose of the children, you must let me take you to a doctor.' She was patently uninjured but this, he decided, was as good a device as any to continue in her company.

'I really think . . .' She frowned.

'If you need my credentials,' he persisted, 'I'm really quite all right. My father is Amas Holder, the owner of the Premier Mine in Pretoria.'

'Holder!' There was a friendlier look now in her wonderful eyes. She knew the name, then. A slow, enchanting smile broke out over her face.

'I am Martin Holder,' he said.

'And I am Anjanette Ryn.'

Anjanette. The name suited her, he thought, savouring it; it

205

sounded as feminine and dainty as . . . ruffles.

'Then, Miss Ryn,' he said triumphantly, 'now that you have my *bona fides*, may I have the privilege of escorting you?'

She nodded, shyly. 'Yes. Mr Holder. You may. We must take each of the children home. Then I must go home, where you will meet my aunt. She will be extremely interested to meet the son of Amas Holder.'

Martin was tantalised by that and she did not enlighten him until all of the children had been safely delivered. But none of that had import for Martin Holder; his whole self was possessed now of a great singing, of a vast uncharted wonder.

Anjanette Ryn, eager to forestall her Aunt Margit, called out, 'I will answer,' and ran to the door.

The Martin Holder who stood there, smiling down at her with burning, eager eyes, bore little resemblance to the raffish fellow she had literally collided with two weeks before. His Bond Street clothes enhanced his strong, reedy height, the grace of his tensile body, yet did nothing to disguise that slight roughness, the muscularity she had never associated with elegant men. His mane of tawny hair was freshly barbered and tamed to accord with the classic features of his eager young face.

But Anjanette could not miss the wild intensity of those golden-brown eyes, like a lion's; that look of passionate apartness that had undone her even during that first hour. She did not recognise herself now, either, she had so wholly changed.

This Martin Holder, like the first, aroused sensations in her body that she had never known when she was still the impervious, demure and dedicated Anjanette Ryn.

'My darling,' he whispered, and took her impulsively in his arms.

Fearful of her aunt's imminent entrance, Anjanette tried to protest, but her own overpowering tenderness defeated her. That weak liquidity had taken possession once more of her flesh and, acquiescent, overjoyed, she gave herself up to him, softening into his firm embrace as her mouth submitted to his hungry mouth.

'Anjanette!'

Startled, Martin loosened his hold, feeling Anjanette quiver. Over her golden head he met the small, outraged eyes of Miss Margit Ryn.

'Mr Holder, what is the meaning of this?' she thundered.

Keeping his arm about Anjanette, Martin replied calmly, 'I have come to ask for your niece's hand, Miss Ryn.'

The respectful formality of the statement did nothing to smooth Margit Ryn.

206

'Her hand!' she repeated. Her tone suggested that he wished to sever that member from her niece.

Unruffled, Martin said, 'Yes. We love each other, Miss Ryn. We want to be married.'

'But . . . but . . .' Margit Ryn spluttered, 'you have been acquainted little more than two weeks. Two *weeks*, Mr Holder. What have you to say to all this, Anjanette?'

'It's true, Aunt Margit. I want to be married to Martin.'

Margit was rendered speechless by the even retort. She shook her head again and again, observing them with annoyance and something akin to pity.

'Well, come into the sitting room,' she grumbled. 'This must be fully and thoroughly discussed.'

Anjanette felt a quick flare of hope, and was proud of Martin when he responded quickly, 'Thank you, Miss Ryn. That is exactly what I am most eager to do.'

'Sit down, young man.' Margit plumped herself aggressively into a high-backed chair which gave her the height of an inquisitor and waited for the two to settle themselves on the opposite sofa.

'Now,' she said sternly, 'what do your parents think of this?'

'I haven't told them yet,' Martin admitted frankly. 'It was only yesterday,' he gave Anjanette a melting look and touched her hand, which set off a delicious quiver deep inside her, 'that Anjanette gave me her consent.'

'Well, then, the whole thing is impossible. I dare say Mr and Mrs Holder will deny you their consent.'

'I dare say they won't,' Martin countered. 'They themselves were married within a month of their first acquaintance.'

Anjanette enjoyed the twinkle in his brown eyes and felt an answering smile twitch at the corners of her mouth.

'This is not a matter to be treated with levity, Anjanette . . . Martin.' Her niece was encouraged by Margit's inclusion of him in her reproach, by her use of his first name.

But her glowering expression had not disappeared. 'I will never grant my consent, Mr Holder,' she went on stiffly, reverting to her earlier formality, 'without your parents' equal consent. You are both far too young to know your own minds. Furthermore . . .' she held up her worn, scrubbed hand to forestall any disclaimer from them, 'even in the unlikely event of your parents' agreement, I must know what you intend to offer my niece.'

Baldly Martin stated the amount of his wages at Dunkensreuter, impressive in themselves, adding the full extent of his share in Holder Mines. Then he casually dropped the information about the discovery of the Holder Diamond, now safely in London at Dunkensreuter's. For security reasons, none of the Holders felt free to mention the discovery until that was so; Martin had even sent his cable in code.

Anjanette, who had known of the diamond's existence, almost laughed aloud to observe her aunt's stunned face.

Margit cleared her throat. 'I . . . I see,' she commented rather weakly. Then, resuming her inquisitorial manner, she added, 'All this wealth, Mr Holder, commendable as it may be, will not compensate my niece if she finds herself married to a wild, reckless youth whose devotion is uncertain.'

Anjanette glanced sideways at Martin; he raised his head and met Margit's scrutiny with a level, pleading look. 'Miss Ryn,' he said solemnly, 'I have never even known what it was to love before. All I want is to devote the rest of my life to making Anjanette happy.'

Anjanette's heart thudded; she could hear its wingbeat in her dazzled ears, and a wide hot flood of tenderness and longing swept throughout her body. She was so weakened by it she began to tremble; she leaned against him for support.

It was apparent that her aunt could not help being moved. A slight relaxation of her stern features approximated a smile, and there was a kindlier light, almost an affectionate warmth, in her small, deep-set eyes.

'You speak well, Martin. I can only hope that your actions will match those pretty words. In any case, I still cannot agree to this marriage until I confer with your parents.'

Martin scrambled to his feet. 'I will ask them to come here this evening,' he offered, eagerness and hope shining from his every feature.

For the first time the dour Margit smiled. 'Very well, Martin Holder. My foolish niece has already consented. Now, if your parents follow suit, then so shall I.'

'Oh, Miss Ryn, thank you, thank you.' Martin stooped to kiss her lined cheek. Then he turned to Anjanette.

She rose and went to him, her joy like a titanic surge of soundless music that surrounded all of her being; vibrating to the very pores of her skin, it racked, it dazzled her.

Waiting for her in the luxurious stateroom of the *Union Castle Scot,*

Martin Holder watched the pictures of the last few hectic days flash across his inner eye – the interview between his parents and Margit Ryn, their warm embrace of Anjanette.

And Anjanette, that dream on earth, standing by his side in something white, only flowers and not a veil on her hair; the hasty celebration and then – when Martin felt even more surely that he was not awake but walked as people do in dreams on water, without the least effort or percussion – the boarding.

It had all gone so fast, so fast. Therefore this night he must go slowly. She was so utterly without experience, so unknowing. If anything in this magic ritual pained or frightened her it would shadow all their lives together.

He had a sudden and irrational wish – that he could be as untouched as she, could bring to this solemn moment the same purity she had.

And the bitter, shameful memory of his interlude with Bea returned to him in lurid detail like the garish paintings he had sometimes seen of the congress of howling witches and demons, the recording of some dread All-Hallows. The images whirled past his inner vision, recalling his first besotted days and nights with Bea four years ago, and then the gradually dawning horror and disgust, the realisation of what he was committing. Vividly at last he remembered their final encounter, when he stammeringly declared to Bea that he could not go on repeating his wrong, and she had greeted his earnestness with raucous laughter.

Waiting breathlessly now for Anjanette, Martin felt the full pain of his regret. If only, if only it had never happened. Now it would always be a terrible secret from her that he must carry like a stone. He prayed that it would not mar their perfect closeness, or cast a pall over this hallowed night.

Martin paced the carpet. The door to the dressing room began to open.

He could only stare in wonder.

Neither of them spoke a word; he was too overcome, and she was patently too shy for anything but a bright greeting of the eyes that served for a smile. Her mouth was quivering, solemn, and he saw the faintest hint of fear.

Again he warned his leaping senses: slow. Go slow.

He was capable only of a sharp, swift intake of the breath. For the first time her body was plain to him under the clinging ivory gleam of her low-cut gown, between the frail and drifting fabric of a cloud-

209

like garment. He marvelled at the nipples of her breasts, erect sweet buds that thrust out the glimmering cloth; the softness of her loins and belly, that maddening suggestion of a precious mound of luxuriance, as she moved soundlessly towards him, with her loosened hair like a ripple of golden moonbeams spilling on the whiteness.

Martin held out his arms and very lightly, fancying now that the lightest touch could make her disappear, circled his shaky fingers about her upper arms and drew her gently towards his pounding body.

Liquid and submissive, she raised the arms veiled in drifting white and slid them around his neck, raising her quivering mouth to his.

He covered her mouth with hunger, so feverish with that conflagration of desire that his skin almost pained him, as if it burned; she was so soft, so soft and small and sweet that he was almost afraid to hold her closer, but then, through some miracle, she was moving closer, to him, into him, and he sensed that she might be impelled by a longing urgent even as his own. The feel of that clinging softness now was robbing him of all control.

At last he managed to whisper her name and, muffled in her shimmering hair, his own hoarse whisper reached him, 'Lovely, you are so lovely, my darling, my beloved.'

There was an answering throb in her soft flesh. And in the rosy dimness, solemnly, she was allowing the outer garment to fall away from her shoulders; deftly, with that mysterious gift of women he had never fathomed, was gracefully undoing the shiny gown which he saw now had tiny buttons down its side.

The gown slid down her, settling into glistening folds around her feet, and she looked like a gold and white lily blooming from a giant alabaster rose.

He gasped. She was like a garden to him in his fever, possessed as he was by visions of flowers. Her naked body was of such perfection that at first he could only stare, not even touching – she was poreless, pure as a lily newly opened. The breasts with their rosy aureolas, the secret gold of her loins and the slenderness of her shapely legs robbed Martin of all speech or sense, of the very power of motion.

Then at once his hands burned to know what only his eyes had discovered: with enormous gentleness and caution he stepped to her and learned the shape of her shoulders. She was like hot silk to the fingers, the texture of her flesh was living ivory. He was making all the sweet discoveries of her body, in an instant, palming the unreal softness of her breasts, her belly and her curving hips; that fragile luxuriance met his fingers' tips like shining foam, it had the feel of milkweed down.

She moaned slightly, her cheeks dyed, her eyes alight as he repeated the caress.

A throaty cry escaped him; he lifted her off her feet. Glorying in the feel of that warm silk in his arms, he took her to the bed and laid her down. Throwing off his dressing-gown he saw a greater brightness flame in her wondering, longlidded eyes.

With excruciating leisure and slow care he started to salute her satin nakedness with his nibbling mouth. Now he could taste her breasts and all the wonders that had been offered first to his eyes, then his hands, and downward, downward over the ivory swell of her shuddering nakedness his lips roamed, savouring and worshipful until he found the pulsing golden heart of that white flower.

It came to him once more, in his rising frenzy, how like she was to a pulsing garden, a place of hot, live sweetness, and he began a rhythmic new caress, steadily, steadily, with ecstatic delight; glancing upward he saw through glazed eyes that the moonlike hair was spilled in two outspread and polished wings on either side of her, that the silver eyes were closed, her small face stricken with the wonder of this unknown pleasuring. She was smiling a quivering smile and making narrow sounds as he savoured the scents of new-mown hay and remarkable spices, breathing and tasting the heavenly perfume of clove, of apple blossom that she always seemed to have about her.

He listened to her cry and felt her shudder, knowing then that the moment had at long last come when there need be no further hesitation, when he could drown his burning, bursting body in that writhing sweetness: he was entering, to the fine jumbled madness of a thousand new sensations. He was stealing into an enchanted grotto, running with naked feet on the sponginess of pungent moss, into the interior of a brilliant sanctum where swiftly door succeeding door parted like magic, and she was there, she was there. For a heartbeat there was a faint impediment, a slight, sharp cry from her, and then the impediment was gone, his whole self plummeting, plummeting downward into diamond light, even as he mysteriously rose on pumping wings, flying and drowning at once into the welcome pulsations of that silken declivity, and deeper into the magic cavern.

All of Martin broke and quite dissolved, until he dreamed, half-knowing, that he was no longer himself and whole, but a consciousness of many fragments, departed from his flesh, although his very flesh had never been more vibrant and alive.

His body and his mind came gradually together with his gasping breath and he found that he was lying close beside her, holding her with bruising nearness in his arms.

He had no courage for more than silence. He was afraid to break it, until he could gather enough sense to tell her of the wonders he had dreamed inside her body.

But with gratitude and disbelief he knew that she herself, even with all her letters and her grace of speech, was powerless to find a single word.

He could hear her small, quick breathing, feel her fine hair tickling the vibrant skin of his damp chest; his heart was still thudding like a fast, barbaric drum. He listened to it slow and squeezed her closer.

Her little mouth opened against his skin and she began to speak; the nibbling, negligible pressure sent a new convulsion skittering across his flesh, still resonant from that mighty clashing of release that had pounded him like cymbals.

'My husband,' she murmured into his chest, and he felt another delicious shiver, 'before I was asleep in darkness.'

She raised her head and leaned over him, smiling, worship in her eyes.

'Now I am born.'

CHAPTER FOURTEEN

On that grey November morning in 1910 when the Stirlings' liveried chauffeur handed her into the family limousine, Vanessa had little thought to spare for the transformation of New York.

But Amas even in his anxious sadness, was looking about with bright, inquisitive eyes, and the seven-year-old Megan was fairly feverish with excitement, wriggling and craning to see everything.

Vanessa could think only of the crumpled cable that she still had with her, in her handbag, like some kind of pathetic talisman, the last artefact of Martin Stirling. For the hundredth time she prayed that they would not arrive too late. Her every nerve was strained to breaking-pitch, and she was deeply exhausted from the frantic rush to depart, the seemingly endless voyage.

As the great motor car smoothly turned and began its purring journey uptown, Vanessa was aware that Amas was changing places with Megan.

'Now,' he said gently, 'you can look out the window.' He reached for Vanessa's gloved hand and, squeezing it, held it on his knee. 'Twenty-five years, Vanessa,' he commented so softly it was almost a whisper. 'Can you credit it?'

'No.' Momentarily distracted from her anguish, grateful to him for what he was trying to do, she smiled.

'The ship was a far cry from the *Walmer*, too,' he added in the same low voice, exerting new pressure on her fingers. She looked up into those fierce, familiar eyes and was overcome with tenderness and sweet recall, reflecting how very much the same he was, with his strong, muscular body kept in trim by the years of hard and grinding work. His face was deeply seamed now, it was true, and burned almost mahogany from the African sun. But the voice, the savage passion of the eyes, the smile, were every bit as young as they had been that afternoon she had seen him standing on the deck of the *Walmer*.

His own concern was patent in the lines of strain around his mouth, the shadows under his eyes. But her heart swelled with love: he was making a mighty effort to distract her as much as possible from her gnawing anxiety and guilt, a guilt that had nearly felled her when they received the cable from New York telling them that Martin Stirling was gravely ill.

With that seventh sense of those grown close as each other's very epidermis, Amas had read that paralysing guilt in her, flailing her once more now.

'What's that?' Megan demanded suddenly. 'Is it a palace?'

'That is the City Hall . . . something like the Government House at the Cape,' Amas explained patiently. The child fell silent again, fascinated by the passing scene, and Vanessa was thankful.

'Darling,' Amas murmured. 'We will be in time. Think . . . think of all the happiness you brought him, Vanessa, with the wonderful letters and gifts and pictures, over the years. We fulfilled his dream for him, out there. And he lived to see Martin . . . and Lesley.' Amas seemed almost to regret mentioning that name, but his hand was firm on Vanessa's, his gaze steady. 'Already your father has led a long and happy life.'

213

He spoke as if her father were already dead. 'But Amas, all these years, the years that I neglected him.'

Amas shook his head. 'It wasn't like that, Vanessa. It wasn't. We are what we are, we do what we must do.' He was speaking to her in the same patient tone he took with Megan, and she was suddenly consoled. And shamed that his patience and endurance were so great, hers so inferior. She returned the pressure of his big hand and tried to smile.

'Thank you, Amas.'

She could hardly believe that they were already approaching that familiar house. The limousine stopped before the well-known veranda and the chauffeur was emerging, opening their door. With a blank, respectful face he handed Vanessa to the kerb.

'Thank you . . .'

'Harris, Madame.' He gave Vanessa a proper smile and she thought of the old coachman with a tug at her heart. 'Thank you, Harris.'

Another strange young servant had come out to help Harris with the bestowal of their luggage. Vanessa looked up at the elaborate marble entrance, with its stained-glass windows. A vast dread overtook her, causing her to tremble.

Amas grasped her firmly by the elbow to steady her and, with his other hand holding Megan's, he led them up the stairs.

A stiff and unfamiliar butler opened the door.

He bowed with great solemnity and said, 'I am Gardiner, Madame.' Absently Vanessa noticed that he had said no word of welcome; his eyes had faintly reddened rims.

'How is my father?' she blurted out.

'Madame . . . he is gone.' There was the slightest break in his even and proper tone.

'Gone?' Her legs and arms began to tremble horribly and Amas put his arm around her waist.

'Yes, Madame . . . only . . . about a half hour ago.'

'Oh, Amas, Amas.' Vanessa collapsed against him, feeling the dry, tearing sobs begin to rack her, still unable to cry; the pain was almost unendurable.

'Come, darling,' Amas was saying gently. A young maid had Megan by the hand and was leading her off towards the kitchen quarters. Megan was all right, Vanessa concluded dimly. 'Come, Vanessa. You must sit down and have a glass of brandy.'

She stiffened her spine and took a deep, gulping breath. 'No,

214

Amas. I must go and see my father.' She asked the sorrowful Gardiner calmly, 'Where is my mother?'

'She is in her room, Madame. The . . . doctor gave her something to make her rest.' Vanessa silently thanked the doctor for that; the sight of her mother's grief, at this moment, would be more than she could well endure.

'Mrs Seton-Prince is with . . . your father, Madame.'

Vanessa stared at the butler, uncomprehending. He was unable to conceal his surprise. 'Your sister, Madame,' he prompted, 'Mrs Beatrice Seton-Prince.'

Dear God. Vanessa looked up at Amas, who could not control his expression of dismay. Beatrice. Now, in the midst of this cataclysmic horror. Her father had been dying just as they disembarked from the ship. And Beatrice, whom he detested, had been with him. It wasn't fair, it wasn't right, Vanessa thought wildly, feeling the weakness assail her again.

'Vanessa. Are you sure you won't rest before you go . . . upstairs?' Amas pressed her.

'No. Come with me, Amas.'

Slowly they mounted the curving stairs and she walked unsteadily ahead of Amas into her father's room.

She could see nothing but his wasted figure on the bed, the shining coverlet folded with an awful neatness under his joined hands. Vanessa swayed, feeling Amas' strong fingers around her waist. Then she went forward on her wobbly legs and knelt down by her father's bed. He looked so old, so pitifully old, and smaller than she remembered, shrunken somehow in his age and death. Vanessa reached out a quaking hand and touched her father's lifeless fingers. They were cold, horribly cold, and they would never respond to her warm touch again.

For the first time in her life Vanessa Stirling Holder crumpled backwards, fainting, with no awareness of the woman sitting in a shadowed corner, elaborately decked out, staring at it all with bright, rapacious eyes that were quite dry.

When Vanessa opened her eyes, she was lying in her old bed. Amas was sitting on a chair beside her. Her first conscious thought was, Amas is here. How blessed I am. But he was in her own room – how could that be? They must have given her some kind of soporific dose, she decided, because her mental processes were still very hazy.

In all these years her room had remained unchanged. How

remarkable that was – her father had seen to that.

Her father.

The recollection of that stark death struck her like a fisted blow; something hard in her throat began to melt away and she felt the healing gush of tears, surging to a paroxysm of sobbing. Amas got up from the chair and sat next to her on the bed, cradling her head on his lap. Gratefully, like a child, she clung to his strength and firmness; gradually the sobbing slowed, then died, the relieving tears ceased to fall. The awful pain in her chest and her throat were eased now; she felt the kind of sadness that was settled in but not so agonisingly sharp, the beginning of a sorrow that would be endurable.

And she was shamed to feel, too, a great and inappropriate hunger. She was shy of saying so to Amas.

He mopped her face with his handkerchief and waited while she blew her nose, smiling a little at her.

'I think you should eat something, darling. You know, you've had hardly anything for nearly twenty-four hours.'

It was so; she had barely been able to touch her food on the ship.

'It must be very late,' she murmured, watching him bring a bed-tray from another table, submitting as he set it before her.

'It is rather,' he said. 'Nearly nine o'clock. I'm glad you rested, Vanessa. You were completely done in.' He seated himself again in the chair.

As she sipped some coffee, then took a few spoonfuls of soup, she asked anxiously, 'What about your dinner?'

'I had it here with you, about seven,' he told her with a rueful inflection. 'I had no strong desire to dine à deux with Mrs Seton-Prince. Megan was already asleep and your mother is in her room. I looked in on Mrs Stirling and she was still sleeping. The doctor told me she was completely devastated.'

'My poor mother.' Suddenly the food seemed repulsive and Vanessa made no further attempt to eat. 'Oh, Amas . . . Bea here. Now.'

'Of course now,' he said drily, disposing of the tray. 'She would not miss the reading of the will.'

Vanessa lay back on the pillows, fighting waves of nausea and revulsion. 'Beatrice Seton-Prince. She has married again, then. I wonder what happened to poor Tony?'

Amas sighed. 'Apparently Tony took a very bad toss at polo. Beatrice, you see,' he explained, 'leaped on me like a flea while I was seeing to Megan and your mother. Before I could make my escape,

216

she told me about Tony. Knowing her I almost suspected she'd had a hand in his accident, especially with a Harold Prince in the wings.'

'Who is Harold Prince?' she asked, glad of this small distraction.

'One of the richest men in England, a financier. Much older than the Queen Bee, and characterised by a monumental ugliness. The Queen Bee flew very high this time, indeed. And she'll have to wait a much shorter time to be a widow,' Amas concluded with a sardonic look.

For the first time in a long while Vanessa really felt like smiling. 'But Seton-Prince?'

'The "Seton" of course has very aristocratic overtones, which I'm sure she was not going to lose.' Amas studied her closely. 'How are you now, my darling? Are you feeling a . . . little better, at least?'

'Yes. Yes, I am. Thanks to you, Amas. Always thanks to you.' He leaned over and kissed her. 'But you look so tired, my dear.'

'I am. I'm very, very tired. I think I'll come to bed, right now.'

As he prepared himself for sleep, and came to join her, Vanessa said with self-reproach, 'You've been so good, Amas. So very good. And all this is almost as hard for you. Come here, come to me, darling.'

He turned out the lamp, got into bed and moved close to her. She took him in her arms and held his head against her breast, aware that a wetness was penetrating the thin fabric of her gown. And she knew that Amas was weeping, too, for Martin Holder, who had been for that brief time like the father he had never had.

She felt a tenderness for him so strong it almost made her sore. She held him more tightly, kissing his head. 'Amas, oh, Amas, of all things in my life you are the most precious to me. I am blessed with you.'

He raised himself and gathered her into his hard embrace. 'You bless me, too, Vanessa.' After an instant, he added, in a broken whisper, 'I will . . . miss Martin. I will miss him like hell. It felt as if he was with us all these years when he and I exchanged so many letters.' Then, after another small silence, he said, 'In the midst of death, Vanessa, we are in life. And somehow, still, "my heart is sweet".'

When Vanessa visited her mother the next morning, Hester Stirling was awake. But she greeted her daughter with blank eyes and a terrible indifference, as if she had already detached herself from the world that no longer housed Martin Stirling.

And Vanessa, pitying, knew the true depth of her mother's devotion to her father. For all their amiable jousting, and Hester's irritable disapproval of Martin's irreverent ways and unconventional comments, Hester seemed utterly lost now, as empty as a husk, and very frail.

Overnight, it appeared, Hester had lost all her fractiousness and anger. She will have no one to quarrel with now, Vanessa thought sadly, and it was likely that very thing that had kept Hester's blood pumping smartly in her veins. Vanessa could hardly bear to see this now helpless and querulous old woman, who had once been tart and upright, full of the stimulus of small vexations.

Gently Vanessa attempted to consult her about the funeral, but Hester responded weakly, 'You and . . . your husband will see that everything is proper.' After all these years, evidently, she still had not quite mastered the peculiar name of 'Amas'.

'Yes, Mother, we will see to it,' Vanessa assured her and went sorrowfully away.

To Vanessa's enormous relief, there was no sign of Bea today. Gardiner told her that Mrs Seton-Prince and her husband were staying at the Plaza Hotel; she had left word to be summoned if anything were required of her. This evidence of unfeeling conduct had apparently lowered Bea in Gardiner's estimation, but his correct statement gave but a bare hint of that judgment.

Vanessa thanked him with a fervent overtone that could not have escaped him and went to join Megan and Amas.

Now that she had fully absorbed the shock of her father's death, her anxiety began to centre on her mother. When Hester kept to her room for another day and evening, the doctor was summoned. He pronounced her very weak and strongly suggested that she should not suffer the ordeal of the funeral. To Vanessa's surprise, Hester was compliant.

Vanessa was grateful that there was so much to see to that she hardly had time, for the moment, to grieve. The servants, flustered by the death of their master and the inattention of the mistress, turned to Vanessa with almost pathetic eagerness for direction. One of her immediate tasks was to see to Megan's new quarters, and make certain that the child was occupied. It was a relief to notice that Megan, in her remarkably adaptable way, was settling in chameleon-like to her strange surroundings, reacting with particular warmth to the pretty young maid, Millicent, who spent a good deal of time with her.

218

Amas, consulting Vanessa, made all the arrangements. He was like a rock in this, she realised, as in everything, and she looked to him, loving him more than ever.

Then, during the stately ceremony in St Thomas' Church, where the Stirlings had worshipped for so many years, Vanessa found her strength was beginning to fail her. She was but dimly aware of the other mourners, clinging to Amas like a lifeline, barely seeing Bea beyond a dim image of black feathers, festoons of jet beads and rapacious eyes; Vanessa could not have described Harold Prince, except to recall a large, red-faced presence with a walrus-like moustache at the side of Bea.

After the ordeal of the burial, Amas was insistent that Vanessa go to bed, leaving him to receive the guests at the house. She must save her strength, he warned her, for the day after tomorrow, the reading of the will.

Submissively she obeyed, falling almost at once into the blackness of exhausted sleep.

The next day, refreshed, she felt a measure of peace return, and some vitality. That evening when she and Amas went to bed she faced the following morning with somewhat less dread.

But when she and Amas were waiting in the library for Beatrice and her husband to appear, the dread returned in full force. And by the time Gardiner announced them, Vanessa was fighting a queasy, inner tremble of sore anger. This was without doubt the moment that Bea had come for.

The library doors parted and Amas and the attorney got to their feet. Beatrice Seton-Prince swept into the room, her husband lumbering close behind. Now, with clearer eyes, Vanessa could see her plainly.

The intervening years had not been kind to her face; it was sallower than ever, had grown more sharp, and even her skilful make-up could not conceal the ill-natured lines about the sullen mouth, the scored mark between the brows that evidenced a constant frowning. But her great, black, greedy eyes were glittering as they surveyed the room as if it were her prey, and her narrow gown, with its surplice-topped overdress of sooty black, its underskirt of amber, revealed a form still shapely for a woman of forty-five.

'Vanessa,' Bea fluted with that sham sweetness that always made her gorge rise, 'I would hardly know you. You're as brown as a little berry.' No, Bea had not changed; this was the old code language for the 'weathered colonial'.

'She's so *healthy* looking, isn't she, Harry-Bear?' The owner of that grotesque endearment, Vanessa thought, looked more like a puzzled hippopotamus, but she managed to smile and extend her hand to Harold Prince. 'Isn't she delicious?' Beatrice demanded, as if she were pointing out a child.

'She is indeed.' Harold Prince's answer did not seem to please Bea, nor his heavy-lidded, bestial gaze that swept Vanessa from her bright hair to her feet. He was, as Amas had so aptly said, a man of monumental ugliness; his wide-set bulging eyes, his awkward ears and rough skin, the gaping mouth under the walrus moustache, were beastlike. He looked enormously stupid and uninhibitedly sensual, almost lewd. However, Amas had said to Vanessa yesterday that he was one of the shrewdest men in Europe, remarking that his abilities at finance were doubtless inferior to his judgment in choice of a wife.

'We hardly got to introduce ourselves at the funeral,' Bea twittered on. 'And then you ran away afterwards, you naughty thing.' Which was Bea, Vanessa translated, for: how very rude you've been, Vanessa.

'It was not the best time,' Vanessa responded drily. She glanced at Amas; his face was a study. He had told her yesterday that he'd had his fill of the Princes at the gathering after the funeral.

The attorney cleared his throat in a significant fashion. 'I beg your pardon, for intervening. But I must remind you that I have another appointment . . .'

Prompted, Bea gave a hideous, coy little shriek, and said, 'Here am I, running on and on. Do let's begin.'

With horror, Vanessa thought, she sounds as if we're beginning a parlour game. But they began to take their places – Bea and Prince on the sofa, with her hand on his heavy knee, Vanessa in a high-backed chair with Amas standing behind her.

Vanessa could not help another glance, with a kind of awful fascination, at the gross body of Harold Prince, the spraddled haunches, the pendulous belly thrusting out his elegant vest. Fleetingly she wondered how there could *be* that much money, but then, embarrassed by the thought, recalled herself to the measured opening remarks of the attorney.

He intoned, 'I will, with the concurrence of all present, dispense with the actual reading of this monumental testament' – he raised it for their inspection; it was ponderous, clearly numbering several hundred pages – 'inasmuch as each of the beneficiaries will receive a copy from me today.'

There was a general murmur of agreement.

'Very well, then, I shall outline to you the primary bequests of Martin Stirling.

'The widow, Hester Stirling, is to receive during her lifetime an annual income of fifty thousand dollars in addition to the cost of maintaining this residence, which with all its contents are to be Mrs Stirling's until her decease.

'The residue of Martin Stirling's estate, aside from certain bequests to servants and employees, including real estate holdings, stocks and bonds, and the control of Stirling Enterprise, have been bequeathed to Mrs Vanessa Stirling Holder and her heirs. On the death of Mrs Stirling the residence and its contents revert to Mrs Vanessa Stirling Holder.'

There was an outraged gasp from Bea. 'What about me?' she cried, her face mottled with the blood of anger. Harold Prince shushed her and shook his massive head. She subsided.

'I will get to that, Mrs Prince,' the attorney retorted in a repressive manner, 'in its proper order.' He cleared his throat, plainly annoyed, and went on, 'The possession of Stirling Enterprise has attached to it a certain condition. The late Martin Stirling expressed a wish that his son-in-law, er, Am . . . Amas . . . Holder serve as its president after a three-month period of . . . exploration to determine if he wishes to continue in such capacity. Should Mr Holder decide that he does not wish to do so, he is to arrange for the sale of Stirling Enterprise, the profits therefrom accruing to him and to Mrs Vanessa Holder.'

Vanessa darted an uneasy glance at Bea; she was livid.

'Now,' the attorney began, with a reproachful survey of Bea, 'Mrs Beatrice Stirling Dillon Seton Prince, presently known as Beatrice Seton-Prince,' he amended drily, 'is to receive a lump sum of two hundred thousand dollars . . .'

'Is that all?' Bea demanded.

'. . . and no further bequests,' the attorney concluded with a vexed frown.

Vanessa heard Prince mumble to his angry wife, 'Now, now, Honey-Bee, you don't need it, anyway. You have your Harry-Bear.' With distaste she glimpsed the hairy hand caressing Bea's thigh.

'That is not the point,' Bea said clearly, so everyone could hear. 'My father has left me out in the cold.'

'Just a minute, Honey-Bee,' Prince said. Then, raising his voice, he announced to them generally, 'I think it only fair at this point to advise Mr Amm . . . er, Holder of certain facts.'

'And they are . . .?' The attorney raised questioning brows.

'When Mr Martin Stirling . . . passed over,' Prince said with an awkward try at delicacy, 'naturally the stocks of Stirling Enterprise took a plunge.'

Vanessa thought, sickened, that great beast was snuffling around Wall Street while my father was drawing his last breath. No wonder Bea was so often unattended; she had wondered about that.

'And I,' Prince went on slowly, 'thought it wise to buy up a good block of shares. Now, if Holder announces his presidency – and everyone knows Holder Mines, and the Martin Diamond,' Prince smiled grotesquely at Amas, 'the stocks are going to shoot up again like fireworks. So you see, Holder, you'll have a kind of partner. Or partners,' he added, smiling at Bea. 'Harold and Beatrice Prince. I didn't want to keep you in the dark any longer.'

Amas responded for the first time, 'I think, Prince, we had better discuss this at a more appropriate moment. Say at the offices of Stirling Enterprise. Tomorrow morning.'

Vanessa leaned back and looked up at Amas, about to speak. Could he mean that he was willing to take over the business . . . that they would stay in New York? It didn't seem possible. He hated cities, he . . .

Bea broke in, 'I couldn't agree more! I will not stay in this house another instant, Harold. Let's go.' She flung off his heavy hand and rose; fumbling in her small black bag, she withdrew a fragile black-bordered handkerchief and held it to her face.

She rushed from the room, slamming the great doors to. Embarrassed, Prince heaved himself to his feet and, without a farewell, followed her.

'Oh, dear.' The old attorney wiped his brow with his large and pristine handkerchief. 'These affairs are sometimes very trying. The Princes, I fear, have rushed off without their copy of the testament. Could you tell me where I should direct it?'

'The Plaza Hotel,' Amas said briefly.

'Thank you, Mr Holder.' The attorney began to gather up his papers, putting them into a briefcase. He nodded towards the ponderous will on the desk. 'After you and your wife have read the will, sir, I dare say you may have certain questions,' he commented drily. 'It is a complex document, as you will see; the full estate of Martin Stirling amounts to some eighteen million dollars.'

'Good Lord.' Amas stared at him. 'I had . . . no notion.'

'Well, that's what it was. You will probably do well to continue

222

with Martin Stirling's present advisors; their probity is unquestioned, and they are highly capable. However, as I say, if you have any particular questions, please call on me at any time.' He handed Amas his card.

'Thank you.'

'Then I must be on my way. I wish you every success.' He went out.

Vanessa was still sitting in the high-backed chair, trying to digest the full import of the conference. Her father's wealth seemed unimaginable; the main thing now was Amas' wishes in regard to Stirling Enterprise.

'It's early in the day,' he smiled, 'but I think I'll have a brandy.' He went to the sideboard and poured some into a glass. 'Will you join me?'

'Under the circumstances, I think I will. A sherry.'

He supplied her with a small glass of the wine, then took a swallow of his brandy, sinking down onto the sofa facing her. 'Vanessa, what do *you* want me to do?'

'What I have always wanted,' she replied promptly. 'What you must do, Amas.' She smiled. 'Remember, I went with you to Kimberley once.'

'I haven't forgotten that, for a moment, for twenty-five years.' He sounded sober, deeply thoughtful. 'I've remembered that, watching you waste your wonderful gifts; watching the children grow up, longing for other sights and places. I see it now in Megan; she is delirious with the city.'

'Yes,' Vanessa admitted. 'But you, Amas . . . are you certain you could endure the city life, the restrictions of an office, an administrative routine? How could I be happy, ever again, knowing that you were like a lion in a cage . . . the way you seemed in New York the first day I met you?' She was trying to keep her query humorous and light, but she could not conceal the deep seriousness in it; not from him. He read her too well by now.

'Don't you think I *owe* you something, Vanessa . . . and Megan? Don't you think you deserve some recompense for all that you sacrificed for me, for all the glorious happiness you've brought me? I've had a good long run of it, anyway,' he grinned, 'with my wife allowing me to grub in the dirt, grubbing along with me . . . a hell of a lot longer than any other man's ever had, more than your father *ever* had. No, wait now,' he ordered, stemming her comment, 'hear me out.'

'There's Megan, too. Why can't you let me do for her what I never did for her mother . . . my own child? Here Megan will have luxury and opportunity, fine schools, interesting society. She loves it here already. Who knows? If we had lived in London or New York, instead of Kimberley, perhaps Lesley never would have . . .' He stopped.

Vanessa could see he was reading her expression of pain. She erased it from her face with a mighty effort.

'All right, Amas,' she said in a steady voice. 'You are offering very good arguments. But how do you *feel*, my darling? How do you feel about altering your whole life?'

'I feel that any man who is a man must pay his debts,' he said firmly. 'And I have them . . . to you, to Megan, even to Martin.'

'That's not an answer, Amas.'

'It's the only one you're going to get, Vanessa.' He set down his glass and came to her, ruffling her hair. She looked up at his smiling face, uncertain.

'Besides, you know I've always loved a fight. And now I'm offered one on a platter – a battle with Harold Prince, the biggest financier in London Town.'

Amas' eyes were bright and mischievous; it was clear the stimulus of that challenge pleased him.

'And what about the mines?' she demanded. 'Can you run Holder Mines from a distance, Amas?'

'This won't all be settled in an instant,' he admitted. 'But I have a strong feeling Martin's goals might be changing. You know how he's told us that he's gone as far as he can at Dunkensreuter . . . that Anjanette is not wholly satisfied with city life herself?'

It was certainly true. Anjanette, who wrote them faithfully, made occasional references to the 'awful' climate, with assurances that her 'wonderful' husband had provided her with sufficient furs to keep her warm; but there was always a wistful undercurrent there, and in Martin's letters, too, which were critical of the sophisticated London society, the people with whom he and Anjanette had 'little in common' in their simplicity.

'It sounds like a marvellous solution,' Vanessa admitted. 'But just too good to be true, Amas.'

'Maybe not. I am going to cable him at once.'

He went to the telephone. There was a light tap at the door. It was Mariette, Hester Stirling's ancient maid; she looked anxious and grim.

'If you please, Madame Holder,' she said in her precise Gallic fashion, 'your lady mother requires you. At once.'

Vanessa hurried after the maid and followed her upstairs to Hester's room. 'Have you called the doctor, Mariette?'

'Of course, Madame. I summoned him at once.'

Hester was lying back against the pillows, deathly pale; she hardly seemed to be breathing. Frightened, Vanessa approached her and took her frail hand.

'Nessa,' she said, so weakly that Vanessa could hardly hear. 'Nessa.' Vanessa was touched by her use of the old childish name that she hadn't heard in years and bent close to her mother's lips. 'I am very bad. Promise . . .'

Vanessa nodded immediately.

'. . . promise that you won't let them take me to the hospital.'

'Mother . . . Mother, perhaps . . .'

'No. Please. I want to die in my own bed, in Martin's house.' A bright, stubborn light flickered for an instant in the pale old eyes.

'I promise,' Vanessa whispered. 'I promise,' she repeated firmly, in a normal voice. 'But you are not going to die, Mother.'

However, after the doctor had arrived and examined Hester, and was conferring with Vanessa in the corridor, he said gravely, 'I will not keep the truth from you, Mrs Holder. I do not think your mother has a great deal of time to live. She doesn't want to, you see.'

Vanessa tried to swallow the great lump in her throat, and repeated her promise to Hester that she would be allowed to remain at home.

'I concur,' the doctor said. 'There would be no point in sending her now. It would be a needless cruelty. She has become so anaemic there is no longer any hope, you see. And she may as well have the consolation of remaining here, especially since, fortunate as you are, you can provide her with care in her own house.' He gave Vanessa a sad smile.

'I will arrange for the nurses,' he added, 'and whatever is necessary.'

He gave her one last keen look and departed.

In the midst of life, Vanessa thought, they were once more in death.

She visited her mother's room again later in the afternoon, and before she went to bed. Hester seemed quite peaceful and resigned.

Lying in Amas' arms that night, Vanessa murmured, 'What bothers me the most, Amas, is still what you want and need . . . are you sure?'

'That I want us to stay, Vanessa? Yes, very sure now.'

She relaxed a little. He did have a certainty now that he had not had before.

'And when . . . when all these tragedies are behind us a while,' he

225

said slowly, 'then you can begin to study with Bufera.'

'Bufera!' She raised her head from his shoulder, staring at him. 'What do you know about Bufera, Amas Holder?'

Among the world's great teachers of the piano, Giuseppe Bufera stood alone. After a lifetime of brilliant performing, throughout the world, he had chosen New York, in his old age, as his home. He spent his time composing and teaching a select few of only the most gifted. That Amas knew of him, or paid attention, confounded her.

'I *do* listen to you, you know,' he twitted her. 'You've spoken of him a dozen times . . . and I've done some research since we came to America.'

'But Amas, that's outrageous, that's absurd,' she protested. 'I haven't studied, properly studied, for nearly twenty-five years. It's not possible.'

'Not *possible*, Vanessa?' He gave her a challenging look. 'Did you think it possible that you would follow me to my ship – and give me my life – or that we would survive the war . . . or Lesley? And all the other things we've endured together? It wasn't even possible that we would feel like this about each other, after all these years, yet we have. Or *I* have, at least.'

'You're fishing, you're fishing, Amas Holder.' She leaned over and gave him a tender, lingering kiss. 'And so have I, as you well know.'

He held her close. 'What have we ever counted impossible, Vanessa?' he pursued in his relentless fashion.

'You don't give up, do you, Amas?'

'Never. And neither do you.'

He was right. She lay back against his shoulder. To study with Bufera. It was the dream of a lifetime.

As they drifted off to sleep, Vanessa thought, he has done it again – he has distracted me from another dragging sorrow. For a time even the shadow of her mother's imminent departure had been lifted, through the unyielding strength, the unending magic of Amas Holder.

Harold Prince, né Persiliba, soaped his sagging flesh in the hot, scented water, preoccupied with a number of things – his encroaching age; the coming interview with that colonial fellow, Holder; the enticing woman who would be waiting for him in bed.

As usual, the image of the Honey-Bee blotted out all the other matters. It was wonderful, like coming home every night to the

226

Whore of Babylon. As he continued to lather his titillated flesh, Harold Prince let his hot thoughts caress her wonders, the trick she did sometimes with the rose and the cigarette; the sharp, arousing scrape of her thin little shoe heels against his haunches.

Prince shivered pleasurably. He still couldn't believe that, out of all the fellows in London, she'd chosen old Harold Prince. It certainly hadn't been for his money; he knew her old man was filthy with it.

Now, however, remembering that idiotic will gave him pause. She wasn't so filthy rich now at all, not in her own right. A chilly draught from somewhere struck Prince's massive shoulders and he shivered.

Nonsense. That was then. Although he would have thought the old devil, considering what he'd done to his child, would have left her everything, and not lavished it all on that great colonial and Bea's older sister. Funny how young the older sister looked; oh, well, there was no telling with women.

Mustn't sit dreaming here while his delicious piece was waiting in the boudoir; he didn't want to find her pouting. With a grunt, Prince heaved his massive frame from the tub and reached for a towel. A suspicious little twinge shot down his arm; he felt bloody tired.

Towelling himself, he then observed his sagging self in the several mirrors. That damned doctor might be right. He ought to take off several stone.

Jove, he was sixty years old and looked like something out of the zoo. The minute pain was still there.

But damn it all, he didn't feel like sixty, not a bit. He chuckled. That's what came of marrying a girl nearly thirty years younger than himself; kept a fellow young. As for his weight – his little Honey-Bee didn't think he was too heavy. She always said it gave her more to love.

Besides, how could he stick to a diet when she smeared them both with the filling from the pastries and . . .

Prince shuddered lightly, this time not from cold but from sheer lust.

He was no old man. And he mustn't keep her waiting, not his sweet girl who had had such a wretched time of it in life – degraded by her own father, her fiancé stolen by her sister, then the abuse by that colonial maniac who'd done himself in; finally, the dreadful marriage with that stick Seton, who was impotent with everyone but boys.

Faugh. Jolly fortunate for that Dillon he was planted; Seton, too. If

Harold Persiliba got his hands on either of them – now why in hell had he called himself by that declassé old Syrian name?

Prince patted cologne on his sagging breasts and pendulous belly, then carefully smoothed his moustache. Odd. Well, anyway, odd that Dillon could have been fool enough to shoot himself when Bea was in his bed . . . and Seton. That had been a lucky toss for Prince.

With one last uncertain glance at his image, Prince opened the door and strode into the adjoining boudoir.

Ah! The slight pain was forgotten. There she lay. Prince was gratified to feel the quickening of his flesh, helped along by that new stuff he'd found in Paris. God, she made him wild.

The light in the room was livid scarlet; the minx had covered the lamps with thin red scarves. She lay spread-eagled on the bed, vivid against the amber satin sheets that they took everywhere on their travels. The salient point was her lower body, clad only in one of those black harnesses that got him so excited, attached to black lacy stockings. On her feet were dainty shoes with high, sharp heels.

And she was doing that trick again with the rose. He recalled, his flesh itching and heating with new lust, that bizarre dinner party at the notorious pair's mansion in London, where each guest was instructed to remove his clothes, then was given a thornless hothouse rose to 'wear', the women one way, the men another. His Honey-Bee, he judged, must have fallen in with the children of his hosts because she was aware of that device, too, and once greeted him at the door wearing nothing else.

'Where has my Harry-Bear *been*?' she demanded in that mewing, kittenish voice that affected him like fingernails tickling the skin, hinting as it did at small feminine mysteries, secret hiding places. And when she used that little girl intonation Prince could fancy that he, too, was a boy again, with a boy's tireless abundance. 'Honey-Bee wait so *long*,' she whined sweetly, and the infantile tone made him feel hot as fire.

'Harry-Bear very bad,' he responded heavily, falling in with the game of which she was always mistress.

'Yes, he is, and he will have to be punished.' Prince's heart hammered against his ribs; this was the part that always excited him the most.

'Bad Harry-Bear,' he growled playfully and, falling to his knees, crawled over the carpet towards the bed.

She was so delicious, so enticing he wanted to throw himself upon her there and then, but knew he did not dare, not yet. First he would

228

have to take his punishment, and that in itself had charms.

Wordlessly she sat up in the bed and handed him another rose, waiting until he put it to the use she had intended. When he had, she laughed, calling him a very bad bear indeed. He crouched submissively until she had mounted his wide back. She kicked him sharply with her pointed heels; they struck and pierced the hairy flesh of his upper legs. He thrilled to the painful sensation.

Then she tightened her legs around him and kicked him again. 'Growl, growl and ride Bee.'

Feeling her against his back, his titillated flesh was even more alerted; he obediently gave a great growl and began to crawl around the carpet with her on his back, kicking him again and again, beating at his skin with her ringed fists until he was aware of the tiny cuts the rings had made; perversely, his desire became hotter and hotter.

At last she rose from him and, striking the top of his head, commanded, 'Now, love Bee.'

Kneeling, gazing up at her, he put his hairy, huge hands first on her ankles, then on her shapely knees, his heart hammering, hammering as he stroked the rough lace of her stockings and surveyed the seductive harness with its little apronlike arrangement of sooty lace.

She was making little mewling noises of anticipation, and his massive hands ascended, stroking, until they found the ultimate goal. Bea emitted a low, shrieking moan, and then he was staggering to his feet, picking her up roughly, throwing her on the bed again to carry out her clearly stated directions.

Her body arched upward; she squealed, letting out a high, swift series of staccato cries.

Panting, Harold Prince grunted, 'Harry-Bear wants his honey, wants his honey.'

'Good bear, good bear can have it,' she told him in a husky, panting whisper and he fell upon her, almost maddened by the need to ease his bursting body.

When he was relieved, he fell from her almost on the instant, feeling a great fatigue descend upon him. His body felt like lead; he couldn't keep his eyes open any longer.

But she was pressing herself against him already, grumbling in that kittenish high voice, 'Harry-Bear asleep already? Old, old, *old* bear.'

Stung, the drained, exhausted Prince forced his eyelids open; her huge, ravening black eyes were very near his own, half-shuttered by their blue-painted lids. 'Honey-Bee still buzzing,' she lisped.

And Harold Prince heaved himself upward, sensing that minute pain shoot through his fat chest and heavy arm. But she was insistent, and for an endless interval, it seemed to him, he enacted the required caress.

His head was pounding, his neck muscles strained to agony, but still she commanded him to go on. At long last she seemed somewhat appeased.

Prince fell backwards, ready to sleep where he lay. 'So tired, so tired.'

As he dropped into quick, all-embracing slumber, he thought he heard her comment, 'Old bear . . . old, old Harry-Bear . . . fat, revolting bastard.'

But that, he reflected hazily, half-asleep, could not be possible.

He dreamed a vivid dream of his mother, and his first wife, Marya. In the dream she was as gentle and tender as she had been in life; she seemed so near.

And in his dream Harold Prince told his dead wife, 'I wish we were together, Marya. It was so sweet, then, and now I am so tired, I am always so weary.'

That was all of the dream that he remembered.

CHAPTER FIFTEEN

Amas was overjoyed when Martin cabled back not only his willingness, but his eagerness, to return to Kimberley and take over both the Big Hole and the Premier mine.

A long, excited letter followed from Anjanette, telling them of her happiness. 'The only thing lacking now in our lives is the child we are still awaiting.' To her great disappointment, Anjanette had still not conceived; in her letter she confided to Vanessa, 'I think, now, we will have a son, when I am home again, away from the big, cold city of London.'

Amas, with an almost boyish eagerness, turned to the running of

Stirling Enterprise. For the first time in their lives Vanessa was not deeply involved in his work, even if he discussed everything with her at length, fully acquainting her with the business. His only source of worry was the large block of shares owned by Harold Prince who, he told Vanessa, had worldwide interests, like a 'vast spiderweb'.

When she suggested that they buy him out when the stocks increased in value, Amas told Vanessa that he didn't think he could – that money was not the issue here at all. Amas felt that Beatrice wanted to be connected with Stirling Enterprise simply to be a nuisance to the Holders.

But there were too many preoccupations now to let Vanessa spare much thought to Stirling Enterprise: there was the constant problem of her ailing mother, the care of Megan and the supervision of the house. In only weeks, however, Vanessa had mastered the latter with her usual expertise, charming the staff into such perfection that the house, before they knew it, was running itself again.

Megan had adapted with remarkable speed to the swifter tempo and the disciplines of New York. Vanessa registered her in a private school, where the reports of her academic and athletic endeavours were glowing, if the comments on deportment were a bit less so. But her teachers, like Vanessa, took an indulgent view of that, taking into consideration the sharp contrast of the circumscribed life of the city and the child's early freedom in the mines and on the veld. All in all, Vanessa was reassured.

Beyond her daily visits, always accompanied by little gifts, there was nothing Vanessa could do for her mother. The doctor came each morning and two nurses kept a vigil around the clock.

So, after a few delighted shopping sprees, Vanessa suddenly found herself strangely at a loss for occupation. She had been reluctant to resume her ardent scales and exercises on the Steinway for fear of disturbing her mother. But now the doctor ridiculed her fears, declaring that the noise from the music room was barely perceptible in Hester's quarters. Early on Vanessa had discovered how sadly out of tune the magnificent instrument was and almost automatically had seen to its tuning.

Now she recalled her conversation with Amas about Giuseppe Bufera. And she realised that it had been fear, not preoccupation, that had kept her from seeing the great master.

The time had come, and she must face it: she would never know the extent of her gift until she made the dreaded visit to Bufera.

*　　*　　*

There was a hint of snow in the wind that bright December morning when Vanessa left the house for her appointment. She had been so nervous that she was dressed and ready far too early; almost without volition she'd found herself choosing dark, unobtrusive garments, somewhat studentlike, for her meeting with the great Bufera, observing some peculiar sumptuary law of her own.

She'd said nothing to Amas and little to the servants except that she would be away for several hours and would telephone to check on her mother's condition. Megan of course was in school. Vanessa knew her secretiveness was born of deep uncertainty; she had no notion of what her reception would be, but surmised it would not be encouraging.

Hesitating at the corner of Fifth Avenue, she weighed the advantages of finding a taxi against those of walking, and opted for walking. It was a long trek – about nineteen blocks north and several west – to Carnegie Hall, where Bufera kept his studio. But the exercise might calm her.

And in any case, it was a new joy to join the teeming ranks of pedestrians in the city that was her home, and yet the place that had grown so strange to her.

As she moved with her almost floating stride up Fifth Avenue, slightly impeded by the narrowness of her skirt, Vanessa was once again surprised by the number of motor cars. America was indeed on wheels this year. She could not help being amused by the stares of passing men; understated as her ensemble was, it was undeniably fine, and she imagined that 'fine' women did not walk habitually in these times. They were driven in automobiles.

And for the first time it occurred to her that the Stirling limousine, as well as two other cars, were always available to her, yet she had not thought of them. Part of that had been sheer distraction; also, she supposed unconsciously, she did not want Bufera to see her in a limousine – his studio faced the street – and take her for one of the idle rich playing at, not working at, her art.

She was already passing the great Public Library and Bryant Park, and suddenly gloried in her unique vitality, the tensile grace of muscles oiled by years of riding, climbing, grubbing in the mines. She judged that few women of forty-four were half so young and energetic as she.

It was foolish to be so fearful of Bufera; she was at her peak, the prime of her existence. It was *not* too late to start again. That conviction, and the long walk, fired her cheeks and brought a new shine to her eyes, heartening her when she glimpsed herself in a mirror in the corridor outside Bufera's studio.

However, as soon as she knocked and heard the gruff command to enter, all her optimism, her high hopes failed her.

At last she was in the presence of the mighty Giuseppe Bufera. Now she could understand in full the terror he inspired.

He was seated behind a piano with his back to the light; at first all Vanessa could comprehend was a huge, shaggy shape, a veritable monster of a man with a rough grey aureola of untamed hair.

'Miss Holder,' he growled, and she perceived the Italianate shading of vowel, the lingering consonants. He half-rose from his seat and then resumed it. 'Come in, come in. Sit in that chair.'

She obeyed, no longer a forty-four-year-old woman with a grandchild, or a pampered lady. All of a sudden she was a quaking student again, facing her first music master.

Bufera turned to her, and the light illuminated his face. It was all sternness and crags, not at all what she associated with the operatic handsomeness of Italians; it was as hard and granitic as the mountains of Wales.

And his deep-set eyes, black as coals, would have been almost invisible below his cavernous brow-bones, his prolific brows, had it not been for their extraordinary brightness. Black fire blazed out at her. His mouth was the greatest surprise of all. He was clean-shaven, and it was clearly revealed, at once grim, yet with a passionate softness.

'Well, Miss Holder.' He studied her.

'It is Mrs Holder,' she said quietly.

'Ah!' He ran a hand through his tangled hair and she marvelled at the length of the fingers. 'That is bad, very bad.'

Her courage almost failed her, but she demanded bluntly, 'Why?'

Bufera chuckled; it sounded like the playful growl of a huge beast that had discovered a new toy. 'You are not timid, anyway. Because, Signora, I do not teach idle wives who are bored with their husbands and children, and need a new form of game to amuse them . . . and who, in the last analysis, are more concerned with little Willie's measles than with their practice.'

She could not contain her annoyance. 'My "little Willie", Signor Bufera, is enrolled in an excellent school and is carefully seen to by others in my household. I assure you that I am not an "idle wife". I am here to find out if you will teach me. I have been playing the piano for thirty-one years.'

Bufera, obviously impressed, raised his beetling brows. 'Thirty-one *years*, Signora. Why, then, do I not attend your concerts? Why have you then presented yourself as a . . .' he shuffled among disordered papers on the top of the piano, made a sound of satisfaction as he found and consulted her letter '. . . beginner? Surely if you have met no success after thirty-one years, is it not hopeless to start again now?'

Vanessa's timidity had evaporated. She retorted sharply, 'If you read your mail, Signor Bufera, you would have comprehended my letter. I have stated that for twenty-five years I lived in South Africa, without proper guidance or instruction, yet practised constantly, performed in local concerts and learned to tune my own piano.'

This time Bufera let out a guffaw. 'Bravo, Signora Holder! *Bravissimo*.' He rose from the piano stool, applauding lightly. Then he approached her and held out his hand.

'Forgive me,' he said softly. 'You see, I always put my prospective pupils through this unpleasantness, to sound out the depths of their seriousness. And you, I must say, look like a serious woman.' His fiery glance took in her sober, elegant ensemble, the neat hat on her brief golden hair devoid of ribbons and plumage. 'Now,' he said briskly, 'come to the instrument.'

She rose at once and went to sit down at the piano.

Bufera took a chair. 'Play.'

She launched into the first of Schoenberg's 'Three Piano Pieces', performed for the first time only last year. It was a difficult one, but Vanessa had chosen it for its range and power, even though she was more adept at Mozart, Bach and Chopin.

Vanessa glanced at Bufera; he seemed to be suffering from a migraine. But then he began to stare at her. When she was through, he said only, 'Let's try some accompaniment. Have you ever accompanied?'

'Rarely.'

He picked up a violin from a table and came to stand by the piano. 'Do you know Arnold's "Verklarte Nacht"?'

Arnold. This man was Arnold Schoenberg's *friend*. Awed, she nodded. 'An orchestral piece . . .?'

Bufera waved his hand. 'Originally a sextet for strings. I've transposed it. But remember what Liszt said – a man's ten fingers can reproduce the harmonies of two hundred performers.'

She waited.

'This is certainly not my instrument.' He smiled. 'But you must have *something* to accompany. Sound your B flat.'

She struck the note as he tuned the violin. Then he placed a piece of music on the piano.

'You've given me the violin part,' she said hesitantly.

He looked at it. 'Careless of me. I fear I am getting old.' Annoyed, he shuffled among the pieces on the table where he kept the violin. '*Dio*, where is the piano part? Ah, well, I cannot find it. We must make do.'

Desperately Vanessa began, transposing the string notes as best she could. When Bufera's uncertain violin joined her, however, she found she was not only keeping up, but that her melody dovetailed precisely with the end of his.

When they had finished, he declared, still holding the violin, 'You are excellent at harmony, Signora.'

She glowed at his praise.

Slowly he walked to the table, put down the violin, and sank into a chair facing her.

'You have a great gift.' Her heart began to thud with excitement. 'I did not think you could read the violin part at *all*, even if you certainly did not do it well. However, your technique is atrocious; you bring a sentimentality to the music of Schoenberg that would make him ill.'

Her hopes sank again.

'You are more adept at Chopin, I take it?' he inquired with an ironic smile. '*And*, I'm sure, also sentimentalise that helpless dead man, who was never sentimental though full of sentiment. You also play a great deal of Bach.'

She nodded dumbly, dazzled by this display of intuitive knowledge, by the witchcraft of the great Bufera's flawless ear. 'Yes,' she murmured, 'Chopin. Chopin and Bach.'

'Ah. Your fingering leaves much to be desired; it is, in fact, abominable. You have developed slovenly mannerisms; you do not play at your full strength. You think you are weaker because you are a woman. That is nonsense, Signora. Your hands are natively a bit too small – you have developed, them, however, how . . .?'

She found herself telling him of the exercises she'd done for years to lengthen her fingers and increase the power of her hands, diverging into the story of the past quarter century, the constant exercise of her hands at work in the mines, riding. He blanched.

'It is a miracle you still can play at all. From now on you must take the greatest care of your hands, although the finger stretching you mentioned is fine.'

Her heart was going like a trip-hammer; did he mean, then to take her as a student? She was too overwhelmed to speak.

'You have money, I take it?' he asked bluntly. She nodded. 'Good. I don't come cheap, Signora. And I assume, then, you have no need to injure your hands in futile chores around your house?'

He did mean to. He did. Her heart fairly sang. She grinned at his last question. 'We have a staff of more than ten servants,' she said.

'Excellent. And your daughter – how old is she?'

'She is my granddaughter. She is seven.'

'You are very young for that, Signora.' For the first time he sounded almost tender. Then he reverted to his questioning. 'Your children? Where are they? Do they consume your time, your thoughts?'

'My only son is married, living in South Africa now. He does not consume my thoughts. My daughter,' she blurted out, 'committed suicide because she did not consume enough of them. Apart from my husband, I have always been consumed by my music, Signor Bufera.'

He was studying her keenly. 'And your husband? Does he approve of this course?'

'Whole-heartedly. But even if he didn't, I would still go on trying,' she admitted.

'That is all I need to know. You have suffered tragedy, and life's experience. You have an unusual gift. I will take you as my pupil.'

Involuntarily she clapped her hands together, feeling an enormous elation flood through her every vein.

Bufera held up his oddly delicate hand. 'But I warn you, Signora, it is going to be very difficult indeed. I am going to work you, work you so hard that you will ache and weep; it will be tantamount to bodily torture. You will suffer pains and fatigues you have never imagined. For, you see, we have many years of wrongdoing to undo before we can even begin to work at the positive side of your performance. You will have to practise at least seven hours a day – are you prepared for that?'

'That will be no problem,' she said calmly. 'I will do anything.'

'Then let us begin. I will instruct you two hours a day three times a week, and one hour a day on three other days. Is that agreed?'

'Yes,' she said fervently. 'May we begin, Signor?'

He looked at her with approval and grudging admiration as he gestured towards the piano.

Bufera's prophecy did not begin to describe the extent of her exhaustion. But doggedly, with Amas' delighted approval, Vanessa stuck to her gruelling routine, day after draining day; her back, neck and arms burned, her legs grew numb.

Hester continued to fail and at last, just before Christmas, died peacefully in her sleep. Amas took most of the burden of the arrangements off Vanessa's shoulders. Even on the afternoon after the funeral he insisted that she return to her routine. She was grateful for his insistence, not only because the action – which seemed callous to the unknowing – distracted her from the overpowering sorrow of her mother's end. They had always been strangers to each other, and remained so until Hester's death; the terrible waste was devastating, would have felled her had she not had the blessed discipline of her instrument.

The well-regulated household prepared for Christmas almost without a thought from Vanessa; Megan seemed happy and glowing with health. Amas was busily occupied with Stirling Enterprise and appeared to have reached a measure of content. He gave her a gold, gem-studded clef on a chain.

And thus, as day succeeded day, Vanessa found with joy that her power and skill, her authority and confidence, increased with her excruciatingly slow progress, and she was living for her music now, living for the hard-won and rare praise of Bufera. Her body was gradually adjusting, too.

By the spring of 1911, their master-pupil relationship had warmed almost to a kind of friendship. When Vanessa detected in Amas a faint restlessness, and wrung from him an admission that he longed to spend more time at the Stirling country place in Long Island, she concurred. A piano was purchased for the house in the country; she would travel into the city each day with Amas to study with Bufera, then practise at the city house until they returned together to the country in the evening. Amas was reluctant for her to waste her strength in this way, but she soon found that she was adapting to it easily, that a school could be found for Megan in the country as well.

As far as that went, the child went almost wild with delight in the fresh, new atmosphere and Vanessa surmised that she was benefitting by it, looking healthier and more vital than ever.

The coming summer would be an idyll, Vanessa discovered. Bufera preferred to spend the summer in the country, too, and was within easy travelling distance of the Holders. Amas himself planned to take a whole month's vacation from Stirling, which hummed along now under his able administration.

They had heard almost nothing from Beatrice and Prince; she was biding her time, Amas commented with irony. In April, however, they learned that Harold Prince had died of a massive coronary occlusion. Amas remarked that 'the poor devil died of Beatrice', and the sordid implications did not escape Vanessa even if neither of them said it in so many words. Beatrice still clung like a limpet to her Stirling shares, now vastly increased in worth, and Amas and Vanessa also learned with dismay and bitter amusement that Beatrice Stirling Seton-Prince now occupied her late husband's seat on the London Exchange and threatened to become something of a force in the diamond world.

Anjanette and Martin wrote them frequently; both seemed to exude happiness in their letters.

All was going well, Vanessa reflected; the worst was behind them. And the matter of Bea, even Martin, Anjanette and Megan, were far away concerns to her now, lost as she was to the world of her music, consumed by it entirely.

Vanessa was to look back on the years preceding 1917 through a kind of golden haze, an interval of national innocence, of Holder contentment.

She realised that her personal joys and preoccupations coloured her wider view, yet she was marginally aware of the country's mood, one of unbounded confidence that the future could only get brighter. The income tax, imposed in 1913, did not yet have much of a bite; the avant-garde in art was born, felt in the music world through the names of Skriabin, Stravinsky and De Falla. Vanessa felt Bufera's excitement echoed in herself.

Vanessa was finally free to pursue her musical career with a light, whole heart – Martin and Anjanette still flourished, Megan was growing as slim and lovely as a young sapling. She was studying dance now with great enthusiasm, developing into a near acrobat. And Amas, the one dearest to Vanessa's heart, was totally immersed in his advisory communications to Martin and the operation of the business, now called Holder-Stirling Enterprise at Vanessa's suggestion.

After the first gruelling year of study with Bufera, which Vanessa later wondered that she'd survived at all, he eased her regimen. In another six months her habituated body, her fine ear newly tuned and her more practised fingers fitted her for wider exploration in her music. And in the second year the admiring and astonished Bufera, who had come to address her by her first name although she continued to call him, respectfully, 'Signor', declared that she was ready for a recital.

'Not a concert yet, Vanessa,' he warned with the hint of a smile on his fierce, craggy face, 'but a recital, certainly.'

Her triumph knew no bounds. And on the afternoon of her first recital, shared with other pupils of Giuseppe Bufera, she received a cable from Anjanette and Martin, and thrilled to the sight of Megan and Amas, standing in the audience to applaud her performance.

Afterwards, at a small party for Bufera and the other pupils and friends held at the Stirling house, she managed an instant alone with Amas.

'You've been so good,' she said. 'I owe all this to you. Oh, Amas, you've been so patient, these last two years. Sometimes I wonder how you've stood it, the nights I've collapsed into bed, without enough strength to . . .' She flushed, in her old way.

Amas put his arm around her. 'You've done this, Vanessa, not I. Besides, we're together. That's all that's ever counted, you know. And I look on this as a way of making things up to you.'

' "Making things up . . ."?'

'All the years in Africa, Vanessa. You gave up everything for me. And now, finally, I can begin to repay you in this small way.'

She marvelled at the strength of their love, which had endured so much, and yet never lessened or changed. It was that, as much as anything, that impelled her onward.

Then in 1914, when war broke out in Europe, the Holders were preoccupied with happier things. Martin and Anjanette had a son. They named him Anthony, for Martin's closest friend. The whole family was so overjoyed by the event that even the shadow of the war could hardly touch them. 'It will be over soon,' Amas assured Vanessa. 'We'll never get in it.'

There was a financial slump in Europe that forced diamond dealers to liquidate their stocks at very low prices, and both the Big Hole and the Premier mine were forced to cut back. Yet even that event could not mar the Holders' new happiness.

Now Vanessa was preparing for her first concert; as always every other consideration was marginal to her mind.

Vanessa stood in the wings, alternately chilled and burning, waiting to go onstage. She repeated to herself, like a comforting rune: this is the Town Hall, it is only the Town Hall, this is not Carnegie Hall. The smaller, more intimate space had a consoling cosiness.

But a small swift flock of freezing butterflies still fluttered inside her. Amas was out there, with Megan and his mother; out there were hundreds of people. Vanessa took several deep breaths and put her hands behind her back to flex her fingers, shy of letting Bufera, who was standing a short distance away, see her full terror. He smiled at her; for some reason the smile gave her much more confidence.

She returned his smile and, at his signal, walked into the lights. For a horrible instant she was certain she was going to faint; her body ached all over and she was convinced the audience could see her trembling. Her knees were positively knocking against her narrow skirt.

But in the brightness she could see nothing but a mass of vaguely flesh-coloured knobs that must be faces. Then, miraculously, she caught sight of Amas. His face was suddenly clear to her, and it was transfigured by love and pride.

She sat down at the piano, feeling utterly alone in the world under the glaring lights, in the centre of the now vast and empty stage.

But her hands were warmer when she placed them on the keys: the Chopin phrases were sure and true.

It was going to be all right.

Vanessa heard the front door close with an unaccustomed sharpness; she lifted her hands from the keys, still deep in triumphant reflection even as she noted the sound of the car.

It was amazing, almost miraculous, she was thinking, that whole new sound that Chopin has for me now. She smiled to recall Bufera's acid comment on that first visit – well, there was nothing sentimental about her rendition today.

That must be Megan, she decided. At this time of day, Vanessa generally left the door of the music room ajar, used to Megan's habit of stopping to wave at her from the door, and then going off to her room to rest and study before Vanessa dropped in on her at five for their daily visit.

Usually Vanessa was able to see at a glance how Megan's day had gone, and she counted on that little barometric reading.

This afternoon, however, Megan did not pause or wave. Vanessa glimpsed her passing, then heard her light footsteps on the stairs.

Vanessa got up and hurried to the door. 'Megan!'

The child, arrested halfway up the curving flight, did not turn. There was something in the way she stood there, in the very posture of her proud head, that alerted Vanessa.

'Megan,' she called out softly again. 'Are you all right?'

Megan slowly turned. Her small, pointed face was stiff and tight;

she did not smile. There was a wounded look in her odd golden eyes.

'Darling, what is it?' Vanessa came out into the hall. 'Please, come down here and tell me.'

Megan descended the stairs with her remarkable grace and, even in her anxiety, Vanessa had to admire her. She was far taller, more lissome and mature than any other ten-year-old, Vanessa reflected, with an eccentric beauty. Her slim, fine-boned face recalled nothing of Lesley; she invariably reminded Vanessa of a feminine version of Amas, yet there was a hint, too, of the narrow, arrogant features of Mitchell Farley.

Recalling that hated name Vanessa was distracted by another anxiety, gripping her out of the nowhere of the past – they had told Megan her father and mother were both killed in an accident, and she had never questioned it. What would happen if Megan and Farley ever met?

Vanessa shook off the tormenting notion; that was not too likely. In any event, the present was what she must deal with.

'Darling,' she said softly to Megan, 'come in here a moment. Let's talk. Please.'

With a light touch on Megan's shoulder she urged the child into the music room. 'You haven't finished for the day,' Megan said quickly.

'That doesn't matter at the moment. It's been going very well. Even I deserve a break some time, don't I?' Vanessa smiled, trying to lighten the heavy atmosphere.

But Megan did not respond in her usual fashion; generally her fey, impressionable temperament answered others' moods like a mirror. A mirror – Vanessa briefly examined the simile. A mirror reflected all that passed before it, but hid all that was behind.

'Sit down, Megan. Relax a little. You look all . . . tense,' Vanessa said uneasily. 'Darling, please tell me what's the matter. Something happened today. I know it did.'

Defeated, Megan tossed her books onto the sofa and threw herself down beside them. 'Oh, well, you'll soon know anyway.' She looked down, as if unable to meet Vanessa's eyes.

Vanessa sat down on the other side of her and put her arm around the child's narrow shoulders. How fragile she felt, and yet how strong she was, with that athletic, tensile little body almost as hard as a boy's. Vanessa waited for her to go on.

'Miss Abernathy is going to telephone you and Ampus tonight.' It had been years since she'd used that childish name for Amas; she

241

called both of them by their first names now. Somehow this reversion caused a deeper uneasiness in Vanessa. Some kind of confession had to be in the offing. In essence Megan was asking her not to be angry at their grandchild.

'About what, Megan?'

'About my . . . taking something.' Megan mumbled her reply, her eyes still downcast, a faint pink colour dyeing her white face. 'And about the way I . . . am with the others,' Megan blurted, her voice resentful.

'Tell me exactly what happened,' Vanessa said quietly, stroking the girl's tawny, abundant hair.

Megan moved her head a little aside, with that rebellious, coltish gesture that always touched Vanessa. She said. 'The girls are always complaining that I have a "big head",' Megan offered. 'I can't help it if I'm better than they are at games. Can I?'

'You certainly can't help it if you're better,' Vanessa agreed. 'But you can help . . . emphasising it, my dear,' she added delicately. 'Is that what you do?'

Vanessa was thinking of all the comments about Megan's deportment.

'Well, I guess so.'

'Well, then . . . and now, what about this other thing? "Taking something?" What is all that about, Megan?'

'Oh, it was a damned bracelet.'

'Megan!'

'I'm sorry, Vanessa, but it makes me so . . . annoyed. You know we're not allowed to wear jewellery at school, but Merry Morgan does it anyway. She wore a bracelet today that had pearls in it . . . my own birthstone,' Megan added with a queer reflection, and Vanessa's uneasiness grew. 'Miss Abernathy made her take it off, *of course*,' Megan said bitterly, 'and Merry put it in her desk, and then it was gone later and Merry said I took it.'

'But that's outrageous!' Vanessa protested. 'In the first place, that was very foolish of Miss Abernathy, and I shall tell her so. Why didn't she put the wretched bracelet in her office? I'm sure it just got lost.'

'But there was something else,' Megan offered with painful slowness. 'Felicia Boerum's pencil case. Something that happened before. I didn't tell you about it, because it all got straightened out and Miss Abernathy didn't call you because Felicia admitted she lost it.'

Vanessa was aghast.

'And this woman is accusing you of thievery? *Why*, Megan? It's all too absurd. We give you everything you want; you have three or four very handsome pencil cases, if I remember – there was the one Anjanette sent you last Christmas, then the . . .'

'I . . . I did take it, Vanessa.' Megan coloured and looked away. 'It had a wonderful bird on it.'

'But . . . but *why*, dear heart?' Vanessa was stricken. 'If you wanted one like it, why didn't you just *ask* us, and we would have bought you one. You know that.' She realised she was near tears.

'Oh, don't cry. Vanessa. I *do* know that. It wasn't the case . . . or the bracelet. It was the *fun* of taking them, right under all their snooty noses. That's why I did it.'

'Then you did take the bracelet.'

'Yes,' Megan admitted and there was a twinkle in her golden eyes.

'This isn't funny, Megan,' Vanessa admonished her.

'I guess it isn't,' the child said uncertainly. 'Anyway, I put the stupid thing back in Merry's desk. She'll find it tomorrow.'

'If the cleaner doesn't, first,' Vanessa said sharply 'and take it home.'

'Oh, that'll be all right.' Megan asserted with great confidence. 'Mrs McGinty is "honest as the day is long", they all say. She'll give it right to Miss Abernathy in the morning.'

Vanessa's head was starting to ache. 'Megan, that was a very . . . wrong thing to do. This is not a nice kind of joke.'

'All right, Vanessa, I guess it isn't, really. I . . . I won't do it again.' Megan was looking at her with strangely blank, secretive eyes.

'Promise me you won't. Don't you see, if you . . . do these things, it'll spoil everything for you. There are people who won't understand that it was just in fun. You could even be asked to withdraw from school. Now wouldn't that be awful?'

For the first time Megan seemed truly concerned. 'Oh, they *can't* make me do that!' she cried. 'We've got the games . . . and the dance recital, and . . .' She started to sob.

Vanessa gathered Megan into her arms. 'Now, now. It won't happen, if you behave, darling. I'll take the whole thing up with Miss Abernathy right now. I'll call *her* before she even calls us. And for the time being we won't mention this to Ampus.'

Megan brightened. 'Oh, thank you, thank you, Vanessa. You're the best mother anybody ever had!'

Megan put her thin arms around Vanessa's neck and planted a number of light kisses on her cheeks. Vanessa's annoyance melted and her anxiety began to ease.

She would explain the whole thing, she resolved, watching Megan run up the stairs. It was probably a tempest in a teapot, only a childish prank.

As she picked up the phone she indulgently recalled Megan's early ways – she'd been like a little bright-eyed jackdaw, secreting the diamond pebbles and later, other items, in tin boxes in her room, arousing great amusement in Amas and Vanessa. This prank was all of a piece with those.

CHAPTER SIXTEEN

The reluctant Miss Abernathy succumbed to Vanessa's persuasive charm, and the very next day Vanessa bought Megan a gold bangle bracelet set with pearls that she would be allowed to wear on 'state occasions'.

Reared in the austere tradition that forbade jewellery to nice young girls under sixteen, Vanessa found that the gift went against her own grain; it seemed a gross violation of good taste. And yet she'd observed that these days some girls of twelve and thirteen were being allowed to wear modest items of jewellery. So she shrugged it away, conceding that Megan was very precocious in many ways; after all, what did it really matter in the cosmic scheme of things? Something cautious and uneasy in herself had caused her to buy the bracelet; it would do no harm to demonstrate to Megan that she could have whatever she wanted, and need not take others' possessions, even if it had been a prank.

Vanessa was reassured when the incident was not repeated, that year or the year after, and decided that it had been a good idea, this once, to keep it all from Amas.

In May, 1916, Martin's second son, Clinton, was born. 'Oh, I do wish we could visit them . . . or they could visit us,' Vanessa said to Amas.

'This is not the best year for voyages,' he remarked grimly, and the shadow of the imminent war fell over Vanessa again. Last year the Germans had sunk the *Lusitania*; Britain's merchant shipping losses during the year had been a million tons. And just this last March an unarmed French steamer, *Sussex*, with American passengers aboard, had been sunk by Germans in the English Channel, followed by President Wilson's warning last month that America would end its relations with Germany if their submarine warfare continued without notice.

Try as she might, Vanessa was no longer able to dismiss this spectre from her consciousness; men were dying in Europe, innocent passengers drowning at sea. That uneasy, fragile peace could not be preserved much longer.

It took all of Vanessa's strength of will to keep her at work, preparing for the next concert. What was music now, in the face of that terrible slaughter? If the world were being torn asunder, how could it matter that one woman perform at the piano?

Bufera, while raging with her at the senselessness of the costly conflict, raged even more when she expressed those gloomy thoughts to him.

'What does it *matter*?' he bellowed. 'Good God, you foolish woman! You have endured so much, and come so far – you have coped with the nonsense of submitting yourself to marriage, and fiddling about with these grandchildren' – Bufera, a confirmed bachelor, believed that no artist had the right to marry – 'and now your name is becoming known. What business have you to despair? What does it *matter*? I tell you now, nothing else *does* matter. Music is all; it represents the unconquerable spirit of man. Is Mozart dead, because there were little wars? Is Bach? Does Skriabin cease composing? Let me hear no more. You have work to do.'

It was the longest, most passionate harangue he had ever subjected her to, but there was a glimmering hope, a truth in it that at once heartened her and ended her uncertainty.

Subdued, she returned to her practice and exercises, concluding that the great master was right. Like Voltaire, he knew that the only thing possible, in the face of destruction and despair, was to cultivate one's garden.

New York people were cultivating actual gardens in that summer of 1917, at the request of Herbert Hoover, National Food Administrator, the summer that Megan Farley became fourteen. America was in the war.

245

Apart from city gardens and the sight of khaki-clad soldiers heading for the trains, sleek-haired young officers escorting their filmy ladies into the flowery dining rooms of the hotels, the war did not seem real to Megan. She recalled her grandparents' grim, horrified reaction to the President's announcement in April; endured the patriotic lectures at school, but beyond that could see little difference in New York.

The Kaiser seemed a mythical bugaboo in this city still busy and prosperous, still a safe place in which to work and play. Megan's uncle Martin, fortunately, would not be going to fight; she was deeply impressed by her grandmother's tears of relief. Her grandfather went to his office every morning, as usual; her grandmother still practised daily at her piano, and was even planning another concert soon. So, apart from the meatless Tuesdays the family had elected to observe to help the war effort, Megan found herself oddly unaffected.

There were two things, she realised guiltily, that she could thank the war for: one was the fact that they were staying in town this summer. Amas decided that, apart from a few weeks in July, they would occupy the city house; he said that it was unpatriotic to crowd the commuter trains, possibly causing a soldier to have to stand, and that overmuch driving wasted precious fuel.

That first boon delighted Megan. The country had been nice enough, but nothing contained the excitements of New York, where it was possible for her to play the exciting new game without interference.

The other advantage of the war was that all over the metropolis there was now a pervasive feeling of feverish urgency, almost hysteria, that aided Megan further in pursuing her new enjoyment. Few people, in these tense new days, gave much thought to the actions of a quietly-dressed girl of fourteen. Everyone seemed to have more important matters on his mind.

And in the stores which Megan haunted the women assistants, swept up in the excitement of the war, were too busy flirting with soldiers to pay any attention to people like Megan.

She had been stealing regularly for more than a year.

At first, subdued and shamed by the incidents at school, she had resolved never to do such a thing again. But then it happened again one afternoon in a department store.

It really hadn't been her fault, she reflected. She had such a hard time getting served that the store deserved it. Megan had glimpsed a particularly attractive little handbag; her clothes allowance would still allow her to buy it without strain. It was totally unsuitable, of course, according to her grandmother's standards, a dainty item of soft leather with a handle studded with false gems. Megan could never resist anything that looked remotely like the diamond pebbles.

She'd waited patiently for a time with the handbag but then, ignored by two gossiping assistants, simply put her hand over the price tag and slowly walked out of the store. She'd brought her money in a pocket and didn't have a bag of her own on that occasion; fortunately the stolen bag matched her ensemble rather well. So when she reached the front door of the place, the doorman checked her smart appearance, smiled, and opened the door for her with one hand, touching his billed hat with the other in a respectful salute.

Megan had walked hurriedly down the street, stepped into a doorway and detached the price tag from the bag. She felt wildly buoyant, tingling with the thrill and funniness of it; there was an odd heat in her body, down in her very depths. It was the most satisfying feeling she'd ever had; quite physical. The only thing she could compare it to was winning a game, or performing a particularly difficult acrobatic feat with special grace. Or eating something quite delicious.

She transferred her money to the bag and went into another store, where she bought a pair of stockings so she would have a sack to conceal the bag in when she went home. She was sure Vanessa would disapprove of the gaudy little bag.

Her first success encouraged her mightily; thereafter she appropriated things that were more tasteful, so she would be free to use them. Her grandmother hardly seemed to notice that Megan was collecting a large amount of possessions, probably assuming that her clothes allowance covered them, or that she had used one of the various accounts she was allowed to utilise.

This last spring, though, had been the best of all. When the wear fever struck the city, and the assistants seemed to become more and more indifferent and absent-minded, Megan grew bolder.

One chilly April day she'd crept away from school at the lunch interval without a coat and taken a taxi downtown and west to the stores along Fifth Avenue. In the coat department she told one sales assistant that she had checked her coat in the ladies' parlour, for convenience. Then she chose the coat she wanted – wishing it were a fur, but knowing full well that her grandmother would forbid that until she was at least seventeen – and at last was able to walk right out of the department, covering the price tag that dangled from the sleeve with her curled hand.

She hurried to the ladies' parlour and in one of the stalls removed the tag, walking out unmolested, receiving the same respectful salute from the doorman that she always did. And again there was that rush of excitement, that gnawing, itching fire in her body. She had fooled them again; they were too stupid for Megan Farley.

Why she had taken a coat, which she really didn't need, puzzled Megan. But somehow taking anything at all was something she needed to do now, something that compensated for the fact that she was different from the others, disliked and stared at because she had no mother and father; envied because she was so bright at her studies and good at games and, by some, because her family had so much money and her grandmother was becoming famous.

Megan hadn't made many friends at all; most of the girls seemed more interested in boys than anything else, and Megan found that incomprehensible. When she was forced to dance with them at dancing school she judged them rough, awkward and silly, no matter how many good manners had been forced on them by their teachers and parents.

Megan was aware that this bothered her grandmother and grandfather a good deal; sometimes they would observe her worriedly, she thought, but then, seeing that she looked healthy and all right, concluding that she was doing well at school and appeared content, never pursued it much.

The Holders themselves, as a matter of fact, were not very social people, so Megan supposed they could hardly criticise her for the same fault. Amas was so involved in the business, and Vanessa so wrapped up in music, that they didn't entertain people that much, apart from an occasional dinner or gathering for their business friends or Vanessa's musical people, all of whom were too old and boring for Megan.

This last birthday her grandparents had asked her if she wouldn't like to have a party of her school friends, but she politely declined, telling them it would be fine if they'd just take her and Pamela Longstreet to dinner.

They were overjoyed to do that; they took Megan and Pamela to an elaborate dinner and to the theatre afterwards, giving Megan a beautiful string of pearls and a generous amount of money, even giving Pam a bracelet for the occasion.

Pam was the only girl at school Megan cared for at all; she was athletic, too, and she and Megan shared an equal passion for books like *The Scarlet Pimpernel* and stories about great jewel thieves and detectives.

Sometimes Megan thought she might even tell Pam about her Game, but then she decided not to; she was a little afraid. Pam's father was a lawyer, her grandfather a judge, and Amas said she came from 'very upright people'. Doubtless Pam had been raised to disapprove of things like Megan's Game, despite her addiction to raffish adventure stories.

Of one thing Megan was sure: the Game had become her favourite occupation, central now to her daily life.

At last she decided to take something really valuable. Today she'd go to the fine jewellery section of her favourite department store.

'These . . . ah . . . are not for yourself, Miss?' The sales assistant examined the young girl with surprise. She was a nice-looking girl, not at all cheap. Her clothes were excellent and the trim ear-lobes below the bobbed, tawny hair, were intact, not pierced. Generally much older women made such purchases. The assistant wondered for a moment if the girl were playing a joke; surely such a young girl would not walk around with that much money. But then, these days, you never knew.

'Oh, no.' The girl blushed a little, and the assistant thought her odd golden eyes had an abashed expression. 'They're for my mother's birthday.'

'Ah! Well.' The assistant unlocked the case and brought forth the tray of diamond earrings. 'What, er, price range,' she inquired tactfully, 'interests you?'

'Just about any,' the girl said airily to the woman's surprise. Good Lord, she reflected, she might be one of the Astors. I'd better watch my step here.

'Well, these are very lovely,' the assistant said, indicating an intricate pair of drop earrings consisting of one large pear-shaped diamond surrounded by a multitude of smaller ones that twinkled like minute stars.

'Oooh,' the girl said, and the woman was struck by the fervency in her voice, almost a . . . passion, she decided, when the girl surveyed the earrings.

'These,' the sales woman said softly, 'are three thousand dollars.'

It seemed to her that the girl changed colour; the lovely golden eyes met hers with dismay.

'Oh, my.' The girl smiled a little and made an awkward gesture, upsetting the tray. It fell upside down on the marble floor. 'Oh, dear!' she cried and, stooping down, began to gather up the fallen trinkets before the horrified sales assistant could free herself of the counter.

'Oh, dear,' the girl repeated, sounding tearful, 'I'm so sorry.'

'It's all right,' the sales woman said with desperate courtesy, stooping to join her, frantically trying to count the earrings replaced on the tray.

'I think I'd better look at other things for my mother,' the girl said hastily, red with chagrin. 'Thank you.'

She headed for the nearest exit. The distracted sales woman, keeping an eye out for her supervisor, looked at the tray. A pair of earrings was missing; there were two empty slots on the velvet tray.

She shrieked, 'Roberts! Roberts!' and pointed towards the exit.

The tall, dark-suited man took Megan Farley by the elbow and led her back into the store, and towards the jewellery assistant.

'Is this the . . .' the man surveyed Megan, 'young lady, Miss Wood?'

'Yes.' The woman looked at Megan reproachfully.

'Look, Miss . . . I'll have to ask you to empty your pockets.'

With trembling fingers, Megan took the earrings from the pocket of her long, loose pongee jacket and put them on the man's palm.

'How old are you, Miss?' he asked her in a gentle voice.

'Four . . . fourteen,' she stammered. The man's brows drew together in a frown.

'Are you a resident of this city?' he asked her.

'Yes. I live with my grandparents.'

'What is your address, please, and the name of your people?'

He looked shocked when Megan gave him the address. 'What is your grandfather's first name?'

She told him. She could fairly read his reaction – the grand-daughter of Amas Holder, of the prestigious Holder-Stirling Enterprise!

'Miss Holder . . .'

'Miss Farley,' she corrected absently.

'Miss Farley, I'm afraid you will have to come with me upstairs. We will have a word with the manager.'

There was no escape.

Megan walked at the man's side to the lifts, thankful that he was not a policeman in uniform. She would have died of the humiliation;

250

now she was cold with dread. What would the manager do to her – would he have her arrested?

When the two reached the top-floor office of the store's manager, the dark-suited man escorted Megan into his sanctum. She was painfully aware of the curious and scornful glances of the typists and clerks in the outer office.

'What's this, Roberts?' The manager, a heavy, scowling man with a huge moustache, looked up from his mahogany desk.

'This is Miss Megan Farley, sir. She is fourteen years old.'

The manager made a sound of consternation.

'Miss Farley made off with these.' Roberts opened his hand and showed the glittering earrings. He laid them on the desk. 'Miss Farley is the granddaughter of Mr Amas Holder, of Holder-Stirling Enterprise. She lives with Mr Holder and his wife, the pianist.'

Megan saw the manager's nameplate on his desk – Herman F. Grower. The name certainly suited him; it was quite as forbidding as the man himself.

'Well,' he ejaculated, frowning. With a keen glance at Megan that made her feel undressed, he said, curtly, 'Sit down, Miss, er . . .'

'Farley,' Roberts supplied.

'. . . Farley. I am going to call your home. Will you give me the number?'

Megan swallowed painfully, then gave it to him.

When Grower was connected, she heard him say, 'Mrs Holder?'

Her heart sank into her shoes and she trembled. How on earth would her grandmother take this news? She listened to the fearsome Grower detailing her malfeasance to Vanessa. He hung up the phone.

'We will wait here,' he said sternly to Megan, 'for your grand-mother's arrival.'

'Why did she *do* it, Amas?'

He heard her voice shake and, although her back was to him, imagined the wetness of her eyes. She had been calm and restrained throughout dinner, not telling him about it until afterwards, when Megan had gone up to her room.

Now he could understand in full the dread and misery on the child's face at dinner, her pathetic attempts to eat; her tearful reply, when he asked her what was troubling her – 'Vanessa will tell you' – before she fled upstairs.

'I can't fathom it,' he answered Vanessa. She turned from her

251

unseeing survey of the cold hearth, decorated with a basket of flowers for the summer weather, and looked at him with beseeching grey eyes.

He thought parenthetically how beautiful she still was, with her rich, slender body made softer and somewhat more abundant by the years, but the wonderful face so little altered that he sometimes imagined they were newly married again; that there were no children yet, no Megan.

Vanessa's flawless skin had lightened under the pale northern sun, but the huge grey unchanged eyes were as brilliant as ever – more brilliant now with tears – and that sweet mouth was still young and vulnerable. Strands of silver had crept into the brief golden hair, making it look like a cloud of gold and silver fire.

'It isn't,' Vanessa insisted, 'that she was ever *deprived*. Good heavens, we've given her a most generous allowance; I've bought her everything she ever expressed an interest in, or allowed *her* to buy it.'

She look so wearied that he said gently, 'Darling, sit down. Sit down here by me.' He patted the sofa.

As she joined him, he added, 'This has been too much for you. You should have called me at the office. Perhaps I could have spared you the unpleasantness.'

'I couldn't do that,' she murmured, putting her hand on his knee. As always, he was amazed at his strong reaction to her lightest touch, after all these years. One would think a man would finally burn out a little, he thought, distracted. But not with Vanessa . . . he pulled in his wandering thoughts. She was speaking again. 'You have so much to do these days – the contracts for this horrible war, and . . . oh, Amas, Amas, I am so worried. And so *tired*.'

She laid her head against his shoulder.

He put his arm around her and gently pulled her curly head onto his chest. Stroking her hair, he said, 'You *should* be tired. You've been working like a slave at the music. Sometimes I've wanted to take that Bufera and . . .' He paused, smiling ruefully.

But she was not to be diverted. 'Amas do you think . . . do you think that Megan's a . . . bad seed?'

'What on earth are you talking about?' Absently a part of his mind noted the parted door, caught a slight sound in the corridor.

'I meant . . . because of poor Lesley . . . and Mitchell Farley. He was always bad, bad all through, Amas. And Lesley – I think she must have inherited my mother's weakness, helped along,' she amended bitterly, 'by my criminal neglect. Why else would she have killed herself? And my God, what kind of a man *is* Mitchell Farley, not even to look at his own child, then to abandon her almost the day she was born?'

Now Amas was certain that he heard someone in the hall, but Vanessa's desperate questions, her look of deep anxiety, erased all other matters from his mind. She must not be allowed to go through this self-flagellation again, not while he had breath in his body.

'Vanessa . . . Vanessa. In the first place, sweetheart, I don't believe in this inheritance nonsense much.' Passing over the question of Lesley, he went on, 'Megan has had every advantage and a lot of love from you and me. She's been a very happy child. True, she's a bit of a hermit – but then, so are you and I. We've given her that example, I'm afraid.' He smiled. 'But otherwise we have nothing, nothing to reproach ourselves for. We've spoiled her rotten, if anything. What happened today was only another prank. She'll get over all this, I assure you. Someday, when she meets the right young man . . .' Amas smiled again, and ruffled Vanessa's hair.

'All kids take things,' he said easily. 'I did. Didn't you?'

'Never.' Her face was pressed against him, muffling her answer.

'But then I was a poor kid,' he said thoughtfully. 'I had to steal a lot of times, on the road, or I would have starved.'

'That's sad. Poor Amas.' She stroked his chest. 'But Megan's hardly poor,' she protested, 'and not that much of a "kid" any more.'

'Yes, she is, Vanessa. Anyone who had Mitchell for a father is poor. And she's still very young, in so many ways.' Suddenly he was very tired of the whole subject, tired of business, tired of responsibility; for a fleeting instant he even wished that they'd never had any children at all.

Oh, the old days, the old days, he thought, when she and I had only each other. And they had been so pitifully brief, so very beautiful.

'No more,' he whispered. 'No more tonight, my darling.'

Now he was sure of it; he heard that sound in the corridor again, imagined the almost soundless padding of bare feet on the carpet of the stairs. Good Lord, he hoped it wasn't Megan. He wondered how much she'd heard.

But determinedly he dismissed that from his mind. Damn it, he had rights, too. He and Vanessa were people. No more worry, no more responsibility; not now, not this night. Their lovemaking had been so infrequent lately. He was with his woman and he wanted her.

Sensitively she had read his mood, and was stirring in his arms, raising her head from his chest to kiss him on the neck, under his ear. Bless her. She knew him like a book.

And at once, as it had never failed to do, her caress aroused him to a new energy and strength; the adrenalin of his desire coursed through his body, filling him, expanding him. He sure didn't feel like a fifty-six-year-old man; and she, looking up at him now with those great glowing eyes, seemed more like twenty than fifty-one.

'Oh, Amas, my dear one, my dear,' she whispered, raising her mouth to his. He was fairly singing with desire; he could feel the vibrations of it in flesh and tendon. He lowered his mouth to hers, slowly, aware of her closing eyes, glimpsing the thick crescent of her golden lashes on her satiny cheeks before he took her mouth with his, savouring, glorying in that submissive sweetness that his tongue tasted, trembling, like a young, freshly-fallen, vivid fruit. My God, she was so lovely, so lovely.

And, impelled as strongly by remembered frenzies of the past as by present delight, Amas prolonged the hungry, seeking kiss, tasting her mouth just one more instant, then an instant more, feeling her strong, soft hands reach upward to stroke his face.

Then his own eager hands were stroking her, from her smooth shoulders down her bare arms, returning to her breasts, stroking and kneading, hearing her excited murmur; descending again, quickly, to caress her thighs.

He could feel an arousal in her equal to his own.

'Come,' she said in a low, urgent voice. 'Let's go upstairs.'

'Let's stay here,' he whispered, his whisper sounding thick, almost desperate, in his own ears.

'Oh, Amas,' she reproached him with a hint of a laugh in her, 'what if someone should . . .? We are disgraceful, for a grandfather and grandmother, you know.'

'Damn grandparenthood,' he growled, holding her tightly. 'If you are going to argue, I'm going to carry you up those stairs.'

And he pulled her almost roughly to her feet, stooped and picked her up in his arms.

'I'm not light enough any more,' she protested, beginning to laugh.

'You're saying I'm not strong enough any more?' he demanded with mock anger, but he could feel himself smiling. All of a sudden, then, there was no humour in it, not any more. He wanted her too much now to smile.

And, ignoring her murmurs, he walked with her to the door, pushing it ajar with his foot, and started up the stairs.

'Amas . . .'

But now she was no longer unwilling; now she cared as little as he if someone saw them, and he could feel that surely in his bones. A wild, warm feeling of triumph enveloped him, and he knew in that moment that they were back on the *Walmer*, that a quarter-century of living and suffering and fatigue and worry had never been at all.

They were so young again, so young, he exulted; that powerful adrenalin drove him, buoyed him until he felt his strength was unending, his endurance like a boy's.

He opened the door to their room and, still carrying her, shut it softly with one hand. She was hiding her face against his chest. He lowered her to the bed.

He tossed away his smoking jacket, ripped at his cravat as she lay gazing at him, her mouth and eyes, her whole face, he thought, like a lovely opening flower.

She raised her body, leaning on her elbows, as he sat down on the bed and, wordlessly, let him unfasten her filmy dress. As he lifted her lower body gently to pull the dress away and toss it aside, he almost blurted, 'Thank God women aren't wearing so many clothes these days', but he didn't want to break the spell now with anything so banal; he didn't want to speak at all.

She, too, was silent, and breathing with quick, shallow breaths; triumphant, he realised that her state of excitation was akin to his.

Now he was ridding her of her chemise, and she lay naked to his sight in the rosy illumination of the one dim lamp, plain to him in all her glory.

'Vanessa,' was all he could say now. 'Vanessa.'

He stood abruptly and undressed himself to the skin, letting his clothes fall everywhere; he saw the fiery brightness of her eyes, the darker hue in her cheeks and his desire filled him to bursting.

Once more he surveyed her lovely body, the generous, sprawling breasts, the soft but firm stomach, the shapely legs, the golden, sweet luxuriance, before he knelt upon the bed to begin that caress that would awaken her to frenzy, to an unendurable pleasure as overpowering as the dissolution of his loins.

Her flesh carried the scent of nameless April flowers, the smell of mimosa and new grasses on the rain-washed veld. In the wondrous senselessness of desire his every sense was still awake, each sense transmitting messages to his need-hazed brain; unthinking, he was

255

yet capable of wild, poetic thought: this magic, this magic that her body exercised confounded him.

He was aware of her shuddering and leaping response to his caress, her pleasure murmurs striking his astonished ears just as the music springing from her fingers rang, always, along his very marrow.

And then, feeling the last convulsion of her joy, her final, wordless exclamation that had the timbre of a small animal's keen, or the faint mourning of a far December wind, sharp in his ears, Amas raised himself and pressed full length upon her quivering softness to enter the yearned-for country of his peace; with almost lightning suddenness he found his easement, the vast concussion, the shattering, the letting go.

Poised in a kind of wonder, he felt her arms around his moistened body, felt the small, strong fingers trace the form of his quaking biceps, his shoulders, his haunches and back, his neck and ears and hair.

Then he was lying beside her, half-turned, studying the happy, drowsy face beside him. Her eyes were heavy-lidded with satiety, the lips parted, bearing the trace of a lazy smile.

He could find no word now to express that depth and height, that fleeting wonder of the instant when he had been so young again, at the apex of his powers, the sap of boyhood shooting through his veins.

At last he said, 'It was like . . . like the first time, Vanessa,' feeling the inadequacy of it.

'Yes, oh, yes, Amas.' She petted his hard-muscled stomach with her hand. 'You have not changed. *We* have not changed. I find that . . . wonderful.' He sensed that she, too, was finding it difficult to say what was in her heart.

Then all in a moment they were close and familiar, without the need for flowery speech, and she was burrowing nearer to him, chuckling against him as she fanned his skin with her warm, companionable breath, 'Disgraceful for grandparents, Mr Holder.'

He smiled, but he answered soberly, 'I still say damn all that. We're people, too, you know. We have the right, Vanessa . . . the right to this. The right to be as happy as any of our children are. In the last analysis, this is the greatest thing we have, the only thing we have. Children leave; but lovers stay.'

She raised her head and looked into his eyes, and he saw a deeper, more joyful look there than he had ever seen before in all their time together.

'Yes. Yes, you're right, Amas.' Her whole face was alight, the shining cloud of her curly hair like sun-touched silver.

He thought, she is unyielding; brilliant and unyielding as the enduring fragments of that silver fire we've wrested from the ground. And yet, compared to her, that vast treasure was a mound of dusty pebbles in a world of desolation, with its madness of markets, wobbling demands.

This, Amas Holder thought, this is the only treasure that will never be rendered meaningless by the whim of commerce, the vicissitudes of time.

Megan Farley lay wide-eyed, staring into the dark.

They had lied.

For fourteen years they had lived a lie to her.

Her mother had committed suicide; her father was 'bad all through'. And her father, Mitchell Farley, was alive.

For all these years the great, frank, honest Holders had lied to Megan Farley. She burned with resentful anger; she was sore.

She'd wanted so much to burst in and confront them, crying out that they had lied and now she knew. But she had glimpsed them close together, seen them kissing, heard their murmurs.

It was . . . disgusting. Old people like that, acting like . . . animals on the veld. Megan had never forgotten her feeling of sick bewilderment when she had seen the quachas mating. Her grandfather told her it was just a natural thing.

Perhaps. Perhaps it was natural to quachas. But to her *grandparents*. She'd thought old people did not act silly any more. Why, Pamela had told her that her own mother and father had separate rooms, and they were not even as old as Amas and Vanessa.

Megan had long ignored the whispers of the girls at school about this mysterious and distasteful subject; she'd never felt the things they did. Some of them had kissed boys.

Ugh. To imagine kissing the boys at dancing school, with their awful smell of old brown corduroy, turned Megan's stomach.

Then, tonight, after she had heard that dreadful thing, while she was still almost sick from it and dizzy, and had taken refuge in her room, she'd heard them.

Or she'd heard him, her grandfather, walking with strange, slow steps towards their room, but she hadn't heard her grandmother's steps. What could they be doing? How could her grandmother be there, talking, but walking in the hall without a sound?

It had been too much for Megan's curiosity. She'd got up, stolen to her door and opened it a crack.

257

Her grandfather was *carrying* her grandmother! At first Megan thought she might have fainted, or something; might be ill. But she wasn't. No, she was giggling, leaning her head against his chest, as silly as any of the girls at Megan's school.

It was . . . awful.

Feeling even dizzier, Megan had crept back to bed. For the first time in her life she was fully aware of what was going on in her grandparents' bedroom. It was nothing she actually *heard*; but she knew. Oh, yes, she knew.

And, feeling astonished, she tried to reconcile this with the public picture of Amas Holder, tall, strong and grave; respected, full of dignity, so self-satisfied and sure. And Vanessa . . . this could not be the goddess in the flowing draperies, bowing on the concert platform, stately and beautiful, her fine face glowing as she heard the waves of applause.

If this revolting exhibition is what they meant by 'love' . . . her own mother and father had done that. They'd had to, or Megan would never have been born. But it had made her mother so miserable she'd taken her own life. Her father had been so disgusted he went away without even looking at Megan, they said.

Well, she didn't blame him. What she knew of the birth of babies was so hair-raising, so revolting that she thought it was unfair . . . unfair that everybody had to come into the world so filthy and disgusting right from the very start. And that other indignity that was yet to begin.

And rigid, sore with indignation in the lonely darkness, Megan Farley made a vow.

She would shut herself away from all of it, hide what she knew from Amas and Vanessa. She would be free and stainless as a mirror, even when that moon-sickness came.

A mirror. She recalled some of her great-grandmother's letters to her mother, Lesley Farley, when the old woman had learned that Megan would be born in June. Vanessa had thought the letters were amusing, but Megan took them very seriously. Her great-grandmother Hester had written, 'You will have a little Gemini, whose star symbols are the crystal, the mirror and the pearl. She will be as pure and lovely, as stainless as all of those.'

I am a silver mirror, Megan repeated to herself, consoled. I will go on reflecting them all, and they will never see what is inside. And men will never touch me at all.

Part V
The Grading

CHAPTER SEVENTEEN

On that August afternoon in 1920, Megan Farley stood with Amas and Vanessa in the crowds along the Avenue de Keyser, waiting for the Antwerp Festival parade to start. Three years, she thought, had changed her as drastically as the world had changed. And for Megan, like America, there was no turning back. She was sensation-hungry as the rest, and the meeting in London with Beatrice Prince-di Gamba had titillated Megan with its glimpse into an even more exciting world. Now she fairly burned to lose that adamant innocence she had once clung to like armour.

Glancing at Vanessa, Megan smiled to remember her horrified reaction to that love-scene she had witnessed on the night she learned about her father. With the coming of the following autumn, Megan had tardily reached her womanhood, and with that natural phenomenon the hot new emotions, the softer sensations came.

The last three years had been so all-absorbing, with their discoveries and inner change, that Megan's childish feeling of betrayal had evaporated in life's urgent warmth, like morning mist in noonday sun. It had been a long time since she had even thought of her father, or where he could be. Next month she would enter Hunter College . . . unless she married Roger Kimball.

But that was still not settled in her mind. She was haunted by the notion that what she felt for Roger was nothing like the feeling that Amas still plainly had for Vanessa, just now, on this late summer day in the Belgian city; when even at the awkward age of fifty-four, her grandmother was as attractive as many of the younger women about them.

American as she had become, Vanessa kept a cosmopolitan air. Today her brief silver-blonde hair, never tinted, was almost hidden by her soft turban. Huge earrings hung from her covered lobes and her body's voluptuous lines were hinted at by a long olive-green redingote with an underdress of black. She was carrying a small pouch bag in which she had casually brought a fortune in diamonds for their visit to the Antwerp Exchange.

'What do you think of the Diamond City?' Amas smiled at Megan.

'I love it.' Megan grinned at him, catching the faint sound of the band, approaching now from the direction of the river and the Hôtel de Ville. Belgium, neutral during the war, had hardly been touched at all except when the Germans crashed across its borders to fight France. This was Megan's first trip abroad – Vanessa's and Amas' work, and then the war, had put paid to the earlier journey they planned.

Her grandparents were still a puzzle to Megan. She could never understand why people so rich could choose to work all the time. They rarely took a real vacation; their only hobbies were music and the diamonds. Now, for them, the magic was in negotiation and the find. The power that diamonds carried had become their game, like the pathetic game, Megan thought, that used to absorb her childish days.

And yet, to Megan, the diamonds were a magic in themselves. Vanessa rarely wore them any more; when she did, they were only the rarest coloured stones. But Megan loved the silver brilliance of the pure 'white' stones, after they had acquired their 'city polish'. In South Africa they had been dirty pebbles. Only in the cities could the diamonds take on the glitter that thrilled Megan – just as she had taken on that glitter, she had come to realise in the last few weeks, herself. The expansion and stimulation she vaguely remembered on first entering New York as a child, had been multiplied a thousandfold in London. She itched to get to Paris the day after tomorrow.

And here in the Diamond City, which had bounced back after the war, they said, with an amazing quickness, Megan had encountered for the first time in her life the vast collection of brilliant diamonds at the Antwerp Exchange. It had been as magical as walking through the Milky Way. And at that moment she had not been able to help remembering the diamond earrings at the store; that old, lost challenge and excitement.

Even now, swept up in the anticipation of the parade, Megan felt an irrational twinge of something lacking, caught a vision of a glimmering, flying something always just ahead, waiting to be caught, not yet experienced.

'They're coming!' Vanessa cried. Megan could see it now, from far away, winding down the broad Avenue de Keyser – the splendid 'procession of jewels', with its thousands of participants dressed in period costumes, riding decorated chariots among the camels and zebras, elephants and horses. On many of the men's tunics and the women's robes were gems of extraordinary size, whether paste or real it was impossible to tell at this distance and yet, as Amas had said, in the Diamond City 'anything was possible'.

For one mad moment Megan had an impulse to join the procession, but her clothes, as Bea had remarked, were 'so plain'. It chafed Megan that she was considered too young yet to dress as glamorously as Vanessa, and she resented her drop-waisted dress of taupe and black shadow-plaid, its neck inset with blue-green, even if Vanessa claimed the ensemble gave Megan's eyes and hair a wonderful 'value'. Megan's lion-coloured hair was shingled now in the shadow of her broad-brimmed cream hat with its black crown. Examining herself in the mirror that morning, Megan admitted to herself that her hair looked nice below the drooping hat brim, her golden eyes almost bronze from the reflection of the gown.

But she longed so wildly, hotly, to be wearing a crimson robe with twinkling gems all over. She noticed a striking young man; he was almost near enough to touch with her fingers.

He was dressed like the figure on the posters all over the city advertising the *Juweelenstoet*, the jewel parade in the *Feesten Van Antwerpen*, a sign that had caught Megan's imagination. Not only the strange Flemish words but the vivid colours and antique costume were utterly typical of the city's paradoxes – fifteenth-century guild houses juxtaposed with modern buildings, narrow ancient streets full of motor cars. Here the poster was, alive, in the person of the black-eyed man; the only word to describe him, Megan realised, was beautiful.

Beautiful used in the old, high heroic sense for splendid men with godlike bodies; unique men embodying all the impossible myths, the fabulous old tales of love. That flashed through Megan's mind in the brief instant their eyes made contact – his were black as jet, piercing, glittering; they surveyed her with a Gallic frankness, their colour enhanced by his jaunty scarlet hat to which a dashing white feather was attached by a jewelled pin.

He was wearing a black wig, she judged, because his hair looked like that of a medieval youth, reaching the high white collar of his tight crimson tunic.

The belted tunic, edged in fur, had trailing sleeves so long they brushed his stalwart, shapely legs in their red and white striped tights. The man was mischievous and virile with that strong yet delicate leanness she associated with French men.

Megan had never seen a man before who affected her with such immense force. He seemed to realise his own beauty, and carry it with a matter-of-fact grace.

Megan heard someone call out from beyond Amas, 'Hugo! Hugo Bouwer!' And the young man raised a lean-muscled arm in its tight red and white undersleeve, responding with the casual poise of a prince accustomed to public appearances and adulation. He smiled slightly; slowing his pace and moving deliberately nearer to Megan, he continued to stare into her eyes. Then she saw the jet glance dart away for a second, observing her arm linked with Vanessa's, taking in her grandparents with a fleeting look.

At that very moment the event happened that impelled Megan Farley on her course; she was to think of it later as something fated, the incident that determined her life's direction. So suddenly that she could hardly comprehend it, there was a cry in the crowd, 'Thief! Thief, there!'

The press of bodies shifted and somehow Amas was shoving his way through, grabbing for the man that the woman had pointed to, Vanessa was desperately trying to hold onto Megan, calling out her name; it all happened in the wink of an eye, but every image was vivid, brilliantly clear to Megan.

She heard Vanessa call out, 'We will meet back at the hotel! The hotel, Megan, if we get separated!' And in the roiling shift of bodies, Megan found the young man in scarlet close to her, grabbing her arm, saying in accented English, 'Careful, careful, mademoiselle!'

He led her through an open space in the crowd; she looked back, seeing Amas now with Vanessa, apparently in fear for her safety. He, too, was leading Vanessa away but in the opposite direction.

Madly the band played on, the glittering procession continued down the broad avenue. Vanessa was straining to see Megan, wildly waving her arm; Amas was saying something to her, still urging her out of the mass of people.

'But . . . but my grandparents,' Megan tried to pull away from the beautiful young man named Hugo. He tightened his grip on her hand, and the dry heat from his strong fingers swept into Megan's, darting up her arm. Her heart hammered.

'I will take you to them,' he said easily. 'But now we must get out of this.'

'You are in the procession . . .' she protested.

'The procession will proceed without me,' he said carelessly, and then Megan saw that she had lost sight of Amas and Vanessa. 'Come.'

She looked into the glittering onyx eyes. 'Yes. Yes, I will,' she said abruptly, smiling at him. An answering smile broke out on his swarthy face, his square, even teeth so white they fairly blinded her.

'Excellent.' He steered her through another widening space and she realised now that a vast number of people separated her from the crowd in which she'd last seen her grandparents. The police had arrived; there was a passionate discussion among those who had evidently seen the thief, and a great deal of milling about.

'Where are we going?' Megan asked Hugo Bouwer.

'Towards the Hôtel de Ville.' He had her by the elbow, propelling her along.

'But our hotel is in the opposite direction.' She paused; this was the maddest thing she'd ever done in her life, going off like this with a perfectly strange man in a foreign city. At least she knew French, which was the official language here, and many of the residents spoke English. But she was still at sea when she heard the frequently spoken languages of the people, Flemish and Walloon, the former a kind of French incomprehensible to Frenchmen, the latter a Dutch that few Dutchmen could understand. It was a scary sensation.

'I know,' he said, smiling, staring down into her eyes. He seemed immensely tall and strong and, near like this, a hundred times more appealing than he had before. His eyes admired her with total frankness; when she spoke he had a way of resting his look caressingly on her mouth. That excited her so much she was frightened by it.

'What are you saying?'

'That I want to kidnap a so beautiful lady . . . for a little while. I have never seen anyone like you, mademoiselle, never. You have the eyes and hair of a little lioness, all golden.' He examined her hair and eyes again as he spoke, then stared at her mouth.

Somewhere in the crowd from which they had fled there was another commotion and, turning to observe it, Megan thought she saw Amas and Vanessa in the middle of it again.

She wavered; she ought to go to them, right now. And yet, she stood near Hugo Bouwer, her senses were assaulted by his closeness. His penetrating eyes, his smile served to confound her; she felt dazed. There was something in him that reminded her of that poignant ache for the unknown; he himself, at this moment, might have been that very glimmering, winged ghost always darting beyond her vision, taunting her.

And almost without volition, she blurted out, 'Yes. Yes, I think that would be a magnificent adventure.'

He beamed. 'Magnificent indeed. Let's get out of this. I will show you something of my city . . . and then I will deliver you back to the Holders.'

Megan was startled. 'You know them?'

Leading her across a winding side street, Hugo laughed. 'Who does not? No one who loves music can have failed to hear of the great Vanessa Holder . . . and Amas Holder is famous in Antwerp. Especially to me. You see, I myself am employed at the Beurs – the Diamond Trading Bourse, you say in your country.'

'The Bourse . . . I see.'

'I got a look at you there, only yesterday, with your grandparents. You are Miss Megan Farley, they told me. And I determined then, Miss Megan Farley, to meet you, no matter what happened.' He pressed her arm close to him.

Her heart began its wild hammering again; nothing, nothing like this had ever happened to her before. It was like . . . it was like her grandmother's descriptions of her own meeting with Amas Holder. A sudden warmth suffused Megan's cheeks and neck, washing downward to her breast, shooting out through her arms and finding the very centre of her astonished body.

'Ah! The Stadhuis already,' he murmured. 'The Hôtel de Ville.'

They must have been walking very fast, because already, as he pointed out, they were approaching the Grand Place, and she saw the notable Renaissance façade of the great building.

'I live right over there, in a pension near the quai, on the Rue aux Cheveux.'

She broke out into a merry laugh, 'Hair Street. It is a funny name.'

He answered her with a smile, but she felt that he was not amused. 'Indeed, a funny little place on a funny little street. But I will not always live so, I assure you.' His strange eyes glittered.

'I'm sorry,' she said quickly. 'I meant no . . . criticism.' She felt deeply disturbed; she was afraid that her comment had been construed as a snobbish one. It had to be obvious to him, if he knew the Holders, that they had a great deal of money. 'I think it is charming.'

That apparently satisfied him, because he smiled widely, and then said, 'With your permission, we will go to my pension for a moment so I can get rid of this ensemble. It is very conspicuous and not too comfortable.'

She slowed her pace, hesitant, wondering why he did not want to appear conspicuous. But that was foolish; in free-thinking America it was not unknown for a girl to visit a man's apartment house and wait for him in the lobby. She was sure that was all he meant. Trying not to think of what Amas and Vanessa might be going through, Megan nodded.

'All right.'

He looked so pleased, however, that she began to wonder. European men sometimes considered American girls a little too careless and often 'took advantage'. It disturbed her to realise that she might *want* him to take advantage, and the idea made her flush.

But she preceded him into the pension. A great number of people were already occupying the chairs in the parlour. 'Ah!' he said, 'I'm afraid it is very crowded. Perhaps . . .' he hesitated. 'At least you could be seated in my rooms. I apologise for this.'

'It's . . . it's all right,' she said reluctantly, yet she followed him up the stairs. He opened his door and gestured her into a small, plain sitting room, furnished as austerely as a student's, with many books. The only salient piece of decoration was an enormous bowl of fish by the windows. The afternoon sun ignited them to gemlike colours.

'How lovely!' She wandered towards the fish bowl and leaned down to look at it. On the bottom, half-buried in the sand, were innumerable chunks of glimmering crystals.

Hugo stood staring at her an instant with a peculiar smile. 'So you like my aquarium?'

'Very much.'

'But please,' he urged her. 'Please sit down. After I change clothes I will make you some tea.' He removed some books from a chair and made a gallant gesture.

'Thank you. Take your time,' she said easily. Now she felt more at ease, somehow.

He excused himself and went into a room beyond, shutting the door. She took off her hat and put it on a table, running her fingers through her glowing shingle of tawny hair.

Almost before she knew it, he was back, dressed in a shirt and trousers, and she observed him with surprise. His hair, without the wig, was so utterly different, cut almost *en brosse* high above his ears, coal black and shining with life. If anything, he looked more appealing than ever; she had half-expected that without the romantic medieval costume he would lose his dashing look, but he had not.

Far from it. Even in the ordinary clothes, he looked as lithe and tensile as an acrobat; the severe cut of his hair, rather than detracting, enhanced the shape of his head, the striking eyes, the fine nose and rather full soft lips. He was slightly Mephistophelean.

Hugo stared at her from across the room. '*Voilà*,' he grinned, 'transformation. Are you . . . disappointed?'

She looked at him soberly, fearing that her emotions were plain to read. 'Disappointed? Oh, no. No.'

'Well, then,' he said softly. 'Let me put on some tea. Then we can go out and see something of the city. Unless . . . it is very crowded with the Festival, at this time of day. Perhaps you would honour me by letting me serve you here.'

'Of course,' she said formally. 'I would be delighted.'

She noticed that peculiar look of beaming triumph, thinking, I may be committing myself to more than tea. But somehow she no longer cared; nothing mattered. She had never felt like this, never been so charmed, so magnetised by anyone before. And she knew that she just wanted to be with him. It was as simple and surprising as that.

Watching him put a kettle on a small gas ring, and then pour out the tea and arrange some cakes on a plate with his slender, strong fingers, Megan was overcome more and more by that flooding, warm carelessness, by alien emotions.

So it was almost without astonishment that she felt him bending over her and, setting down the cup and saucer, lift her chin and lower his mouth over hers. Megan was lost utterly, opening her lips to that knowing and passionate fullness.

'I don't think you understand,' Amas Holder said to the agitated gendarme, first in English, then in halting French. Amas was still searching desperately in the milling throng for Megan while at the same time trying to comfort Vanessa, who was crying. 'Damn it, man!' Amas yelled. 'My granddaughter is *missing*!'

'Ah, *mon Dieu*,' the officer breathed. 'A *petite* – a little child?' His English was as thick as Amas' French.

'No, no,' Amas said angrily. 'A . . . a *jeune fille*. She is seventeen.'

Ha. The gendarme, Hector Lelot, had heard much of these intractable American girls. They were capable of anything, absolutely anything, in his experience.

'Well, now, sir,' he temporised in his halting English, making an indescribable Gallic gesture, 'the young ladies these days . . . perhaps she has met a . . . *friend*, yes?'

'We are strangers to the city,' the man's wife intervened sharply. She was an original, if Hector had ever seen one. Not young, certainly, but possessing extraordinary attractions. Hector had a memory of seeing her picture somewhere not long ago. 'As a matter

268

of fact,' she went on in perfect, Parisian French, 'we have reason to believe she was abducted by one of the young men in the parade, in the red costume of a page.'

'Madame,' Hector addressed Vanessa sternly, 'the young men who march in the procession are persons of undoubted probity, the most respectable. They are employees of the Beurs, members of the Diamond Club itself.'

'Don't take that tone with my wife,' Amas growled.

'Amas,' Vanessa took his arm, speaking to him in a low voice.

To the great relief of the sweating Hector Lelot, his captain appeared with two gendarmes. 'One moment.' The imposing captain held up his hand. 'Now, what have we here, Lelot?'

As best he could Hector explained.

'And your name, sir?' The captain addressed Amas neutrally, but there was a belligerent gleam in his small dark eyes, the thin mouth grim under the drooping moustache.

Amas gave it. The grim lines of the mouth relaxed, and the captain's face underwent a remarkable change. He looked deeply chagrined. 'M. Holder. Madame . . .' he bowed a little to Vanessa, adding with a faint smile, 'it is an honour to meet such a fine artist. I saw you perform in Brussels.'

'Thank you,' Vanessa murmured, inclining her head slightly.

'M. Holder, if you and Madame will be so kind . . . as to come with me to the constabulary. It is only a step away. I think we can arrange this matter to everyone's satisfaction.'

'Not until I find my granddaughter,' Amas barked. 'I'm not leaving this spot.'

'Amas,' Vanessa said in a low, coaxing tone. 'Megan is obviously nowhere to be seen. I think it's a good idea.'

'. . . and,' the captain continued as if Amas had not spoken, 'we shall then be able to get the particulars about your granddaughter, M. Holder . . . with a measure of quiet and comfort for Madame,' he concluded meaningly, glancing at Vanessa.

Amas followed the direction of his eyes. Vanessa did look exhausted already from anxiety and nervous upset. 'You're right,' he admitted sheepishly. 'I beg your pardon. We will of course accompany you.'

As they moved slowly along towards the constabulary, the captain promised Amas, 'Be assured that we will locate your granddaughter. There is no way, no chance of evading the police of Antwerp.'

*　　　*　　　*

The sunset's colour struck the panes of the little room like a great fiery rose and burnished Hugo Bouwer's naked skin. He lay in half-sleep, smiling, and Megan leaned on her elbow, staring at his body. More than ever his beauty struck her; she blinked in the burning light that pierced the shabby curtains, trying to comprehend that rapid interval of dazed submitting and forgetfulness when he had brought her so abruptly to the act of love.

She was still dazed, dazed and sore and throbbing with unsatisfied longing. It had all been so quick and new and bore no resemblance at all to the two brief and fumbling experiences she had had before – once, two years ago, with the boy in New York; then the abortive but thrilling encounter with Pamela, from which both had turned away, knowing that it had been a freakish, forbidden thing. And least of all was the passage with Hugo anything like the incomplete, respectful overtures of Roger Kimball. Roger, she knew now, had touched her no more than the charms of an affectionate puppy.

The orange light of the sun was suddenly snuffed out; the window panes looked grey all at once, heralding the chill of dusk, and Megan shivered.

She could not comprehend what all the lyrical clamour of her wondering years had been about. There was no difference in her now at all, only that nagging dissatisfaction, the bodily unease, the sinking knowledge that that glimmering, winged image still eluded her, somewhere ahead, beyond.

And yet she was puzzled, knowing a painful new tenderness for the man beside her. She had experienced a strange joy in his mighty pleasure before she had fallen into that cool and empty aftermath of lonely disillusion.

Resentfully Megan reflected that Vanessa Holder had lied to her about far more than her father – she had let Megan live with the far more serious myth of love. Was this, then, the glory that had sustained her grandparents all these many years? Surely it could not be. Surely they possessed a magic that she had not been blessed with, perhaps never would be.

But why, in that event, did her heart melt within her now when she contemplated Hugo Bouwer – why this dragging tenderness? Perhaps . . . perhaps next time, she thought with wistful hope. There was a timid awkwardness in her when she covered herself with the sheet, moved towards him to kiss his face.

'Lovely Megan,' he murmured, opening his black eyes. 'Megan who has never loved before. How charming that is.' He caressed her face lightly with his hand, and it chilled her blood. He sounded as if he were complimenting her on a dress, and had not said a word of love.

Her heart felt like a stone within her body, and the faint tenderness evaporated. She wanted to be far away from him, never to see or think about him again.

She made a restless movement, pulling away from his hand. 'I must go,' she said.

'Go?' He sat up in the bed, staring at her. 'No, no, my charming Megan. Not now. You will not go now.' He reached for her and imprisoned her with his arms.

An odd feeling of fear mingled with her renewing and reluctant tenderness. Now she was no longer sure. His magnetism was so strong, his lithe body and Mephistophelean face so beautiful that she lay down again, hesitant, pondering him.

'Ah, that is better, my dear little Megan.' He stroked her face and, throwing the sheet aside, began to stroke her narrow body. Her aroused senses began to overcome her fear, and she let herself relax in his knowing embrace. Perhaps this would be the time of magic, perhaps this time she would know all that she had puzzled over. With wild anticipation, she submitted to him, thrilled by the closeness of his smooth, hard body, the murmured foreign endearments uttered in his growling and persuasive voice; now they were coming together, this time with a greater warmth for her, a deeper excitement. Now she thought triumphantly, I will know, I will reach the place of contentment and knowing.

But when he fell from her with a cry, it was even more maddening than before. She was filled with a deeper desolation, a gnawing pain and restlessness. And as he lay beside her in content she heard within herself an awful weeping. This was the greatest bewilderment, the most profound dilemma she had ever known – his beauty aroused her to such longings, cancelled out her will. Yet here it was, ending in this nibbling sadness.

Nevertheless she could not deny him, was powerless to resist him. This must be what they had all meant by love. And even now, already, she was defeated by it, no longer able to think of going away. Contemplating him, Megan felt an awful ache of tenderness, an unrelenting sweetness.

With another timid, unpractised motion, she moved towards him and laid her head on his chest. 'Hugo, Hugo,' she whispered. 'I love you.' She hid her face against him.

He tightened his arm around her and she could sense a new wakefulness in him. 'I know, Megan, I know,' he murmured, stroking her brief hair. She waited, breathless, for him to say the words she had said, but he did not. 'You are a lovely lady.'

She raised herself and looked down at him. The black eyes gleamed, unreadable, and a smile was on his full, arrogant and shapely mouth. She thought sadly, I will have to be content with that. It was too late now to turn back. She knew she could not leave, that it would be unbearable now to go back to the hotel, and ultimately back to the world of New York, to the dull and limited Roger. All that seemed impossible now.

'I want to stay with you,' she said impulsively.

The dark eyes brightened, the smile grew wider, and it seemed that her statement had given him extraordinary pleasure and satisfaction. 'Of course you do. And you will. You will go to Paris with me tomorrow.'

'To Paris!' She stared at him, realising that now she had cast her lot with him; her whole existence rested in his hands. For an instant she wavered. It was terrifying. 'But, Hugo, I . . .'

'You said you loved me, Megan.' His look of reproach, almost of anger, made her uneasy.

'I do, Hugo, I do!' she protested, half-weeping, throwing herself against him, kissing his face wildly.

He hugged her in an absent, indulgent fashion, as if she were a troublesome child, pushing her ever so slightly away from him. She wondered if all men were like this after the act of love; perhaps they were. Once the goal had been attained, she supposed, they didn't care as much any more. That's what some of her friends had told her. Once again Megan had that sinking sensation. It was unimaginable that this cool encounter could be called love.

And it was equally impossible to imagine leaving all she knew to run off to Paris with Hugo. Because she had a feeling it might be for good, and not just the adventure of a moment. 'I . . . I'm not sure.'

'Of course you are.' She was amazed at the calm way he was taking it all. He kissed her neck, and a little shiver of excitement ran through her. 'We won't be poor, dear Megan.'

She wondered exactly what he meant. The salary of an employee of the Bourse could not be immense, and he lived so plainly. The matter of money had never occurred to her until he mentioned it. 'What do you mean?'

'Come. Come with me, Megan Farley.' He threw back the covers and held out his hand.

She made a sound of protest. 'I'm not . . . not wearing anything.'

'So much the better,' he chuckled. Shyly she got out of bed and followed him, naked, into the shabby sitting room.

In the first moments she felt her nakedness sorely, suffering great discomfort. But then, when he took it all so matter-of-factly, she relaxed a little and almost began to enjoy it. It was titillating; they were free spirits.

'Come,' Hugo said again, and gestured her to the huge fish bowl. 'See the pebbles in the sand?'

She nodded, mystified.

'That is two millions in diamonds,' he said casually, 'valued in English pounds.'

Megan gasped. She sank down in a chair, unconscious now of her nudity, forgetting everything but his astonishing announcement. 'But . . . but how . . .?'

'Wait.' He laughed and sat on the arm of her chair, and she was thrilled by the sight of his bare body. But somehow she did not dare to touch him, not now. 'I will have to go to Paris tomorrow morning. Monday, no doubt, the discovery will be made. But by tomorrow they will be all nice and dry, reposing in a courier's portfolio, for which I have the credentials. And you will go with me. In fact, you must, now that I have told you.'

There was something cold and threatening in the last statement, but perversely it excited her as much as his nakedness so close to her now. 'I can't believe it,' she said slowly. Her hand stole onto his upper leg, and she could feel him reacting.

'That I am a thief?' He smiled down at her and his face was demoniacally attractive. She was swept with another wave of heat, then coolness, like fever followed by chills.

'I can't believe it, because I am, too. I have been for years.'

'Megan!' He was smiling broadly. 'You are more delightful than I could have hoped. What a marvellous confederate you are going to be.'

'But how – how did you manage?'

'Never mind that now. I think you deserve a little reward, my Megan. I did not do right by you.' She did not know what to answer to that, and he went on, 'I was far too carried away. But now . . .' He leaned over and took the tip of one of her breasts in his mouth, and the fever in her body became a frenzy of longing, a wildness of unknown desire. She quivered at the caress.

Then he took his lips away and suddenly was kneeling before her on the floor, parting her trembling knees with his hands, leaning into her, doing what she and Pamela had done together and Megan began to shake all over, to moan; her whole body shook and leaped as she moved towards that amazement of narrow pleasure, that pleasure she had known only once, and furtively, afterwards stricken with the guilt and terror of an unnatural sin. But now, with Hugo, it was not the same. He was a man, and her lover. She loved him. And the marvellous skill of his caress was beyond anything she and Pamela had managed in their fearful fumbling; her whole body was on fire, the needle-point of pleasure piercing her, piercing her now, like a tiny blade of fire and growing, growing bigger and wider until it was unbearably, overwhelmingly sweet. With tightly closed eyes she leaned back, shuddering, shuddering and abandoned to it.

Now her legs were trembling so, her flesh so frenzied, that she felt the great convulsion of her soft limbs and let forth a screaming cry.

Then he was urging her downward, and he was lying on the floor, holding her tightly upon him, giving her quick, urgent directions which she hastened to obey. They were in the other closeness now; he was leaping and writhing below her, moving her, guiding her with his strong hands until he, too, emitted a long, strangled cry and collapsed backwards under the frail weight of her.

'Oh, Hugo, Hugo, it is so . . . wonderful,' she gasped, and he murmured, pulling her flat against his slackened flesh as she gloried in the feel of him, still quaking, vibrant with her magical new appeasement. This, then, *was* love, she decided. This was truly love at last; she belonged to him forever. If it were always going to be like this, nothing could make her leave him.

And now, she marvelled, they were going to embark together on the greatest adventure of her whole life. Nothing else mattered at all, not her grandparents or New York, not college or her vast possessions, nothing. Certainly not Roger.

From that moment everything he said to her was like a sacred order. When he suggested, smiling, that they dress and have some food, she fairly leaped to obey. What they ate, which was sparse and simple, no longer mattered either. Nothing did but Hugo, and the thrill of what would come tomorrow. Megan had never felt so alive, so tingling, so chock-full of excitement in her life before.

He told her that they could not go out that evening. Doubtless the police of Antwerp would be searching for her by now. Fortunately her grandparents had seen Hugo only in the comparative disguise of his costume and would certainly not be able to identify him to the constabulary.

Here was the plan, he told her: tonight he would go out to buy more food, and some wine, also the other things they would need for their journey. Submissively she agreed.

When Hugo returned, after an anxiously long interval for Megan, he was bearing a number of parcels.

'*Voilà!*' he greeted her with his demoniac smile. He put the food away and uncorked the wine; they drank several glasses. 'Now here's the important part.'

He opened one of the parcels and took out some bottles. 'We have got to dye our hair,' he stated. 'Wigs are too suspect. This is for me,' he held up a bottle of bleach, 'and this for you.' Her bottle was black. 'You will make a charming dark-haired beauty. I will also do something about your brows. And your own clothes will have to be disposed of,' he added.

Interested, she watched him take a woman's ensemble, suit, blouse and shoes, bag and gloves and a soft, crushable hat from a big sack. 'The gloves will cover your rings . . . it would be a pity to abandon them,' he added shrewdly, 'and you will be a different person in these.'

Megan held up the clothes. They were not bad; the ensemble combined black and an orange-gold that were quite attractive. Eagerly she submitted to his ministrations, as he explained that his sister was a dresser of hair in the provinces and he had learned these matters from her. Megan examined her new self in the mirror and felt the delight of masquerade. Then he dyed his black hair blond, which took several hours. But, when he was through, she thought he looked handsomer than ever, something like a young Prussian.

'I think we are going to do very well,' he commented with satisfaction.

'So do I,' she grinned at him in the mirror.

This was going to be a thousand times more diverting than her pathetic little Game. This would be the greatest game that Megan Farley had ever played.

CHAPTER EIGHTEEN

The Holders had chosen the Grand Hotel on the Rue Gerard for its central heating, small garden and the likelihood of a room with a bath. The fact that it was less convenient to the Bourse, where they had had a good deal of business to transact, was offset by their liking for the Old Town section where the hotel was situated, with its ancient guild houses and fairy-tale air.

But this grey morning, when Vanessa awoke abruptly to a shrill reveillé of birds, she was conscious of hating the hotel, resenting Antwerp. Oh, I wish to God, she thought, we had never come to this wretched country.

Amas was deep in exhausted sleep. Moving cautiously so as not to wake him, Vanessa got out of bed. Her body felt as heavy as if it had turned to stone, the result of her anxiety and sleep deprivation. They had been up very late the night before. She had to admit that the constabulary was remarkably quick to begin the search for Megan. Everything that could possibly be done was being done, she knew.

Amas Holder's status with the Exchange, she realised cynically, was speeding the investigation. Yet they had turned up nothing yet. The police had of course first inquired of all the hospitals and even – Vanessa's heart gave a painful jolt – the places where the dead were brought in. They had also scoured the usual cafés and taverns, the milk shops and confectionaries, which were the gathering places of the young in Antwerp. The stations and quays were being watched.

Today, the captain had told them late last night, his men would start at dawn to inquire at every hotel, pension and boarding house in the city, in the event that Megan was being . . . forcibly held.

Vanessa could hardly bear to think of that. She sank down wearily into a chair by the window and stared with unseeing eyes at the garden. The offending birds still chirped and shrilled, worsening Vanessa's headache. For the hundreth time she questioned, what could have got into Megan?

And the dreary answer was always the same – that old rebellion born of insecurity, the neglect of Vanessa Holder. The indifference and neglect that had killed Lesley, as surely as if Vanessa had given her the laudanum; the selfish blindness that had caused Vanessa Holder to take too much for granted.

Our status did not rise in her eyes, Vanessa judged wryly, when she found out we lied to her about Mitchell. And all those years that they had blithely ignored the 'childish prank' of thievery, taken calmly the fact that Megan was an isolated, strange child with two few friends, passed lightly over the phenomenon of her very late menstruation, which had to have damaging effects on her psyche, as people were calling the mind these days.

Vanessa, hearing little but music for the past ten years, had been more than glad to file Megan away, as it were, marking her for the solid, likeable Roger Kimball, reassured by her consent to attend Hunter that autumn. What fools they'd been!

And what an utter fool *I* was, Vanessa added mentally, not to go after her yesterday, drag her back if necessary, no matter what was happening in the crowd. At the same time, she had to admit that Amas had done the rational thing, holding her tightly like that. She could have been trampled, injured in that mob.

Vanessa flushed with sudden guilt, remembering that her first care had been to protect her hands, the phenomenal hands that Bufera said had been strengthened by the previous work she'd done, not hurt.

Vanessa held them out before her and stared at them, thinking of the years of concerts, the indescribable joy she'd known when she felt she had created beauty and pleasure for her audience through her own very personal, lyrical interpretations of the masters, old and new.

Enough of that. It was part and parcel of the sweet, unending madness that had so possessed her it had brought her to this hour – this grey and lonely, chill dawn, brooding over the empty garden of an alien city.

Restlessly she got up and dressed herself. She would go down and sit for a while under the indifferent trees.

'It's almost time,' Hugo said to Megan. He was dressed in a dark and unobtrusive suit and hat, with a leather portfolio under his arm, a small bag in the other hand.

Megan took a final glance in the mirror, hardly recognising her image. Her ebony hair peeped out from below the small helmetlike hat, which was the colour of a nectarine. That colour, and the jet black hair with her darkened brows and lashes, made her golden eyes stunning. Under the trim black suit-dress she wore the blouse that matched the hat, with black shoes and gloves and a chic little bag shaped like a censer in black and gold. She looked, and felt, as glamorous as Vanessa.

The thought of her grandmother brought on a twinge of guilt; she would send her a postal card from Paris, telling her that she was well. At least she could do that.

'This won't do at all,' Hugo added, staring at Megan.

'Why not? Is something wrong?'

'Yes. You are far too pretty. Everyone will be staring at you, and consequently may remember me. We had better travel separately and meet in Paris. Here, I will give you the address now, Megan. It is the only thing to do.'

Reluctantly she took the scribbled address from him.

'Memorise that on the way to the station,' he directed. 'Then burn it in the public convenience. *Remember*. You have cigarettes, do you not, and therefore matches?'

'Yes.' She did. She carefully concealed her smoking from her grandparents.

'Very well. Now let's run through it quickly again. With this change of plan I want you to be sure you know. Tell me again.'

Obediently she repeated everything he had told her – she was carrying a false passport made out to Michel Choisnet, which Hugo had carefully altered to 'Michele'. But the only thing he had slipped up on was the picture. That space was blank. Megan was to charm the customs official into accepting the passport without a picture; she would pose as an Antwerp assistant to a couturier who was visiting Paris briefly to see her brother. That would account for the male garb Hugo had filled her suitcase with, the old Megan Farley possessions at the bottom. It was a plausible story; few young women with any means at all *took* many clothes to Paris, leaving room for those they would bring back.

Megan's French, Hugo judged, was so excellent there should be no problem.

Hugo nodded, at the end of her recital, satisfied.

They kissed hastily and she stole downstairs alone, relieved that the concierge on duty was fast asleep at the desk. She closed the door without a sound and found a taxi. As it was pulling away she saw Hugo emerge from the door of the pension; he did not give her a glance.

Soon his taxi was driving off a few blocks behind hers. She paid off the taxi and then bought her ticket with Belgian francs she'd already possessed added to others that Hugo had given her. He reminded her that it would be disastrous to have any American dollars changed,

278

with the police looking for her. Besides, the worth of the American dollar was now so high that change in francs, he said sardonically, would fill her suitcase.

Megan arranged for her bag to be left at customs and went into the public convenience for women. There were few there at this early hour, but she waited until all of them had left before she went into one of the stalls and, memorising 27 Rue Chanson, set the note afire and flushed the ashes down the drain.

When she returned to customs, she imagined that the knot of Antwerp police were staring at her. But she felt an overpowering relief when she heard what they were saying, such a great relief that a trickle of perspiration ran down her back.

'*Non, non,*' she heard one policeman say. And she caught the murmured words, '*Blonde, Américaine.*'

The other officer seemed to relax, and he gave her a gallant salute, saying, '*Charmant, très charmant.*'

She allowed herself a half-smile and a roguish glance, then turned to the customs official.

'Mademoiselle,' he chided her, but he was smiling. 'What is this? Your passport lacks your picture.'

She explained to him with a nervousness that was not all feigned that she had lost the picture the very night before; only through his very great kindness would she be able to visit her poor brother in Paris who was awaiting her with such anxiety. Out of the corner of her eye she caught sight of Hugo, down the line, talking to another official. Her heart leaped into her throat.

'Ah! You are naughty, Mademoiselle.' The official smoothed his large moustache, surveying Megan from head to foot. 'I will have to confer with my superior.'

She waited breathlessly, trying not to look as terrified as she felt. And, to appear that she was bored with the wait, she began to look about; she glanced at Hugo again. The official was examining the contents of his portfolio and looking at the documents Hugo had forged. Then the official nodded, once, and handed it all back to Hugo, touching his billed cap.

At least that's all right, Megan thought, her relief making her legs feel weak and trembly. She watched Hugo walk away towards the second-class compartments of the *Oiseau Bleu* that would take them first to Brussels, then to Paris. They would not have to endure another examination at Brussels, she knew; the Antwerp stamp of approval was all that was needed.

279

At last the official with the big moustache returned. 'Very well, Mademoiselle.' He was smiling, 'Apparently no man can refuse such a beautiful young lady. All is well.' With a flourish he stamped the passport of Michele Choisnet, and handed it back to her, saying, 'I wish you a very pleasant visit with your . . . brother.'

His grin after the last word was supremely Gallic. She grinned back. 'Thank you a thousand times,' she said effusively and, on an impulse, kissed him on his swarthy cheek, inhaling a horrible scent of tobacco, garlic and wine, even at that ungodly hour. The group of watching gendarmes broke out into applause.

Flushing, Megan hurried to her first-class compartment, an attendant in her wake with the bag. She must be more careful from now on, she decided. There had been something decidedly American about that gesture – she doubted if a Belgian girl would have done it.

Settled in her compartment, she waited eagerly for the whistle of the *Oiseau Bleu*, the great asthmatic exhalation of the steam. She and Hugo were so near freedom now. Nothing, nothing must go wrong.

And when the awaited noises broke forth, they sounded like music to the ears of Megan Farley. The *Oiseau* was in motion. They were free.

The name of the train was a wonderful omen – the 'Bluebird'. In Paris she and Hugo would surely find that elusive bird of happiness.

Obdurately and at enormous inconvenience to them both, Vanessa and Amas prolonged their stay in Antwerp. The police reported, two days after Megan's disappearance, that there was no trace of her in the city. No young woman of her description had been seen leaving the city by boat or train. They feared that the young woman might not be alive.

Vanessa cried out, 'I will not accept that.'

Nevertheless Amas insisted that the rivers be dragged, that a search be made for the body.

'We have searched, M. Holder. As to dragging the river – ' the captain shrugged, raising both hands palms up in a despairing gesture – 'the good God himself could not do that, with the currents and the river traffic. No body has ever been discovered in those waters.'

But Amas Holder was far from through. He went to Brussels to consult a private inquiry agent, bringing him back to Antwerp. After a week, the man reported dolefully that the young lady had either left the country or was dead.

Vanessa, feeling quite ill by that time, could not get out of bed until the following evening. Amas stormed and raged, infuriated both by Belgium and by Megan, who he felt was still alive, and considered further alternatives.

Combing the newspapers for a clue, he ignored the large headlines proclaiming that a young employee of the Beurs, a trusted employee of twelve years' standing, had got away with diamonds worth two million in English pounds.

If Megan had left the country, he figured she would go to Paris, because they'd already visited England which did not excite her, and she had talked of nothing but seeing the City of Love.

He hurried upstairs to discuss this with Vanessa, hearing someone call out behind him. 'M. Holder!'

He paused, turning. One of the assistants to the concierge was holding out a postal card to him. 'A communication for Madame,' the man said.

Amas snatched at it eagerly, fumbling in his trousers for some francs, almost throwing them at the assistant.

He saw a garish representation of the Eiffel Tower. Flipping the card over, he scanned the message.

'I am well and happy. Do not try to find me. Forgive me.' It was signed simply, 'M'.

For an instant Amas was stunned. Then, realising in full the glorious import of the card, he ran up the rest of the stairs and burst into their room.

'Vanessa, she's alive!' he shouted, waving the postal card.

She shrieked with joy, and took the card from him, reading the message. Neither of them, he recognised, was paying any attention to the second and third sentences, only the first – 'I am well and happy'.

'Let's get packed,' Amas said buoyantly. 'We'll leave tonight for Paris on the *Étoile du Nord*.'

Megan and Hugo had been in Paris for more than a week by the time the card reached Antwerp's Grand Hotel.

She had never loved any place so much, never found such enchantment in any other city; she revelled in the thin, silvery light of the City of Love. There was nothing about Paris she did not love, from the glittering elegance of the Champs-Élysées to the winding streets of Montmartre. Dazzled, she gazed on the fiery fountains near the Arc de Triomphe, explored the Luxembourg Gardens and the Invalides.

Most of all, however, she loved the Left Bank, with its raffish air that answered something gypsylike in her depths; was charmed almost to disbelief that there could be a street named for 'the cat that fishes'.

Hugo's confederate, who had purloined the stationery and the official stamp of the Paris Exchange, and had mailed the note to customs in Antwerp to add credence to Hugo's forgeries, had found them a flat near this on the Rue Chanson. The very name of that cobble-stoned street, 'Song Street', rang with the song in Megan's heart.

There was so much furtive excitement, their constant motion so stimulated Megan, that her brief guilt had disappeared. The sending of the postal card, without Hugo's knowledge, had been enough, as far as Megan was concerned, to fulfil her responsibilities.

Nothing existed any more, beyond the nights with Hugo and the present whirl of gaiety and recklessness. Megan, living her greatest adventure, was titillated by the night clubs of Montmartre, thrilled by the Moulin Rouge whose crawling spotlights of poison green made wild ghosts of drunken, laughing faces; painted scenes for her like those the great Lautrec himself had rendered.

The diamonds, Hugo told her, would have to be fenced out very gradually; the Sûreté would leap on them like a hungry flea on a dog if they slipped up. By now it was well known that a false 'courier' had bought a ticket for Paris.

His bleached Prussian hair would not fool that relentless body of men, whose worldwide fame equalled Scotland Yard's. Therefore, on the night of their reunion, Hugo had dyed his hair auburn and radically changed his style of dressing. Megan, who was not being sought as a brunette, was free to remain dark-haired, at least for the time being.

The aroma of freshly baked bread, it seemed to the buoyant Megan, seemed to scent all of the Rue Chanson that day when she hurried up the stairs to their little flat. She was carrying a basket containing an enormous loaf of bread, a bottle of wine and an aromatic cheese.

Setting down the basket by the door to reach into her pocket for the key, Megan was startled to hear voices and laughter from inside. Hugo had told her that he would be quite late; he planned to meet a fellow in Montmartre who could direct him to a safer receiver for the next batch of diamonds, half of which now reposed in the sand of another big fish bowl in the flat.

She recognised Hugo's voice. He was speaking in English. Megan started to put the key in the lock, but something made her pause and lean against the frail door to listen.

Hugo sounded very drunk indeed. 'Of course I've tried women for a change,' he was saying loudly, his voice thick and slurred. 'But you know there's no one like you . . . there's nothing like this.'

Bewildered, Megan caught the murmur of another man's voice, and then soft laughter. Following that there was a rustling silence, a creaking, then a muffled outcry. She started to tremble. What could it mean?

Now she was fairly paralysed; she felt no power on earth could move her from the door. She kept leaning against it, feeling faint, catching new and unmistakable sounds of creaking springs, the rustle of cloth and loud, ecstatic sighs.

Hugo was making love to someone – and it was a man. Sickened, Megan felt her whole body shudder, as if she were suffering a seizure; even her mouth was shaking. Her teeth began to chatter. She closed her quivering mouth with her own hands to still the faint, hysterical clicking. The voices were heard again.

'As soon as this is over,' Hugo was saying, 'and the trail is cooler, I'm going to get in touch with the mighty Holders. I'll have to work out a way. It will take time. But when that time comes, my dear Charles, we will buy a villa in Cannes. I have a feeling the Holders will pay a pretty penny to know the whereabouts of the kid.'

'But why not now, my love?' The sound of the other voice, very British and young, aroused such ire in Megan, such nausea, that she feared she was going to vomit.

'Because it is too soon, sweet boy.' There was another silence, another rustling. 'Because the prices aren't as high as I hoped; I've got to sell the rest of the diamonds. I want us to be secure for life, Charley.'

In the midst of her sickness, Megan thought, Hugo always has an answer. Something steel-cold, rational, that had not been dulled by her shock and horror, told her that even now Hugo was probably lying to this boy as he had lied to her.

Now, more than anything, she wanted to leave. She must get out of here. She could not bear the thought of their discovering her. But good sense reminded her that she really had nowhere else to go, not at this moment. The only hope she had of independence lay in the fish bowl of the flat. That was it.

Picking up the basket cautiously, she heard the invisible Charles say. 'Let's go out.'

Hugo answered, 'A splendid idea. She might be back at any minute. Let's make it the "Deux Magots"; that should be safe enough. Get cracking, love.'

Megan tiptoed to the end of the hall and concealed herself in the water closet used by the occupants at the other end. Leaving the door slightly ajar, she heard the door of their flat opening, and Hugo giggle drunkenly, 'Nature calls, Bonnie Charley. *A bientôt.*'

The door of the other water closet banged shut. In a moment it opened again, and Megan heard the two men descending the stairs, Hugo still laughing as his body bounded against the stair walls occasionally.

Megan crept out of the place of concealment and, when she heard the downstairs door bang, into the flat. She would take nothing, she decided, except the diamonds. With those she could buy anything she would ever need, once she had fenced them. And she still had the American dollars; she would just have to risk changing them. She would leave the ensemble which she had worn to Paris, just wear what she had on.

But how in the name of heaven could she safely transport the diamonds? With trembling hands, she scooped them all out of the sand and dried them. Then an inspiration struck her. Taking a large knife, she cut the bread and laid the diamonds inside the split loaf as if making a monstrous sandwich. Snatching up some green vegetables from a shelf in the tiny kitchen, she spread the greenery over the diamonds.

She hurried out, closing the door without locking it, and went quickly down the stairs, hailing a taxi to take her in the direction diametrically opposite to that of the 'Deux Magots'.

She knew quite well that even with the American dollars she could not check into a good hotel carrying a basket of bread and cheese (she had left the wine behind to lighten her burden), without baggage. So she asked the driver to let her off not far from the Moulin Rouge. There were hotels here, she'd learned, who were quite accustomed to odd patrons.

As predicted, the concierge of a small, ratty hostelry hardly gave her a glance after she had presented her American dollars. Live and let live, she saw thankfully, was the motto of the house, it was clear.

She went to her room and freshened herself, then lay down. Already she was cold with fear, drained from the shock of what she had heard at the flat. But there was no time now to dwell on Hugo's faithlessness; she was utterly alone, and she must look out for herself.

Hugo might kill her.

That thought made her break out in a cold sweat and her teeth start to chatter again. Yes, he might well kill her; his plans for blackmailing Amas and Vanessa would be nothing beside his desire for vengeance. She would go to Bea.

But she must get rid of the diamonds. Bea was on the Riviera. She had left for it, as a matter of fact, before Megan and her grandparents had left London. And it might be impossible to get beyond the checkpoints with the diamonds.

Megan had to sell them. And she had to get that passport picture done. There was no time to waste, none at all. She got up, feeling weak and heavy with dread, and went out. An utterly incurious photographer took her passport pictures and told her they would be ready the next morning. Megan ate a hasty meal at a small café and struggled to remember the name of Hugo's contact in Montmartre. It might be mythical, she realised angrily; perhaps he'd just invented that errand to excuse his time with Charles. But she had to take the chance. What *was* that name?

At last it came to her. She'd remembered because it was so comical – Clacque. Henri Clacque. The place she knew well – the 'Fille Verte', the Harsh Girl; she and Hugo had been there often together. Unfortunately it was also a favourite hangout of his confederate, Armand. But she would have to risk it. A disguise, perhaps . . .

It occurred to her that she could disguise herself as a young man – an effete young man, perhaps, with her frail build, but a young man all the same. She would have to cut her hair and buy clothes. She took care of both that afternoon – the barber was as incurious as the concierge and photographer, in the strange and cosmopolitan atmosphere of modern Paris. But just to play safe, she made up a tragic story of buying funeral clothes for her dead brother when she purchased the man's suit.

Brothers were very convenient relatives, she thought with amusement, remembering the story in Antwerp. However, she repressed her burgeoning smile and managed to look properly grief-stricken in the shop. She thanked the proprietress for her condolences and went out with her bundle.

There was no place to change except the hotel, and she shrank from the idea of the concierge's cynical reaction when she appeared in such clothes. But there was no help for it, and her ears burned that night when she passed the desk, hearing the woman murmur to her husband, 'Another of those freaks, hiding out down here. Ah, well, the money is good, so what does it signify?'

285

Megan was aware she presented a peculiar image, with her deli-cate face, her pierced ears and shorn hair in the men's garments. But at least it gave her a new idea; no one was going to take her for a man, obviously. She would just pose as a *phenomène*, as they were styled by the *petite bourgeoisie*. And she began almost to enjoy the masquer-ade.

Her courage almost failed her in the 'Fille Verte', though; it was particularly sinister-looking tonight, and when at last she accosted Henri Clacque, he shouted loud enough for everyone to hear, 'Why do you approach me? Surely you don't want a *man*.'

In a low voice, she told him what she wanted. Suspicious, he asked her how she'd got his name.

She decided to try the last great, dangerous bluff. 'I am acting for Hugo Bouwer,' she said calmly, 'and Armand Noir.'

'Oh, that's different. Why didn't you say so?' And in a lower voice he gave her the name of the contact.

She hurried out of the 'Fille Verte' and took a taxi to the dark street near a quai, her heart in her mouth, praying that she would not be attacked by apaches. But to her astonishment she arrived without mishap at the small chandler's shop which showed only one dim light from the rear.

Even more amazing was the appearance of the receiver; he was a fat, small man with a voice as gentle as St Nicholas', but he was unmoved when she protested at the small price he offered. 'They're worth at least a million pounds,' she cried.

'Ah, but they are worth nothing if I don't buy them . . . are they now, *mademoiselle*?' He nastily emphasised the form of address and Megan felt her face flush.

'Very well,' she said at last. She had no choice in the matter. She received the combination of dollars, pounds and francs in which the cherubic receiver paid her and stuffed the money into a small bag she'd purchased for the occasion.

But at least she'd come out of it with the equivalent of about twenty thousand American dollars, a fraction of the stones' worth but more than enough to outfit herself well and take the next *Train Bleu* to Nice.

And that she fully intended to do. She'd had enough of bohemian living and posing as an oddity. First thing in the morning, she decided, I'll go to the best stores on the Champs-Elysées and get something elegant.

If she got out of here alive, she amended, looking about her. She heard footsteps and started to run, racing desperately until she reached a brightly lit street, where she collapsed, almost sobbing, into a taxi that hurtled her back to the cynical little hotel.

A young brunette of striking *chic* stepped aboard the Blue Train in the early afternoon while Amas and Vanessa Holder were checking into the Crillon.

'This may be the right side of the river to Parisians,' Amas commented drily, 'but I think it's the wrong one for us.'

'What does that mean?' Vanessa demanded without turning from the dresser mirror. She pulled off her black, close-fitting hat and combed her brief hair with her fingers.

'Where do all the young runaways go these days . . . the "*Rive Gauche*", I hear.'

Vanessa picked up her hat again. 'Let's go there, Amas.'

He chuckled. 'Not so fast. How would we know where to start? I've never been in this town and you haven't been for . . . how long?'

'Don't remind me. I feel like a pterodactyl today to begin with.' She turned away from the glass.

'Come here,' he said. 'You're still tired from all this upset. Believe me, no pterodactyl could make that awful dress look so good.'

They both laughed at his peculiar figure of speech; her shapeless chemise dress with its grey embroidered top and dark blue skirt reaching halfway to the ankles could not disguise the very feminine contours of her body: the sombre colours merely enhanced her fresh skin and big blue-grey eyes. Amas was pleased to see her looking a little more rested.

There was less of that painful urgency now to their errand, oddly enough; Amas had a notion Vanessa felt that way, too. Just knowing Megan was alive at first had been sufficient to raise their spirits high. Then, on the train, the significance of the rest of her message had penetrated to both of them and they had discussed it at length. She'd said, 'Don't try to find me'.

Megan was only a girl of seventeen and they had no choice but to ignore that; yet it had hurt, had taken a bit of the edge off their eagerness somehow. Well, it was useless to debate the matter. He'd better get moving.

'Do you want to come with me to the Embassy?' he asked Vanessa. 'Or wait for me here?'

She sat down on the bed, feeling indecisive. 'You think that will be best . . .' Her tone was questioning.

287

'No doubt about it,' Amas could picture their reception at the Sûreté – the officers' reaction, he had no doubt, would be a more polished version of the Antwerp captain's initial reception. The Sûreté would not be eager to pursue one of America's flaming youth, off to discover Life on the '*Rive Gauche*'. But a word from the American Ambassador, a delicate hint of the Holders' status with the International Exchange, would save a lot of running back and forth. Amas had a suspicion the Sûreté would send him to the Embassy, anyhow.

'You know best. I'll wait. I'm . . . losing my second wind,' she admitted. Looking at her more closely he realised she had dark shadows under her eyes and was looking a little pale. He'd been too distracted before by the general picture of her loveliness to register that.

'You rest,' he said gently. 'I shouldn't be long. If the Ambassador decides to send me right to the Sûreté, I'll give you a call. Then you can have the option of going with me or staying here a bit longer.'

'You're so nice, so sweet,' she murmured, getting up and going to him to put her arms around his still hard waist. She leaned against him a moment, as if to absorb some of his strength, like a cold child coming close for warmth, and the gesture touched him unfailingly, as it always had. He felt a great wave of protective tenderness and a new resentment against the fleeing Megan.

He thought, Vanessa is still the only one who means anything to me, when push comes to shove. He squeezed her and kissed the top of her head, then released her and put on his hat.

'*Au revoir*, as they say in Paris.' They both grinned at his appalling accent.

Amas and Vanessa stood on the balcony of the Crillon Hotel, looking down at the Place de la Concorde. The fountains were playing and, as the sun sank, the outlines of Paris assumed the blue-mist colours of a city from a dream. The outlines of the Eiffel Tower were smudged, not sharp, and the trees in the Tuileries billowed like smoke.

'So beautiful,' Vanessa murmured. 'So mysterious. And she's still out there somewhere, Amas, like a . . . like a pebble thrown into the water. A little ripple, and . . . vanished.' Her voice broke, and he put his arm around her.

'Vanessa, it's been three weeks, and they haven't found a trace.

288

The Ambassador assured me that the Sûreté employs the best men in Europe.' He hesitated and sighed. 'If you think we should try another private man . . .'

She shook her head. 'It could take forever.' He heard the resignation in her voice, the dawning acceptance. 'My God, Amas, we've looked ourselves, so hard . . .'

He considered the long, wearisome days of their combing the Left Bank. Amas had even checked out the Sorbonne, on the wild chance that Megan might decide to go and study. They had investigated every likely and unlikely possibility. The result was always the same – no trace.

'I think we've got to conclude she's left the country,' he said as he had a dozen times before. 'And I think we've got to get on with our lives, Vanessa.'

She looked up at him in the blue, failing light and nodded slowly. 'Yes. Yes, you are right.'

He was aware of her torment away from the piano; she was not like some artists who could 'practise' without the instrument merely by studying the score. She always said she had to work on her fingering slowly, for a long time; it helped her accuracy and phrasing, all the details. Amas nowadays was conversant with that, being so close to her. And he was conscious, too, that she was itching to begin preparation for Carnegie Hall, which was still years away but would take an enormous amount of work.

There were pressing matters awaiting him, also. If he had time to work them out he could avoid another trip to England and a long separation from Vanessa, a thing he dreaded. Damn it, they must go home.

He said it aloud. 'We ought to go home, Vanessa.'

She smiled. 'We will, Amas. Tomorrow. Tomorrow we will go home.'

CHAPTER NINETEEN

On that summer day in 1923, entering the lobby of London's Ritz-Carlton from the comparative brightness, Amas Holder blinked his eyes. In his last three years in New York, he'd forgotten how dim these European lobbies were. He saw a tall young man approaching with a wide, white grin that fairly split his tanned and weathered face.

'Martin! Good Lord, you're my *doppelgänger*!' Amas hugged his son, his spirits soaring. This was the first good thing that had happened to him since he had reluctantly sailed from New York harbour.

'Dad. Dad.' Amas could hear Martin's deep emotion in the one repeated word. Stepping back, he noticed that he and Martin were of a height.

'Ready for some lunch?' Martin asked.

'More than ready.' Amas could not stop staring at his son. 'Is it possible for a grown man to grow?' he demanded, smiling. 'You have. You're looking very fit, as the Limeys put it.'

'I have, I guess.' Martin laughed a little. 'You're looking "fit", too, Dad. But a bit pale,' he added in a teasing way.

'It's that damned indoor life,' Amas said ruefully. 'But I still manage to get some sun, even if it's only under a lamp. Can you imagine that? I belong to an athletic club now. Vanessa assures me I'd die if I didn't.'

They went into the restaurant, dimly aware that others were staring at them. They both, Amas decided, belonged here like a tiger at a tea party.

They sat down. 'America never ceases to amaze me,' Martin remarked. 'Back home it's still more like 1913 than 1923. Say, how *is* Mother? I was so wound up I forgot everything.'

'She's fine,' Amas said affectionately, but he felt the inevitable twinge of loneliness. 'Working like a beaver for Carnegie Hall.'

'Tomorrow night, isn't it?' They gave their orders to a waiter who could barely conceal his curiosity about them under the trained blandness of his exterior.

When he had gone away, Amas replied. 'Yes. God, how I'd like to . . .' He stopped, chagrined. Martin knew well enough he'd like to be there, would love to be there himself. Amas didn't want to rub it in to the boy that this particular crisis was a bit more than he could handle alone.

But Martin's tanned face darkened with a flush. 'Damn it, Dad, I know. I wish we all were. I can't tell you what it means to me that you came over.'

'You don't have to, son. Since that legislation last year I know how sticky things are right now. Particularly with Madame di Gamba meddling in, with her takeover bid. I had to be here. With the time differential between London and New York . . .'

'Madame *Prince*-di Gamba,' Martin corrected, making a face.

'Oh, yes, I was forgetting. She always keeps all their names.' The waiter set their main courses before them. 'What would it be now?' Amas pursued. 'Beatrice Stirling Dillon Prince-di Gamba? My God, if she keeps all her initials it'll sound like an acronym. She never lets go. She bought her Prince – the Italian one, not Harold,' Amas laughed shortly, 'but even after she kicks him out she still keeps the name. Too bad it's the same way with her Stirling shares . . . and the Corporation.'

The Anglo-American Corporation of South Africa had been formed six years ago, but at this particular point with the new diamond rush and certain international complications, Amas and Holder-Stirling were becoming more and more involved. And Beatrice Prince-di Gamba, by virtue of Harold Prince's wealth and connections, was now a member of the Corporation. Holding on like a bulldog, too, to her Holder-Stirling interests, and trying to buy out those other two members' stocks. How that bitch could retain the old malice, year after year . . .

Amas exclaimed. 'I'm a savage, Martin, I haven't even asked how Anjanette is . . . and the boys.'

'Just great.' Martin seemed oddly relieved by the change of subject, and it aroused an inquisitiveness in Amas. 'We just got a new camera recently, and I took some pictures. Let me show you.'

Eagerly Amas took the snapshots from Martin's hand, the hand so eerily like his own, and devoured the sepia images of his daughter-in-law and grandsons.

'Tony's more like Anjanette . . . you can really tell from this one,' Martin pointed out. 'But how about Clint?' He grinned. 'A chip off *both* the old blocks, isn't he?'

Amas nodded. Clinton already had a remarkable likeness to both himself and his son. 'I should say so.' He handed the pictures back to Martin. 'We'd like to have some of those, too, if you can spare them.'

Martin took a swallow of his coffee. 'Anjanette's already sent some to Mother.'

'That's fine, just fine.' Amas smiled but again he felt that queer pull at his heart just thinking of Vanessa. This was the first time in their lives they'd been apart for more than a few days. He had often gone along with her on her short concert tours when his business permitted.

The sensitive Martin asked, 'What's she playing at the concert?' Amas thought, he learned to read people from Vanessa, the way she always has read me.

'For one thing, the Rachmaninov Second,' Amas murmured. Vanessa always said Rachmaninov was one of the few 'new' composers who realised the power and beauty of the piano.

'The Rachmaninov Second,' Martin repeated softly. 'I've never heard Mother play it, but it's one of my favourite pieces. Somehow it reminds me of the summer we spent with you. You know, I always hear the surf on Long Island when I hear that . . . isn't that funny?'

'Not so funny, boy. I hear the rain on the veld. And your mother hears . . . the music.' Amas chuckled.

Martin was alerted by the reference to the veld. 'You miss it, don't you, Dad?'

'*Miss* it.' Amas had to consider. He realised that it had always seemed so far away, for so long, that he'd almost forgotten. 'In a way,' he admitted. 'I guess I'll always miss it, Martin, deep down. As long as I have Vanessa, I don't miss any place so terribly. And there was a lot of bad in Africa, for us, you know. The war . . . and Lesley . . . and that thing with Sam and Bea.'

Amas' memory drifted back and he stared off into the middle distance for a moment, trying not to let his nostalgia for that country overwhelm him. When he looked back at Martin, smiling reassuringly, he noticed that odd expression on his son's face again.

'Ah, yes, Bea.' Martin sounded bitter. Then he looked at Amas rather sheepishly, as if he'd let something slip.

'What is it, son? Something's eating at you.'

Martin met his eyes and there was a peculiar pain in that lionlike gaze that puzzled his father.

'It's something so damned . . .' Martin stopped, flushing as he had before. 'Say, Dad, why don't we go up to your room for a little while? Where we can . . . really talk. We're not going to have that much chance these next few days.'

'Sure.' Promptly Amas raised his hand for the bill and, after a friendly squabble with Martin over who should pay, the two men went up to Amas' suite.

'Drink?' Amas offered. 'I've got quite a bar set up for the visiting firemen.'

'I think I will.' That surprised Amas a bit; he'd made the offer almost automatically, without thinking. Martin was generally abstemious. Now Amas wondered what he had to say, that he needed one.

'How about you?' Martin asked.

'None for me.' Amas sat down in an armchair.

Martin was still standing with his drink in his hand. He took a hefty swallow, and said, beginning to pace about, 'For some reason I need to . . . tell you something, Dad. Something I've kept dark for years and years.' He laughed in a rather embarrassed way. 'I guess it's all this reminiscence . . . and I haven't seen you in so long. I really feel – pretty close to you this afternoon.'

He paused awkwardly. They had never expressed their affection for each other much in words.

Amas was deeply touched.

'I'm mighty glad, Martin. Sit down, son. Fire away.'

Martin sipped at the drink again and sat down on the couch across from Amas. He put his glass down very slowly on a table and said, taking a deep breath. 'It's about . . . Bea.'

Amas was very surprised. '*Bea?*'

'Dad, a long, long time ago, when I was just a kid, in London, she . . . well, hell, why put it on her? It was as much me as her. Bea and I . . . went to bed together,' he concluded abruptly.

Amas took a quick, stunned breath. 'Went to bed. Christ! Why, that bitch. That rotten, depraved bitch – with her own nephew, Jesus. Jesus Christ.' He could not contain his astonishment.

'It's a hell of a thing to tell you, Dad. But since we're going to see her, I didn't want her to have that to blackmail you with. Which she is capable of doing. I didn't want you to go into this thing without all the information. It would put you at a disadvantage. Forewarned, you know, and all that.'

Amas nodded once. 'I get your point. But my God . . . how old were you, son?'

'Fifteen.'

'Well, God almighty.' Amas felt incapable of anything but oaths for the moment. 'It sure as hell wasn't your fault, Martin, not at that age. There are women like that. Once, a long, long time ago, before I married your mother, she was after me.'

293

'I suspected that.'

'But her *nephew* . . .' It still sickened Amas. 'And now Megan's in her neck of the woods,' he muttered, recalling Vanessa's anxieties about that.

'You've heard from Megan!' Martin's face cleared; he was very excited. 'I just didn't want to . . . bring it up before,' he explained.

'A letter, about six months ago. Not telling us much of anything . . . except that she was "on the move a lot", whatever that means. But it was postmarked Nice.'

'Madame di Gamba's watering hole,' Martin commented. 'The word is she buys young fellows now.'

'I can well believe she has to,' Amas said drily. 'She must be . . . what, nearly sixty now.' But that was a highly distasteful topic, so Amas said quickly, 'You know, Martin, what I can't figure out is, how the hell is Megan surviving? She's never asked us for a penny. God knows we would have been delighted to send her money, still would, for that matter.'

They were silent. Then Amas went on, 'I have the damndest feeling it's something . . . illegal.'

'Why do you say that, Dad?'

Amas hesitated, then began to tell him what he never had – Megan's early penchant for thieving.

Martin looked thoughtful, then he said, 'Good Lord, Dad. She couldn't be this "Chameleon", could she? It's not possible. She's only about twenty years old now.'

'Exactly twenty, Martin.' After a pause, Amas added, 'I've thought of that, believe me. And I think she could be. Stranger things have happened. It all seems to . . . fit somehow. Don't you remember,' Amas went on, looking earnestly at Martin, 'how she used to shinny up and down the mine walls back in Africa? Why, the very day you came to see us in Pretoria, Vanessa was chiding her about that very thing. Megan never had any more fear of heights than a bird.'

Martin chuckled, nodding.

Amas resumed, 'It's the damnedest thing, but ever since I read the first "Chameleon" story in the papers, I had the strangest sensation. I kept remembering that she used to take bright, shiny things like a little jackdaw . . . and one of the incidents in New York involved her stealing a diamond thingamabob.'

'Talk about a shoemaker stealing shoes,' Martin remarked wryly.

'That's right . . . it was such a crazy thing to do. And this

Chameleon has taken crazy chances.' Amas gave a short, sudden laugh. 'Good Lord, I wonder if we've all got larceny in our souls? Everybody I know has read the Chameleon stories and is interested. Even my mother, if you can believe it. There's something about those exploits that appeals to the daredevil in us all, I guess. You read about this last incident, I suppose . . . the French police finding that earring at the scene of the last robbery? The Sûreté thinks it could be a woman, ever since they found that earring.'

'Yes. I loved that quote,' Martin said, unable to help his amusement. ' "Either a woman or a very odd man", according to Inspector Sagittaire. Did they describe it, the earring, I mean?'

'A yellow diamond stud. Just the kind of thing Megan used to go for, even before she was allowed to wear that kind of stuff. I remember once she said to Vanessa the yellow diamonds looked like lions' eyes . . . and she made some reference to her eyes, and mine.'

'It's fantastic,' Martin murmured.

'Not so fantastic, son, when you recall she studied acrobatic dancing in New York; she could twist herself into a pretzel. And early on – I forgot to mention – we got a postal card from her, from the French Alps.'

'The Alps! Good God, Dad, she could have been learning to climb . . . to rappel . . .' Martin's words trailed off.

'That's right. You know, Martin, you said she's "only" twenty. I'll tell you, son, you've got to *be* twenty to have the nerve of the "Chameleon" – rappelling up and down the walls of those villas and hotels.'

Martin nodded.

Maybe it wasn't the world's happiest conclusion, Amas considered wryly. But it had taken their minds off other things.

Such as the Corporation. And Bea.

And his own unending ache for the presence of Vanessa.

Vanessa lay on the *chaise longue* in her dressing room, wishing the concert had begun. Her face burned, her hands were freezing with nerves; she felt that familiar empty ache in her middle, the stabbing of shivers of not-quite-pain that heralded the familiar stage fright. She never tried to calm herself, because it was no use. Tuned high like this, she knew it would go better. It always did.

But this night was different from all the others. Another cold flutter swooped in her stomach like a roller-coaster: this was Carnegie Hall. And Amas was so far away. Out front, she knew that the ancient but indomitable Ellen Holder would already be seated in her orchestra chair, on the first row.

Over her physician's protests Ellen had come from Philadelphia, declaring that she'd already lived a very long time; that she would die happy after hearing her daughter-in-law perform at Carnegie Hall.

Vanessa smiled to remember that. Ellen would be staying with her for a while after the concert, and Vanessa looked forward to it greatly. She and Ellen had become quite close in the last thirteen years; the Holders had visited Ellen frequently and were in constant correspondence. Vanessa hoped she would live to see Martin and his children, because her joy in Megan had been unbounded.

Megan. Better not think of that now.

Vanessa flexed her hands and took a series of deep breaths, trying instead to concentrate on Diana Stirling, who would be occupying a prominent place in the dress circle. Diana had delightedly used the concert as an 'excuse' for another visit to New York, and would act as hostess after the concert at an elaborate reception at the Plaza.

'Oh, Amas, Amas.' Suddenly the thought of him assailed her. She was shattered by his absence, sleepless and lost. Even now she could feel the depth of her fatigue. For one horrible moment she questioned that she could even play.

She got up from the *chaise longue* and went to the dresser, automatically checking her appearance again.

The Doucet dress, at least, was fine. It had been designed especially for her and, like many Paris gowns, was almost a year ahead of New York, from the 1924 collection. Its sliplike, simple lines, the glowing orchid-pink satin lustre which moved and changed in the light, were good for her. The colour flattened her pallor, casting a healthy shade on her skin. With it she wore no ornaments except her customary rings and a pair of rose-diamond drops that peeped out from under the brief froth of her silver-blonde hair.

She glanced at the watch on her dressing table. Only twenty minutes remained. She got up and paced restlessly back and forth, her satin slippers a mere whisper on the dark red carpet.

A knock at her door made her jump. She called out, 'Come', her voice sharp and high with tension, and the call-boy stuck his head tentatively around the frame of the door. 'Phone call, Miss Holder,' he said. 'Transatlantic.'

Her heart could be felt in her very throat. 'Thank you,' she gasped and hurried out, forgetting even to be amused at the usual address of

'Miss', and Bufera's comment that there were 'no Mrses at Carnegie Hall.'

The call-boy respectfully handed her the phone.

From very far away she heard his voice. 'Vanessa, Vanessa, my darling.'

'Amas, Amas,' she breathed into the phone.

'Are you there, my darling?' His voice was desperately anxious, and she knew then in her excitement she had almost whispered.

'Yes, yes, beloved,' she said, raising her voice.

'Oh, Vanessa, I miss you, I miss you so damned much.' A great warmth flooded her and suddenly she felt alive and strong again.

'I miss you, Amas. More than I can say. Oh, my dear, I'm so happy you called. So happy. Everything will be wonderful now. Your mother's here . . . and Diana . . . and . . .'

'*You* will be wonderful, I know you will.' His voice sounded clearer now, happier. 'And I'll be back with you in just a little more than a week.'

'Things are going well?'

There was a slight pause, and then his voice came to her again. '*Very* well. Play the Rachmaninov for me as if I were there.'

'I will, oh, I will.'

'I'm sorry I called so late, but the damned cables were . . .'

'Never mind, never mind, darling. I love you. I love you so much.'

'And I love you. Always.' His words were inexpressibly tender. 'Goodbye for now, Vanessa. Martin sends his love. Good luck!'

'Thank you, thank you. Give mine to him.'

'*A bientôt*, darling.' The badly pronounced French was very touching.

'*A bientôt*,' she answered caressingly. Then there was a crackle and a silence on the cable.

But it was all right. Now everything was going to be all right. Better than all right. She replaced the phone.

The orchestra was tuning up.

Her face was cooling off, her hands warming. As she walked into the wings Vanessa could feel the spring and strength returning to her limbs, and her fingers felt wonderfully loose now, yet wholly ready.

Bufera was standing in the wings. His old eyes, under their shaggy brows, were bright with pride and anticipation. All at once, in that instant, Vanessa saw how much he had aged. And yet his power was undimmed.

'Rachmaninov was never so beautiful,' he teased her, his habit at times of great stress and importance. 'I think you were right to schedule the Second first.'

He had been surprised to learn that she was planning to play the draining concerto in the first half of the programme, the less demanding solo music during the last, quite opposite to the practice of most artists. But Vanessa wanted to start, she said, in a 'blaze of glory', and leave the gentler strains of Schumann and Chopin and Mozart in the departing audience's ears . . . and hearts.

'Thank you,' she said simply. Pressing Bufera's outstretched hand she walked onto the stage. There was a great, resounding wave of applause, like the clatter of a multitude of shutting wooden fans, and her heart swelled with gratitude, exhilaration. In her customary pre-performance blindness, under the brilliant lights, she could make out no one in the audience, but after she had bowed to them, and then to the conductor, and sat down at the piano, she could feel them.

The whispers and rustles and murmurs fell to silence; she could hear them as if they drew one huge, expectant breath. Confidence, like heat, flowed into her hands, together with authority. And she knew that it would be good.

She struck the eight solemn chords with which the concerto began, each individually shaded and coloured, each of her ten fingers producing a different quality of tone – those glowing, yet sombre utterances of the keys which were one of the great exordiums of music.

Vanessa felt her power grow with the second movement, felt lost in the music, carried by it like a bubbling of foam on a wave of the sea, yet paradoxically in total control, reining and guiding the sound with her hands, playing a passionate song of piercing beauty, a curious descending dialogue between the piano and the horns and woodwind in brief sharp phrases.

The second theme returned, was dominant as the close approached her, the keys commenting to the chant of strongly bowed strings.

And then the end, with its powerful and rhythmically eccentric figure, to which Vanessa Holder brought all the passion and the might of her body, mind and heart.

There was a crashing silence for an instant; she bowed her bright head above the keys. And abruptly the stillness broke, exploded into the wide, pounding surf of applause, and cries of *Bravo!* as Vanessa rose, trembling, from the bench; with her hand on the piano's surface, she bowed and bowed.

The ovation went on; smiling, she gestured to the conductor and the orchestra, which rose in a body to the continuing applause.

Attendants began to come forward with baskets of flowers, and someone tossed roses on the stage from the dress circle. Such a thing had never happened to her before; these extravagances always came at the end of a concert, not like this, before the intermission.

A slight dew of moisture broke out along her forehead, on her arms; she bowed and bowed again, and smiled, her heart fairly bursting with happiness.

I have brought them beauty, she realised in her transport, I have given so many people joy.

And now her eyes, accustomed to the light, could make out faces: Diana's glowing, from the dress circle, where she stood still applauding, ecstatic when Vanessa saluted her with a special smile, a particular inclination of the head; Ellen Holder, standing with apparent difficulty on the first row of the orchestra seats, weeping with pride.

And not far from Ellen, a young woman as slender as a willow wand, dressed in glittering dark brown. Her hair was brief and vividly auburn; her eyes were golden, like those of a young lioness.

Golden.

They were Amas' eyes.

It was Megan.

Megan Farley stared at the splendid figure on the stage, almost breathless with her emotion. In that moment it was hard to believe that this slender goddess in shining lilac, who had coaxed such magical power from the keys, was her grandmother.

Then she saw the goddess' huge grey glowing eyes narrow as that gaze locked with hers; Vanessa Holder's face broke and changed. Megan could see her turn pale with shock, and then the lustrous eyes ignited with recognition.

Vanessa had recognised her.

How could that be? There was no resemblance at all between the Megan Farley of three years ago and the Michele Fournet who had travelled to New York. Everything had changed – the colour of her startlingly-cut hair, in its *garçon* style, the swoop of her brows, even the shape of her nose and mouth through the art of cosmetics.

It must have been her eyes. There was nothing that the former Megan Farley could do about her eyes; even the exotic make-up on her shadowy lids that subtly disguised them could not change the lion colour of her eyes. Her grandfather's eyes . . . and Martin's.

She would have to leave. Right now. It broke her heart; she had longed to stay for the second half of the programme, to hear Vanessa play the Schumann and Chopin that had made a glory of Kimberley and New York when Megan was still a child.

Yet almost without volition she stood there a moment longer, unable to tear herself away, staring into Vanessa Holder's eyes.

But now Vanessa seemed to have pulled herself under control; she stood there bowing with her brilliant, charming, professional smile and, when the applause began to diminish, walked off the stage.

Excusing herself to the indignant, surprised people on her right, Megan slipped past them and hurried up the aisle, almost colliding with those who were leaving for the intermission.

She rushed through the rapidly filling lobby, hearing the comments of the dazzled audience, 'superb', 'magnificent', and went out to the street.

Her luggage was already at the pier; she would go to the ship now, early, just as she was. In her sequinned bag that matched her striking gown was the passport of Michele Fournet; in the hollowed-out Cuban heels of her shoes and in tiny pockets sewn on her underwear – unnoticeable under the chemise style of her Lanvin gown – was a fortune in rubies, emeralds and diamonds.

She should have sailed two days ago; she was taking a terrible risk. Already the police force of the entire East, she knew, was combing the coast for some trace of the famous English stones; the gems she had prised from their settings, leaving the settings in a laundry cart at her Boston hotel before she drove to New York in a hired car.

She had been a blonde then, thanks to an excellent wigmaker, dressed like a homely German governess, registering as Maria Freischutz. She always kept to the same initials; there were certain possessions she could not bear to part with and they were monogrammed. Besides, she had found that sticking to the same initials as her true ones made things easier. It was not so strange to adapt to the false names when they had initial sounds that were the same.

Megan hailed a taxi that took her to the pier. The *Statendam III* would not be sailing for nearly two hours, but she said with false gaiety to the officer on watch that she was hostessing a celebration which would start early. He took it all very much for granted, and she was certain he would never know that she spent the hours alone, and not in celebration. Only the stewards were really aware of those things.

300

The officer, giving her an appreciative glance, smilingly referred her to customs. She waited calmly while the customs officials checked her luggage and glanced at her passport, then at her. The living face of Michele Fournet was identical to that of the pictured one. She had thrown Maria Freischutz's passport into Boston Harbour the day before yesterday.

The custom official's knowing eyes ran up and down her Lanvin dress. He saluted, smiling, and wished her a fine celebration.

When Megan was settled in her stateroom, she stripped off the gown and unscrewed the heels of her shoes. Then, removing the custom-made heels from a pair of plain black calf shoes, those she would wear on the rest of the voyage, she poured the gems into the heels and donned the shoes. The brown satin shoes, to her regret, would have to go overboard during the voyage.

Retaining the same taupe underwear – she had a dozen duplicates in various colours; the pockets always escaped the sharp eyes of customs, adroitly disguised in lace and appliqués – Megan put on a black skirt and a taupe and black twin sweater set, designed by a new, eccentric couturier named Coco Chanel.

The deceptive simplicity of the outfit would make her less conspicuous on deck. And she needed desperately to get out in the air for a time, in a shadowed spot; just to sit alone and smell the sea.

And digest what had happened in America. She had wanted so badly, so badly to stay at the concert hall, to touch Vanessa once again. But it was too late now for that. To go back would be impossible.

From Paris she would go back to Nice, where it had all begun three years before.

Megan would never forget her introduction, at seventeen, to the villa of Beatrice Prince-di Gamba.

It was not one of those scintillating days she had always associated with the Riviera. As her taxi rattled along the road beside the Promenade the sea looked grey, not blue; a faint haze lay over the water, giving it a touch of mystery that was unexpected on the garish Côte d'Azur.

The taxi slowed for a sand-cart; it had to be emptied before they could proceed. Then a wagon of fir cones stood in the way, refusing to move for an endless time, and a company of soldiers on unkempt mounts formed a barrier. At last, however, the taxi had left the huge, gay, expensive city and was ascending a twisting, intricate, thickly wooded road, so steep it made Megan gasp for breath.

Finally they drew up before the villa. It seemed to be deserted. The driver slammed to a halt, got out and removed Megan's luggage letting it fall with a thud to the ground. She paid him and he left without a word.

Leaving the baggage where it lay, Megan went to the entrance door and pulled the bell. There was no movement within. And then from somewhere on an upper terrace she heard voices and laughter. A harsh cry succeeded: 'Who's there?' It was a woman, speaking English.

'Megan! Megan Farley!' She shrieked to make the person hear.

'Who? *Megan?* Oh, good God!'

Looking up, Megan recognised the dyed black hair and shocked face of her aunt, Beatrice Prince-di Gamba. The strengthening sun was unkind to her; the glamour Megan had so admired in London was gone. The light mocked her heavily made-up eyes, the carmine of her lips. She looked a little like a startled witch, Megan thought, and her shoulders were bare. As Beatrice strained to see over the parapet of the terrace, raising herself a little higher, Megan could tell that her breasts, too, were naked.

Megan felt an almost electric twinge of shock.

'Megan! I can't believe it!' Beatrice cried. 'Just a moment. Someone will be right down.' She disappeared.

Megan heard a scuffle and a laugh, caught some words in French, apparently her aunt Bea's: '*Vous avez fini de me peloter?*' Roughly translated, it had to do with playing ball, but Megan was fairly certain that no ball game was in progress on the terrace. She was not at all familiar with the expression.

She waited patiently, however, at the front door until it was opened by a sullen, roughly handsome young man wearing only white trousers. His feet and chest were bare.

'*Mademoiselle*,' he said with sarcastic respect, looking her up and down. '*Entrez.*'

Glancing beyond her, the man sighted her baggage. Cursing under his breath, he brushed past her and went to get it.

'*Entrez, entrez*,' he repeated impatiently, using none of the polite forms. If he were a servant, she thought, he was a very peculiar one. She wondered just who he *was*.

Her answer came from Bea, as soon as she entered the cool, dim entrance hall. Her aunt came clattering down the imposing stairs in heelless clogs; Megan gasped. Through her aunt's diaphanous robe, Megan could see her sagging, naked body.

'Megan! Well, welcome . . . unexpected as you are. I see you've already met Georges. Georges . . . takes care of things.'

And, Megan remembered, as Beatrice came forward to embrace her, she wondered just what she'd got into.

She was to find out soon enough. It was all too plain that the insolent, greasy-haired Georges enjoyed many privileges beyond that of an ordinary servant; that so did Jacques, who waited on them sloppily that night at dinner.

And after dinner, for which Beatrice had changed into a more opaque but hardly less revealing garment, the first wave of guests began to arrive. Megan, for all her fancied liberation of spirit, was horrified by them.

They were ugly and corrupt and old; those who were not, it seemed to her, had flat, dead eyes. And all of them, men and women, seemed to undress Megan with their scrutiny, as if to evaluate her for some mysterious role.

'Is this one of your little protégées, Bea?' The question came from a flabby, deeply tanned old man in raffish trousers like a fisherman's; his fat, hairless chest was bare almost to the waist in an open shirt the colour of a frosted grape and his veined feet were sandalled. Megan couldn't keep her eyes, however, off his rings – an immense Brazilian aquamarine, a giant blood-red ruby, an emerald of vivid clarity and a large honey topaz surrounded by amethysts. Around his corded neck he wore several heavy gold chains set with those gems, and with diamonds.

'This is my niece, Montclair. Miss Megan Farley. Megan, the Duc du Montclair. We call him Monny.'

The grotesque man called Monny took Megan's hand in his and kissed it with an unpleasant pressure of his moist lips. 'Ah, Megan.' He pronounced it MAY-gann. 'What a lovely child you are.' His English was quite fluent. 'She is really enough,' he smiled at Bea, 'to make me change my ways.'

Bea laughed harshly.

'For a moment there,' Monny continued, 'I had hopes you might be dispensing with Georges and Jacques.'

'Not bloody likely.' Bea gave him a poisonous look. 'Not while they behave themselves.' She raised her voice and shot a glance at Georges, who was lingering as he served a drink to one of the jewel-laden women.

The conversation was full of references to places and things Megan had no knowledge of. There was a good deal of talk of

'Monte', which she finally gathered was Monte Carlo, where the casino was, but she was unable to follow the various *double entendres* in rapid French and Italian. The whole thing was oppressive and wearisome. Finally it came to her that Monny's 'ways' had something to do with what she'd discovered about Georges and Jacques.

When two of the women, whose hair was cut in the *garçon* style of her own, began to stare at her, whispering between themselves, Megan's gorge rose. She excused herself as gracefully as she could, saying that she was very tired from her journey, and went to her room, where she locked the door.

Several times during the restless night she imagined she heard fumblings at the knob, and muffled, drunken exclamations from her aunt Bea. Once, she woke to hear wild laughter, and screams. She lay awake for a moment, wishing she had never come to the villa.

But she couldn't forget the exquisite gems that ornamented that company of grotesques. Apparently they even wore their jewels to the beach.

And Megan Farley had nowhere else to go, for the time being. The next day the whole party drove to the shore. Megan lay apart from them in the sun, fending them off with an apparently dull and listless manner. While one woman's back was turned, as she sported with a much younger man in the water, Megan snatched up a few pieces of her discarded jewellery and buried them in the sand. She came back later to get them, and secreted them in her room.

The suspicious woman accused Georges and Jacques of the theft, and left the villa in high dudgeon. Megan had few regrets; she had disliked Georges from the moment she set eyes on him and didn't have much more use for Jacques. Bea scoffed at her guest's accusations, concluding that she'd lost the gems in the water, being too befuddled from drink to remember.

Megan invented an errand in Paris and took the jewels to the man who looked like St Nicholas. When she returned to Nice she took a small house of her own, but every now and then she would drop in at the villa. Beatrice Prince-di Gamba's friends possessed much valuable information.

And from there – the woman with the passport of Michele Fournet lay back in the shadowed deckchair of the *Statendam III*, smiling – it had been a hop and a skip to the Chameleon.

Part VI
The Brilliance

CHAPTER TWENTY

'What is it?' Amas growled into his interoffice phone. He was feeling extremely grouchy today, the full weight of his sixty-four years hanging on him.

Damn it, this year of 1926 was a young man's year, he decided – the biggest diamond rush in years, men racing, literally, on foot to stake their claims; these fellows were flying aeroplanes. Martin was enjoying himself in Oranjemund.

His secretary's intimidated silence made Amas even more irritable. 'What is it, I said?'

'It's Mr Jamison Burke for you on the wire.'

Amas snapped, 'Put him on, put him on.' Jamison Burke, his friend on the big international news service, was probably calling to set up a date for golf. And Amas wasn't in the mood at all. Nevertheless, he liked Jam Burke and tried to sound more pleasant when he answered.

'Jam? How are you – itching for the green?'

'Amas, something's happened at Oranjemund. We just got it over the wireless.'

It was bad when Burke didn't even say hello. 'What is it?'

'Your son's out there . . . isn't he?'

Oh, God, he was stalling for time. 'Tell me,' Amas said curtly.

'The sea wall over the diamond-bed was breached; part of it collapsed,' Burke said briefly. 'About twenty men were drowned, more injured. There's no list yet of survivors.'

Amas was stricken dumb.

'Amas?' Jamison Burke sounded harried, but he spoke very gently. 'Are you still there?'

'Yes.' Amas forced the word out, still too stunned for a sane reply.

'Listen,' Burke went on urgently. 'I've got to get out of here, right now, Amas. They want me in Florida to cover that damned hurricane. There were six thousand injured there. Never mind that, though. Here's what I've done; I've made arrangements with another fellow here to keep in touch with you. Or better still, if you want to hang around the office for a while, my desk is at your disposal. It's all set up.'

'Thanks. Thanks very much,' Amas managed to stammer. Then he thought of something else. 'This'll make all the afternoon papers, won't it?'

'Sure. They're working on it right now. I didn't want you to . . . learn about it like that. But look here, pal, I'm going to miss my connections. Do you want to come to my office?'

'Yes. And thanks . . . more than I can say. I'm very grateful.'

'Forget it. And good luck, Amas.'

Amas hung up the phone and put his face in his hands. If Martin were dead . . . he would have died in Amas' place. I would have been there, Amas agonised, if it hadn't been for our staying here because of Vanessa's music . . . but that was a damned fool notion. Martin had hardly been able to wait to get back to Africa. His decision had been his own; he'd have gone back to Africa no matter what anyone else did.

What must be done now was more urgent. He had to get home to Vanessa right away. Tell her before she saw the papers. Then he was going back to Burke's office to stay there until doomsday, if need be . . . until there was some word of Martin.

He went out of his office, telling his secretary briefly what had happened. She gasped.

Notifying her about where he could be reached, Amas took the lift to the street and got his car. Driving uptown he was cold with dread. They had lost so many in the last few years, his mother and aunts, Bufera among them.

And they still had no idea where Megan was, although after that strange night at Carnegie Hall, three years ago, she'd begun writing more regularly, sending presents; never saying much, though, never writing a return address.

But this – this was the most unbearable blow of all. And now he would have to be strong for Vanessa, when all of his strength seemed to be ebbing away.

Except for those who might have reason to fear him, few of the patrons of the casino at Monte Carlo would take the aristocratic stranger for Jean Sagittaire, Chief Inspector of the Sûreté.

The tall man was so elegantly dressed that some thought he might be a nobleman; there was an arrogant reticence in his narrow features, a superb self-confidence in that face with its hawklike nose, its chiselled lips and penetrating, dark brown eyes. The sharpness of the Inspector's face, which matched his mind, had earned him the soubriquet of 'Flèche' among his Sûreté associates. The play on the word 'arrow' referred to Sagittaire's legendary skill at pinning his prey with a lightning shot of relentless deduction, but it also had a connection with his odd surname, the French for the astrological sign Sagittarius, the centaur-human letting forth his arrows into the air.

No Parisian bore such a family name, but Sagittaire had come from Alsace-Lorraine, and he was very differently cut from his peers. He combined a dogged endurance and peasant shrewdness with a princely air and a fastidious nature inherited from a high-born mother who had, according to her relatives, married 'beneath her'.

Jean Sagittaire surveyed the Casino while giving the appearance of being intent on the roulette table. Not long ago he had left the bright dusk blazing outside, the vagrant early summer breeze, the twittering of birds.

Here there was silence – a silence, he thought with amusement, far deeper than one generally found in a cathedral. This congregation was far more devout. Now the quiet was broken by a strident cry: '*Messieurs,*' *dames, faites vos jeux!*'

Sagittaire placed his bet; the other offerings came raining down on the table as the mysterious black bowl began to turn, the little ball started to click and spin.

'*Rien ne va plus!*' The bets were closed.

Sagittaire glanced up from the wheel. There she was at last, the silly creature, the bait he had come to keep an eye on – the Honourable Mrs Reginald Marleigh. She was staring at the wheel, dressed in a sliplike silk dress of deceptive simplicity. The dress was a vivid greenish-blue, and on its front, worn as casually as a string of cheap glass beads, was her famous pendant cross.

It was copied from the Great Cross of Diamonds of François I; set in the cross's heavy enamelled gold were nine magnificent diamonds. Sagittaire, who had become even more conversant with the stones since the Chameleon affair, evaluated them with a practised eye – five huge mirror-cut diamonds, and below them the big cushion-cut stone, one that had been garnered from the huge Holder diamond. Below that, three rose-cut stones and, dangling alone below a smiling golden cherub at the bottom of the pendant, a gigantic baroque pearl.

'*Dix, noir, pair et manque!*' the croupier whined in his beelike drone. Black ten: Sagittaire gathered up his chips with a faint smile for the murmurs around him, thinking, it is women like the Marleigh who make policemen's lives so difficult. Monte bored him to distraction, and he would have infinitely preferred the mountains or the country, away from the heat. But this was no holiday.

Jean Sagittaire had not taken a real holiday for nearly ten years, since the death of his wife. His work was his distraction and amusement. But all the same he wished The Notorious Marleigh had chosen a more congenial spot.

However, she was wearing just the bait he hoped for; the cross was no paste imitation. Its owner was famed for her indiscretion. She scorned paste replicas of her famous gems and wore them everywhere. No insurance company would touch her.

And there the cross was, winking at Sagittaire. If ever there were a temptation for the Chameleon, it would be this trinket belonging to the Honourable Mrs Reginald Marleigh.

Sagittaire was wearied of the game, but he had to keep his eyes peeled. His senses were a little bewildered by the display of wealth in this luxurious sanctuary. Watching the notes and gold being flung on the tables, it was hard to realise one was playing more than an innocent game, where in actuality pounds and dollars were no more than so many *sous*.

Restless, Sagittaire noticed the opening of the door. Two women entered, one young, the other not so young. It was the young one who captured the bored Inspector's attention. He met the young one's eyes – golden eyes. His pulses leaped.

Following Honoria Grey into the dark casino, Megan was assailed by the tall, lean man's dark stare, and a peculiar weakness invaded her narrow body, a crawling sensation of electric surprise over her bare, tanned arms, gnawing at her.

She could not quite read the meaning of that odd sensation. He was attractive, to be sure, in his elegant leanness and height, with his air of a scholarly nobleman. But there was something about him that made her uneasy; the eyes were no drowsy scholar's, the hard face was not self-indulgent. He looked like a man who had been in tight places and could take care of himself; something almost like Amas Holder. And yet he seemed, somehow, threatening.

Megan looked away and walked with Honoria towards the lemonade bar. The refreshments of the casino had always amused Megan; nothing stronger than lemonade could ever be obtained, despite the decadent, almost sinister atmosphere. Indifferently she sipped the bland drink and with feigned idleness looked about her.

There she was. Helena Marleigh, at the roulette table. And of course she was wearing the François pendant.

'You are very thoughtful,' Honoria Grey remarked. She studied Megan with her keen blue eyes; they were bright against her weathered skin which seemed even darker below the short, crisp, snowy hair.

'Am I?' Megan smiled at the other woman. She was very fond of Honoria Grey, soothed by her intelligent silences, almost awed by her dazzling gifts. Only the *cognoscenti* knew that the daring and ironic novels of Michael Ballantine were written by this quiet woman.

Megan had been amazed, two years ago, to find her at Bea's villa. But soon enough she had seen that Honoria was there as an observer, much like Megan Farley. Though not quite, Megan amended drily now – her own observations had far less innocent results than the making of novels.

Nevertheless Megan and Honoria had become very friendly; each woman kept a solitary house in Nice, and kept herself essentially apart from the activities of Bea's set. This spring, though, Megan knew she would have to steel herself for frequent visits to Bea's.

Helena Marleigh was Bea's guest at the villa.

She would remain for another week.

This week Megan Farley would steal the François pendant. In a way, with its Holder diamond it already belonged to her.

Sagittaire positioned himself so he could watch Mrs Marleigh and at the same time that other remarkable creature, the woman with the bright golden eyes.

At this moment the man was warring with the policeman: Jean Sagittaire had not been so bowled over since the day he met his wife Camille.

At the cry of '*Faites vos jeux*' he placed his chips – on *une noir*, black one – surprised at his own boyish act of sentiment. The golden-eyed girl had deep black hair, black as night but so glossy that the lights made little pools of silver on it as she turned her head and smiled at her companion.

Sagittaire summed up the other – an original, certainly, and perhaps a lover of women. He hoped not with a queer desperation, for then the beautiful one might be . . .

Good God, what was it to him? He was here to work, not to let his imagination run amok. Nevertheless he could not, without difficulty, turn his eyes away from the girl with the shiny onyx hair cut like a boy's. She was dressed in a simple-looking dress of some rough material in a golden-orange color; it seemed to be little more than a homespun shift, belted with a kind of rope plaited with strands of golden-coloured metal. But the Parisian Sagittaire was well acquainted with expensive *couture*; it was a very costly garment he would wager.

It set off her slender roundness to perfection; she had a remarkable figure, high-breasted, with waist and hips and stomach so little and slender that in contrast the breasts were startlingly soft and emphatic. The knee-length dress revealed legs of delicious shapeliness, those of a dancer . . . or an acrobat.

Sagittaire was overtaken with an idea so disturbing that he felt suddenly hot, as though someone had thrown boiling water on his back. A narrow rivulet of perspiration began to trickle down him; he shifted his shoulders uncomfortably in his thin, well-tailored jacket.

An acrobat.

She was staring at the Marleigh now, and quickly looking away.

The Chameleon, he recalled saying to the eager press, was either a woman or a 'very peculiar man'. The Chameleon had made just that one mistake – dropping the stud earring in the Ritz when that awful fat woman . . . what was her name? . . . Hooker. Dorothy Sue Hooker, the pork queen, Sagittaire remembered with a smile.

The yellow diamond stud, which he'd examined and re-examined time and again. His men could still not trace the jeweller who had made it; it was of foreign manufacture. Sagittaire had taken to carrying it with him everywhere; it had become an obsession, just as the Chameleon had.

He reached into his pocket, feeling the stud with his fingers.

And that girl had amber eyes, almost the colour of the yellow diamond, a tawny, brownish-gold, like sun-warmed wine.

Jean Sagittaire pulled himself together, snapping to alertness. What was the matter with him? He never maundered like this.

The girl with the lovely body and her white-haired companion were approaching the roulette table.

Glancing at the Hon Mrs Marleigh, who was so intent on the wheel she did not look up, the white-haired woman murmured something to the girl, and raised her brows.

The girl shook her head. The two women took their places at the table, across from Mrs Marleigh. Sagittaire moved a trifle nearer. Now he was only the length of his arm from the striking girl.

Seen close, she was even more magnetic: the black, winging brows

312

and heavy lashes served to emphasise her aureate irises, making the colour utterly startling. Her skin looked as poreless as a flower-petal, lightly touched by the sun. And if she wore make-up at all, he estimated, it was so skilfully applied it might be non-existent.

Sagittaire's police glance, perfected by years of habit, took all of her in within seconds; his sharp scrutiny also picked up a peculiar hint of bronze at the base of her thick lashes. She dyed them, he decided, as well as her brows and hair. Interesting.

He pretended to be deaf to the conversation that followed. The white-haired woman, catching Marleigh's eye, said neutrally, 'Hallo there, Helena.'

'Why, Honoria, Honoria Grey! How are you, my dear?'

Ah! So that reticent lady was the notorious Michael Ballantine. Sagittaire felt a whimsical pleasure. Who would have thought it? And she knew the notorious Marleigh.

'Do you know Megan, Helena? Megan Farley, Beatrice's niece?'

Megan, Sagittaire repeated to himself in silence. *A propos* – she was the finest of the Anglo-Saxon type with Celtic overtones.

Marleigh acknowledged the introduction, he observed, with cool civility. Jealous, doubtless; Sagittaire almost had the instincts of a female in these matters, another asset of his that not only surprised others in concert with his toughness, but set him apart from his fellows. He repressed a smile.

'Will you be staying at Bea's villa?' the Marleigh asked negligently.

'No.' The girl named Megan had a voice like rough honey, and it chafed the inspector's heightened nerves. She had only murmured before, but now he could hear her voice plainly. 'I keep my own house in Nice. I'll be . . . dropping in now and again. Tonight, probably.'

Sagittaire was disturbed to realise that the voice affected him like the stroke of a soft, electric hand. This was something he had not counted on; this job must not be complicated by such emotions.

For this woman, particularly. His peculiar intuition marked her as someone different from the general run; someone perilous. But he was unable to control the leaping of his pulses, the bodily discomfort aroused by her proximity. *Quel dommage.* Tonight.

For an interval the players around the table did not speak; there was only the whine of the croupier, the click of the little ball.

'*Trois, noir, trois, noir!*'

Sagittaire raked in more chips; black was good to him today. Now he could feel those magnificent eyes on him, and he looked up.

Just for the space of a heartbeat he met that splendid gaze that was the hue of brandy, and his very loins reacted; the swift stare was marked by intelligence and daring . . . and something more. Fear.

Now Sagittaire was certain; the girl named Megan Farley feared him. Why? And his wild suspicion returned.

'Oh, damn it!' Helena Marleigh cried out. 'I've been losing steadily ever since I began this wretched game. What about you two? Let's go out and have a drink, shall we?'

Honoria Grey hesitated, looking at Megan. Definitely, Sagittaire judged, there was something there. Grey had a carefully restrained passion for the girl Megan, who did not return it. Sagittaire was boyishly, fatuously glad.

Megan shrugged, and he was impressed that even that minute gesture revealed the unusual suppleness, the grace and looseness of muscle one saw in athletes. Once again the suspicion surfaced; he was becoming more and more certain. 'Very well,' she murmured in flawless Parisian French.

Keeping the three under close, discreet observation Sagittaire rushed to cash in his chips and followed them at the regulation distance from the casino.

Now they were passing a tobacconist's which displayed newspapers. 'Excuse me a moment,' Megan Farley said quickly. Sagittaire lingered before a flower stall, as if weighing choices deeply, thinking: when she speaks English it is with a cosmopolitan non-accent. She has lived long in France and travelled in many other places.

The other women halted. Megan snatched up a newspaper, staring at its front page, and absently handed coins to the vendor.

'What is it, my dear?' Honoria Grey inquired.

'Oh, just something I wanted to look for – the race results.' Sagittaire's trained ear caught a mendacious overtone. That was untrue. The girl's eyes were glowing; she looked as if she'd just won an enormous lottery.

As they moved on, he picked up the same paper and threw coins on top of the remaining pile. He divided his attention between its front page and the three women as he strolled along.

What was it? His glance flicked over the newspaper. Hardly the dull international news or the ponderous reportage of the doings of the French government. Then at the bottom he saw a smaller item: 'Holder Heir Survives Oranjemund.'

Briefly, one Martin Holder, son of the American millionaire

314

miner, supervising the bed-mining of diamonds on that lonely African coast, had been caught in the wash of waves when the sea wall broke. Not only had he survived by leaping on one of the giant conveyors, but he had saved ten other men from drowning. Communication, the article stated, had been broken down, and only now had the news come through.

Sagittaire looked up again. The women were taking chairs in an outdoor café.

He wandered with seeming negligence across the cobbled street and into an unusual bar – unusual for its plainness in Monte Carlo, where even the churches seemed too rich for the poor to enter – and sat down at a table near the window, ordering a brandy.

He must find out, at once, what that girl had to do with the Holders. There was some connection. He was sure now that her joyful expression had some connection with the survival of this Martin Holder; little else on that front page could have produced that joy. And it was obvious to him that the name was familiar to her; the article, with its brevity and smaller headline, would have attracted the notice only of someone who knew that name, and knew it well.

And the François pendant contained one of the Holder diamonds. *Curiouser and curiouser.* Jean Sagittaire was very fond of *Alice*, and indeed of much English literature. He had long been interested in solving the puzzle of the strange Anglo-Saxon character, as evidenced in his good friends at Scotland Yard.

He asked the proprietor if he might use the telephone.

'Not,' the man said, eyeing him, 'if you are calling a distance.'

Sagittaire covertly showed the man his identification. 'Paris,' he said briefly, 'but it will be charged to that city.'

'Ah!' The proprietor looked interested, respectful. 'Please.' He made a polite gesture towards the instrument. Luckily for Sagittaire it was in a private spot. Still keeping his eye on the café, the inspector spoke tersely into the phone.

'Danton? Flèche. Charge this to the bureau and get me this data, at once. Family of Amas Holder, American millionaire. Last name of rich Beatrice, villa in Nice, connections with Holders. Now.'

He smiled at Danton's protests. 'I'm waiting. Call me at this number. If I've left, at my hotel.' He hung up and returned to his chair.

The three women were ordering another cocktail. Danton was good, Sagittaire reflected, when in an amazingly short time the phone shrilled and the proprietor came to him.

'A telephone call for you, Inspect . . .' At a minute gesture from Sagittaire, the man amended, 'sir. Paris.' He seemed childishly pleased to be involved in this apparent cloak-and-dagger operation.

Sagittaire smiled and went to the phone. Listening, he nodded and his smile broadened. After a brief but sincere compliment to Danton, he replaced the receiver.

So the Beatrice of the villa, Megan's aunt, was the sister-in-law of Amas Holder, with as many discarded surnames as a crook had aliases. And Megan Farley, her niece, was the granddaughter of Amas and Vanessa Holder, actually the grand-niece of di Gamba. No doubt, Sagittaire thought in his cynical way, 'niece' made the ageing Beatrice sound younger.

The women were leaving the café now and Sagittaire tossed money onto his table, leaving a generous gratuity. He stepped quickly onto the street where he immediately slowed to a saunter. The women were getting into a shining new silver-grey Rolls, an aluminium torpedo tourer very like the one the Indian bigwig from Bahadur had used in Paris.

A beauty, Sagittaire judged parenthetically . . . built on a Phantom chassis to last for forty or fifty years. Helena Marleigh of course would tire of it in a year, as she had tired of leading a leopard on a leash around the streets of Rome, or having a turbanned blackamoor for an escort. The English were truly mad.

He dared not follow them now in his car. But they were taking the road to Nice. Tonight, he promised himself, he was going to lurk outside the villa.

If ever there were an irresistible target for the Chameleon, it was that eccentric English lady who defied all sense and caution.

Fortunately for the inspector, the villa of Beatrice Stirling Dillon Prince-di Gamba was an isolated one, with no security measures at all, surrounded by concealing woodlands of oak, chestnut and umbrella pine. There had been no point in arriving early; di Gamba's guests, Danton had said, caroused sometimes until dawn.

Concealing his car in a wooded patch, Sagittaire took the path to the villa on foot, thanking the outraged former guest who had complained to the Sûreté about di Gamba's servants stealing her gems three years ago. One of the other men had handled it, but Sagittaire, alert to such thefts ever since the Chameleon's little reign of terror, had kept tabs. He recalled that the Nice constabulary had investigated and come up with nothing. He'd give a lot to know if Megan

Farley had been in residence three years ago; he did not doubt she had.

On the whole, he had little doubt now that she herself was the Chameleon. He felt it without evidence, in his very bones, with that sharply honed, instinctive knowledge that had made him the pride of the Sûreté. He had long since abandoned pointless modesty about his gifts.

Arriving earlier than he'd calculated, Sagittaire hid himself in the trees and sat on the ground. He was dressed in a dark but lightweight shirt and sombre trousers, his feet in dark canvas espadrilles for silence and comfort. He longed for a smoke but knew that was absurd; even a match flame could give the game away. He checked the sleeve-hidden radium dial of his watch, however, and saw that it was two in the morning.

The rowdiness of drunken voices and laughter still proceeded from a hidden terrace of the villa. Patiently he settled down to wait, thinking of the girl Megan with an ache of regret. He almost hoped he was wrong.

And then he wondered, quite suddenly, why he had chosen to come to this assignment on his own, when it was proper to enlist the aid of the Nice men. It violated every tradition of the Sûreté, working like this alone.

He did not have to consult his watch again; he was amazed that his varied and wandering thoughts had so distracted him that he heard a huge bell from somewhere toll three times. A whole hour had elapsed. The sounds from the villa were at last diminishing.

At three-thirty silence reigned.

His watch indicated a quarter to four when he heard a faint rustle in the grass. His heart thudded and he leaned forward, peering into the moonlight.

He saw a slender, dark-clad figure steal towards one of the great oaks whose branches almost brushed the villa's second storey. The pale white illumination clearly silhouetted the furtive figure's outline: it was boyishly slender, lithe and lean, but undeniably a woman's. No mistaking that. She must have bound her breasts for the other jobs, but now they were not inhibited, and their roundness, the curve of the hips, gave her away.

She was dressed in black from head to foot, something tight, yet with a give, for she shinnied up the oak with the ease of a monkey and then made a dangerous, silent leap onto a balustrade. He saw her listen an instant, then enter the open window.

317

Sagittaire felt the thrill of a big-game hunter closing in on his prey, the excitement he had only known with the prey of man. He heartily disapproved of blood sports himself, but acquaintances had told him that sometimes the prey was so magnificent it seemed a pity to kill it. Sagittaire felt just that now, at this moment.

She was magnificent, superb. What a woman! He sighed, waiting for her to emerge. In a very short time she did; he wondered why she simply hadn't gone through the victim's room and into the hall. But she must have a reason. Perhaps there were servants still awake.

In any event, he watched in admiration as she made her descent, thinking drily, this must be like a stroll compared to the walls of those hotels in Biarritz and Paris. A hundred to one she'd climbed in Switzerland.

At the moment of her contact with the ground, Sagittaire rushed forward and grabbed her around the waist. He could smell her faint perfume, and even in the excitement of the capture was sharply aware of that tensile softness, that sweet slenderness in his grasp.

She merely took one quick, startled breath. His unwilling admiration flamed: she was remarkable. Her nerves were pure steel. Any other woman would have shrieked. Not this one.

He said softly in French, 'Good morning, Chameleon.'

Sagittaire felt the lithe body go limp in his hold, but it was only for the flick of an eye. After that momentary reaction of defeat, he could feel the body stiffen to a wariness, an alertness of muscle.

He looked down at her. A soft dark cap covered her hair; in the moonlight her delicate face had an ironic, austere appearance.

'You were in the casino,' she whispered. 'But I don't think we've been properly introduced.'

Once again his admiration almost overcame his policeman's caution. He quietly gave her his name and full title.

She was silent for a long moment. Then she asked, with smiling defiance, 'Where do we go from here? To the constabulary?'

'Mademoiselle, if you please, may I see the contents of your pockets?'

'Why?' she demanded softly. 'Surely you know.'

'The François pendant, without doubt.' He could not help smiling. There was no need, he decided, to hold her so tightly; after all, she was only a woman, for all her comparative strength. But even that strength was no match for his. The man in him was reluctant to bruise that exquisite skin. He relaxed his grasp ever so slightly.

But, to his astonishment, she had wrenched herself away and was

318

running like the wind towards a small, powerful car and leaping into it; the motor growled, and she was driving away, speeding down the road from the villa.

He took off down the hill, through the woodland, towards his own concealed car, cursing himself for a quixotic fool, first of all to come on this job alone, which had been egomaniacal nonsense, and then to let her slip away. She must have had the key in her car already; he threw himself into his own car and sped off after her.

She had outwitted him, for a moment; he'd be damned if she'd outclass him, too. He was driving like a madman along the winding road, and prayed that no car would come in the other direction. That could finish him . . . and her . . . and some poor innocent besides.

He was catching up with her a bit; the sound of her powerful motor was louder. But then he heard a noise that chilled his blood.

A car crashing with a horrendous sound over a precipice . . . and the titanic splash in the harbour-water, far below. The shock made him swerve for a split second, but he righted the car somehow and, sweating copiously, gradually slowed down.

He drove on very slowly, for another mile, his whole body shaking. When he got to the place he had calculated from the noise, he stopped and looked down. Her car was almost swallowed up in the water.

'*Mon Dieu*,' he said aloud, and it came out in a kind of grieved croak. He was incredulous at the depth of his pain. Could she really be dead?

But no. His policeman's mind was still busy; crooks had pulled this kind of thing before. She had put the car in gear and let it go over. She was hiding in the woods, and he would damned well find her.

He tried not to admit that it was hope, not determination, that made him scour the woods for another several hours. At last, exhausted, he gave it up. She was nowhere to be found. Either she was dead . . . or she had escaped him.

And even if it were the greatest blow to his pride he'd ever suffered in all his career, Jean Sagittaire prayed that it would be the latter.

Beatrice was drinking coffee on the terrace about one in the afternoon, having just awakened, when her peace was shattered by two amazing events: one was the shrieking entrance of Helena Marleigh, in *déshabillé*, with the news that the François pendant was missing; the other was the almost simultaneous announcement by Jacques that the chief of the Nice constabulary was below, asking to see Madame.

'Oh, Christ,' Bea complained. 'This is just too much for the first thing in the morning.'

'Never mind that!' Helena screamed. 'What about my pendant?'

'Shut up, Helena,' Bea snapped. 'We'll get to that. I'd better put something on; the police are so goddamned *bourgeois* they're capable of arresting me for exposure.' Her harsh laugh exposed her yellowed teeth to the maddened Helena, who cursed and sank down on the *chaise longue*.

'Damn the police,' she muttered.

Bea threw a robe around herself and pulled her hat down over her aching eyes. 'Send them up, Jacques.'

Honoria Grey had come into the terrace, unblinking in the sun, fully dressed for the day in a short-sleeved shirt and immaculate duck trousers. 'What's going on?' she inquired, glancing at Helena. 'Megan still asleep?'

'I don't know how, with all this racket,' Bea responded sourly. But she smiled in an automatic way when the chief appeared. After all, he was a man, if old and fat.

Jacques said to Bea, 'There's something you should know, 'Trice, about the pendant . . .'

'Not now, Jacques.'

'What about the pendant?' Helena shrieked. 'Good God, man, *tell* me!'

The chief had not even been given the opportunity to address Bea but, hearing that exchange, he was suddenly all alertness. He stood, waiting.

'I chased a man off the property last night,' Jacques said quickly. 'I had not yet had the chance to tell 'Trice . . . Madame,' he amended. Forestalling Helena's questions he hurried on. 'I heard something, then saw a man running down the hill. I chased him, but he was too fast for me. He got into a car and drove off, like a madman. And there was another car, farther along, driving very fast.'

'What kind of man, what kind of car?' the policeman demanded abruptly.

Jacques turned and looked at him. 'I do not know, sir. A tall man only, dressed in dark clothes; I could see neither him nor the car clearly.'

'And you say there was . . . another car?'

'Yes, Chief Inspector.'

'Were there any cars missing from here?' the man demanded of Jacques.

'I did not really notice. I was too interested in that man. I think, Madame,' he said to Helena, 'that it must be he who took your pendant.'

'We will get to the matter of the lady's pendant in good time,' the chief said firmly. 'But now, I fear I am the bearer of terrible news, Madame di Gamba.'

'What terrible news?' Bea asked sharply.

'Your niece's car, Madame . . . was seen to go over a cliff late last night.'

'Good God!' Only Bea cried out. The other women were apparently speechless, and Jacques stood silent, his lips ajar. The white-haired one, the inspector noticed, was pale as milk. 'Have you found . . . did you . . ?'

'We have not found the . . . your niece, Madame. It is not certain that she was driving.'

'Jacques!' Bea shrilled. 'Go at once and see if she is in her room.' He rushed out.

'That is an excellent idea.' The inspector spoke in a solemn tone and waited, as silent as the others, for the servant's return.

Jacques came back to the terrace, muddy under his tanned skin. 'She is not there, 'Trice . . . Madame. Her bed has not been slept in.'

The inspector sighed. 'Ah, Madame, that is not a good sign. We have definitely identified the car. The force of the impact, you understand, when the car struck the rocks in falling, detached the number plate. The plate was found lodged in a crevice. It matched the licence number of the car belonging to your niece, Miss Megan Farley.' The conclusion was like an elegy.

Jacques, Beatrice and Helena Marleigh could find nothing to say at all.

But Honoria Grey, who was generally so controlled that they hardly knew she was there, let out an agonised cry like that of a wounded animal.

Startled, the others stared at her; the inspector of the Nice constabulary was overcome with pity.

CHAPTER TWENTY-ONE

Megan was so tense and sore she was hard put to hold onto the bough; she heard the car stop, and listened to Sagittaire crashing around in the underbrush below her, almost afraid to breathe.

The famous Sagittaire, the relentless Flèche. Surely he would discover her.

But he did not, and she was fairly dizzy with the slow acceptance of that miracle. After what seemed an entire morning she heard him leave. She knew she must get down; she could not hold on much longer. At least, she decided, he would be searching another part of the wood. But she must use the greatest care.

Very cautiously she looked about and listened, then slid down the trunk, scraping her palms badly. She threw away her shoes and crept forward in her stockinged feet. Her house was hardly a stone's throw away, but she couldn't linger.

As soon as he found out about the house, he would be on it like an ant on a pear. She would have to race for dear life. Her heart was almost jumping out of her mouth when she came in sight of the little house. She stayed behind a tree, listening again. There was a vast silence, but it could be the silence of a hidden man.

Well, she had to take the chance. All her money was back at the villa, except for an emergency amount she kept at the house; and her cheque books were inside, the cheques of Michele Fournet. Good God, what he wouldn't make of that! She had no car now, either. She would have to take the train back to Paris, and not come back to Nice.

Her head was pounding with a sharp pain now. And the first thing she must do, in Paris, was to cable Amas and Vanessa. Bea would notify them that she was believed dead; she could not put her grandparents through another agony so soon after their fear for Martin.

Dear God, if he were hiding in the house! But it was possible he didn't know yet where it was; she recalled vaguely having said something to Helena at the casino about keeping a house in Nice. That was all. He, she knew now of course, had heard and noted that without doubt.

But he might have assumed she would have a house nearer the town, as most women indeed would. There was no way that Sagittaire could have discovered her hermitlike habits. Not already.

Or had he? The notorious Flèche seemed to know everything, according to the gossip of her shady companions.

Well, she would have to take the chance; there was no other way. Megan dropped to the ground and crawled through the shrubbery towards the house. Finally at the back entrance she crouched for an instant, listening hard again.

With a muffled oath she stood up and went in. She never bothered locking the house – foolish, perhaps, in this lonely area, but so far she had had no difficulties. The house had a blessedly empty feel. Now her sharpened senses let her know that she was, at last, alone.

She raced into the front room and retrieved all the Michele Fournet papers from the desk; in the bedroom she put them in a hidden lining of her suitcase, along with the pendant. Then she fairly threw off the dark sweater and trousers and cap and, taking them to the fireplace, set them ablaze. She ran back to her boudoir, took the first travelling clothes that came to hand and dressed with great rapidity. She donned the bronze wig that she took from its box on a shelf and with swift, practised fingers removed the black paint from her lashes and substituted brown. She dusted powder over her brows and repainted them in a dark brown colour, choosing a lighter lip pomade, no rouge.

She looked at the auburn wig. For good measure she took it to the front room and added it to the pyre. Tossing some high-heeled shoes into her capacious bag, she slipped on some low-heeled ones and, assuring herself that the fire-screen was in place, hurried out of the house.

To make assurance doubly sure – she smiled, for the first time, at the old Shakespearean expression which, heeded, had stood her for so long in good stead – she slipped on a loose, concealing summer coat and some thick-lensed spectacles, together with an ugly hat. She knew a shortcut to the town and she took it, all tiredness gone now, her spirits rising.

However, when she went into the train depot, her heart nearly stopped beating. Jean Sagittaire was sitting on one of the benches reading a newspaper. She went quietly back out and, a few blocks down the street, hailed a taxi to take her to Cannes. She would entrain from there. The taxi driver at first let forth a flood of protests, but the sight of thirty English pound notes made his eyes bulge. At that point, Megan considered with amusement, he was ready to carry her to Cannes on his back.

With a horrendous clash of gears the taxi hurtled off towards Cannes with the passenger who would now be called Marta Franz.

In the station Sagittaire shifted restlessly. He was half-dead with fatigue and furious at himself for not calling in an aide; he could hardly check the boats and trains at once. He had found a house he suspected was hers because of certain burnt items. She would have to get out soon, because there was hardly anything left at that house. And she would not go back to the villa.

He had at least alerted the car-hire places and she still might show up here. But so far there was nothing – only one woman, a dowdy creature at least ten years older than Megan Farley, in a too-large coat, an unspeakable hat and spectacles over faded eyes. Untidy bronze hair.

A coat – in this weather.

Bronze hair. He had seen a trace of golden-bronze at the base of Megan Farley's lashes when she looked down at the wheel in the casino. He could have sworn that she had a blonde's complexion, too. And he should know. He smiled sardonically. He specialised in them; his very darkness hungered for their brightness. That awful-looking woman could have been his prey.

Cursing, he got up and hurried out to the street.

No trace, anywhere, on the street, in the shops or cafés. Somehow he knew it had been she, and she had slipped out of his grasp once more. Had he . . . *wanted* her to?

He had mishandled this damned thing from the beginning – the relentless, the great Sagittaire, who had never lost anyone before. And in this he had been more inept than the greenest recruit to the force.

Yet all the while he felt a strange elation: this could mean she was still alive.

CHAPTER TWENTY-TWO

But Sagittaire was no longer sure of that on the May morning in 1932 when he was suddenly assailed by the old memory. His train was leaving Strasbourg, the ancient, gracious capital of the Alsace, to which he had paid a sombre visit for the funeral of his mother.

She was the last one who'd really mattered, Sagittaire gloomily reflected. The whole thing had left him with a sensation of desolate loneliness; and that, of course, was what reminded him of Megan Farley. He'd thought he'd had her when he discovered she'd sent that cable to America, but she'd slipped away again.

Sagittaire laid his proud head back on the seat of his luxurious compartment and let his memory wander. He closed his eyes; there would be little to look at, certainly, before Nancy, the centre of Lorraine. And the blossoming orchards, the emerald woodlands flashing past had too poignant a beauty for his present mood; everything but him seemed to be renewing itself, making him by contrast feel empty and dry.

Empty as the last six years had essentially been, despite his professional successes and a measure of personal content. Berthe was a charming mistress – chic, gifted, and independent by means of her fashion designs. And yet he was left with a sinking sense of blandness, almost boredom, when he contemplated their three-year association. It could drift on and on until they married out of sheer apathy. Sagittaire could not accept that, not even now, though at thirty-nine he was ready to make some move. Otherwise he might never even have a son of his own.

To 'carry on the title'. That expression brought a sardonic smile to his narrow lips. It was of prime concern to his mother's people. Then he sobered, recalling the unpleasantness before the funeral; his mother's stiff relations – the château set, as he contemptuously called them – who had been so cruel to her in life, became very proprietary about her death. They wanted her buried with the family in the burial ground adjoining the château. It had only been through Sagittaire's intervention that her last wishes had been carried out. She was buried beside her husband in Alsace, the country of her only happiness. At least if Sagittaire had accomplished nothing else, he had seen to that.

And now his hateful older brother, the present Comte de Lille, was failing; his only heirs were daughters. That left Jean Sagittaire in line for the title. A Sagittaire, the next Comte de Lille! The thought was too absurd. The only thing he would get out of it was the satisfaction of placing a burr under their tails.

As for the rest – he knew it was more than his mother's death, and the disturbing state of France and the rest of Europe, that was troubling him. Of a certainty, that shrill little vulgarian in Germany, Mussolini's copycat, was enough to depress anyone. Two years in succession the Nazis had won a huge majority in the Reichstag; France had constructed the Maginot Line, a system of fortifications along the eastern frontier extending from the Swiss to the Belgian border. Matters were not improving.

But even that, grave as it was, was not the source of Sagittaire's depression. It was far more personal.

In these years since he had last seen Megan Farley in the moonlight outside the villa, slender and defiant in her black masquerade, Sagittaire had met no other woman who so affected him. He had lost the youth of his heart.

How dramatic, how extreme! Sagittaire mocked himself.

Nevertheless, it haunted him: no other woman, no other criminal, either. It was absolutely *fou*, but much of the zest had gone out of the eternal chase, with the Chameleon quiescent all this time. Except for last winter, in Munich. Those thefts had been just her style (to himself Sagittaire still referred to the Chameleon stubbornly as *her*, still privately kept the case open, even if the Commissioner now considered it closed).

That had been an awkward little *contretemps*; despite the increasing pressure of other business, Sagittaire had kept a number of men on the Chameleon affair, and it leaked to the Commissioner, which would have cost Sagittaire his rank had he not been been so essential to the organisation.

Finally he'd had to yield, and let the investigation die. It was too quixotic, anyway; he had probably been chasing a phantom all these years.

Sagittaire opened his eyes. Enough. Rested now, he had a sudden impulse to limber his legs. Yawning, he stretched and rose, straightening his clothes before he went into the swaying corridor. Perhaps he would kill a little time in the bar car, farther on.

In the next car, a sudden lurching of the train sent him careening into a *wagons-lits* attendant standing at the open door of a compartment.

There was a simultaneous apology. However, before Sagittaire could fully right himself he was awarded a glimpse of the compartment's occupant.

He blinked his eyes in utter disbelief: the woman was slender as a wand, dressed in a fluid ensemble of sooty black that made a flaming glory of her brief cap of vivid auburn hair. He saw the shock of recognition in the amber eyes.

It was Megan Farley.

He could hardly think, but he decided to act quickly. 'Mademoiselle!' he cried with amiable surprise. 'What an unexpected pleasure. I have just come from a visit with your uncle!' He'd said the first thing that came into his head; anything to make the attendant step aside on the assumption that it was a fortuitous meeting of old friends.

The amber eyes had a trapped expression; the smiling attendant waited politely, standing by.

'May I join you?' Sagittaire asked coolly.

Now the remarkable eyes flashed with frustration and anger, but Sagittaire already had one foot over the threshold of the compartment. Megan Farley's slender body seemed to sag with defeat. But she said with admirable calm to the attendant, 'Thank you for the information. That's all I need for now.'

The man touched his billed cap and moved away.

Sagittaire stepped in to the compartment and closed the door.

Now he was tongue-tied. All he could do was stare. She was paler and thinner than he remembered, but a thousand times more enticing. The fiery hair, the honey-coloured eyes and the small lips like the petals of a crimson flower were startlingly vivid against the deep, matt black of her Lanvin ensemble.

The black chiffon blouse, tied high at her delicate throat with the trailing scarf ends floating over her back, highlighted her firm, untrammelled breasts; the long black skirt, reaching halfway between her knees and her graceful ankles, hinted at supple hips and long, delicious legs. Megan sat with her body in half-profile as if she sat for a photographic portrait, her proud chin raised.

For a long, stunned instant Sagittaire's mind snapped the image as a camera would; an instant he would always treasure. He was as speechless as a young, smitten boy, his awareness incapable of anything but her. Everything was simple: she was alive. They were alone for the first real time together, speeding through the greening countryside towards Nancy and the pastoral region of Lorraine. Paris was far away.

And then, as swiftly as the flicker of her long lashes, the moment was gone.

Sagittaire regained his sober senses. With a slight, ironic bow, he murmured, 'The Chameleon is resurrected.'

Meeting his stare head on, she said, 'The Chameleon died in Munich, Inspector.' She was looking at him too steadily; he knew she was lying.

'At the height of her success?' He raised his brows. 'You were fortunate, Mlle Farley. The German police, these days, are too busy with more important matters' – his reference to their political duties was heavy with sarcasm – 'to bother with an Englishwoman's pearls. The Sûreté is more fortunate. Where are they?'

He shot the question out. He was himself again, but he did not yet know whether that made him feel relief or sadness. Likely both.

Sagittaire had to admire her calm when she answered, 'In Stuttgart, Inspector. The Nazi police are also too busy to bother with fences. And a woman named Marta Franz, with the proper political ideas' – this time it was she who gave him an ironic smile – 'is treated very indulgently by customs. I'm afraid I have only money. Are francs illegal these days in the region of Lorraine?'

'No, But a forged passport is, mademoiselle.'

She laughed. 'I am carrying the passport of Megan Farley. Would you like to see it?'

He burned with disproportionate anger and frustration. She skittered away from him at every turn, like a small, mischievous wild animal too fast to capture. What evidence did he have, after all? Now he lacked even the approval of the Sûreté to reopen and pursue her case. But it had been a black mark on his stainless record.

And suddenly Sagittaire knew what was behind his frustration – sheer wounded vanity. This magnificent creature was maddening, impossible; there was just no rational way to deal with her. He had no doubt at all that she had disposed of her Marta Franz passport and, when she got to Paris, might assume some other name. Name of names, what was he supposed to do – scour Paris for an unknown alias, a woman with black, red, blonde . . . who knew, even white hair, next time?

Sagittaire began to laugh, wildly, without volition, and the unaccustomed sound astonished him. He felt as if he were observing the actions of another man. No, there was no reasonable way to deal with Megan Farley.

No *reasonable* way: the way that occurred to him had to do not with reason, but sheer emotion, a state that was anathema to Jean Sagittaire.

She looked, if anything, even more surprised than he felt. And then a slow, almost unwilling smile broke out on her gamine's face.

It was such a childlike, endearing smile that he heard himself say, 'When you smile like that I know what kind of child you were.' He folded his arms to hide the unsteadiness of his hands. Everything, everything he had thought or said since he had stepped across this threshold amazed him. It had been like crossing the threshold to a new self, a new life. And that realisation was the most unsettling thing of all: he was reacting like an irresponsible boy, with everything vital forgotten, slipping away.

Her expression of surprise deepened; her smile snapped closed, like a shut umbrella. The amber eyes took on a wary gleam.

'Come, come, Inspector. Did you invade my compartment to arrest me or to psychoanalyse me?' That word was less common in France, he supposed, than in America. The way it slipped so casually off her tongue made him wonder if she had undergone such treatment herself. He wondered a great deal, more than ever strangely eager to plumb her depths.

'I have no grounds at the moment to arrest you, mademoiselle.' He made himself speak formally, although at that moment he had an overwhelming impulse to kiss that mocking little mouth. 'Unless, of course,' he added lightly, 'you have the François pendant on you.'

Her eyes twinkled. 'The François pendant, Inspector, will never, never be found.'

Even his natural curiosity was losing its force, in the stronger wave of attraction that quivered over his body now. 'May I sit down?' he asked gently.

'Please.' She waved at the opposite seat, and he sank onto it, their knees almost brushing as he studied her. Her defiant stare dropped before his sober scrutiny.

'Mademoiselle . . . Megan.' He reached across and took her hands in his; he was like a man hypnotised, still not knowing himself. All he knew was that he could not resist the desire to touch her, and the contact of her soft, strong fingers set off in his own hands a small, racing path of fire like that running along a nitrous fuse towards a charge of dynamite. That narrow heat spread from his hands upward into his arms and chest and shoulders, then down, down into the centre of his body. He had never known such a thing before, in all his varied dealings with women.

329

The small hands quivered at the touch, as though physically shocked. She raised her remarkable eyes to his at last.

If he had hoped for a sign of tenderness in them, he was sharply disappointed. They were shuttered now and cautious.

She slipped her fingers from his grasp, and asked flatly, 'Why are you doing this, Inspector? I have heard of the manoeuvres of the famous Flèche . . . is this one of them? What interesting interrogations you must conduct.'

He almost winced at the coldness of her tone, but he said solemnly, 'This is no game.'

'What is it, then?' she demanded. Her eyes blazed with a golden, angry light, like an irritated cat's. 'Do you equate my former profession with the world's oldest one?'

The brutality of it shocked even him. From the first moment he had heard her speak, she impressed him with her fastidiousness. 'Please. Do not say these things.' He gave her a rueful smile and was heartened to notice that her angry expression was evaporating, her face relaxing a little. 'Forgive me, Mademoiselle . . . Farley.'

He leaned back then and gave it up, throwing up his hands in dismissive resignation. 'This is an absurdity . . . a grotesquerie. *I* shall surrender; I don't know any longer what to do. But listen to me, let me tell you.

'For several years of my life my guiding passion was the capture of the Chameleon. I must congratulate you. You were superb. Magnificent.' He was speaking quickly now in French, fearing that his English might not have the fluency to express the stunning complexity of what he had to say. 'While pursuing the Chameleon, I admired him totally . . . even more, I must admit, when I began to suspect that he was a woman. It was very indiscreet of you, my dear lady, to drop that stud.'

He reached into his pocket and then opened his palm before her.

She gasped. 'You . . . kept that, all this time?' Then she coloured deeply. With that she had truly given herself away.

But he was too intent now on his monologue even to consider that fact. He rushed on, 'Yes. Yes. All this time, Megan Farley.'

This time there was no coldness in the golden eyes, but a dawning softness, a look that gave him hope. Exhilarated, he felt quite drunk.

'And then,' he went on softly, 'when I . . . caught you outside the villa in Nice, I think the pursuit took on quite another aspect.'

She looked away and nervously reached into her handbag, bringing out cigarettes. She lit one; her hand was shaking. Belatedly she held out the case to him.

He shook his head. 'At first I felt . . . I *hoped*,' he said frankly, 'that

330

you were not in the car when it went over. That disguise, by the way, was masterful.' He grinned. 'I didn't know you at all.'

There was a trace of a smile on her lips but she did not answer. She was still canny, hesitant. As who would not be, in this situation? He admired her control.

'Then, after a while,' he said, 'I feared you might be dead after all. Until Munich, last year. Where were you all these years . . . why so inactive?'

She answered him with a question of her own. 'What are you going to do, Inspector? Are you still trying to trick me into a confession . . . wasn't the stud enough?'

'What am I going to do?' He queried himself in that moment. He was still amazed that he did not even know.

'Stop the train?' she pursued ironically. 'Haul me off at Nancy and turn me over to their constabulary . . . or, better yet, escort me to Paris in handcuffs?'

She was not so brazen as she sounded, he knew, because there was the faintest tremor in her husky, caressing voice. Sagittaire had never heard French sound so melodious before. And he knew with an odd, deep certainty that he was going to do nothing. Nothing at this moment except to try and make her like him.

'First,' he said, smiling, 'I am going to ask you if you will do me the honour of dining with me.'

At last he had made some headway. The cautious look in her eyes was changing; a half-smile curved her mouth. 'Why? To interrogate me in front of witnesses?' This time the question was not so cold; she sounded seductively teasing.

'To enjoy the pleasure of your company,' he said with great seriousness.

He was not imagining it now. There was a new warmth about her. He felt at once comically protective and totally at sea. 'Will you join me?' he asked eagerly.

'Yes. Yes, I will, Inspector Sagittaire. I will join you in the dining car in . . .' she consulted her small gold watch . . . 'exactly half an hour.'

He was incredibly elated. He stood up, looking down at her for a long moment, then he bowed. 'There is just one small item . . .'

'Yes?' She raised her swooping brows.

'If you would be so kind . . . no more "Inspector". Not tonight. Do you think you could find it in your heart to call me . . . Jean?'

'I think perhaps I might . . . Jean.' The sound of his given name on her tongue was more musical than he could have imagined. But as he left he wondered if she would meet him.

His relief and delight, when he saw her enter the car, were overpowering. He stood at once and waited until she had negotiated the swaying aisle and handed her into her chair before the attendant could do so.

Seated across from her, Sagittaire enjoyed the sight of her lovely face in the glow of the shaded candle. A vase in the centre of the table held fresh yellow roses and some tiny, unidentified white flower. He could not help thinking that her hidden flesh would have the same purity and sweetness of the white blossoms; he felt his appetite drain away.

Nevertheless he was careful about the wine, attentive to her wishes, even if the food tasted like sawdust to him now. He had got it badly, as the English were fond of saying. On the perimeter of his vision he caught the stares of other men, envious of him, patently admiring her.

'It is a strange world, Megan Farley,' he murmured, raising his wine glass to her in salute.

She raised her own glass of the pale sherry she had requested, and that eerily matched her eyes. 'Yes.'

They were silent for a time, as the Alsace train sped on, approaching the green hills of Lorraine. He noticed that their attempts at conversation were becoming increasingly fewer; words languished, died.

They looked at each other.

She, too, had only picked at her dinner, and he noticed with rising excitement that her lips had assumed a soft, almost vulnerable shape; her eyes blended, now, a sweet consternation, a kind of apprehension with their distant warmth, their glow. She looked down, defensively.

He leaned forward. 'Megan. Megan.'

Slowly the thick lashes rose. Her eyes met his.

He decided to gamble it all on one great throw. 'Will you . . . will you allow me to come to your compartment?'

There was a long silence, and he was stiff with suspense, chilly with fear. He had gone too fast. He had spoken too soon.

But to his utter stupefaction, she nodded, very slowly, the lights blazing on her fiery hair.

'As before . . . in half an hour,' she said softly, and smiled. It was that open, childlike smile again that tugged at his very heart.

'*Merci . . . merci.*' He spoke almost in a whisper, not sure she

332

could even hear him, but certain that she could see his astounded happiness beaming from his every feature.

He stood, staring after her, at the graceful sway of her departing figure, watching all the others gazing at her, too.

Les jeux sont faits, Megan thought. The dice are thrown. She must be mad.

She closed the invisible zipper on the amber robe of slipper satin, feeling its slick caress like alien hands upon her naked body.

At first, when he had stepped into the compartment, she rose to the challenge with a peculiar zest, an enjoyment she had not truly experienced for a very long time. To joust with the famous Flèche was almost as exciting as any hard-won prize in London or New York, in Switzerland or Italy, the Riviera or the coast of Spain.

Megan had read his earnest demeanour as additional evidence of his wiliness; Sagittaire was the best, just as she was, as his opposite. She had relished the continuation of the game in the dining car. She had planned to see just how far he'd go and then slip off the train just before Nancy.

But then he had looked at her like that across the table, wordlessly, his dark eyes hot and pleading in that lean, ascetic face. And against her will her celibate body ignited.

All of it came flooding back – the night at the villa, when he had stepped like a phantom out of the shadows into the moonlight to take her in that accusatory, strangely personal embrace. It had been an embrace, she knew now, and not an attempted capture.

And it went even farther back than that. It must have begun with her first sight of him in the casino at Monte when, stately and detached, he observed her over the clicking wheel among all those ordinary idlers.

Perhaps the doctor in Vienna had been right – she wanted him to capture her because she had sensed in him her absent father, her fated lover, her non-existent home. In all the years since Hugo there had been no one at all. Phenomenal, in these free-wheeling days when it was almost *de rigueur* for women to take lovers, to 'rid themselves of inhibitions'.

Well, she had 'sublimated', certainly; her passion for the theft of those fallen stars had appeased all other passions. She'd never found a single man, or woman, who could make her feel the way she did when she had escaped again after another perilous, self-assigned adventure.

The irony of it dazzled her. Sagittaire, of all the world of men, was being admitted to her compartment.

When she heard the discreet tap she was suddenly stricken with a cold and deep uncertainty. Would it be only an incident, or a beginning? A beginning like this could mean the end of everything she valued, the only life she had come to know. But there was no escape now, no honourable one. In some odd fashion she felt that she could not break her word.

Her hands were icy when she went to admit him.

He stepped into the compartment, sliding the door to again, gazing at her without a word. She stood quite still, looking up at him.

Slowly he reached out for her hand, even more slowly brought it to his lips. He turned it over and kissed the palm, with a tender, leisurely, lingering caress.

Amazed, she felt an instantaneous hotness, like a flash of heat lightning, skitter along her nerves with the pressure of his firm mouth on the skin of her palm; a low, burning ache stabbed her lower body with awful, stunning suddenness.

In utter silence he continued to stare at her with such open-hearted longing that she was dismayed, undone by the sweetness of it, by her runaway feelings. He raised her hand and held it against his face, still looking into her eyes, and his eyes were so deep and dark she could see a place to drown in them, to curl and hide in wakeful sleep.

Drugged with sweet strangeness she found her body moving forward, arms sliding around his hard neck, slowly still. He drew her in his circling arms with a balletic motion, as if to lead her to a fateful dance whose steps were grave and lyrical.

Her mouth began to open under his; with closed eyes she perceived his strong, delicate fingers stroking the quivering small of her back, and the low, aching fire in her renewed, all of her melting, gathering like the titanic dissolution of the mountains' hardened snow. His hands slid upward, kneading her shoulder blades, memorising the slender curve of her upper arms while their bodies ground into each other's, wildly.

Then the strong, tender fingers were lowered again to the inward arc of her waist, outward over the slight, soft curving of her hips, and she was dimly conscious that there could be no turning back.

He released her with a gasp of shuddering breath and stood back for an instant, his look like a kiss on her face and her hair, the shimmering length of the golden satin, from its high, stern collar to the patent swell of her breasts, the hint of curves and shallows and her long, slender legs inside the parted slits of the narrowly shining skirt.

Then, with his lightest of touches on her breasts, she gave a small, astonished cry. He seemed to read her wish.

His dark eyes gleamed. With a delicate, upward stroke and that grave reverence that marked his every gesture, his fingers reached her austere collar's fastening. He parted the collar tenderly and began to slide the gleaming zipper down; her alerted senses, even over the clack and drone of the train, caught that little sound, the distant insect-drone of the zipper's opening, and she quivered with a fearful, renewing excitement.

He bent and kissed her skin in every stage of its revelation, slowly sinking to his knees on the flowered carpet.

CHAPTER TWENTY-THREE

His fervent mouth caressed the bare skin of her feet, beginning on an upward path from her delicate ankles to her satiny knees.

The strong hands grasped the softness of her haunches; the magical, relentless mouth sought out and found the throbbing of her secret places, rhythmically caressing, with a savage steadiness, a fast-increasing tempo, and she began to shudder and cry out.

And there came to her such an ascending throb of pleasure, so sharp an intensity of utter need, that all the universe was centred on the narrowing blade of that demand, there was nothing, nothing left except the labouring flight to that high summit still to be attained; he knew, somehow he knew, assisting her, raising her, urging her there, with a steady and sweet, almost unendurable relentlessness.

With one last, frenzied stroke of ponderous, imagined wings she reached the perilous needle-space, stabbed with a blade of fire, hearing an outcry that she hardly knew was hers; then, vibrant, began to still, with her skin thrumming like the plucked strings of a metal instrument. Her limbs still shuddered; gently, quickly, he rose and urged her with his touch onto the bed.

Through half-closed lids she watched him extinguish the lights, hearing the rustle of discarded clothes, feeling in a moment the naked length of him pressed close to her, his wakened flesh upon her.

And there was a wild, new astonishment, a dazzlement of unbelief; her new desiring had not gone to sleep, not even after the dizzying flight, the momentary easing. For when their bodies were fully entwined, when he was closer than her very heart, she felt a whole new frenzy of flesh and bone and sinew, a fuller joy because this time they came to it together.

Lying tight in his embrace, she marvelled how the whole face of the world had changed for her without a word being spoken. That long silence had given the entire interlude the character of a dream, and yet it seemed more natural than speech.

Sagittaire was the first to break it, his voice resonant and deep with a quality she had never heard in it before. He raised one of his arms from around her and clasped her head to his chest with one of his big hands, murmuring, 'Since Nice . . . ever since Monte, really, I have pictured this, and called myself a fool a hundred times for doing so. Now that we are here together, it almost seems not to have happened, Megan. I cannot help wondering if mere mortals,' there was irony in his tenderness, 'can have so much.'

She could find no answer yet at all, but her lazy mouth opened against his moistened skin, replying with a kiss. She leaned her head back a little, looking up at him. His eyes were closed but, at the instant of the small caress, he responded by a gentle squeeze of her head, followed by a stroking of her bright, brief hair.

'I feel . . . I feel that I have entered an unknown country,' she spoke against him, groping for expression. 'I have been alone so long. Always, I think now.'

His gentle fingers continued to stroke her hair, and she turned her cheek to the blessed touch. He left his hand on her cheek for a while, then ran it slowly down her neck to her shoulder and over her upper arm. 'I know that,' he said. 'I felt it in you. Do you know what you reminded me of, that night at the villa?'

Her eyes were closed but she could feel him smiling. 'No.'

'A little street-child who had just copped something, laughing at the *flic* in Montmartre . . . which was my early beat, long ago . . . and running away.' Now he was tracing the relaxed mound of her hip. 'You have the most magnificent legs in Europe.'

336

She chuckled. '*Merci*. I cannot picture you as a lowly *flic*, Inspector. You were not always, then, the great Flèche of the Sûreté?'

Megan regretted the reference a little; she could feel a subtle withdrawal in his warm flesh, and when he answered her his voice was sad, less confiding.

'Oh, no. I came up through the ranks, completely ignoring the advantages of . . .'

'Yes? Of . . .?'

He kissed the top of her head. '*Rien*. It is nothing of any moment. I am babbling. But I was a very arrogant young fool in those days.' He laughed. 'And just as arrogant in these, although I hope a little less of a fool. So are you – arrogant, *c'est-à-dire* – and I admire that in you. We are very much akin, Megan Farley.'

'Yes. Yes, we are,' she agreed in a drowsy voice. They were silent for a time.

'I began my life of arrogance at birth,' he remarked, 'my career as a hunter for the law very early, too. And you, my dear one, when did you begin your life of blackest crime?' He emphasised the words slightly, in a comic way.

'When were you born?' she asked, evading him. 'What time of year?'

'In the last grey days of November, to match my odd Alsatian surname, as a matter of fact. Are you asking in the name of the stars?' He squeezed her shoulder.

'Perhaps. My grandmother gave credence to such things. She would say that you are my "fate".'

'That's what my mother would have said. You are a Gemini, then, I take it. The sign of thievery and evasion.' She stiffened. Sensitively he felt it, she supposed, because he murmured, 'I'm sorry', drawing her closer.

'Megan, little Megan, you arouse so many questions in me by your so-economical small comments. *Talk* to me, I beg of you. When you spoke of your grandmother, there was so much sadness in you. Will you not tell me something of your life . . . your family? Please.'

'Why? To gratify your policeman's curiosity?' Now the hand upon her body seemed like a stranger's hand and she was stricken with a chill of doubt, the first since he had come to her tonight.

'Megan, Megan. Come. Look at me, please.' He lifted her and stared earnestly into her eyes. 'No, not as a policeman. As a lover . . . as a friend, if you will.'

She was shamed by his tender seriousness. 'I'm sorry about that, Jean.'

He kissed her, and he was beaming. 'I like it so much when you call me by my name.' She returned his kiss with slowly rising desire, and suddenly he was holding her very tightly again to his body, their bodies beginning to move in a leisurely, excruciating contact of fast-heating skin and drumming pulse; they were making wordless sounds of need and longing.

And with what surely seemed a greater passion than before, they came together in new sweetness, already a new familiarity that dazzled, astounded her.

Afterwards again in silence they lay a little apart, only their hands touching. She reached to a shelf by the bed and held out her case of cigarettes. He nodded, his dark eyes heavy-lidded, a faint smile on his ascetic yet sensuous mouth. He took a cigarette. After she had taken hers, he lit them with the matches she gave him.

As he blew out a column of smoke, she studied the paradoxical features of his fine, handsome face. The thin upper lip bespoke discipline and strength, the slightly fuller lower one a leashed sensuality. But only the lower lip's softness and the expressive eyes gave away his power of emotion: the rest of the proud face had the look of sculpted granite, from the high, sloping brow and hawklike nose to the lean cheeks and stubborn jaw.

'Tell me about your people, little Megan. What is she like, the famous Vanessa Holder? I have heard her perform and she was magnificent. But I could not picture her dandling you on her knee.'

'She was never much of a dandler.' Megan grinned. 'But when I was a small child she was very kind . . . and a grand playmate for me.'

'In the city of New York?'

'In Africa.' And she began to tell him about the mines in Kimberley and Pretoria; the journey to New York. And, last, the beginning of the Game.

'*Quelle vie, quelle vie,*' he murmured. 'Remarkable. The small chameleon grew up on the African veld. What strange luxury and loneliness.'

'Oh, yes, I have been rich in that,' she remarked with a lightness she did not feel.

He moved towards her again, after putting out his cigarette, taking the smoking white cylinder from her hand and disposing of it as well. He held her very close, pressing his long, hard body against her, saying huskily, 'I could arrange to bankrupt you in that commodity.'

When she made no answer, he went on soberly, 'It has become my habit, unfortunately, to sound light when I speak of the things most serious to me. Forgive me. I was trying to say, in my awkward fashion, that I want you to come with me. Be with me, Megan. You know that what we have found we could never find with another.'

He studied her expression. 'You look at me so strangely. Do you find it grotesque, then, that a forty-year-old policeman tries to play Pelléas to your Mélisande?'

His smile was so melancholy that it touched her heart. She put out her hand and rubbed his cheek. 'There is nothing grotesque in this, Jean. There could never be. But there are . . . difficulties. Can you trust me – can I trust myself, for that matter – to adjust at once to domesticity in the Faubourg St Germain . . .'

He made a sound of surprise.

'. . . or somewhere like that, and . . .' Her voice trailed off. 'Why do you look at me like that?'

'How did you know where I live?' His question was as melancholy as his smile. 'Do I seem as . . . hidebound, as stuffy to you as all that?'

Her face was hot. She turned away to hide it in a shadow. 'No. Of course not.' All of a sudden she started to relive Antwerp and the Rue Chanson. Twelve years ago, another life. She'd thrown in her lot with Hugo because her body had become a slave to his, her mind a prey to self-deception.

Jean Sagittaire was not Hugo Bouwer; the Faubourg was far away from the Rue Chanson, on the other side of the symbolic Seine. And yet both men held the key to bondage. Her life, until this moment, had been unbearably lonely. But it had been hers. She was uncertain, even now, that she could leave it that abruptly . . . to stay with Jean Sagittaire of the Sûreté.

What if this, like Antwerp, were only the spell of an hour, dissipating in Paris? In these last hours his tenderest declarations, his gentlest questions, had had the character of an interrogation. He had said they were akin; perhaps he was driven, too, by another kind of demon. Maybe his failure to capture her in law had impelled him to capture her in the net of love.

'You are very silent,' he said tentatively. He did not touch her but she could feel the penetrating eyes' scrutiny.

'Yes.' She did not move from her shelter, thinking, it was so beautiful for a short while, until her distrust and doubt got stronger than any other feeling. Stronger than all was her reluctance to give up that life she'd loved so deeply. The cry of 'Not yet, not yet', rang in her ears.

'Megan . . . what are your plans, when you get to Paris?'

'I don't know yet. I have been thinking of going back to America.' That was a lie, but it would throw him off the track at least.

'I see.' She could hear, for all his control, a shakiness in his voice. 'You must forgive me for my . . . rash offers.' She turned and saw him smile, noticing the sad irony on his lean face. 'I was completely carried away, you see. I had no right to assume that you felt the same. It is just that in my whole long life I never knew anything like this with a woman, strange as that may seem to you.'

'Nor have I,' she said softly, touching his arm. 'And you know that well.'

'Then can we not make a small, tentative commitment . . . that you will allow me to see you again?'

'Of course.' She told the lie with ease. This was the way.

'And the Chameleon?'

'The Chameleon is dead. I told you that before.' This was the greatest and yet somehow the easiest deception of them all.

'Then I will leave you now, my Megan,' he said. 'I do it with extreme regret.'

She was exhilarated but very surprised. 'Why?'

'I do not wish to expose you to comment by staying here all night.'

Megan was touched by that courtly remark, and a bit amused. Surely *wagons-lits* attendants knew everything. It seemed an almost absurd precaution. At the same time it was an indication of the deep seriousness of this encounter. A man used such 'precautions' to protect someone he intended to marry. She had heard her grandfather hint that once to her grandmother when Megan overheard them talking.

When Sagittaire left her with a tender kiss, setting a rendezvous for breakfast in the dining car, she calmly promised to be there at the scheduled time.

But, after he had gone, she threw herself upon the bed again. Her mind was a whirl of doubts and indecision; her very skin still tingled from his nearness, with the remembered wonder of their bodies' meeting.

Was this what she had been seeking, all this time, as the Viennese had so stubbornly insisted – stealing love and security instead of gems, desperately trying to find sexual appeasement in that dangerous excitement?

She did not know. She could no longer tell.

But there was one thing, still, that haunted her. The night in Berlin, when twelve storeys above the street, she had suffered a quick failure of nerve. She had nearly fallen. But somehow she had come through, with the reward of splendid emeralds belonging to a general's pampered wife.

And she had to know if she could climb again. She had to. Until then she could not be sure of what she felt for Sagittaire; it could well be that her surrender to him was the resigned capitulation of defeat and terror.

The Chameleon had never known defeat, so far. When the time came she would throw down the gauntlet willingly. But not this way. Not yet.

On the other hand she was haunted by his wondrous skills, his open-hearted tenderness. She could be making the biggest mistake of her reckless life if she did not appear tomorrow morning.

So back and forth her cold doubts and her reluctance seesawed with her emotions. A long interval ensued before she came to her decision.

When she did she wasted no time at all. Her baggage was largely undisturbed: Michele Fournet and Marta Franz never unpacked more than was needed for the present, always ready to leave.

Neither did Marina Forlenzi. Megan dressed rapidly and took a black wig from a hidden compartment in one of the suitcases, with the Forlenzi passport, thankful that she had got rid of the pearls in Germany instead of waiting for a better price in Paris.

Concealing her hair under a turban-like hat, she rang for the attendant, telling him she had just remembered that she must stop in Nancy. From there she would hire a car, drive to the connection for the train to Basle. From Switzerland she would make her way to Milan.

By the time she descended at Nancy, most of the passengers on the train appeared to be deeply asleep; the blinds on their windows were all drawn.

There was one fleeting ache when she thought of Sagittaire. Then she walked quickly from the station.

Amas Holder felt inordinately tired that summer evening in 1932 when he entered the front door of the house, using his key. It had been a long time since they'd had a butler; like everyone else in America the Holders had tightened their belts. The country was just about at rock-bottom now, still reeling from the '29 crash, but with a glimmer of hope. Roosevelt was taking strong measures to combat the mess. It would have to get better.

But the last four years had taken a lot out of Amas. Like all the other stocks, Holder-Stirling plummeted. But the export part of their import-export trade had saved them, even making a profit. Selling American goods at cheaper prices abroad kept Holder-Stirling well above the water line.

Well, I have to remember I'll be seventy in December, Amas reflected, closing the door. A lot of men are in the box by that time. He counted his blessings.

One of them was always Vanessa. Amas tossed his hat on a side table and loosened his tie, damning that noose of civilisation that he had never got used to, never would, if he lived to be a hundred. Through the closed door of the library he thought he heard strange voices – a woman's and a young fellow's.

Damnation. He was in no mood for company. He was tempted to slip away upstairs until they'd left. But then Vanessa would worry about him, as she seemed to do a lot lately, when he didn't phone to let her know he'd be late. She was so sharp that even when he didn't mention being bone-tired she knew anyway.

Amas sighed and went to the double doors, pushing them open. 'Darling . . . how are you?'

Vanessa must have heard him come in; she was standing right by the doors, smiling at him. She kissed him on the cheek. She was such a refreshment to his eyes that at first he didn't look at the others in the room.

She looked as cool as a rainy garden in her slender two-piece dress of lavender blue and pale grey. It was impossible to credit that she had been sixty-six on her last birthday. He brief, curly hair was still thick and vital, a silver-white colour now. And, unlike so many other ageing women, she made no attempt to disguise her age, thereby managing to look twenty years younger than she was, with her wide, bright eyes and her barely lined skin.

'Fine,' he lied, smiling down at her, bending to kiss her cheek in turn.

When he looked up, preparing to meet the visitors, his heart gave an awful thump and his body felt an unaccustomed weakness.

Beatrice di Gamba was sitting on the sofa. Tony Holder, his grandson, was standing behind her, holding a cocktail glass.

'Good God!' Amas blurted out. 'Bea. Tony . . . where did you

342

spring from? Your father told us you'd just taken off, and he didn't even know where you were, a month or so ago.'

Taking no further notice of Bea, Amas crossed the room and held out his hand to Tony. He hadn't seen the boy in years, and he wasn't too sure that he liked what he was seeing now.

Tony had his mother's light flaxen hair and dark, glittering, oblique eyes. The eyes, they all knew, had by some genetic twist been inherited from Anjanette's unpleasant father. They had certainly not been bequeathed by Anjanette or any of the Holder strains. It seemed to Amas that the boy looked much younger than eighteen, and he had a somewhat bored and effete air totally unlike his father or his brother Clinton.

'I've been with Bea. I thought it would be a lark to come along with her to New York,' Tony drawled.

Amas could not prevent himself from saying, 'You're lucky, then. We haven't been enjoying many "larks" in this country lately.'

A side glance at Vanessa revealed to Amas that her calm demeanour was mostly assumed; there was a sharp tension under her half-smile. She frowned faintly at Amas' bluntness, yet he could read, from long practice, a glint of approval in her eyes.

'Amas, you never change. Still the same rough diamond.' Beatrice smiled and he realised for the first time, with a good look at her, that she had become unattractively stout. Her narrow black dress could not disguise the spread of her haunches, the bulge of her belly. And her piercing black eyes, more than ever, looked like those of a giant bee. Her short hair was patently dyed, for it was still jet black, and she was a year older than Vanessa.

That blackness was harsh against her lined, painted skin, and Amas noticed that when she smiled her teeth were not her own. Deep lines rayed out from her carmined lips. The woman had become a horror.

'Amas, let me give you something,' Vanessa intervened. 'Do you want a drink . . . or lemonade?'

'Lemonade, please.' He smiled at her, noticing that she looked concerned at his choice. Lately he'd thought it wiser to give up his evening cocktail, ever since his heart had started acting so strangely. This minute evidence of Vanessa's unvarying anxiety and love affected him so strongly that for a minute he could hardly gather his thoughts.

But he sank down in a chair opposite Bea and, taking a sip of lemonade, asked as neutrally as he could manage, 'What brings you back, Bea? It's hardly the happiest time to See America First, the way things are now.'

They hadn't heard from her in years. The only contact had been through her lawyers, in business matters. In '29 when the stocks had fallen Amas had scraped up everything and offered to buy her out. Cannily she'd refused. And then when the stocks rallied a little, he hadn't been able to afford it; most of their capital had gone into survival. Furthermore, last year international diamond trading had been suspended because of the world markets' depression. He wondered what the hell she was plotting now.

'I've come to talk business,' Bea said flatly. 'What with one thing and another, I didn't get by the office today, so I thought I'd catch you here.'

He had to admire her lack of pretence. It would have been grotesque for any of them to pretend they were overjoyed by the visit. Amas had never got over what Martin had told him. He had eventually confided that to Vanessa. Intuitively guessing that he was keeping something vital from her, she had finally got it out of him. Ever since the two of them could remember, they had suffered because of this bitch – in latter years, knowing that Bea was privy to the whereabouts of Megan, when she'd sent them that cable about her accident, not knowing they'd already received Megan's; now the additional blow of Tony's hanging around her rotten Riviera set. Already, Amas thought, the boy was marked by it.

'Well, I'm here,' he responded curtly. 'Let's get to it.'

Bea laughed shrilly. 'Amas, you are really wonderful. Twenty years of civilisation have passed right over you, not touching you at all.'

Vanessa made an involuntary motion; her face was tight with anger.

But Bea went on, her voice becoming flat and hard again. 'I've come to make you an offer. I'll sell you my shares . . . at a very good price.'

'What's the catch?'

'That you won't tell Martin where Tony is.'

Amas glanced at the boy; he was smiling. When he looked at Vanessa, she had paled.

'Why do you want that, Tony?' Ignoring Bea for the moment. Amas confronted his grandson.

'Because with Bea I can live my own life,' Tony drawled. 'Mother and Dad . . . and my wonderful, upright brother,' he added sarcas-

344

tically, 'won't ever leave me alone. They won't ever let me be myself.'

'And what is that, Tony?' Vanessa spoke for the first time; her question was soft, but her voice trembled.

The boy had the grace to look chagrined. 'Just myself, that's all,' he mumbled. His tanned face darkened with a rush of blood.

'It's no deal, Beatrice,' Amas said coldly.

'I thought it would be worth anything to you to get me out of your hair,' Bea said sharply.

'It is . . . practically. Anything except the destruction of my grandson. You killed Sam Dillon and Prince . . . you tried to destroy me and my whole family. You're not going to do it to Tony, at least not with my help.'

'What the hell does all *that* mean?' Tony cried to Bea. 'What is all this damned *bourgeois* nonsense?'

'Never mind, *mon cher*.' The look that Bea exchanged with Tony chilled Amas' blood, and he saw that Vanessa had her hands clenched into fists. She was quivering, and as white as paper.

God in heaven, Amas thought, is that boy sleeping with this old painted witch, as Martin had been tricked into doing? He felt sick at his stomach, and now there was a big clenching fist of pain in his chest.

'Get out of here,' he said tightly. 'Just get out, Bea. Tony, you stay here.'

'I'll be damned if I will,' the boy retorted. Enraged at his impudence, Amas got up and was on him in two strides. He grabbed Tony by his collar and slapped him across the face.

Tony reeled backwards in shock. But then a mocking smile curved his weak young mouth. 'Thanks for the welcome, Grandad. Come on, Bea, let's get out of here.'

'With pleasure, sweetheart.' Bea hauled herself up from the sofa and grinned at Amas and Vanessa. He noticed even in his ire and shame that she looked still more grotesque standing. Her lumpy body bulged under her smart black ensemble, and the resemblance of that swollen body to a bee's was very pronounced, filling Amas with a kind of horror.

'But first,' Bea added with poisonous sweetness, 'I must deliver a message. From a very old friend of yours – Mitchell Farley.'

Amas and Vanessa were both speechless.

'Mitchell has been a frequent visitor of mine,' Bea continued, smiling. 'In my set he has also found the freedom to . . . be himself.

And he and Tony have a great deal in common, as uncle and nephew. You might say he's acting as Tony's . . . tutor.'

With a toss of her head she went to the double doors and slid them open. Tony followed without another word or look.

They heard the front door slam.

And suddenly the fist in Amas' chest tautened, clenching ever tighter. The big fist struck him, and he felt a quick, sharp, stabbing pain before he was conscious of nothing more, except Vanessa's outcry of sheer terror.

When he came to he was in bed, in the master bedroom. He opened his eyes, disoriented, seeing Vanessa's face close to his. Her red-rimmed eyes and anxious expression evidenced a long, wearisome vigil.

Amas gathered that he had been medicated; his sight was fuzzy, he felt limp, overcome with languor. 'What time is it?'

Vanessa's worried eyes brightened and a smile broke out over her face, lighting every feature. 'Thank God.' She sat carefully down on the edge of the bed and put her hand to his face. 'It's late,' she replied to his question, her hand quivering against his cheek. 'Nearly ten. Oh, Amas.'

She leaned over and kissed him. He tried to raise his arms to embrace her, but they felt heavier than iron. 'Good Lord, what's the matter with me?'

'Dr Cleary said you had a heart attack. Not a grave one, he told me. But enough to frighten me out of my wits.' She gave him a trembly smile. 'He'll be back in the morning. Meanwhile he says you've got to stay in bed for a few days.'

'A few *days*! God almighty, I'll go out of my mind.' He struggled to sit up. She put her hands on his chest, and urged him to lie down again. He obeyed without protest.

'What in hell did he give me?' he demanded weakly. 'I can hardly keep my eyes open, and sitting up is like lifting a dumbbell.'

'A mild sedative,' she answered softly. 'That's the way you're supposed to feel. Cleary said you'd overworked until you're exhausted, that any other man your age would have been dead by now; that you have the constitution of an "ox", I'm happy to report.'

'I *am* tired,' he admitted. 'Awfully tired. But I know I'll be all right by morning. I'll be damned if I'm going to lie here for *days*.' Already, however, his lids were becoming heavily weighted, and he was having trouble seeing her now.

'We'll talk about it tomorrow,' she hedged. 'Now go to sleep, darling.'

'But what about the office?' he mumbled. 'There are things tomorrow I've got to . . . '

'I'm going in myself,' she reassured him.

'*You*?' He smiled, his eyes nearly closed now. 'And what are you going to do about it, Madam?'

'Don't be smart, Amas Holder. Do you think I've been deaf all these years when you've talked to me about the business . . . deaf and dumb?' Her tender eyes belied the sharpness of her tone.

'All right,' he said, his voice so thick by now he could barely enunciate. He slipped away in peaceful waves of darkness.

When he woke up again, the room was bright with sun, and Vanessa and Cleary were standing by his bed.

'Well, hello,' Amas said. He slid up a bit in the bed, feeling stronger and wide awake compared to the heavy drowsiness of the night before.

'How are you feeling?' Cleary asked him, opening his pyjama top to position his stethoscope.

'Great,' Amas lied. He still felt weak and tired.

'Oh, sure.' Cleary was not taken in. 'Now, be quiet.' He moved the instrument over Amas' chest and back, listening intently.

Cleary straightened up, putting the stethoscope back in his bag. 'Not bad, I must say. However, I'm coming again tonight, and if it's not a lot better I'm going to send you to the hospital for tests.'

'I don't have time for that,' Amas grumbled.

'Oh, yes you do. Mrs Holder told me she went in this morning to your office, and she's going back this afternoon for a while. From the way she talks, I'd say the place will be in good hands. I'll put it this way – you have complete freedom of choice in this matter.'

'Oh?' Amas inquired drily. 'And what might that be?'

'You can stay in bed for a couple of days, take it easy for two weeks; or you can go back to work right now, and die.'

Amas heard Vanessa gasp, saw her face breaking up. Cleary's bluntness was not pleasant, Amas thought, but he never minced his words. That was the very thing that made Amas respect him so much. It also made him willing to listen.

'Sorry, Mrs Holder.' Cleary turned his back on Amas and spoke to Vanessa. 'He's a hard case; I had to put it that way.'

'I realise that.' Vanessa sank down in a chair, in better control. 'You heard him, Amas.'

His eyes met hers. 'I heard him. Don't worry, honey. He's sold me.' He was almost pained by her look of relief. 'Tell me, doctor, will it put me under the grass to have a conference with my wife every day, about the business?'

'Hardly.' The doctor's sharp eyes twinkled. 'Not if you don't get yourself in an uproar. It's the pressured atmosphere of the office, with the phones, the schedules . . . and the Stock Exchange . . . that worries me. I don't want any conferences with your brokers for a while. Let Mrs Holder and the lawyers handle that. You must have some good men you can rely on, for heaven's sake. Why do you pay them otherwise?'

Amas had to laugh at Cleary's acerbity. He'd always liked this fellow; in some ways they were two of a kind.

'You've got me there, all right. I do, of course. But it's a pretty sad thing to feel totally inessential.'

'I wouldn't worry about that. Just don't let your vanity kill you, that's all. You're pretty damned essential to this lady. Put that in your pipe and smoke it.'

The crusty doctor got up and lifted his bag. 'I'll see you this evening. Take it easy – or else, Amas.'

He stomped out of the room.

Amas met Vanessa's eyes and they both laughed. But he couldn't help noticing that her laugh wasn't as hearty as his, that under her calm demeanour there was a gnawing anxiety.

'Please, my darling, don't worry. I'll follow his orders to the letter, this time. I swear it.'

'You've got to.' She came to him and sat lightly on the bed, kissing his forehead and cheek. 'If anything happened to you, Amas . . . I can't even think about it. If you have any love for me at all – promise me, Amas. Promise me to be careful.'

'I promise.' He turned his head so his lips could find her mouth.

It was a full three weeks before he felt like himself again, but even at that point he was advised by Cleary to go in to the office no more than two days a week. He chafed under that routine, but Vanessa was taking hold wonderfully, and mingled with his pride in her was a kind of relief.

He was tired of it all – not so much physically, now that he was recuperating, but he found in himself a profound mental tiredness that would not go away.

About a month later, after they had returned together from the

348

office, Vanessa remarked casually what a shame it was that diamond trading had been suspended.

'It makes it so dull for Martin,' she commented.

Amas grinned. 'You're leading up to something, my dear. Why not go on and spill it?'

'I can't ever keep anything from you, can I?'

'Not much. What are you leading up to?'

'How would you feel if Martin took over Holder-Stirling?' she asked abruptly.

He was really surprised. 'I've never thought of it. But, what about Africa? He loves it there . . . so does Anjanette.'

'You'd be surprised about Anjanette, Amas. Don't you remember how she loved it here on their last visit? It's been a long time since London. I have a feeling she thinks she's been missing a lot out there.'

'And Martin?'

'You know as well as I do he's always loved cities . . . he only went back for Anjanette's sake. He was wild about London; he loves New York. I think she realises something else – how much she's deprived Martin of by taking him away from a big city. She wrote me that, just the other week. What do you think, Amas?'

'I think it sounds good,' he said, feeling exhilarated. 'To be free of it at last, perhaps to . . .

'Then I'll write to them now,' she said excitedly.

'And what about us? Will you plant me on a golf course somewhere and go on with your work?' he asked her, only half in jest.

She looked at him with a glowing, serious expression. 'I have better plans than that for us, Amas Holder. I'll tell you about them when we hear from Martin.'

He was delighted but puzzled over her mysterious, stimulated air.

CHAPTER TWENTY-FOUR

Jean Sagittaire built up the fire in the grate of his austere living room, with the strains of Prokofiev climbing, crashing into gold and scarlet brasses from the phonograph. He poured himself a *fine* and sat down in a winged chair by the fire, preparing to forget that it was Christmas Eve.

A grown man should not be so strongly affected by a thing like a holiday, he ridiculed himself. Certainly there was nothing in the flat to remind him; it was barer, more cell-like than ever, now that the visits of Berthe had ended. Nothing to remind him but his overweening loneliness. Even the crooks were going home tonight to their families, he reflected with a sardonic smile. They had already done all their stealing for the occasion.

He could have stayed at the office, of course, but somehow the thought made his gorge rise. And inevitably he remembered the Christmases of his childhood in Alsace, the warmth and the closeness and the gaiety. The de Lilles had pressed him to spend the holiday at the château and he had been almost tempted. But in the last analysis, when he considered his alienation from them and their circumscribed life, he had known it would be futile. It had been a duty invitation, anyway, simply because he was the present Comte de Lille; a reminder that his own duty lay in a holiday appearance at the gloomy ancestral pile.

The recorded piece had reached that antic progression of notes that inevitably reminded him of a harlequin at mischief; he should not have chosen the Prokofiev. It painted too clear and painful an image of Megan Farley.

Idiotic, to keep brooding on that interlude. She had failed the little test he had set up for her. His memory drifted back to that spring night, his own half-hopeful, half-cynical face pressed to the window of his compartment, peering through the slightly parted blind. And he had seen her disembark stealthily at Nancy. He had not left her for the reason he gave – only one of the stuffier de Lilles would have been impelled by that hypocritical motive – but to see if she would go or stay.

Well, he'd seen. His pain and disappointment had been intense. A disappointment of his vanity as much as anything else, a dismay that

Flèche could have lost again. He'd been a bigger fool later, even going to Milan on a thin pretext to follow up that theft at the big hotel. Again, there had been no trace of Megan Farley. It was time he forgot, and let it die.

It was late enough to go to bed. He was certainly tired, after the usual spate of pre-holiday crimes, wearily prepared for those that would result from tomorrow's family quarrels and certain criminals taking advantage of the general air of relaxation. He'd invent an excuse to go to the bureau; that would pass the time.

There was always sufficient work to do. These days, besides the old-fashioned crimes – which Sagittaire had come almost to regard with affection – there was the new political guerrilla warfare on the streets of Paris, where the royalists and socialists were beginning to fight out their differences.

France had her own traditions of liberty and freedom, not like the Anglo-Saxons, with their development of parliamentary forms, but derived from the combats and uprisings of French politics in the tradition of the Revolution nearly a hundred and fifty years old. Small revolutions, inflamed by the threat of that fellow Hitler, were gathering momentum.

A policeman's lot was indeed not a happy one. Turning off the phonograph, Sagittaire began to whistle the Gilbert and Sullivan air, but the whistle sounded so lonely he stopped. He poured another small *fine* and swallowed it quickly. Then he knelt down to check the firescreen again, making certain it was secure. He'd leave the blaze burning. The freezing wind outside, the quiet night, made him feel unusually cold, though customarily he liked the winter.

He was startled by the sound of his bell. It was hard to imagine who could be ringing; Sagittaire was not one of those who encouraged droppers-in.

He got up and strolled to the door, glancing through the peephole. The opening was high to match his inordinate height; he could see nothing. Then he looked down.

An unbelieving exclamation broke from him. He saw a woman's hat, a small, dark, snug affair like a brown helmet, strands of dark gold hair escaping over the brow. Then the eyes – wide, uncertain amber eyes with thick brown lashes. Sagittaire thought he was suffering from an hallucination. It could not be; it was too wildly improbable.

But the bell had not been imagined.

Still staring, he saw the neat head turn. She was going away. Good

351

God, she was leaving. He had waited too long to answer, in his bemusement.

He snatched open the door and called out, 'Wait! Megan . . . wait!' He stepped into the carpeted hall.

She was standing by the lift; arrested like a surprised deer, she turned her head. He drew in his breath sharply, overcome by her beauty.

From head to toe she was dressed in a rich, sombre brown velvet, the sleeves of her coat cuffed in tawny fur that echoed the colours of her hair and eyes, the small, delicate face framed in a towering collar of the same autumnal fur.

The short, curling tendrils of hair escaping from the velvet turban were a warm, rich golden-bronze, with the gleam of ancient, polished brass.

He strode towards her and said softly, 'Please. Do not run away this time. At least come in and get warm.'

She gave him a hesitant smile and murmured, 'I should not have come like this at all. It is unforgivable. I didn't even know whether you would be . . . alone.' She still looked ready to flee.

'I am alone,' he said soberly. 'Almost always.' He stared into the wonderful eyes and caught from them a hesitant glimmer of change. Her body relaxed a trifle.

'Alone . . . on Christmas Eve?' She smiled that childlike smile he had never forgotten, the one that had the power to drag upon his very heart, speaking with a hint of a teasing manner.

'You, too, are alone on Christmas Eve,' he countered. 'Therefore I see no reason why you should not come in.' He held out his hand. She put her gauntleted fingers in his and even through the thick cloth he could perceive that odd, electric flow between their two bodies. From her expression of surprise he sensed that she had felt it, too. 'Come,' he repeated.

Letting her hand remain in his, she walked down the hall beside him to the door of the flat, which was still ajar. He pushed it open, gesturing for her to enter.

Her amber eyes lit first on the orange fire, then she glanced about with curiosity and something like pity. It was as if she knew at once what his whole life was from the look of the room. And he was struck anew with their remarkable and peculiar kinship, after so many months' absence the quick meeting of their thoughts.

He closed the door soundlessly, watching her. She was standing with her back to him before the grate, and her slender outline, the vulnerable look of the small head in its *chic* velvet covering, struck his every nerve.

'May I take your coat?' he asked her formally.

She nodded, without moving. He walked towards her and she turned, unfastening the garment. He removed it from her; the lining was warm from her body, and he felt again that rising, running heat, that racing excitement along the fuses of his veins.

Coatless, her slender, curving body was revealed in all its perfection under a close-fitting, simple brown velvet dress, its floating hem like a flower's petals.

'Take off your hat,' he suggested gently. She pulled the small turban from her hair, its bronze gleam vivid above the sombre colour of the dress, her amber gaze regaining more certainty as he smiled at her.

He laid the coat carefully over a chair and placed her little hat upon it. 'Will you have a drink?' He was still speaking in that cautious, formal way, absurdly afraid of scaring her off by revealing the tumult of his feeling.

'Yes. Thank you.'

'A *fine?*' He began to wonder just how long he could maintain this charade, but he warned himself to go slow.

'*Parfait*. I am so cold.' She smiled less certainly this time, and yet he wondered if there were some kind of invitation in the statement. His hopes shot up, suddenly as high as that Piccard fellow's stratosphere balloon, and he himself was smiling.

'We will remedy that.' A bit unsteadily he poured the brandy into a tiny crystal stem, one of the treasured bits he had brought back from Alsace.

She took it from his fingers with murmured thanks, regarding the little goblet with appreciation before she sipped from it. Her look met his for the space of a heartbeat over the delicate rim.

'Please,' he said. 'Sit down.' He was still holding on desperately to his calm. She did so, putting the glass down on a table without a sound.

He sat down beside her, trying not to lean towards her, asking quietly, 'Why have you come?' He could contain that burning question no longer.

'Because I have been racing and hiding, floundering. I have come to surrender, now that it may be too late.' Her voice quivered over the final words.

He shook his head slowly, in dazzled disbelief. He could find no word at all sufficient to dispute her. His reply was to gather her into his arms, devouring her soft, vulnerable mouth with his.

Finally, he whispered, 'It would never be too late.'

After that, there seemed to be no need for talk between them; the small flame that had been ignited in the casino, and burned brighter in the pale light of the moon outside the villa, blazing into that conflagration on the spring night in Lorraine, leaped higher now in the Paris winter, consuming them with greater force than either had imagined.

Gently he urged her upright with his hands, and they walked very close together towards the boudoir of the flat.

He stood for a long moment in the morning, watching her in sleep, overjoyed now that he had done that quixotic thing – taking possession of the de Lille jewels from the bank. What a splendid Christmas he would give her now.

Feeling like the Alsatian boy who had stolen into his mother's room and put his modest gifts upon her bed, Jean Sagittaire opened the casket of de Lille gems. Very quietly he began to lay them about Megan on the bed – the lovely *parure* of topaz and pearl, that was set with his birthstone and hers; the sets of rubies and aquamarines, diamonds and emeralds and amethysts.

It was done, this lovely absurdity, this thing he'd dreamed of doing for the last seven months . . . and on such a perfect day. The grey of yesterday's skies was gone; through the narrow, curtained windows there was a brilliant stream of December sun.

He waited. Her eyes were opening. She saw him and smiled, moving her small hand on the coverlet. Her fingers struck the necklace of topaz and pearls; the matching ear-drops made a minuscule chinking sound when they touched the necklace. She stared at them, and then all around herself at the gem-laden bed.

She blinked. 'What . . . what is this, Jean?'

His heart, as always, warmed with her use of his *petit nom*, his given name. He was not Flèche now, not at this moment, and she was no longer the Chameleon. They were lovers, close, sweetly familiar, warm.

'The ancestral baubles of the family de Lille,' he intoned with a comic solemnity. 'For the future comtesse.'

'Comtesse . . .?'

'A dark secret I have kept from you.' He grinned. 'Of course, these don't come up to the booty of the Chameleon . . . but I think they'll have to do.'

'I think,' she said softly, with a glowing look, 'that it's time for me to give you your gift. Please . . . bring me my bag from the living room.'

Mystified but smiling, he obeyed. When he returned and handed it to her she reached into its depths and brought out the François pendant, that famous piece containing the enormous Holder diamond. Grinning, Megan held it out to him.

With trembling fingers he accepted the pendant, staring at her with astonishment.

'I think,' she said softly, 'that this is what you always wanted, even more than me – the ultimate symbol of the triumph of Flèche.'

'*Inexacte.*' The brief, precise word sounded indescribably tender now. He tossed the pendant on the bed and, leaning forward, took her face between his hands. 'I have never in all my misspent life wanted anything as much as you, my Megan.' Their kiss, this time, had a sweetness beyond all longing and passion. When he was able to speak, he murmured, 'This item will be anonymously returned to its owner. And you were wrong, my love; it is not the symbol of my triumph. It is the ultimate sign of your love for me.'

With that all his questions were answered; as he took her in his embrace he knew, for certain, that their long, cold loneliness had come to its final end.

Amas heaved a great sigh of content and leaned his grey head back on the tapestried sofa in the grand salon of the *Île de France*.

'This was a fine idea,' he said to Vanessa. They were sitting close together, completely alone in the vast salon with its towering, gilt-corniced columns, fantastic mirrored walls and clusters of cut-velvet chairs. Most of the other passengers were still on deck, waving to those who were waiting on the pier for the enormous liner to sail from New York harbour. 'It's a far cry from the *Walmer*, though.'

She laughed, elated by his look of returning health. The last nine months had been hectic, anxious ones, months when she had the persistent feeling that they rode a bubble about to break. But it hadn't . . . not yet. America was recovering a little from the big depression, but Europe was heading inevitably towards war. And diamond trading was still suspended. But Amas, the centre of her life, was regaining his strength day after day. Vanessa's world still revolved on its axis, because he was alive.

'Not that far,' she responded wickedly, giving his hand a squeeze. He laughed again and the hearty sound of it reassured her.

'I still can't believe it,' she murmured. 'It was just too good to be true, too tidy to accept.'

'Martin, you mean.'

'Yes.' She looked up at the huge, circular chandelier; the salon was exactly like a room in a castle. 'Swapping houses, even.' Smiling, she turned back to him and their glances locked for an instant; she could read an incredulity there as strong as hers.

'How will it feel, to be living in the house at Kimberley again?' he asked her soberly. 'Vanessa, you are giving up so much.'

'Giving *up* . . .' She leaned over and kissed his face. 'You gave me my life, Amas Holder, nearly fifty years ago. What kind of exchange is this?'

'Uneven,' he said ruefully. 'But God, it will be good to see it again.' After a moment's silence he asked her anxiously, 'Can you really cope with the African summer? You remember what it was like in February.'

'I did before,' she said calmly. Then of course she'd been a girl and not sixty-seven years old. But she dismissed the thought and remarked, with incipient laughter bubbling in her, 'What I can't accept is Megan as Madame Sagittaire.'

'It proves my pet theory – crime does pay, every time, in the end.' His grin was so young it astonished her.

'Don't start again with those tales of the road, Amas Holder. I can tell them better than you can by now.'

They were companionably silent, the sounds of merriment, the uproar of voices, the bustle of comings and goings drifting to them faintly from the mighty decks.

Vanessa let her hand lie in his, closing her eyes, recalling their wonder over Megan's long, thick letter, revealing that on the twenty-seventh day of December she had become Madame Jean Sagittaire, the Comtesse de Lille. It was all such a splendid joke, an almost cosmic one, but they sobered at the description of her happiness. No one, thought Vanessa, would ever know now that Megan had been the elusive Chameleon; no one but the Sagittaires and Holders. Vanessa hoped fervently that their perilous joy could be maintained.

She was dismayed at the sombre direction of her thoughts, in the midst of all these triumphs. She must concentrate on their arrival in Le Havre, their visit to Paris and to Lorraine; the reunion with Megan, who seemed, in her letters, to have become again the loving child Vanessa remembered from so long ago.

'Did you ever think, when you were brawling in Mexico and

Brazil, that someday you'd have a great-grandchild with a title?'

Amas chuckled. 'Not in a million years. I never thought I'd have a great-grandchild at all. Say, it's nice about Clint, isn't it?'

Martin's son Clinton had elected to stay in Africa. 'It's wonderful.'

'Before we decided to go,' Amas confided, 'I was thinking, well, at least there'll be one Holder left in Africa. Now there'll be three of them.'

'There will always be a Holder in Africa, Amas.'

When she saw the anticipation and the grateful love in his eyes, Vanessa was surer than ever that they had made the right decision.

'Madame Sagittaire, *pardon*.' The head waiter was hovering over Megan's table.

'Yes, Henri?' She smiled up at him; he had become such a familiar fixture in their lives, because they dined here so frequently.

'Monseur l'Inspecteur has telephoned, Madame. He regrets . . .'

'. . . that he will not be able to keep our engagement. An emergency has arisen; he may be late returning home.'

Henri beamed at her. 'Precisely. Madame has learned the art of life, very young.'

'And that is?'

'The art of gracious acceptance.' Henri bowed to express his admiration for her amiable resignation, her great good nature. 'You will nevertheless dine?'

'I will, nevertheless, dine.' She made her selections, and Henri beamed even more until he was fairly incandescent. He approved highly of her abstemious but delicate taste.

She took another sip of her cocktail, quite at ease alone in the luxurious restaurant. People had been staring at her for so long that being the wife of the famous Sagittaire, who had also recently come into his title, had not made that much difference.

All the difference was interior, because she bloomed with happiness. If that inner light broke through she was hardly aware of it. She knew only that she was so happy these days that the very air through which she moved was vibrant. In the three months of their marriage, not quite even that, Megan had become utterly inured to Flèche's demanding schedule.

She smiled to herself; she had come to call him Flèche both because it suited him so well, and amused him, and also for the secret it symbolised, that secret shared only with Amas and Vanessa.

Now, she thought, as the waiter set down her dinner before her, there is another marvellous secret to be shared. Or so she suspected. She was almost sure. Her body had already given her a sign that she might be pregnant. Tonight was to have been a form of celebration.

Just as well, however. It was better to be sure first. All the same she would not order champagne to drink alone. They would have it together when she knew. She was so gladdened, picturing his pleasure, that the waiter blinked a little in the light of her dazzling smile, which she felt like awarding to the whole world.

But the smile faded when she noticed the trio entering the softly lit room – an old, obscenely fat woman with black dyed hair, grotesquely got up in a black ruffled dress and a Spanish mantilla that was cruel to her lined, painted skin; an effete young man with limp, too-long hair and an older man of the same type, big, soft-jowled, his hair also dyed, smoking a cigarette in a long, thin holder and gesturing with his fat, beringed hands.

The dreadful old woman was Beatrice di Gamba; the young man, hardly recognisable now, was her cousin Tony Holder. The older man looked uncomfortably familiar, somehow; she wondered if he had been one of the denizens of the villa in Nice.

Megan, with an almost religious fervour, sent up a kind of prayer of thanksgiving for Flèche's inability to dine. His worldliness would allow him to take such a meeting without surprise and with a certain amusement, but she herself was ashamed of her own shame that these grotesques were her relatives.

She turned her head, looking away from them, but it was no use. She heard Bea's shrill call, sensed heads turning all around them, to survey this strange trio.

'It's Megan!' Beatrice shrieked. 'Little Megan.' The three came trailing towards Megan's table. She thanked whatever gods might be that it was a table for two, that there was no possibility of their joining her.

'My dear!' Bea effused, leaning to plant a moist kiss on Megan's cheek, leaving without doubt a streak of oily carmine there. 'What a marvellous surprise!'

'Bea.' Megan tried to smile, but she was assailed by a sudden, hideous realisation – she had always suspected Bea knew that she was the Chameleon. She deserved a lot of credit for keeping her mouth shut. However, after learning the true state of things from Vanessa in their recent voluminous correspondence, Megan had had an uneasy feeling that Bea might use her suspicions as some kind of club over the Holders. Bea, after all, was *capable du tout*. 'How are you?' Megan asked rather inadequately.

'My dear, you have become positively British.' Bea smiled brightly, revealing yellowed bridges. 'What a greeting after all these years! But you remember Tony, don't you, my dear?'

'Tony.' Megan smiled at him. He did not return her smile, merely regarding her with his heavy-lidded eyes. She wondered if he were taking some kind of opiates; his eyeballs were jaundiced and his colour unhealthy, almost green. 'How have you been?'

'Top hole,' he murmured languidly. He took the older man's hand with a bold, defiant gesture.

Bea bridled. 'And this is someone you don't know, that you *must* know, Megan. This is your father, Mitchell Farley.'

Megan stared up at the soft-faced, strangely accoutred person, for an instant incapable of speech. This . . . this was her father, the man who had driven her mother to suicide, who had deserted her when she was a baby only a few days old. One of the old grotesques in the set of Beatrice di Gamba.

Delayed shock exploded in Megan's body, waves of trembling weakness washing over her.

'Really, Bea,' Mitchell Farley drawled, 'you are sudden. I had hoped to break the news a little better than that.' Dazed, Megan noticed that one of his ears was pierced and he actually seemed to be wearing some kind of liquid powder over his ruined skin.

'Will you . . . won't you sit down?' Megan gasped, endeavouring to hold onto her senses. She no longer knew whether she was going to cry or to break out in hysterical laughter. Either would be horrible.

'Yes. That's very sweet of you.' Farley sank down heavily into the opposite chair, with a sigh of satisfaction. 'My shoes are pinching me horribly. Trying to stay young, my dear child, is a wretched task.'

'We'll go along to our table,' Bea fluted; her dark, rapacious eyes shone like a fed predator's. Megan recalled too well how she had always enjoyed making mischief wherever she had been. 'This is probably the last time we'll see you before we're off to Rome,' Bea went on. 'This is just a flying visit.' Megan felt even weaker with new relief; she hoped that Bea would never return to Paris.

'I hope that you will enjoy Rome,' she managed. Then slowly she turned her head to confront this man who was her father.

'I will not join you for long, Megan.' His bloodshot eyes regarded her with something like pity and a distant tenderness. 'I would not have told you who I am. But the Queen Bee, as you know, will reach out of her coffin and scratch the pallbearers.'

For the first time Megan felt genuine amusement. But she still did not know how to answer.

'I am not so far gone,' he continued, 'that I wish to confront you with an ageing freak claiming paternity. But many times, over the years, I have been very sorry for what I did to you, and to your mother. I want you at least to know that.'

He was so pathetic, so abject and woebegone that she could not help being moved. She reached across the table and touched his hand. 'It's all right. It's all right now. It was so long ago . . . Father.'

The bloodshot eyes moistened. He cleared his throat. Without another word he pushed back his chair and rose, bowing to her. And when he walked off she imagined that his back was somewhat straighter.

She knew that she must leave at once. She was almost ill with conflicting emotions. She signalled for the bill and hurried out. When a taxi was hurtling her towards the Faubourg flat, she said to herself over and over: the bad old days are gone. It is likely that I will never see any of them again.

She almost wondered if there could be hope for her, with such blood in her veins – with such a father, and a mother who had not had the courage to live.

But then she thought of Amas and Vanessa . . . of Clint and Anjanette and Martin. The blood of Amas Holder also flowed in her veins, and would sustain her, and her son . . . or daughter. And soon Amas and Vanessa would arrive.

When Flèche let himself into the flat late that night, she surprised even him, although he was happily used to affectionate welcomes, with the fervour of her delight at coming into his arms again.

CHAPTER TWENTY-FIVE

Giorgio watched from across the street. The old *cornacchia*, the fat old crow, was throwing enough in the Trevi Fountain to keep him for a week. And those two, those *scherzi di natura*, were with her, as usual. He wished they would leave her.

He had started to approach the men once but then his cousin, the teller at the bank, said the old *cornacchia* had the money; she had even bought herself a prince years ago and called herself the Principessa di Gamba. Some princess. Giorgio's full young mouth twisted in his handsome face. He'd be out of these rags tomorrow if he played his cards right.

Finally the three foreign *capricci* started moving off and Giorgio followed at a safe distance, darting in and out of the shadows like a lizard. He hoped the *scherzi* wouldn't go upstairs with the old bitch tonight. Giorgio had found out plenty from the maid, using the ways he knew so well, and he had discovered that the two servants left at night, so the old one was all alone.

He paused again when they got to her gate. 'You'd better lock up, old girl,' he heard the older man saying to the woman in his bad Italian. They were always showing off by speaking it, when any fool tourist knew that most Romans had learned their way around in English.

The *cornacchia* just laughed, and the other two went off. When the woman had gone in, Giorgio tried the gate. It was unlatched. He stole into the courtyard and took off his cracked shoes.

Barefoot he mounted the stairs with the silent litheness of a leopard. He could see light streaming out from a room above.

He tiptoed to the open door. The old witch was taking off her clothes. *Dio*, what a horrible sight she was, fat as a great sow, sagging all over.

The floorboard creaked under him.

She turned without the least fear or surprise. 'I saw you following me, you beautiful boy.' She was actually smiling, the fool. 'How would you like to earn some money?'

Dio non voglia, God forbid, he thought, but he smiled back, saying, 'Very much' in English.

He padded towards her. She took his hands in hers and placed them on her sagging breasts, breathing hard and fast. He made himself touch them. Then slowly he ran his hands up to her neck and closed his fingers around it.

He squeezed hard. Her smile became a kind of croaking, and her eyes started out of her head. She was so awful-looking, with her face changing colour, her coated tongue popping out, that Giorgio closed his eyes.

He let go of her abruptly and she slid to the floor. She was not breathing or moving.

With desperate haste he emptied her purse and began to rifle the room. He found a great deal of money in the dresser drawer and then in the closet, jewellery hidden in her shoes.

Filling his pockets, he was reminded of his own cracked *scarpe* in the courtyard. He must not forget them, even if he would be patronising the bootmaker of Il Duce's mistress soon, when things cooled down.

It served the old bitch right. They'd warned her. The *paparazzi* in Rome were very hungry now.

CHAPTER TWENTY-SIX

'Let's take a break, Bundalla.'

Clinton Holder spoke with the stubborn calm that characterised everything he said or did. His Boer mother had given him his calm; but his father, Martin Holder, and his grandfather had fired him with the dream of finding a diamond mine. He had their lion-coloured eyes and lean, strong height; always their passion for the find had smouldered deep in Clint below that reserved exterior.

His companion was a slender, quiet African with wise eyes. Bundalla, the son of Kossee, nodded. They leaned back on their haunches beside the trench they had dug in the arid Tanganyikan soil of Kisumbe.

Neither man spoke. They worked together so well that the silence between them was companionable.

362

Clint looked out over the desolate plain. It was duncoloured, spotted with scrubby trees. Kisumbe was serene. The workers had gone home, but Clint and Bundalla, his right-hand man ever since he'd been in Tanganyika, still lingered.

They had processed a soil sample by themselves. The soil contained ilmenite, one of the minerals that often indicated the presence of diamonds. So there was a good chance that they were here, plenty of them. Clint had a feeling they were standing right on top of a massive kimberlite pipe.

Soon they would be digging more sample pits and trenches, but it was slow work for two men. Tomorrow, Clint decided, he'd use the magnetometer, too, to measure magnetic fields.

But right now they could both use a breather. They were sweat-drenched, bleary-eyed, in this crazy, fascinating country where everything was upside down, summer was winter, and the reverse.

Clint Holder threw himself on the ground and lay back, making a hard pillow of his clasped hands behind his tanned, muscular neck. He saw Bundalla do the same.

Clint smiled and shut his eyes, hearing the faint rustle of the letter in his breast pocket as he shifted his position. Funny, how he'd taken after Amas and his father from the first, as different from his brother Tony as chalk from cheese.

Clint could remember back to the time when both of them had just about started to walk; already each one was headed in an opposite direction. Tony had never given a damn for the outdoors, for one thing. As soon as he had learned to read, at the early age of four, he was always talking about going to the places he read about. Clint supposed he'd got that from their mother who, after all, had been a teacher and was a great reader herself.

Clint, on the other hand, couldn't stand to be penned up. He'd gone to the mines with his father as soon as he could manoeuvre, and started climbing up and down the shafts the way his father said Megan used to do.

That was really something about Megan, Clint thought, and chuckled. He opened his eyes, glancing at Bundalla. But his friend still had his eyes closed, paying no attention to Clint. He was used to Clint's long silences and musings by now; they worked so well together that they understood each other in many ways by this late date.

Tony . . . the thought of the direction that his brother's life had taken saddened Clint for a moment. And that thing with Bea. Clint had always suspected that something pretty horrific had happened between Bea and his father, from the way Martin reacted when she was mentioned. But Clint would likely never know. It seemed to be a closely guarded secret. Clint recalled the news of Bea's death. Nasty thing, that. He had a strong feeling that hadn't been a 'burglar', as the papers so carefully stated. He'd heard too many sordid stories of indiscreet older women touring Europe. Some family he belonged to. At first he'd been afraid the de Gamba mess would put Ann off. But she was too smart for that, and she didn't seem to be under her conservative family's thumb.

With his eyes still shut, Clint reached up and touched the breast pocket where the letter was. He had much nicer things to think of than Bea . . . things to remember, and to look forward to. His whole body relaxed and tingled at the same time, thinking of Ann Barrett. It was the damndest thing, that reaction.

She would be as near as Mabuki in just two more days. Clint listened to the quickened thudding of his heart. They hadn't been together for four long months, and it seemed like four years. Who would have thought it . . . who would have imagined. Not Clint Holder, for sure.

The first time he'd seen her was more than a year ago, on Stockdale Street, in Kimberley, when he'd been visiting Amas and Vanessa.

They were all three walking down the dusty street, which Amas said hadn't changed that much in fifty years, when Clint first saw her. She was coming out of the old DeVries building, still carefully preserved to retain the look of the eighties, when it had been built.

Clint Holder stared at her when she paused in the shade of the veranda. She looked so delicate and old-fashioned standing there in her fresh white dress, with her luxuriant, pale blonde hair and wide grey eyes, that she seemed to fit, seemed to belong to another, gentler time.

She wasn't wearing any of the paint Clint had become so used to; her brows weren't pencil-thin like most of the other women's. And most of all she seemed unutterably feminine, the way Amas said women used to be, before they got to be such 'free spirits' and decided they didn't need men the way they once had.

Clint laughed at himself for gathering so much with just one glance. When she came out in the sun he realised she wasn't pale or fluttery at all; her skin was fair, but sun-touched, and she had an easy stroll hinting that she was active, not sedentary.

Amas and Vanessa had seen him staring, picked up something in his manner, and he tried to hide his instant excitement, the almost solemn feeling the encounter gave him. But he was unable to help staring after her, as she went off down Stockdale Street with her graceful white calf-length skirt floating about her shapely legs, clinging a little to her beautiful body. She was the most unusual woman he'd ever seen; at first she'd seemed too fragile and dainty even to step on the ground, but now she was moving along with perfect freedom and grace on the rough road in her mid-heel shoes, not mincing and tottering, as if she'd been in this little town all her life.

Clint figured she must be the wife of one of the DeVries executives. She looked very English. He tried to put her out of his mind; he was scheduled to take off in a couple of days to prospect a hundred miles away, and there was no point in getting all hotted up about somebody he might never even see again.

But then that night Amas and Vanessa took him to the Kimberley Club for a dinner and dance.

She was there.

This time she nearly took his breath away. She was dressed in a pale blue satin evening gown with startling lines that bared her magnificent young body; when he watched her dancing, the undulating body was sleek and graceful as a young seal's, and the frank hints of it under the clinging satin made Clint's pulses feel like a jackhammer in operation.

He noticed that Amas was following the direction of his eyes, and before he knew it Vanessa had gone to the girl's table to say hello to some acquaintances, and the Holders were asked to join them.

Clint was introduced. Her name was Ann Barrett. With his heart still hammering, whirring in his ears, Clint asked her to dance.

The orchestra was playing a slow, seductive piece, a new song that had drifted from America to Britain, then to Africa. Clint drew her close. The first contact with that lean yet amazingly soft body fanned his skin's fire like a bellows. He darted a glance at the slim hand he was holding in his; parting his fingers a little, he saw that she wore no wedding or engagement ring.

He felt a disproportionate elation. His spirits shot up like mercury.

She spoke softly near his ear; he was so bedazzled at first that he could hardly understand her.

'I . . . I beg your pardon?' he stammered. He moved back a trifle to see her better.

She was smiling. 'I said I like your grandparents, very much. Your grandmother is beautiful.'

Clint felt absurdly gratified; he loved them, too, with all his heart. And it was satisfying to have relatives who weren't like the grotesque and ill-fated Beatrice. 'Thank you. I think they're pretty great, myself. You . . . you remind me of my grandmother,' he blurted out. It was true. Ann Barrett had the same unusual blend of femininity and strength, the same grey-eyed beauty Clint had pictured in Vanessa when she was young.

But then he realised what he'd said. It sounded pretty silly to compare this lustrous-eyed beauty with an old woman. However, she seemed to take it as a compliment.

She looked into his eyes, and said softly, 'That's a very nice thing to say.'

Clint was so strongly affected by those intelligent, glowing eyes that he couldn't speak again for a moment. Then he said, 'Are you English, Miss Barrett?'

'American.' She smiled that sweet, slow smile and his insides turned over. 'I'm from Virginia.'

'I see.' He felt totally inadequate, wanting to say something clever, like the stuff Tony used to say to girls before he . . . changed. 'Are you visiting here?'

'I'm working here, Mr Holder. I'm a geologist for a company working with DeVries.'

He couldn't help gaping. 'A geologist . . . my God,' was all he could manage.

She laughed and asked, 'Does it shock you that a woman has a job like that?'

'Shock me? No . . . not, not at all. But it does surprise me, Miss Barrett. You're so young and . . . so very beautiful.'

Instead of smiling when he said that, she looked at him with wide, serious eyes, and moved closer into his arms for the dance. Elated, almost drunk with her nearness, he realised that she was drawn to him, and he could hardly believe it.

When they returned to the table, they sat together, and he told her everything about himself, starting with his childhood in the mines, progressing quickly to the present hour, telling her about the imminent prospecting.

She said that she was leaving the next day for Nzega, near Lake

Victoria, the opposite direction to Clint's destination. His heart sank; he imagined he heard a faint regret in her voice, but that was too much to hope for.

The next time he looked up, he realised that Amas and Vanessa had gone, and that he and Ann Barrett were almost alone in the ballroom. They danced the last dance, to 'Goodnight Ladies', and he walked her slowly back to her small hotel.

'It may be a long time,' he said huskily, 'before we meet again.'

She nodded, looking up solemnly into his eyes. He bent quickly and kissed her upturned lips. The kiss began as a gentle, tentative caress, but in an instant it had caught fire, and they were kissing each other with enormous hunger, clinging together, his hard body aware of her melting softness. He felt a positive ache to hold her in the ultimate nearness, to make love to her.

'Oh, Clint Holder, I don't want to go,' she whispered when he raised his mouth from hers.

Clinging to her, he answered hoarsely, 'And I don't want you to go, Ann Barrett.'

'But I must. I know I must,' she said reluctantly. 'There is no way out of it now.' She laid her head against his chest, and he absolutely hurt with the thought of letting her go away.

'How long will you be in Nzega?' he asked her anxiously. 'Of course I guess there's no way, at this point, to be sure.'

She shook her head. 'No, there isn't. You understand.'

The hell of it was, he *did* understand. The most unpredictable thing in the world was a geological survey in Africa. 'I'll come to *you*,' he said eagerly. 'I'll get away as soon as I can. You see, my grandfather's sunk a lot of money in this project . . . he's counting on me. I . . .'

She put her fingers on his lips, and he felt a trembling, deep in his guts, at the light touch. 'I understand,' she said softly. 'Of all people, I ought to.' She smiled at him, but it was a trembly, sad smile and he kissed her again with a new, hungry fervour.

'I'll come to you in Nzega,' he promised again. He could feel his very heart plummet to the middle of him when he watched her go.

But he had gone to her there, and it was something Clint Holder would never forget.

He opened his eyes slightly to gauge the position of the setting sun, sensing Bundalla's restlessness. But he would daydream just a little longer . . . just a little, let himself savour that wonderful day.

Clint had raced through the prospecting job, he recalled now with some guilt, in record time, using only a part of his concentration. But, he consoled himself, it had been a failure anyhow, and wouldn't have turned out any better if he *had* put all his mind to it.

He recalled his desperate hurry to get to her location, remembered the first heart-stopping sight of her, labouring in the bitter sun. She was wearing a helmet over her bright hair, and was dressed in a khaki shirt and trousers that accentuated her slender femininity. He stood on a rise, watching, with his heart pounding, until at last she saw him.

She held up her hand in greeting; even from that distance he could see her eyes glow. She said something to a fellow worker near her – Clint felt an immediate, irrational jealousy – and put down her tools, hurrying towards him.

He burned to take her in his arms, kiss her sweet mouth; the weeks of their absence from each other were the longest he'd ever endured. But he understood her shyness, because they were being observed, so all they could do was clasp hands and look into each other's eyes. And the touch of hands, to him, was like a kiss.

Clint remembered very dimly the interval between their meeting and the blessed time when at last they contrived to be alone. His meeting with the others and their conversation were a blur; it seemed hours before the dark.

But at last it arrived. And like someone from a dream she appeared at the arranged meeting place – a wooded spot not far from the roaring falls. That was the part Clint Holder would never forget if he lived to be a thousand years old.

She came into the shadows dressed in white and they ran to each other. He grabbed her so hard he was almost afraid he had bruised her skin; she smelled of roses and immaculate cloth and said his name over and over again, with that precise yet melodious inflection he had taken for English but which he had come to learn was the speech of the high-born southerner.

He was suddenly awkward and hesitant with her; she was no longer the independent, easy-mannered girl he'd met in Kimberley. He had a crippling sense that she was the lady of the manor stealing off to meet one of the servants on the estate. It was insane, he realised, to feel such things, when she was warm and melting in his embrace, but he knew then he could not make love to her this way. Until they belonged together before the whole world, until she was his wife, his desperate longing and hers would have to go unappeased.

He drew her down onto the cooling grass and held her close,

trying to tell her what was in his heart. And she said, with a soft matter-of-factness, 'Then we must be married, right away.'

Clint was so moved he could hardly speak. But finally he was able to say, 'I can't come to you, shame you before your family, with my hat in my hand. I've got to make a find, Ann, got to know that I can give you everything you've always had before.'

'What does that matter?' she cried. 'How do you know what I've had before, Clint?'

'My grandparents told me.' He was miserably silent for a moment, then he mumbled, 'My grandmother says it doesn't matter.'

'She's right – it doesn't. Not if you love me.' Clint could hear her soft voice break.

'I do love you, Ann, more than anything in life. That's the very reason I feel the way I do.'

'You don't love me,' she said, stricken. 'I was wrong about you, Clint. I think I must have seen something in you that didn't even exist . . . only something I hoped for.' Her voice was so sad it tore his heart.

'Don't say that, please don't say that. You don't know how much I love you, how much I've been just . . . dying to be with you.'

'I can't believe that now.' She rose. 'I'm going back now. Please, Clint, just go.'

He had been unable to dissuade her. He watched her go off in the moonlight, felt all the life going out of him. Wretched, he left that night.

The savour had gone out of everything. He felt so empty that most of the time he just wished he were dead.

He wrote her a long, desperate letter, begging her to see him. There was no answer. But then after a month a letter came from her. His letter had followed her to two additional sites, finally reaching her. She confessed that she still loved him, and always would, asking for his forgiveness. They would wait to be married, if it must be, but she had to see him, must be with him.

There was one wonderful reunion, and then they were both off again. Finally he wrote her that he had been a fool. He wanted them to be married whenever she decided it was the time. They had become very close with their correspondence, falling in love more deeply with every letter.

And now, Clint Holder exulted as he lay on the arid soil of Kisumbe, she was coming to Tanganyika. He was almost wild with anticipation.

Amas and Vanessa had told him they would be coming to visit too. They would be there for the wedding.

But now the project before him prodded, scattering his images of happiness, his remembered pictures of Ann. They'd better get on with it.

If ever he'd needed the find it was now. Vanessa had teased him gently about being a conservative Boer, like his mother Anjanette. But it still mattered a lot to Clinton Holder. Things were tight now with his father, and Amas had invested more of his money in this project.

I can't let Amas down . . . or myself . . . or her.

Clint got to his feet.

Bundalla opened his eyes, stretched and rose.

'Let's get to it . . . shall we?'

Bundalla nodded and smiled.

They went back to their digging. For an awful space that seemed like hours, as they laboured, sweat blinding them, Clint thought he'd been wrong. There was nothing there.

And then, just as the sun was about to sink, he felt something. 'Bundalla!' he shouted.

His friend came running.

Clint was stooping by the trench; his knees were shaking so hard he nearly fell backwards. He stared and stared at the thing in his dusty palm.

It was a magnificent two-carat octahedral diamond.

Clint was so jubilant he was about to burst. Bundalla let out a mighty yell, grinning from ear to ear. Both men squatted there together, unable to take their eyes off the diamond.

'It's here, Bundalla. It's here. The pipe. Come on, let's look some more.'

'If it gets too dark, we'll work by lamplight,' Bundalla said quietly.

They went back to their digging. In about half an hour they had found three more stones.

They were so intent on the find that they didn't even hear the sturdy Land Rover until it was almost upon them.

Dusk was about to fall. Clint jumped up and automatically drew his pistol from the holster on his belt. He aimed it at the Land Rover.

The vehicle drew to a halt. Two people got out – a tall, lean old man and a woman.

'Good God,' Clint ejaculated. 'Amas . . . Vanessa!'

In his surprise he was still aiming the gun.

The two walked towards him. Amas was grinning. 'Hold it, hotshot. I'm not wearing a bulletproof vest. Neither's your grandma.'

Clint tossed the pistol on the ground and reached them in three long strides, holding out his arms to embrace them both.

He kissed Vanessa. She looked almost absurdly young in khaki shirt and trousers, her brief hair like a foam of silver.

'I didn't expect you this soon.' Clint peered at them in the failing light. Amas looked exhausted, and a deep anxiety underlay Vanessa's cheerful expression.

Amas looked out over the twilight plain and filled his grateful lungs with air. 'Now I've seen Tanganyika,' he murmured. Clint wondered why he'd put it that way.

'Hello, there,' Amas said to Bundalla, who was standing a little apart. 'Where are your manners, Clint?'

'Sorry.' Clint gestured towards Bundalla. 'May I present Bundalla . . . the son of Kossee.'

'Kossee's . . . *son*?' Vanessa stared at the young African. 'Why, your father and my son Martin were the dearest friends.' Clint saw her mouth tremble with her deep emotion. She went to the boy and hugged him to her. Bundalla, despite his stately reticence, seemed very moved.

Amas shook his hand in a ceremonious way. 'This is a great pleasure, Bundalla.' Then, as if embarrassed at his own emotion, he said briskly, 'What are you boys doing here at this hour, anyway?' Clint said softly, 'Don't move. Stand right there.'

He went back to the spot where they'd piled the diamonds and picked them up, returning to Amas, holding them in his clenched fist.

'Here's the first return on your investment.' Clint held out his hand to Amas and let the diamonds fall on his grandfather's outstretched palm.

Amas stared at the rough diamonds, blinking in the fast departing light.

Then he looked at Clint, grinning, and slowly let the stones fall back in his grandson's dusty, calloused hand.

'Another Holder's done it, son.'

Vanessa's heart was fairly singing. This was the one thing she'd waited for, hoped for, prayed for since the moment they had first set foot on the Cape Town pier.

That Amas would have another find.

For more than a year she'd been holding her breath, watching him like a hawk but taking great care not to let him know. She couldn't chance that again, not after the time when she'd cautioned him once too often. And he'd said, 'My darling, don't make me dead before I die.'

He hadn't realised how much that had hurt and she hadn't let it, not for long. She couldn't. He was the one whose life was in the balance.

After that she'd quietly waited, hoping, hoping, her spirits battered after every unsuccessful search of Clint's, clammy with terror the time Amas had gone along to the site, against the Cape Town doctor's orders.

But he'd come back to her. When he'd mentioned coming to Tanganyika it had taken all her control not to protest; the trip had tired him horribly.

All the same, he'd been right . . . as he had always been, about so many things. Because they had come in time for the find.

'Clint,' she said, going to the boy and taking his arm, 'this is the best thing that's happened to the Holders in a long, long time. Only one thing could make me even happier.'

And overjoyed, with her hopes flying, she saw that tough young giant beam at her with Amas' smile and Amas' eyes. 'I know what that is . . . and it's coming true. Ann will be here tomorrow or the next day. And you'll be attending a wedding.'

Vanessa, to her chagrin, burst into tears. Amas put his arm around her, and teased, 'What's this? Changed your mind? I thought you wanted this all along.'

She smiled through her tears. 'Oh, be quiet, Amas Holder.' But she said it so tenderly it sounded like 'I love you'.

Then she addressed Clint, wiping her eyes. 'It's a damned good thing. I've got a small fortune in family jewels to give the bride . . . on the strength of your last letter.'

'You do beat all, lady.' Clint hugged her to him. 'I've heard of people being prepared for the worst . . . you're always prepared for the best.'

'Always,' Vanessa retorted. 'Ever since I met this grandfather of yours.'

Looking at Amas, she saw the same fire in his eyes that had burned a half-century before, and a deep, abiding joy, the same joy that had shone from him since the day they'd sailed on the *Île de France*.

Clint was blinking and Vanessa suspected it was because his eyes stung with something more than labour's sweat. 'There's not enough light now to find the rest,' he said rather awkwardly. 'But tomorrow . . .' He swallowed. 'Not quite enough light now.'

'There's never enough, boy; it never goes on quite long enough to suit me.' A faint grimace twisted Amas' mouth.

Vanessa knew him so well she knew he didn't mean the light of that single day.

No, she answered in grieving silence, there's never enough light for anyone. It goes so quickly, the way I just seemed to wink an eye and fifty years passed before I knew it. Never to come back, ever again.

There might not be that many more days for Amas to feel the sun on his back; not many more nights for her to know the warmth of his long, hard body pressed close to hers.

How wise you are, my love, she reflected. There is never enough light or time.

We must make our own light, she decided.

And eerily, as if she had been heard, Bundalla lit a lamp and the three men walked along the trench, peering down into it in the gathering dark.

We have made our own light, Amas, Vanessa called out to him in silence.

In truth they had triumphed over everything that was death and darkness – even over the endless machinations, the poisoned sting of Beatrice. If she had infected Megan and Martin and Tony for a time, two of them had been healed, and the third might soon be. Tony was at home again, and he seemed to be changing.

They had won over their despair after the deaths of Lesley and Sam and Martin Stirling; they'd lived through the Boer War and she, Vanessa concluded drily, had lived through her battle with the piano which even Bufera at times had called impossible. Yes, they had won over death and loss and separation, won out over the stubborn earth itself, wresting a fortune from its profoundest depths, knowing always a passionate delight in the quest as well as the finding.

Riding the crest of this new happiness, Vanessa realised something else – she had even found it in her heart now to grant a last forgiveness to Bea, whose tawdry and pathetic death lacked the dignity that every end should carry, the dignity that would be accorded to the Holders.

Poor Bea had clung to everyone she considered a little piece of Amas; he was likely the only man she could have ever loved.

There was no room for malice any more, not after that last dark departure; they would all go, in time, to that dreadful escort.

But something far happier, more remarkable came to Vanessa: not

373

a jot of her former guilt remained. She'd thought she'd been a neglectful mother and grandmother, that she had been selfish in putting Amas first, too long. What he'd said to her often was absolutely true: the children would leave to pursue their own destinies, and a man and wife must cling together. This was what was meant to be. She knew that now more certainly than she had ever known it before.

The men were coming back, talking of leaving.

Still in her deep, private dream, Vanessa took Amas' arm and they walked back to the Land Rover with Clint and Kossee's son in their wake.

Clint said to Amas, 'Do you mind if I drive? I haven't had that much chance at Rovers.'

Vanessa hid her smile. Clint asked it as if Amas were doing him the greatest of favours. She listened to her husband give the expected consent. A great wave of love and pride swept her; the boy had such a gentle heart. He would make a wonderful husband for Ann Barrett, that lovely girl who reminded Vanessa a little of herself and yet was just different enough to add a welcome spice to the lives of all the Holders.

In the back seat of the Land Rover she took Amas' hand and murmured, 'I'm glad we have a chauffeur. I can sit and hold your hand the way we used to do, a long time ago.'

He smiled down at her, his beloved and familiar face almost fading now in the encroaching darkness.

In the time that remained, as it had been from the beginning, they would take the cup of life in both their hands and drink deep. Perhaps it was her imagination, but she seemed to see his lion-coloured eyes take on more fire.

That same unyielding fire that had captivated them all . . . the long unquenchable brilliance of the very diamond, that would live on after them, in Clinton and his children. None of the Holders had ever rested until they had attained, in their various ways, that glittering star just beyond them, the adamant symbol of the heart's desire.

And tomorrow they would register the new-found Holder claim.